# Marines on Top

## A Novel by

## A.X. WyKat

TurnKey
press

Marines on Top

ISBN: 0-9741858-1-7

TurnKey
press

2525 W Anderson Lane, Suite 540
Austin, Texas 78757

Tel: 512.407.8876
Fax: 512.478.2117

E-mail: info@turnkeypress.com
Web: www.turnkeypress.com

# Prologue

*Marines on Top* is the story of Sergeant J.E.B. "Jeb" Hussar, USMC, and the Marine Rifle Squad he leads into combat in the War on Terror.

The War on Terror is the first global conflict of the 21st century. Early "battles" in this war have already triggered tremendous changes in our conventional thinking on national security, the use of force, and the structure of the military. As this conflict is destined to continue for many years, additional changes, possibly of even greater scope, should be expected in response to specific new threats and attacks.

We face a ruthless enemy whose actions have redefined the word "heinous." Bound by an extreme and murderous interpretation of Islam and sworn to the death to destroy our way of life, these fanatical, transnational terrorists gleefully target innocent civilian populations. Other groups of criminal malcontents, and some rogue nations, salivate at the thought of our demise and openly, or covertly, support the terrorists. To counter these threats, America has once again called upon the U.S. Marines.

Sergeant Hussar and his squad of intrepid Marines, as part of a forward-deployed Marine Expeditionary Unit, have answered the call to arms and are hunting down the terrorists. Ride along with these gunslingers as they bring justice to the bad guys.

<u>The Marines</u>

For well over 200 years, the United States Marine Corps has consistently produced fierce warriors flamboyantly consumed with a fraternal *esprit de corps* and a love of liberty. Less-recognized, but often just as critical to their legendary success, has been the Marines' willingness to adapt and use new technologies and tactics to support the grunt in the field. On occasion, these changes have been quite severe, not to mention timely, such as the amphibious doctrine and exercises developed and mastered in the years immediately preceding World War II which shaped the winning strategy in the Pacific. Dramatic forces of change in conflict with unique identity and spirit have destroyed many civilizations and cultures, but the Marines morph without an external ripple to their core intensity.

Today's Marines, again working through a period of transformation, are busy inserting the most useful of the ever-expanding information technologies (IT) into key leverage points in their force structure. Characteristically, the Marines bucked the trend and bypassed much of the frenzy over the smoke-and-mirror IT promises of the past several years. They chose not to buy a bunch of seemingly cool stuff they didn't really need and that didn't really work. Instead, they focused exclusively on getting capabilities truly useful to the grunt in the field—the same poor grunt who is already carrying too much crap. This philosophy of "if it don't work, ain't no one gonna carry it" cuts to the heart of the technology insertion issue and is the mantra for those working to improve the combat power of future Devil Dogs. This approach will pay off. Some kid in boot camp right now, just starting the process of becoming a Marine, will one day lead a Marine Rifle Squad and live the exploits of Sgt. Jeb Hussar. I envy him.

## The Hussars

A bloodline of independent, hard-working, and honest people, the Hussars confidently live in casual, but complete, rejection of any pinhead telling them what to do, how to live, or what to feel. With a hearty appetite for adventure and an uncanny ability to seize the moment, the robust men of this family live large and without regret. Indifferent to trends or fads, these men have the rugged constitution to boldly meet life's challenges head-on. Strength of character more than compensates for their ignorance of Italian footwear. To have such men as friends guarantees at least one constant in your life.

Remarkably, and often tragically, each American generation of this family came of age during a period of great national distress. Without fail, Hussar men vigorously participated in the events that shaped our country. Thus, the history of the Hussars in America is the history of America and Americans.

Look for future manly books from the American Hussar Chronology, exciting stories of Hussar families in Prussia, Austria, and Norway; and incredible adventures on the continents of Africa, Australia, and South America.

## Author's Note

Growing up in a blue-collar neighborhood in a medium-sized town in mid-America in the 60's, I had the street smarts to know the men I should show a little respect to and the ones I could blow off without a second thought. I wouldn't have been able to articulate this knowledge—I didn't possess the necessary verbal and reasoning skills at the age of 8—but I nevertheless had a solid sense of what was appropriate behavior, entirely defined as getting away with as much as possible without getting my ass kicked. Today, with marginal improvement in my ability to reason and speak, but probably no better intuition, I realize that what I somehow knew to respect as a young boy was the quality we call character. As I now think about this quality of character, I marvel at its power to non-verbally communicate the demand for respect from a person who possesses character to another person who can't even spell the word.

You probably have similar recollections of some of the men you encountered as a child. And when you became an adult, if you bothered to recall those times, perhaps late one night after a few beers had made you philosophically intoxicated and provided the brief luxury of floating beyond your own self-centered world, you realized it had to be innate—that the ability to recognize strength of character in another person, and its associated effect of automatically triggering the respect gene to become momentarily dominant, was a natural part of us. That strength of character was not about knowing the difference between right and wrong but about actually living the difference between right and wrong without ambiguity or regret. That a guy with character was solid, reliable—in a way very difficult to explain—but still solid, like being able to recognize the Hoover Dam is going to be around for a long time even if you're not a civil engineer. And you also realized respect for character wasn't just a thing for kids—we all have it, but we've mostly got in the habit of burying those feelings of respect under a shell of indifference in our modern, politically correct world. And, yet, we still yearn for those feelings.

Something else I remember from that time years ago. Just being around one of these "character" guys gave me a brief rush and made me feel older, more important, part of something powerful, especially if the guy actually acknowledged my existence. When the moment passed, I was certainly confused about exactly what had just happened, but I still remember the rush. I realize now that I have spent my entire adult life subconsciously seeking to re-experience this feeling. Trust me, it took a long time to figure that out. But retro back to the 60's …

Back then, you could run into these men in many places. They didn't all end up in similar jobs or as company presidents or with any other obvious professional similarity. You might have seen him on a construction site or walking a beat or plowing a field or cutting meat or working in a bank or teaching a class or standing a shift down at the firehouse or sitting in a generic office doing something or mowing his grass or fishing on a lake or at a kid's ball game. Maybe you were really lucky and saw him every night at the dinner table. This guy didn't have an earring or blown-dry hair or manicured fingernails. He might have a faded tattoo somewhere on his arm, possibly an eagle—a remnant of his youthful zeal—when it just felt great to be alive, to be on top of the world, with limitless opportunities and potential—but still prescient enough to realize life may not always be so great, and he ought to get a permanent reminder of how good it once had been. I remember the laugh, a hearty laugh of someone who has seen good times and bad and is now somewhere in between but believes things are looking up. And he was taking care of business, man's business, providing for a family and looking after his community.

Today's version of this old guy from your childhood—the not black, brown, white, yellow, red but just tough, middle-aged, backbone of the community guy—is alive and well. If it doesn't seem like there are as many around as when you were a kid, you're probably right. But here's what I know about him ...

-Every once in a while, he grabs a beer or two with some buddies at a local beer joint, sports bar, pool hall, whatever.

-He wants his son, and maybe his daughter, to know what it's like to chase down a long fly ball on a perfect spring afternoon when it's finally turned warm and green and there's not a cloud in the sky. Maybe his father would have wished his son could have a shot in the majors, but he's seen how money has destroyed the simple joy of sports and has no such thoughts. He just wants his kids to know the pleasure of being young and alive.

-He wants his kids to walk tall and straight, stand up for what is right, respect their elders, take care of business.

-He can be fooled. He let down his guard in the 90's, sucked in by the bogus economic bubble and tolerated the crowd of clever, condescending, media-savvy, progressives who ripped the social fabric of this country with their politically correct, touchy-feely crap. When it was all over and the country woke up to a charred NYC skyline, he realized that there had been a strong sense all along that something wasn't quite right. And he finally realized what it was—no character. He doesn't like being snookered. He vows never again to vote for any cute, let's sit down and talk it out, in love with his own voice jerk who can't wait for the next photo op.

-He's proud of his ethnic heritage, appreciates jokes that highlight differences of his and others ethnicity but doesn't hate anyone just because they come from somewhere else. And he doesn't feel like just because he was born into whatever circumstances, over which he had no control, he owes anyone anything either—not hate, money, special opportunity, or intolerance.

-He served his country—somewhere, somehow. He knows what it is to put on a uniform, salute a flag, and get along in crummy living conditions with a bunch of other guys he would have otherwise never met or befriended. He has seen or imagined death on a large scale. He knows the military is necessary to fight our enemies, but even more, it's necessary to give a bunch of young guys a common sense of what it is to be an American, a realization that there are kids from all over the country who can be buddies. He discovered a resolve, a discipline—not by accident but by emulation. Because at some point in his military service, he encountered a man, probably a non-commissioned officer, who epitomized the whole military ideal—professional, tough, decisive, courageous, adventurous, matter-of-fact—and he, and the other young Americans in the unit, derived character from this man. After their service was up, they all went back to their farms, villages, towns, and cities as better men.

And, finally, to the point of this story. The professional, tough, decisive, courageous, adventurous, matter-of-fact man described above that others draw strength from—who impacts so many, whose legacy is carried forward throughout the land by all who knew him, whose character shapes a new generation—what do we know about him?

We know that, throughout history, in tight situations when death was near, people have gathered around the strength of such near anonymous men to do the great and not-so-great things that had to be done. In such times, the policies and regulations subordinating these men to faceless bureaucrats giving orders from hundreds, perhaps thousands, of miles away became immediately irrelevant. Only the resolute courage of the men at that place at that time could preserve or lose an entire nation. And often the situation hinged on the character of a single man.

The Hussar family produced men of this rare breed of character.

Their American story follows.

# Chapter 1

Boner, what'cha got?" followed the faint crypto sync-up chirp in Corporal "Boner" Danzig's earpiece, as the hushed whisper of his squad leader, Sergeant J.E.B. "Jeb" Hussar, came over the squad intercom link. Boner, the First Fire Team Leader, had just started to scan, for what seemed the thousandth time, a narrow alley 400 meters away that his fire team had been eyeballing for almost three hours. The alley ran behind a row of building facades bordering the souq, or market square, of Al Bazterd, a small town northeast of Zinjibar, Yemen, and looked pretty much like every other dirty alley in the ugly, little towns scattered throughout western Yemen. But Boner realized immediately that this scan was different—even before his scan eye had completely focused on the already familiar building shapes centered in the faint green display fed from his night vision device, he spotted a change from his previous peeps of the alley. Reflexively, his whole body tightened as he caught a "flash"—a line of pixels showing a spike of momentary brightness on the image screen of his heads-up display eyepiece. Like the flash you would see if someone had tried to check out the alley by quickly cracking open and then shutting a door from a room that was just slightly more illuminated than the darkness outside. With the sensitivity and light amplification capabilities of the 4th generation night vision equipment he was using, the relative brightness of the interior space over the outside ambient illumination could have come from a minimal light source, such as the backlight of a radio or VCR, the power light of a coffee pot, the

13

drag of a cigarette, or even a slightly lighter shade of interior wall paint. The gear was that good, the best yet to come out of the Night Vision Laboratory at Fort Belvoir, VA. Of course, the flash was almost, but not quite, immediately dampened by embedded image processing software to prevent the sudden relative intensity spike from blinding him with "sunspots" or, the more likely scenario, to prevent a local "flare" on his viewing screen from masking potentially important intensity changes in the neighboring pixels. The algorithm was significantly more sophisticated than what the tankers used to momentarily, and completely, blank out their night vision equipment when firing the M1A1 tank's main gun. But the tankers had old stuff. Boner knew he had the latest night vision technology in his AN/PVS-9. He didn't know exactly how it worked, but he had been on the test team evaluating the new imaging software for field use and had been stunned at the improvement in feature recognition and general viewing quality of the AN/PVS-9 when compared to the raw images provided by earlier generations of equipment. Plus, the device had been integrated with other parts of his personal gear. Boner was actually looking at the output of the AN/PVS-9 on the eyepiece image screen of his new, as yet undesignated by the Federal Supply System, Integrated Display System (IDS). The IDS came with either the low-profile monocular eyepiece he was wearing or a set of wrap-around goggles for the total combat geek experience. Although the screen was presently being fed images from his helmet-mounted night vision device, Boner could, at the touch of an integrated mouse button, change the background image source to one of several other video inputs or could even "tile" multiple video inputs onto the screen for simultaneous viewing. He could also turn on a network-generated data stream, which used intelligent agents to track mission-related activities and was specially configured as a "cueing" function to alert his attention or stimulate him to perform some action when certain key events occurred. As soon as an important event was detected, a message would immediately be superimposed on his screen and an audio alert would be sent through his earpiece. But this "feature" was still a little too high-tech for most of the Marines and Boner had it disabled. It was somewhat overwhelming to consider the fact that in one rapid acquisition cycle, the grunt in the field had overtaken 30 years of heads-up display technologies developed for combat aircraft.

"I just caught a flash down the alley. Nothing else, but … hold on, I'm seeing some movement! Wait one, over," Boner replied.

Boner quickly toggled the display to the new, also undesignated from a military nomenclature perspective, thermal sight on his M-16 and watched as two shapes came out of the same doorway previously opened and began shuffling awkwardly down the alley towards him, carrying a large bag between them. He softly pressed his foot against the leg of Lance Corporal Jim "Oddjob" Trah, the designated squad ◁ sniper lying next to him, to make sure he had also seen the men. Already coiled in a tight prone shooting position, Oddjob immediately rewarded Boner with both a return foot press and the almost imperceptible, but reassuring, sound of him tweaking the focus adjustment on his scope as the two bad guys began closing the distance between them. When given the green light, Oddjob would initiate the ambush by taking a head shot and then follow-up with suppression fire, as required, to silence any threats and cover the squad's egress. The Marines had always prided themselves on marksmanship, and Oddjob was the present generation of that long tradition. The average joe got his knowledge of marksmanship from watching Hollywood action movies or perhaps from the manly challenge of capping stupid deer at a feeder from a braced position at 75 meters in daylight—both of these were about as relevant to combat marksmanship as playing golf—and had absolutely no idea how hard it was to engage a moving target at night at 400 meters with a fuzzy thermal sight. But guys like Oddjob lived the marksman's credo—Sight Picture and Sight Alignment. He was rock-solid from several different positions and was very comfortable with night shooting. Oddjob was so aware of shot accuracy factors that he carried a small meteorological sensor to help him correct his aim for trajectory roll-off and visual distortion from atmospheric conditions when engaging targets at long distance. He also was tuned in enough to personal biological functions that he subconsciously adjusted his shooting "rhythm" to compensate for a combat-induced accelerated heartbeat. This would ensure he still squeezed the trigger on the desired diastolic blood pressure moment.

"OK, two shitheads carrying a dime bag out of Number 5," Boner finally reported back to Hussar. He had waited until the images had sharpened on his screen, as this wasn't the time to be guessing at what he was seeing.

Number 5 was the third building on the west side of the alley. Several low-angle, high-resolution satellite photos had been used to generate an accurate GPS-referenced electronic rendering of the souk, complete with marked and annotated buildings and exit points. Since the local Arabic signs were meaningless to most of the Marines, the squad was using the electronic rendering, easily displayed on their individual IDS, to accurately reference locations on a superimposed grid.

"Roger, break, you got 'em, Spike?"

Hussar realized that he probably sounded impatient on the radio and consciously tried to slow his speech. But it was almost showtime and his heart was pounding. Hussar knew he would be fine once the shooting started—he always kept his head during stressful situations. In fact, a part of him was eagerly anticipating the surreal sense of relaxation he knew he would feel as soon as his "adrenalin clock" kicked into high gear. When his brain started racing with the faster clock speed, everything around him would appear to happen in slow-motion, and it would seem like he had forever to evaluate options, make decisions, and take action. The grunts got these danger rushes frequently, even in training situations. The first time Hussar had experienced it, early in one of the stress-inducing scenarios the Drill Instructors had put him through in boot camp, he had remembered a lecture on Einstein and Relativity that a physics professor visiting from the local college had given his high school physics class. Something about time dilation, or time slowing down, when moving at great velocity. Hussar had thought he was onto some fundamental understanding of his brain, but he couldn't quite square the time thing with another comment from the physics professor about an object's mass increasing when moving at great velocity. He knew time was slowing for him, but he didn't feel any heavier during the rush—in fact he felt lighter. After the rush, he might feel a little sluggish, but that didn't really seem to jive with what the professor had been saying. Hussar supposed it would take an

Einstein to explain it, but that didn't keep him from living the experience and figured it was probably one more reason he had joined the Marines rather than go to college. Now Hussar stoically called the danger rushes his re-enlistment bonus—a cynical comment on the fact that many enlisted guys in technical, non-combat, MOSs could get $30,000 to sign up for another four-year hitch, but a grunt wouldn't even rate a new pair of boots for re-upping. Although every Marine was trained in basic infantry skills, it didn't mean every Marine excelled at being a grunt or could effectively lead a squad into action in today's world of non-linear battlefields and asymmetrical threats. You had to take a tough bastard with a desire to lead and train the hell out of him to make a guy like Sergeant Hussar, a fact obviously lost on the technology infatuated weenies working military compensation.

"Got a bead, I like buttboy on the left," came Spike's immediate reply.

Cpl. "Spike" Baker and his Second Fire Team were out-of-sight in a small depression, slightly offset from the axis of the alley but only 100 yards from the men being watched. Baker's team would grab the bag and a prisoner, if possible. The bag was important—experience had shown the prisoner was probably less so.

"Anything there, Gasser?" Hussar polled his Third Fire Team Leader.

"Roger, three rags just out the front of #5, peeped the street, strollin' to a Tonka truck."

"Same three that went in?"

"Looks like it, one fat guy trailing two skinny dudes, but they ain't carrying the big bag they went in with."

"Roger, when we rock, you grab the fat guy and martyr the other two—and you gotta send someone in, Gasser, to scope the place after we strike."

"Q, is this our package?" whispered Hussar to the Marine beside him. Hussar needed target confirmation. He didn't want to take out a couple of locals engaged in some after hours black market goat cheese trading.

Cpl. Dan "Q" Anderson was intensely focused on his heads-up display. His geek set of display goggles were a little larger than those worn by the other Marines in the squad because he was having to watch several inputs simultaneously and needed more screen pixels, or "eyeball real estate," to do his job. Earlier that evening, through the real-time video and command link display, he had remotely piloted a Squad Stealth UAV near each of the access points to the suspected terrorist meeting site and emplaced one of the brand new multipurpose sensors. Now he was datalinked directly to the sensors and was watching the output display slowly increase as the two unsuspecting men approached the sensor located in the near end of the alley. While they were still several feet from it, and about the time Hussar queried him, the alert indicator had moved sharply into the red zone. This was real, he realized, as his throat went dry. He quickly focused the sensor's miniature low-light camera on the bad guys, grabbed and stored a couple of video frames, and began to …

"Q … IS … THIS … OUR … PACKAGE?"

The earnest tone in Hussar's voice jolted Q, and he realized the entire squad was poised for execution, like the lifted blade of a guillotine, depending on him to justify the impending death and waiting for Hussar to give the signal once he had done so.

"I'm in the Red … it's hot or one of those guys is a space alien."

He thought to add, so hopefully the grunts would later remark at how cool he had been under pressure. He was temporarily attached to Hussar's squad for this mission and knew the squad viewed him as an outsider, an office poge, but he desperately wanted acceptance by the grunts. A reputation for coolness under fire would certainly help.

"Take him, Oddjob," was Hussar's immediate order.

As the supersonic crack of the M40A3 Sniper rifle pierced the quiet of the night, Oddjob watched the right bagman's body hurl back several feet in the air and then tumble a couple of times on the ground. Bagman had been shot right out of his sandals, which still marked the location of his last footsteps. The bullet had passed through his solar plexus, entering and exploding the right ventricle of his heart, severing his spine, before exiting his body and then ricocheting off a rock in the alley with a firestorm of sparks before sailing off into the darkness. Oddjob made a mental note that the special armor-piercing rounds he had hand-loaded for the mission were in fact adequate for the job.

18

The Marines from Spike's team each squeezed off a shot at the left bagman, who immediately crumpled heavily to the ground. The entire Fire Team quickly moved into the alleyway, leapfrogging one another in 10 meter rushes until they came to the motionless pair. Two of Spike's Marines, the Scout and Grenadier, grabbed the bag without opening it and ran off towards the team rally point. Spike checked the two bagmen to make sure they were dead, emptied their pockets, quickly took several pictures with his miniature digital camera, and swiped a DNA swab across each of their mouths. He then plastered a picture of a smiling Saddam Hussein firing a rifle into the air across their foreheads and ran off to join up with his Fire Team. *That ought to get the locals talking*, he smiled to himself, nothing like a little dissension in the Arab world to make his job easier. He reached down to scoop up what looked like a pile of goat turds, but was actually the sensor Q had deployed from the UAV, and dropped it into the cargo pocket of his desert camo trousers. With his remaining Fire Team member, the Automatic Rifleman, covering him, they began a reverse set of leapfrog movements to get out of the alley and move to their Fire Team rally point, which was a second small depression about 150 meters beyond the attack point. Finding his other Marines with the captured bag already at the rally point and ready to move out, Spike barely slowed as he motioned the entire team to move out. The team quickly crossed the depression in the direction of the squad rendezvous point, which was another 600 meters away up a small draw.

The action in the front of the souq was just as decisive but took a little longer. Gasser's team had immediately dropped the two skinny dudes. Beside their lifeless bodies, the fat guy was doubled over on the ground, fighting for air. Gasser had bounced two rubber bullets off his large stomach and knocked the wind out of him. Before the guy could figure out he wasn't seriously injured, Gasser's Scout, PFC Benito "Rocky" de la Moya, ratcheted tight several cable tie-wraps around his wrists and ankles, shoved a rag in his mouth, tied a bag over his head, and then fired a morphine auto-injector hypodermic into his leg. At that moment, the sputtering remnants of a 1976 Toyota pick-up, with only the passenger side parking light illuminated, lurched around the corner. Although the little pick-up was still considered a great ride in that part of Yemen, the driver, LCPL Joseph "Injun' Joe" Whitecloud, couldn't even imagine such a piece of shit being seen on the Mescalero Apache reservation where he grew up—and that was saying something. He skidded to a stop near Rocky and the snatch, jumped out to help Rocky dump the fat man into the bed of the truck, and the three of them then sped off for the squad rendezvous point.

Meanwhile, with the remaining Marine from his Fire Team providing cover, Gasser sprinted the short distance to the doorway of the #5 building. Right before all hell broke loose, he had scoped out the space with his thermal sight and was reasonably sure there wasn't anyone left in the building. But the pucker factor was still pretty high as he kicked in the door and stood off to the side to look and listen. Sensing nothing, Gasser quickly ducked through the doorway and executed a rapid room-by-room clearing action. He was alone. Relieved, he audibly released a breath he didn't realize he had been holding and began a second, more detailed, search of the space. His orders were to look for anything unusual or out of the ordinary. That order had seemed perfectly reasonable during the pre-mission briefings back on the mother ship, *USS Tarawa* (LHA-1). But Gasser, being from Baton Rouge, Louisiana, immediately realized that nothing in the building looked normal to him, and it seemed futile for him to search for any telltale signs of terrorist activity. He needed to get the hell out of there. By now, the rest of squad was probably waiting for him at the rendezvous point, but he consciously forced himself to slow down and do a more careful scan of the rooms. After a few seconds, he figured out what was throwing him. Posters, mostly of mosques and with a great deal of unfamiliar Arabic characters scrawled on them, were tacked up on all the walls. Although his ignorance of the language was total, Gasser's natural curiosity and primeval desire to make sense of his surroundings were causing him to focus exclusively on the posters in an attempt to decipher their meaning. Realizing his mistake, he stopped looking at the posters and instead focused on how the rooms were laid out. The place was some sort of small business and was set up with a tiny reception area, a couple of small offices, and, in the back of the building, a small living area. Spartanly furnished, but clean and tidy, it all seemed fairly mundane once you got past the posters. He shot a number of digital pictures through his night vision sight for the Intel guys, and made sure to include shots of all the wall art. Since nothing else looked really unusual to him at that point, he started to leave. But as he walked by one of the offices, he noticed a faint glow from a computer monitor. Curious, he went over to take a closer look and touched what he assumed was the "return" key. The screen flashed to life. *Damn, my eyes!* Before the intensity was automatically dimmed on his display, he had caught a painful bright flash. The computer was obviously still on, just in a blank Screen Saver mode. Apparently, the owner hadn't configured the system to run some cute little personalized program of swimming fish or playful cats to light up the screen and show off the owner's "uniqueness" during periods of inactivity. He hoped he hadn't burned out the sensitive photo-intensifier electronics in his night vision goggles as he tilted them up and examined the computer monitor with his naked eyes. Expecting to see a bunch of unreadable Arabic characters, he instead immediately recognized the language on the screen as French. And the desktop looked familiar—thank God for Microsoft world domination. Like any good Cajun, Gasser could speak Creole, the local quasi-French dialect, and had been forced to take French classes in elementary school as part of some knuckleheaded school administrator's idea of cultural improvement. Although Gasser was a grunt, and a Louisianan to boot, he had a sharp intellect that he went to some trouble to conceal from the other Marines in the squad. With his thick bayou accent, however, it took a lot less trouble than he realized to fool most people. Only Hussar knew that Gasser spent his off-time reading technical journals and tinkering with computers. He would spend hours at a time on a computer, not resting until he had figured out exactly how whatever he was curious about that day actually worked. Gasser had even taken a couple of technical classes at a local community college to help quench his thirst for knowledge. His closet computer hobby is what now helped him notice a modem on the desk next to the computer—he hadn't even realized the locals had phones here. *Wait a minute,* he thought, he hadn't seen any phone lines outside. They must be using a satellite phone. But then the blinding flash of the obvious finally hit him. Even though he would expect to see a computer in almost every office in America, the same was not true in Yemen. So something that would seem perfectly normal to him as an American would in fact be unusual in the Yemeni room he was searching. He had to remember that bit of cleverness during the debrief with the Intel guys—what is normal in America may very well be abnormal in Yemen and should therefore be noted. Realizing the computer may be very important, he wondered what to do—should he carry off the whole computer, just yank out its hard drive, or destroy it where it sat? He had a sudden inspiration. If the computer had critical information to what had just transpired here in the last couple of hours, the bad guys wouldn't have left it here out in the open. But maybe it had some useful supporting information on it and maybe it would be used again in the future. Could be an opportunity if he played it right. He quickly pulled a diskette from his ass pack and loaded it into the computer. Then Gasser did a search to find any computer files that had been modified in the last day. Not much there, but he did copy the last few days of emails he found in the Mail In Box and several temporary Internet files from web surfing. He thought briefly about writing a small script that would cause the computer to report back its IP address whenever it booted up, thus allowing the computer, and any Internet traffic to/from it, to be tracked in the future. But he was afraid that would be too easily detectable, and he wasn't sure where he should have the computer send the message with its IP address. Anyplace cool he could think of that probably existed, like the system administrator for the National Security Agency's website, at administrator@nsa.gov, would pretty much blow the operation if discovered and maybe even cause an international incident. So he rejected the thought. On a final hunch, he double-clicked the modem icon in the Control Panel window and looked at the properties of the modem connection. Gasser copied down as much info as he thought was relevant, especially the phone number in the dialing instructions. He was very surprised to see that the modem connection was set up to use a static IP address. Almost every computer modem connection, and many LAN connections, was set up to obtain an IP address automatically from a server on the network it desired to join. This was done through a negotiation process that used a protocol called the Dynamic Host Configuration Protocol, or DHCP, and was the industry standard way of entering a network. Intrigued by the unusual setup he had found, Gasser quickly jotted down all the network information on the Internet Protocol tab. Then, not able to think of anything else to do, he returned the desktop to how he had found it and made for the exit. As he was passing through the reception area and just about to grab the door, a shiny dish sitting in a small wall alcove caught his eye. *Missed that coming in,* he thought. Checking it out, he was surprised to find it contained what looked like business cards. Gasser grabbed a couple, shoved them into a cargo pocket to examine later and went outside to collect the rest of his Fire Team before heading to the rendezvous point.

By the time Gasser's Fire Team made it to the Squad Rendezvous point, three more of the crapped out little trucks, two Datsuns and another Toyota, were already on the dirt road in a column facing north. Hussar was in the back of Injun' Joe's truck with Q, the bag, and the prisoner. Spotting Hussar, Grasser ran up, reported what he had found in his search of the building, and gave him the notes he had made on the computer configuration, the floppy diskette, and the business cards he had picked up on the way out. The stuff didn't mean much to Hussar, so he passed them to Q to check out. Q snapped a picture of the notes and cards through his night vision sight, copied the files from the diskette, and attached all of them to the electronic message he was already drafting.

Once Sergeant Hussar had seen Gasser's Team nearing the rendezvous point, he knew all of his men were accounted for, and it was time to get the hell out of the area. Within seconds of the assault, other gunshots could be heard in the town and occasional tracers had lit up the sky. Now, almost 3 minutes after the initial action, there was gunfire all over the town. Hussar knew firing off a few rounds into the sky was just the typical Arab reaction to anything significant or unusual, but, entertainment value notwithstanding, there was no real reason to hang around and watch the chaos unfold around the souq. So with Boner's Fire Team in the lead truck, followed by Spike's team, then Sergeant Hussar with Q, the unconscious prisoner and the bag, and, finally, Gasser's team bringing up the rear, the little convoy started up the dirt road into the mountains.

As the Marines settled into their convoy security positions, it was time for Q to check out the goods. He adjusted his night vision goggles, turned on a miniature infrared light, and began to study the bag in detail. Sewn like a satchel, it was made of very heavy, coarse, double-thick canvas. Noting the simple, rugged construction of the bag, Q unbuckled the canvas straps securing the outside flap and pulled it back. The inner surface of the flap was covered with a rubberized substance for waterproofing. There was a second flap also buckled with the double-stitched canvas straps. Once he had unfastened the second flap, he slowly opened the bag. A large, black, circular object filled the entire bottom. Around the inside circumference of the bag, several ominous-looking, waterproofed tags had been carefully stitched. Actually, it looked like two sets of instruction tags had been sewn into the bag, an original set and a newer looking set of redundant tags that appeared to have been sewn into the bag at a much later time. Q thought they were redundant because they contained identical electrical schematics, but the accompanying text on the newer set of tags was in a different language that didn't even share the same character set as the language on the original set. He quickly pulsed his helmet-mounted sensor at the object in the bottom of the bag and was rewarded with a reading high in the red zone. Using the integrated computer pointing device attached to his forearm, Q did a quick frame-grab from his night vision camera of the object and the instruction tags. Then he pulled up on his computer screen a query window for the object-oriented database and searched for reference material on portable demolition devices to see if he could find a match. The images he saw in his night vision camera, with the exception of the new set of tags with Arabic writing, appeared to be an exact match to the stored images from the database, right down to the markings in the Cyrillic characters of the Russian alphabet. He was looking at a SADM-10, the Soviet-made Atomic Demolition Munition (10-kiloton) "suitcase" bomb, variously reported as missing, not existing, etc., in the press for the last 5 years. But the U.S. Intelligence community knew the suitcase bombs existed, had with characteristic efficiency given them a nomenclature (SADM-10 by the Defense Intelligence Agency), and not only had specifications and drawings, but had recovered three of them since the demise of the Soviet Union. He quickly inventoried the satchel's contents and compared what he found to an English version of the SADM-10 parts list stored in the database. There was only a single discrepancy, but it was significant. A critical component, the trigger mechanism, was missing. The trigger mechanism was necessary to properly fire several explosion initiation points in the SADM-10 High Explosive casing. Proper firing of the HE would result in sufficient implosive forces being developed to push the internal-shaped uranium charges into supercriticality. Without the trigger, the device was a dud, at least from a nuclear chain reaction perspective. Q was slightly relieved to know that even the terrorists wanted to control their weapons and were apparently following the two-man rule that had independently, though for identical reasons, been adopted in the military forces of both the United States and the Soviet Union. The two-man rule required the presence of two authorized individuals to arm a nuclear weapon and was adopted to prevent a single, mentally unstable person, or someone accomplishing a partial material compromise, from causing a nuclear detonation. In practice, the two-man rule was implemented by physically separating key components or codes of a nuclear device until the time of actual need. With the terrorists, the concept was being used to keep two courier monkeys, neither one of which was probably "authorized" by the terrorist leaders to detonate the device, from having all the pieces of the bomb. But the trigger mechanism would have to be found.

Q decided against broadcasting the information over the squad intercom link. It was Hussar's call on what and when to tell his squad about the success of the mission. He leaned over the side of the small truck, stuck his face through the open passenger-side window, gave Hussar an update, and got permission to send his electronic report back to the MEU over the Squad Data Link once he had finished it.

As soon as the convoy was out of the immediate danger area, Hussar got on the "Reachback" net back to the MEU command element aboard the USS Tarawa and gave an immediate voice report on the grab of the nuke and its "salesman." Although he expected to hear the S-2 Major Renick on the reply, it was the booming voice of Colonel Steuben, the MEU Commander, that came across the radio.

"Well done, Marine! We'll get you boys out of there in a couple of hours. Here's Major Renick with the details."

"Aye-aye, sir", Hussar answered. He was still a bit in awe of the Colonel and didn't want to say anything that would make him sound like a horse's ass. Best to be brief and not come across like a giddy squad leader gushing his first combat situation report (SITREP) back to headquarters.

"Sergeant Hussar", came Major Renick finally, "there will be an LCAC to pick up your squad from Extraction Point Delta at 0415."

"An LCAC?" Hussar responded with disbelief. A helicopter extraction was in the mission brief. Something had changed. "Delta" was the military phonetic alphabet word for the letter "D," the fourth letter of the alphabet, which in this case represented the fourth pre-planned Extraction Point. In the Mission Brief, it had been identified as the least likely extraction. Something had changed.

"Roger, it was such a hassle for you guys to get wheels that we're going to take them out with you."

That could only mean subsequent missions were already being planned.

"Aye-aye, sir, we'll be at the Extraction Point by 0330."

"Roger, out here." The connection dropped.

He keyed the squad intercom link and told Boner to head for Extraction Point Delta. Boner pulled down the config menu for his GPS on the moving topographic map window of his IDS, found Extraction Point Delta in his list of pre-configured way points, and double-clicked it to start the auto-route calculator. The 30 mile route recommended by the computer would take them over a small portion of the Kru'me Desert. It had been calculated to avoid every known populated site to minimize the probability of running into anyone in the middle of the night. Hussar double-checked the route Boner had laid out and gave him the go-ahead. He was a little surprised the pick-up would happen so close to the Arabian Sea, on what was believed to be an isolated coastal area midway between Shaqra and Ahwar, about 200 miles northeast of Aden. But he knew the site had been carefully selected by Major Renick.

An LCAC extract seemed riskier than a helo at first, but after

Hussar thought about it for a few minutes, he realized it would make his life easier. He wouldn't have to get rid of the commandeered fleet of Tonka trucks, and it would also be less of a hassle with the prisoner. He could just stay tied up in the bed of the truck until they were back on the *Tarawa*.

The trip to the Extraction Point was slow and uneventful. As they passed over the narrow strip of coastal mountains, there were occasional places where Hussar caught a glimpse of the flat horizon of the Arabian Sea. The water would be their way out of here and he was glad to see it. Cautiously coming down from the mountains and moving onto the narrow beach, the Marines found it entirely deserted. For once, the overhead imagery shots had been right. The squad quickly took up security positions to cover all land approaches to the beach. Q unrolled his poncho on the sand, sat down, and continued working on his report. Hussar took a quick tour to check his Marines' positions and also made sure the prisoner was secure with Gasser's team. He then settled in next to a small rock outcropping where he could look out to sea and watch for their pickup LCAC.

# Chapter 2

Whoa, what the heck was that?" Q asked himself aloud. He was reacting to a transient spike that had unexpectedly popped up on his IDS screen while he was reviewing data in "playback" mode.

The IDS had a nifty record and playback function for review of mission data at various playback speeds. For a cursory review of the entire mission, Q planned to look at 10X speed playbacks of all the digitally recorded sensor data sets. He first pulled up the radioactivity measurements recorded from his radiation detector. It had seemed the logical place to start, since recovery of nuclear materials had been the squad's mission. The data playback exactly matched what he remembered from the mission, but since he had monitored the radiation detector's display continuously over the entire evening, this wasn't much of a surprise. Next, Q chose to look at a playback of chem/bio sensor data. Although the intel people hadn't briefed or anticipated any chemical or biological threats to the Marines on this mission, bringing along a new chem/bio detector to alert the squad to any unexpected dangers had been an easy decision. Of course, he hadn't watched its output continuously like he had watched the radiation detector output, but any alarming condition would have immediately rang through whatever he was doing on the IDS. Although no chem/bio alerts had been sounded, Q was still curious as to what the detector had captured and recorded. But it was about halfway through the chem/bio data replay that the spike occurred that surprised Q and caused his outburst. Not only had he seen the sharp rise and fall in one of the spectrometer "bins" used to represent the sensor output, but the bin had also taken on a reddish hue during the same period. Even though the increased level wasn't high enough to generate an alarm, which he certainly wouldn't have missed, it was still an anomaly that he wondered about. Most likely, the new detector he had brought on the mission, called the Miniature Air Sampling System, or MASS, was still a little flaky and the spike was due to a minor software problem. The developers had warned him that the MASS was not yet 100% ready for prime time. Q didn't really know what "not yet 100%" meant operationally, but he was convinced the MASS was the best piece of equipment he could get his hands on. The MASS was a three-year R&D project out of Oak Ridge National Laboratory and was being developed jointly by the Department of Defense and the Department of Energy. It was an interesting technology marriage between three active, but previously unrelated, areas of research in the physics, chemistry, and biology communities—microelectromechanical device fabrication, mass spectroscopy, and fluorescence spectroscopy. Described as an enhanced Microelectromechanical (MEM) spectrometer by the scientists who developed it, the MASS was an amazing device, at least theoretically. It used a two-pass process to characterize the air samples collected either periodically or on command of the operator. In the first part of the process, the MASS used mass spectroscopy to initially type the particulates floating around in the sampled air by their molecular weight. The results were displayed graphically in a bar graph with the individual bars corresponding to different molecular weight groups (or "bins" or "buckets" as the scientists frequently referred to them) of interest and the height of the bars representing the relative density of each molecular weight group in the air sample. The second part of the process consisted of a limited fluorescence spectroscopy evaluation of pre-selected molecules of interest to determine if they represented a potential chemical or biological threat. The fluorescent emission spectrum signature of the air sample was compared against a large library of fluorescent signatures of known chemical and biological agents and the individual bars in the molecular weight bar graph display were then color-coded to reflect the results of the comparison. A strong type match produced a blood red bar. Near-misses, or very low concentrations of suspect samples, produced varying shades of pink or red, proportional to detection confidence. All this may seem like fairly mundane, everyday stuff, but due to the MEM implementation, the device was about the size of a pack of cigarettes. Q had been told that most of the package volume was necessary to support the air pump, device I/O, and tactical ruggedization concerns, rather than the actual new science aspects of the sensor.

Q hit the rewind on the playback to go back and get a closer look, stopped at the time of the increased reading, and then drilled down on the sensor display bin of interest. A technical note popped up informing him that the rise probably indicated a count of potentially dangerous bacteria spores that was higher than the expected background level. He had been dismayed that his limited training on the device had repeatedly used the word "probably" to define results. Athough he would readily admit he didn't fully understand the science of the sensor, he found the uncertainty to be annoying. Seems like if you gave a bunch of scientists millions of dollars to solve a problem, you could get a better answer than "probably." But unlike the relatively large mass spectrometers that have been a staple of research laboratories for years, his new MEM sensor was still in the R&D stage and the results were not fully calibrated and guaranteed. Trade-offs had been made on accuracy and fidelity to achieve the miniature size, and the performance hadn't been verified in a field environment. The use of fluorescence spectroscopy, in this case the strobing of a near-infrared light source and subsequent measurement of the sample's response to the light wavelength for comparison with a library of known responses, was in its infancy as a detection mechanism of chem/bio agents.

Q wasn't sure what to do. Even though the increased level wasn't high enough to exceed the preset alarm threshold he had been advised to set for this area of the world by the scientists at the U.S. Army Center for Environmental Health Research (USACEHR, pronounced "U-SAK-HER") at Ft. Detrick, MD, it was nevertheless a noticeable increase in activity. Q wondered where the recommended alarm threshold levels came from and, more importantly, if there could still be some danger to the squad even if an alarm had not been triggered. He briefly recalled something about the device only accurately detecting specific known threats. But what if the scientists limited experience with the MASS had caused them to mistakenly set the alarm thresholds too high or to not load all the appropriate threat signatures or to not account for the possibility of encountering some new threat? Damn, he had never really thought through this stuff before. And now was a fine time and place to be thinking about it.

He needed to settle down. The mission had gone well, and he shouldn't be second-guessing everything that had happened. The smart thing to do now was to use his brain and try to determine where he was when the higher reading had been taken. He brought up the sensor display log and noticed that all the air sample results had been logged with the time taken and then subsequently tagged with a GPS location. He knew all the different computer clocks were slaved to GPS time, so he didn't have to account for clock discrepancies. He silently thanked Major Renick for forcing the contractors to at least achieve that level of integration with the different pieces of his equipment. After finding the correct entry in the log and noting its corresponding GPS location, Q centered his electronic tactical map on those coordinates. It looked like the higher reading had been taken shortly after they had left the squad rendezvous point and began the egress to the beach.

That was interesting. He had been in the back of the truck with the SADM-10, the prisoner, and the Marine guarding the prisoner. It must have been something off the prisoner—maybe the dude was farting the curdled goat's milk and fried camel crap he had probably enjoyed for dinner. The dietary habit of different ethnic groups was one more factor to consider in the difficult world of biologic detection. To be sure, he re-activated his MEM sensor and walked over and scanned the prisoner. Q spent a good five minutes moving the sensor probe port all around the prisoner while several samples were taken and processed. Nothing showed up on his display that remotely resembled the spike. He was about ready to write it off as a bug in the MASS software, but then his eyes locked onto the SADM-10 satchel. He had been specifically told that the MASS would not be useful for typing the radioisotopes associated with fissionable material and that it certainly shouldn't confuse that material with a biologic threat, but who really knew? Carefully, he opened the SADM-10 satchel and began a scan of the inside of the bag.

Bingo. Almost immediately, he saw the same spike. Not enough to trigger an alarm but an increased reading nevertheless. The computer didn't immediately classify the biologic detected—the classification algorithms still ran about a 25 percent false alarm rate, due primarily to all the naturally occurring biologics in the air—but something inside the bag was definitely stimulating the MASS. Then he had a chilling thought. What if the MASS was actually working properly and there was something besides the nuke in the bag? A shiver went up his spine as he considered all the possibilities. Damn, he hated all this WMD shit. He better just leave the bag alone. But as Q started to gently close the satchel, his hand ran across a slight bulge that he hadn't noticed on his initial inspection. He flipped on the miniature infrared light attached to his night vision device, and the interior of the bag lit up like daylight through his night vision display. Right where he had felt the bulge, Q found a small pocket stitched into the canvas. He had totally missed it before. He quickly brought up the SADM-10 reference material from his database and carefully looked at all the images again. There wasn't any such pocket shown on any of the diagrams he had stored on his computer. He knew the technical guys at DIA were very thorough, so this had to be a very recent modification to the bag. Without opening the pocket, Q carefully felt all around it. There was definitely something inside. And even through his gloves, he noticed the area was relatively warm. *That, too, was very interesting,* he thought. Gently pushing against the canvas near the pocket, the slit top of the pocket opened slightly. He could just make out what looked to be 3 small vials nestled in some sort of insulated wrapper.

As Q was contemplating what he had just seen, a message from the MASS popped up indicating the sample contained a virus classification of unknown type. Strange, the note for the playback spike had indicated bacteria spores, but now there was a virus? This was getting too weird. After acknowledging the message, the computer prompt asked him if he wanted to immediately forward the spectroscopy data to USACEHR for further analysis. *What the heck,* Q thought, with the time change it was only a little after 1900 the previous day at Ft. Detrick, he might as well give the duty research scientist something to do. He clicked on the "Send Now" button and the new software programmable communications module did a complete loopback test of several available communications links to determine the best path for transmission. Because the data file was over 1 Megabyte in size, even after the 5:1 lossless Discrete Wavelet Transform (DWT) compression had been accomplished, two different communication paths were simultaneously selected—an L-band link through the Globalstar Low Earth Orbit satellite constellation and a High Frequency (HF) shot back to the *Tarawa*. His network protocols allowed packets from the same file to be forwarded over completely different paths and still be re-assembled properly at the receiving computer. This wasn't the Muliple Point-to-Point (MPP) protocol or some other Layer 2 inverse-multiplexing technique often used to gang together multiple links going to the same termination point. The communication protocol he had was an enhanced version of the basic Transmission Control Protocol (TCP) layer of the Internet Protocol (IP) stack. TCP/IP were the workhorse protocols commonly used for the Internet, but they sometimes needed a little tweaking to support extremely disadvantaged users, like a Marine sitting on a beach in Yemen. When Q's communication module fired off the File Transfer Protocol (FTP) session with the FTP daemon running on the Ft. Detrick network server connected to the DoD Secure Internet Protocol Routing Network, or SIPRNet, his computer actually established two TCP socket connections for FTP data transfer, one for each comms link. It also set up an associated buffer queue for each socket. As the FTP protocol took file packets and pushed them to the TCP Service Access Point (SAP), the point where communications between different protocol "layers" occurred, they were placed in whichever outgoing buffer queue was smaller. The queue sizes were dynamically managed to maintain the same average wait time in each buffer and could thus tolerate supporting different speed communication links. In this way, the file could be transferred as quickly as possible from a remote disadvantaged user suffering from bandwidth malnutrition, like Q.

The destination FTP server would first be checked to see if it could support distributed TCP. If not, the FTP session would actually happen between Q's computer and an FTP server at the First Marine Expeditionary Force (I MEF) network operations center at Camp Pendleton, California, that supported the distributed TCP and could function as a proxy. A tag would be sent with the file to identify the secure FTP server at USACEHR as the final destination, and the I MEF server would take care of the rest. Just 6 months ago, he would have had to wait to get back aboard ship to transfer the file because he didn't have all the integrated capabilities he presently had access to via the IDS. Plus, he would have had to send an email to an intel analyst at I MEF, and probably even to someone at U.S. Central Command (CENTCOM), to forward the spectroscopy data to the "appropriate party" because he had never heard of USACEHR until two weeks ago. Come to think of it, he wouldn't have had the MEM sensors 6 months ago either, so he never would have gotten the biologic data in the first place. In fact, he would probably be taking a nap right now in the bed of the truck while waiting for the LCAC if he didn't have all this new gear. Of course, without the new capabilities he wouldn't have been welcome with the squad and would still be on the *Tarawa*. "Brace up," he mumbled, "get a grip on yourself." But truth be told, Q was happy to be carrying all the high-tech stuff Major Renick had acquired and quite proud he had been picked to be the first Intel Marine to operationally employ it.

He suddenly realized he had been "zoning" for almost a minute. He better make a report to Sergeant Hussar on what he had found. But just as he started to get up, Q saw that the squad leader was already motioning him over in a very animated fashion.

"What the hell is going on?" Hussar bluntly asked.

"What do you mean, Sergeant?"

"What I mean, doofus, is I got my ass in a crack with the Colonel because an Army doctor at a Bio lab somewhere in CONUS is bugging him for more info about a sample you sent them in the middle of our mission. Did you screw with the SADM-10, and did you send out a friggin' admin report while we were engaged?"

Q quickly explained the MASS, the data playback, and what he had found on his subsequent investigation. He then showed Hussar the vials in the "secret" pocket in the SADM-10 satchel.

"OK, leave them alone, they may be contaminated. Get away from the satchel, get your NBC gear on, and then get on the net with Major Renick." Hussar said, as he turned to get the rest of his squad suited up in their NBC gear.

# Chapter 3

D r. Karen Donnelly, the USACEHR staff research doctor on duty, was making her rounds through the primate area. She was amazed at the number of animals, all in very clean individual cages with little placards announcing the critter's name, the responsible scientist, and the title of the supported research.

A recent hire at USACEHR, it was her first night of "having the duty" alone, and she was enjoying the run of the place. Extremely focused with her own research work in the small Virus Alteration lab, one of many isolated lab areas strewn about the USACEHR campus, Karen rarely left her work space during the day. She was still too much of a "newbie" to know many of her research associates, so she really had no idea what else was going on in the sprawling complex. But given the official responsibility for "holding the fort," as the Adjutant, an Army Lieutenant Colonel, had told the small class of new employees being trained to stand duty at the facility, she now felt obligated to learn as much as possible about the place.

Karen was looking in on Smiley, a rhesus monkey participating in a white blood cell inhibitor evaluation for a Dr. Tony Wei, when her PDA began buzzing. Startled by the vibrations, she quickly checked the incoming message and saw she was required immediately in the CRC, the abbreviation for the Crisis Response Center. Hurrying off to the center, she hadn't gone 10 steps before her cell phone rang. It was the Director of Operations, Col. Danielson M.D., making sure she was responding and directing her to call him once she had discovered the cause of the alarm. She hadn't known that anyone else would be automatically notified of an alarm but immediately realized it was a good idea and just the thing the "military mind" would think of. A single person would never be left alone to do something important, so someone had to follow up. It crossed her mind that maybe she was somehow being tested on her first duty day alone. The adjutant had hinted that not much of an operational emergency ever happened there, what with it being a research facility and all; yet, here she was responding to an alarm barely 2 hours into her watch.

Arriving at the CRC access control point, she swiped her badge, entered her PIN, and impatiently waited for the biometric retinal scan to be completed and the access light to turn green. Once authorized, she waited again as a vent valve automatically opened for a couple of seconds to equalize pressure and then shoved the outer air lock door open. As soon as Karen entered the air lock, she saw a TOP SECRET sign above the inner air lock door that was illuminated red. She hadn't even noticed a sign there before. *This is definitely no drill,* she thought to herself. She quickly duplicated the same procedure to get through the inner air lock and, as she passed through the inner door into the actual Crisis Response Center, two things jumped out at her—a small red flashing symbol in the upper right hand corner of the projected world map, indicating the lack of any specific geospatial information for the alert, and a red flashing "ALARM" message on the Watch Officer's terminal for HAL, the Health Analysis Laboratory (HAL) computer system for analyzing health threats to military personnel. HAL had access to all the data at USACEHR and could also pull data, via the National Science Network, from databases at USACEHR's civilian counterpart, the Center for Disease Control in Atlanta, GA. There is an important, but complicated, relationship between the National Center for Infectious Diseases (NCID) at the Center for Disease Control and USACEHR when it came to tracking organism threats to human health. Basically, USACEHR is the focal point for all Department of Defense (DoD) biological agent issues, but they can reach into CDC and make extensive use of CDC resources. This arrangement not only provided the DoD with an information clearinghouse to track worldwide bio for the military, it also allowed USACEHR to act as a security firewall between the military and NCID to prevent information on sensitive military operations from being disclosed to non-DoD research scientists. Although the CDC researchers were not entirely thrilled at this one-way flow of information, they realized the national security implications and did their best to support USACEHR.

Karen quickly logged into HAL to load her user profile and read the alert summary. An inconclusive field data sample taken by one of the new MEM bio sensors had been forwarded to USACEHR for detailed analysis. HAL had finished the analysis and reported with an 85 percent confidence level that the sample contained the Ebola virus, a viral hemorrhagic fever, and two altered influenza strains. That was a frightening, but very unlikely, bio "cocktail" mix. Having never heard of the 11th MEU, and certainly not knowing that 11th MEU had an ongoing clandestine operation in Yemen by a squad of Marines equipped with a MEM sensor, she wondered where the sample had originated. Pulling up the details of the report, she saw that the originating unit was only identified as CENTCOM. She thought it most likely that the sample was training or test data, mistakenly sent by an operator. She built a query to have HAL try to find the originator. Searching through server logs, HAL found the FTP session in question and the originator's IP address. A reverse DNS lookup showed the session originated with a server in the IMEF.USMC.MIL sub-domain. Karen called up the on-line DoD phone book, found a number for a Secure Telephone Unit (STU-4) line to something called the I MEF Operations Center, and dialed it from one of the Red phones on the Watch Officer's console.

"I MEF Operations Center, Sgt. Jackson."

"Sgt. Jackson, this is Dr. Karen Donnelly from USACEHR," she said in her most official voice.

"Who from where? This is the First Marine Expeditionary Force Operations Center in Camp Pendleton, California, on a secure line."

*So much for impressing the Marines with my Medical degree,* she thought. But now she at least knew what "I MEF" stood for and had a location for the sample. Better get to the point before the Marines sent someone to kick in the door and ask what the hell she was doing calling them on a secure line.

"I'm a research scientist at the Army's Biological Research facility at Ft. Detrick, Maryland. I just received a bio data sample from a server in your facility."

"You received a bio sample from my server?"

"Well, no, not an actual sample, of course. I received an electronic spectroscopy report of a data sample from your server," she corrected herself.

"Stand by, ma'am."

The guy was practically barking at her over the phone. And only a sergeant. She had learned enough about the military rank structure to know that a sergeant was a relatively junior rank. Although she had only occasionally encountered any of the enlisted soldiers on post, the guy on the phone seemed quite different. She made a mental note to try to avoid Marines in the future. They were a little too intense.

"Colonel Jeffries, Command Duty Officer."

"Colonel, I'm a research scientist at the Army's Bio Lab at Ft. Detrick, Maryland. I just received an electronic spectroscopy report of a bio data sample from a server at I MEF. Although this is probably a training mistake by someone unfamiliar with a new sensor, I need to follow up to be sure. Generally, sample results are sent to our facility for further analysis from someone in the field that picked up a possible threat but doesn't have the capability to conclusively characterize the sample and desires more detailed analysis by our powerful computers. Our system here has completed the lab analysis, and I want to get some additional info from whomever sent the sample."

Colonel Jeffries had no idea what the woman was talking about. But with 26 years in the Marine Corps, he knew enough to realize that his ignorance didn't necessarily make the matter unimportant.

"I'm unaware of any situation here that would have caused us to send you a sample, Dr. Donnelly."

"Actually, although I definitely got the electronic spectroscopy report from your server, Colonel, the location and unit ID blocks of the sample report were left blank. It's possible your server was used as a relay by someone else, which also means the sample could have been taken elsewhere." She was thinking, and almost said, that the location and unit ID blocks were "suspiciously" left blank. All the new detectors she had seen had an embedded GPS receiver, or were interfaced to a GPS receiver, and a default Unit Identification was one of the blocks the operator was required to fill in during equipment set-up. That way, both of these important fields could be auto-filled on any of the pre-formatted messages sent out, which should save the operator time and reduce errors.

Then, she noticed something she had missed before. "But there is a reference in the remarks section of the report to a 1-1-M-E-U and a C-P-L Anderson," she offered. Karen had to spell out the unfamiliar jumble of letters in the military acronyms and abbreviations.

One of Jeffries basic principles was that there is no such thing as a coincidence. Just that afternoon, he had heard at the Commanding General's Daily Intel Brief that 11th MEU would be going "hot" in theater with Search & Destroy missions targeting Al-Qaeda attempts at acquiring Weapons of Mass Destruction.

"Assuming this was a real detection, why would you need additional info and what would it be?"

"Even with today's latest technology, bio detection is sometimes an iffy thing. The sample I received had muted indications of several possible biological agents. Since the air volume addressed in a single sample is relatively small, this would be a very unusual situation. In fact, it would almost have to be contrived. On the other hand, a bizarre natural background of biologics, that is to say, a background we didn't encounter or anticipate when we set up the calibration modes for the detector, could have caused the indications received. We need to follow up to account for the readings. Quite frankly, the state of technology is such that our bio false alarm rate is still almost 25 percent."

"What bio agents might have been in the sample?" *Why can't these eggheads ever get to the frigging point,* he wondered. He was going to get the specifics from this woman before he made a decision on doing anything.

"Possible indications of a viral hemorrhagic fever, Ebola HF, and two strains of an influenza virus, something close to Influenza A(H1N1)."

"Ebola? The black vomit?"

"That's correct, sir." The typical response to Ebola, thanks to the many journalists who relished writing of its horrors. "But that's much less of a threat than the influenza we're talking about here."

"How's that?"

She had done a couple of quick searches on HAL and had come up with quite a bit of infomation.

"Well, Ebola HF is not likely to cause a widespread epidemic, as it is most often transmitted through close contact with the rodent reservoir or direct contact with infected people and their bodily fluids. Of course, it's made a lot of headlines and the symptoms are quite severe, but it's not a significant epidemic concern. It's not nearly as casually communicated as the influenza, which is readily transmitted on the airborne particles exhaled by an infected person and subsequently inhaled by another person. More importantly, the influenza strain indicated in the sample appears to be closely related to the deadly strain, commonly called the Spanish Flu, that caused the pandemic of 1918. That influenza is believed to have killed at least 25 million people world-wide and was conspicuous for the high death rate of young adults in their prime, rather than the children, old people, and infirmed who are the most common victims of influenza. The genome map and sequencing for this particular virus was completed last year on some old tissue samples that were recently found in the Armed Forces Institute of Pathology, so I have a good data set for comparison. What's most troubling, however, is this strain is somewhat different and appears to have undergone at least one antigenic shift, which would probably render existing vaccines almost completely ineffective. There are rumors that Russian bio researchers had recently recovered the original virus from victims buried and preserved in the Siberian tundra, successfully cloned it, and then developed a process which seems to require the extended exposure to low levels of ionizing radiation to accelerate the mutation process necessary for the somewhat radical antigenic shift ..."

"OK, Dr. Donnelly, I don't need the PhD version of the story. I need to check a few things right quick. Wait one, over."

Not exactly sure what that meant, as she had never heard anyone say "Wait one, over" on a telephone, she put the call on speakerphone and went back to HAL. In addition to the standard Fast Fourier and Discrete Cosine Transforms typically used for bio spectral decomposition, she decided to try a few of the relatively new Wavelet transforms to decompose the sample data. Although she had never even heard of Digital Signal Processing, or DSP as it was called, before she started working at USACEHR—it certainly wasn't part of her med school curriculum—she had quickly come to realize it was a key research tool. Needing to get smart, but aware of her ignorance, she had somewhat hesitantly approached an associate professor from the Electrical Engineering department of nearby Johns Hopkins University whom she had met at a medical instrumentation seminar in Baltimore. At first, he had rather petulantly answered her basic questions, but when it finally dawned on him that she was a medical researcher at a government lab that was a potential funding source for his own pet research projects, he ended up talking with her for 30 minutes. He had been surprised at her genuine interest and, over the following two months, had occasionally tutored her to the point where she now had a high-level understanding of DSP fundamentals. More importantly, he had become very interested in collaborative research work with USACEHR and eagerly loaned her a few Wavelet algorithms to load into HAL so she could start looking at specific uses of his research. Just as the Wavelet decomposition started, however, she was abruptly interrupted by the ringing of another of the Center's red phones. Seeing Col. Danielson's number in the Caller ID box, she realized she had become so engrossed in the situation that she had forgotten to update him. But before she could give him more than a few details, Colonel Jeffries voice boomed across the speakerphone.

"Dr. Donnelly, who is your Director of Operations?"

"Col. Danielson, sir."

"Is he there?"

"No, sir, he's at home, but I was just starting to fill him in when you came back."

"On a non-secure line?" came the incredulous question.

"No sir, on his STU-4."

"Good, if you have him on the line, why don't you make it a three-way? I want to talk to him direct." Realizing the Marine Colonel was directing her to set up a teleconference and not a ménage-a-trois, she hastily scanned the phone instructions sitting by the phone for how to set up a teleconference.

"Wait one, sir," she smiled to herself for using the jargon she had just picked up as she put him on mute and set up the call with Col. Danielson.

Colonel Jeffries had moved like a bullet after hearing of the potential bio threat to 11th MEU. He was not a computer system administrator, but he had one in his watch section, and the young corporal instantly grasped what Jeffries was trying to explain to him. It only took a few seconds for the "data dink," as Jeffries called him, to verify that the message that had gone to USACEHR via the I MEF server had in fact originated from the 11th MEU. Jeffries knew Col. Bob Steuben, the Commanding Officer of the 11th MEU and wondered what kind of trouble the Marines had encountered. Without a moment's hesitation, he picked up a patch line direct to the automated switchboard for the UHF satellite Demand Assigned Multiple Access (DAMA) controller at the Naval Computer and Telecommunications Area Master Station, Easter Pacific (NCTAMS EASTPAC) in Wahiawa, Hawaii, and punched in the number for the 11th MEU Command Net. The benefit of the direct patch line is that it allowed multiple stations, not even in the same satellite footprint, to use the half-duplex link without incurring the significant time delay penalty of a two-hop satellite connection, since part of the circuit would be through a much faster terrestrial fiber optic cable. His connection from San Diego to Hawaii via a Sprint undersea cable had one-twentieth of the delay of a satellite connection to Hawaii. After about two seconds, the communications circuit was established. Even without a push-to-talk handset, he could join the 11th MEU Command Net because of a voice recognition software daemon monitoring the call that initiated satellite transmission as soon as he started talking and stopped transmitting when he said "over" followed by a 200 millisecond pause. But everyone used a trigger word, like "talk" to initiate their speaking time because the system had a tendency to clip the first word. There was still a learning curve to be able to effectively communicate on a satellite voice net without talking over one another, but anyone senior enough to be standing watch in a high-level military operations center had learned that skill. Managing the word triggers for the keying/ unkeying of the transmitter rather than pressing/releasing a button on a handset took a few times to get the hang of, but he'd long ago mastered that as well. Although the military has had a UHF SATCOM capability for over 40 years, the limited usable bandwidth available for military use in the UHF band had provided a critical but poor quality communications link for most of that period. But advances in Digital Signal Processing had paved the way for the present DAMA system which provided many more users a higher quality link within the same bandwidth restrictions.

"11th MEU, this is Colonel Jeffries, I MEF Ops Center."

"Roger, I MEF."

"Is your actual available?" He wanted to speak directly with Colonel Steuben.

"Standby." But almost immediately, he heard a familiar voice.

"Colonel Jim Jeffries, what's up?"

"That's what I was calling to find out."

"What do you mean?"

"I've got someone from the Army's Bio lab asking me about a data sample that apparently came from a CPL Anderson with 11th MEU. They think it's probably a training mistake, but I thought I better check with you."

"Jim, I don't know anything about a sample sent to an Army lab, but I do have a 'hot' mission going on and the guys took in some of the new WMD detectors." WMD stood for Weapons of Mass Destruction. "They just worked a successful snatch operation and are on the way back. Let me talk to my S-2 and get back to you. But even if my guys did send in a report, why are they calling you?"

"Since we are your reachback point, the report went through an I MEF server. Of course they don't know we are your relay station, so when they did some network tracing and ended up at our server, they naturally thought the report originated here. But the reason I wanted to get you on the horn right away is because several potential bio agents were identified in the sample, and they include Ebola and a nasty strain of influenza. The research scientist wants to ask the sample originator some follow-up questions."

Even with the crypto security of the link, Steuben didn't reveal the exact purpose of the mission because he didn't think Jeffries had the "need to know" for that level of mission detail. 11th MEU's operational chain-of-command had changed three times since they had left Camp Pendleton, and I MEF was no longer in their "chop" chain.

Steuben turned to Major Renick. "Do you have any idea why an Army Lab would be asking I MEF about a data sample that came from Corporal Anderson in the last 10 minutes?" Steuben had been careful to avoid any mention of the word "bio," since there were a number of Marines in the MEU Command Center, and he wasn't about to distract them from doing their jobs with wild talk about a bio threat.

"No, sir, the squad didn't report anything else besides the successful snatch. It's possible there is a default configuration that initiated some kind of auto-report capability back to an Army lab. The MASS is the only thing we could reasonably carry in, but we're not really spun up on the full sensor configuration. Maybe the nuke detection sample was inadvertently sent to the Army lab and they're trying to figure out what to do with it." He offered somewhat lamely, underestimating Q's knowledge level.

Colonel Steuben wasn't about to take a chance with either his Marines or his mission, so he took a few seconds to think through the situation. Then he motioned Major Renick to follow him out of the Landing Force Operations Center (LFOC) and into the small controlled access Joint Intelligence Center (JIC) the Marines shared with the sailors. The JIC was the only place you could access the Top Secret and Sensitive Compartmented Information (TS/SCI) intelligence data that the MEU frequently received from the National Imagery and Mapping Agency (NIMA) and the National Security Agency (NSA). Once they were both inside the secure compartment, Steuben told Renick the full story.

"The sample from Q went to the Army's Bio Lab where it triggered all sorts of alarms. Serious enough that they immediately contacted I MEF. There was some confusion initially on where the sample had come from because it apparently went through our reachback point at I MEF rather than coming directly from us. But something sure the hell is going on!"

"Sir, even though we're sending stuff on the SIPRNET, all our IP addresses are mapped over to I MEF's IP address space through the Firewall we had installed at the I MEF NOC. I didn't want any geek with a clearance sniffing around finding out what we are doing out here, so everything looks like we're at Camp Pendleton. Also, the Sensor Integration Module, or SIM, is set up to deny transmission of any geopositional information to anyone except us. So we've got a pretty good spoof going. But since Corporal Anderson is set up as the default user on the SIM, his name would have still shown up as the sensor operator on the report. That would explain the geographic confusion and everything else you've told me ... except for why the Army got the sample in the first place and what was in the sample. We have had sporadic indications of Al-Qaeda search for bio material, although that has mostly been from Somalia and Sudan. The National Intel guys briefed that they didn't consider bio to be even a remote possibility for this mission, but they could be wrong and it's possible the squad picked up something unexpected. It's still more likely that we have some hosed up configuration on the MASS, and Q sent out a bogus report."

Although he was intimately familiar with the geography of the region, Steuben's eyes flicked to the large wall-mounted map. Sudan was only a few hundred miles across the Red Sea from the west coast of Yemen. Somalia was less than that across the Gulf of Aden. And if anything was first moved into Eritrea or Djibouti, the distance was less than 20 miles across the Bab el Mandeb, where the Red Sea meets the Gulf of Aden.

"OK, let's get I MEF on the sqawk box," he said, referring to the speaker which could be connected to the various voice radio nets, so more than one person could listen in on the conversation.

Renick typed in the code for the MEU command net on the digital display in the Intelligence Center, selected "private" to keep anyone in the LFOC from listening in and depressed the push-to-talk button.

Back at the I MEF Command Center, Jeffries was patiently waiting. He knew 11th MEU was in a prolonged period of very high op tempo, and this was probably the last thing they needed to hear right now. When they were ready, they would get back to him. But he was getting a feeling in his gut that there was something very wrong.

Not wanting to keep the USACEHR people waiting in the dark while he waited for 11th MEU to call him back, Jeffries switched over to the line on which he had been speaking with Dr. Donnelly.

"Dr. Donnelly, are you still there?"

"Yes sir, and I have Colonel Danielson on the line as well."

"Colonel Danielson, I've contacted a unit we have forward deployed that appears to be the originator of the sample. The unit has a team out in the field with one of the new MEM detectors, and they are contacting the team so we can figure out exactly what is going on here. There are more security issues than I can possibly address related to the mission and location of the unit. I can't tell you right now what will happen—whether you will be able to talk directly to the sensor operator now or we end up having to relay the information. Do you understand?"

"Yes, I do, Colonel, but I need to stress the importance of getting timely information here. Lives could be at risk."

"Trust me, Colonel Danielson, there were lives at risk in this unit long before we started worrying about a bio threat. Sorry for the formality and the mystery, but that's the way it has to be. Also, we'll have to skip the science lecture and go right to the meat with these guys. Do you have questions prepared?" he asked, thinking how long it had taken to get the scoop from Dr. Donnelly.

"Yes, we do."

"OK, hang in there until I hear back from the unit."

After a very long sixty seconds, the MEU came back on the net.

"I MEF, this is 11th MEU."

"Roger, this is Colonel Jeffries."

"Jim, I'm here with my S-2, Major Renick," as Colonel Steuben picked up the conversation, "we've moved into the Intel Center to keep the conversation private. I hope you're secure on your end as well."

"I'm the only one here in on this so far. Haven't even called the General yet."

"OK, what else can you tell us?"

"I'd like to patch in the people from USACEHR for the technical details and for any questions you have. Of course, I haven't told them who or where you are, and we can keep it that way. But they do want to talk to a Corporal Anderson."

"We'll play that by ear, Jim."

"Roger, that's what I told them. OK, stand by."

Jeffries switched back over to the USACEHR line and spent a minute trying to explain the connection and the voice-activated transmitter keying. It was clear neither of the doctors had ever used such a link, and he wasn't very successful in explaining the method of operation. Damn eggheads, always made the simple things hard. Finally, in exasperation, Jeffries told them he would act as the net controller and tell them when to talk and when to stop talking. Then he got back on the net with 11th MEU.

"I have Col. Danielson and Dr. Donnelly here from USACEHR. Dr. Donnelly, please provide a quick summary of the results from your analysis of the sample."

She did so in under a minute, Colonel Jeffries observed. He had made some notes from his earlier conversation with her and was checking off items as she provided the summary. It looked like she had covered almost everything. The only item she hadn't mentioned were the rumors about the work of Russian scientists on mutating the Spanish flu virus that had killed 25 million.

While waiting for Colonel Steuben to come back up on the net, he recalled a PBS documentary on the Influenza Epidemic of 1918 that he had chanced upon while watching TV at home one evening. He had been astounded that he had never heard of the monstrous epidemic before, the way it had torn through the country and especially, the terrible toll wrought on soldiers living in close quarters in barracks, on troopships, and in the trenches of World War I. Part of the hysteria was the accusation that the Germans had unleashed "germ warfare" on the Allies. He had found the entire story very unsettling and thought of it now. Though he realized the rumors about the Russians probably weren't important, Colonel Jeffries was, by nature, an extremely thorough man.

"Dr. Donnelly, what about the process for mutating the influenza virus?"

"Right. Over the last several months, rumors have surfaced that prior to the break-up of the Soviet Union, the Russians had recovered the 1918 Influenza virus and had found some success in creating a deadlier version by extended exposure to low levels of ionizing radiation ... over," finished Colonel Jeffries.

He wanted to get a read from the MEU before they went any further, so he quickly took the USACEHR line out of the connection.

"I've temporarily disconnected the bio people from the call. Did you copy all of that, 11th MEU?"

Colonel Steuben and Major Renick had been intently listening and had both been thinking to themselves that there didn't appear to be anything to worry about, the bio threat was highly unlikely in the very rustic environment where Hussar's squad had performed their mission. But Dr. Donnelly's last comment about the radiation-induced mutations had brought both of them to their feet.

"I think we better let them talk to the squad, sir," Renick advised.

Colonel Steuben nodded his head and hit the talk switch. "Give us a minute here, Colonel Jeffries. We need to contact the unit and I'll get back to you."

# Chapter 4

Get Hussar on the hook," Colonel Steuben ordered Major Renick.

Within seconds, Hussar joined the net, patched in Q, and reported to Steuben and Renick about the readings picked up from the strange vials found in the SADM-10 bag. In turn, Renick informed them of the bio lab's request for additional information. When Hussar responded negatively to Renick's question about whether the vials had been opened, both officers exhaled audibly, hoping that the Marines had got into their NBC gear before being seriously exposed.

Renick had a sudden thought, *the MASS actually had two modes of operation.* The primary mode sucked in an air sample, ran it through the full two-pass mass and fluorescence spectroscopy process, and provided a fairly comprehensive analysis. The secondary mode didn't need an air sample but used a small ultraviolet LED to direct energy in the desired direction and a photoluminescent charge-coupled diode detector to measure reflected emission spectra. The results were not as accurate, and the device only had a stand-off range of about 6 feet.

"Q, are you using the MASS primary mode and collecting actual air samples, or are you using its secondary detection capability?" Renick asked.

Once Major Renick asked the question, Q remembered there was a degraded mode of operation with the MASS that he and the Major had been told about at Oak Ridge but had never actually been trained on because the developers thought it was still too fragile.

"Sir, we've only ever used the primary mode." He pulled up the MASS screen to verify the configuration. He couldn't see any obvious indication of which mode he was in. *Damn, where is that setting,* he thought to himself.

"Sir, where is the mode indicator? I don't have anything about mode on my screen, and it's hard to see much with my gas mask on."

"Just a second, Q, I'll go get the other MASS and walk you through the steps." Renick ran back to the LFOC and grabbed the second MASS. He quickly connected it to an IDS and powered everything up. After a few seconds, he found what he was looking for. There was a Mode tab on the Options screen that the operator could select from the Configuration menu. Renick saw there were three options to choose from: Primary, Secondary, or Both. He quickly walked Q through the steps.

"It's in 'Both' mode, sir! What does that impact?"

"Well, based on what you've told me, it seems like we only saw the higher readings when you were looking directly into the bag. Being near the bag or the prisoner didn't do anything. So I'm thinking that since you have both the Primary and Secondary modes operating continuously, you are only getting a hit when you basically have the MASS inside the satchel, and that hit is coming from the Secondary detector. Why don't you see if you can verify that by switching between modes while you are over the open satchel?"

It took a long minute, but they could hear the excitement in Q's voice, even through his gas mask.

"You're right, sir! The vials are a clear plastic and the Secondary must work right through it, but there isn't anything picked up by the Primary detector."

"OK, good, it doesn't look like you guys have been exposed to anything since the air sample came up clean. But keep your NBC gear on anyway until we can check you out back on the ship. This may also explain why you never saw an actual alarm. The secondary detector isn't as sensitive as the primary, and we had all the alarm thresholds set for operation with the primary detector."

Maybe the sophisticated photoluminescence detection capability of the MASS actually could remotely sense biological agents without the need for physical contact with the substance. If it turned out to be true, Renick would have to pass that on to the scientists at Oak Ridge. They would be excited to hear about any success in the field. He recalled one of the engineers on the team telling him if the atmospheric conditions were just right and the bio material was in a plastic or glass container that wasn't too opaque, detection could theoretically occur at 100 meters. The present design, which was only good for a couple of meters, was still pretty remarkable considering the small size of the sensor.

Renick then briefed Q on USACEHR's initial analysis of his sample and repeated several times that with the high false alarm rate associated with bio detection, there was a pretty good chance the analysis was incorrect. Of course, someone had gone to the trouble of stashing the vials with the SADM-10. And only bad guys would have had that kind of access to the device.

It was time to get the guys back in CONUS on the link. Major Renick gave a final warning to Hussar and Q that nothing could be said about the SADM-10 or their exact location because the other people on the link didn't have the need to know. If Colonel Steuben wanted to bring it up, well, he was the C.O. and could pretty much do what he wanted.

But Colonel Steuben had already decided he needed someone stateside who was aware of the situation. This mission was big, but it had possibly just gotten a lot bigger. So, he came clean with Jeffries and told him about the vials being discovered in the same bag as the SADM-10 that his men had snagged. After a short discussion, it was decided that this information was too sensitive to pass on, but they also couldn't do anything to hamper the analysis of potentially very lethal bio material. Major Renick came up with the plan. He would brief the USACEHR doctors that the vials had been discovered in a remote hospital in Southern Yemen. To get in the possibly important point that there had been a radiation source nearby, Renick would identify the place as a cancer treatment facility—probably for all the locals who smoked Camels—that held radioactive materials to provide radiation treatments. That would get in the important points, even if it was an unlikely story. Colonel Jeffries offered that Col. Danielson would immediately see through it but would be smart enough to realize there must be some serious security implications and would not press them. If there were other questions, the doctors would be permitted to ask Q directly.

"Q, are you OK with this?"

"Yes sir."

"OK, we'll be monitoring here, and Colonel Jeffries at I MEF will have his finger on the disconnect button. If they get squirrelly, he'll cut 'em off. Once again, just don't give them any specifics about your mission or location."

"Roger, sir."

As Q was trying to sort through everything that had just happened in the last 10 minutes, the call request popped up on his screen. Verbal communications from pre-approved members of his voice community were configured to automatically connect through to his earpiece, if no other audio was being received at that time. Anyone else trying to contact him would be held behind a call screening capability until he accepted the call. The idea was to be able to potentially communicate with many different people, but only allow a chosen few to cut in during operations. The call request was from I MEF, since they were patching in USACEHR.

Q looked at Hussar, who had the same message popping up on his screen. Hussar gave a nod and they both accepted the call.

Sergeant Hussar was surprised when a pleasant female voice came over his headset. Nobody had mentioned a woman. Considering where he was and what the squad had just been through, it seemed weird.

Things had changed a lot in many parts of the military but not too much in the units especially designed to kill people at close quarters. In spite of all the mind-numbing gender balancing that the military had been subjected to over the last 20 years, when it came to people on the ground pulling triggers to kill people who were within shouting distance, there was still a line drawn beyond which women were not allowed. Hussar was glad there were still some Generals with balls (he smiled at his pun), so that when the "Women in the Armed Forces" discussions started looking at "equalizing" the force structure of units operating at the "tip of the spear," they were able to steer the focus of the discussion almost exclusively to fighting effectiveness. This had marginalized the man-haters social equality argument, and it had been done with brutal dispatch. He had heard about the video the Commandant of the Marine Corps had shown to the liberal do-gooders on the 1994 Presidential Blue Ribbon panel for the "Role of Women in the Armed Forces of the United States." It was a 8mm home movie, captured 20 years earlier, and chronicled the daily life of a band of Viet Cong rebels. Among other disturbing scenes, the film showed, in graphic detail, an ecstatic group of Viet Cong executing and subsequently dismembering two US soldiers found wounded after the Viet Cong had ambushed their patrol. And a scene of an attack on an apparently unsympathetic village, where the village chief and his entire family were disemboweled alive in front of the rest of the villagers. Half of the Blue Ribbon panel, mostly high-brow East Coast Liberals, including a high profile, self-righteous Ivy League law professor who was always available for the evening talk shows, barely made it out of the room before becoming violently ill. The stony-faced Marines in attendance made no attempt to comfort the civilians. The message was clear—there was evil in the world that no amount of bureaucratic action could overcome or billion dollar stand-off weapons systems could eliminate. Marines on the ground would be necessary to root out the worst of it. And when it came to that, and it always would come to that at some point when dealing with true evil, there couldn't be any social engineering limitations on the fighting spirit and effectiveness of the guys that had to go in. And Hussar knew it was true. Although this woman with the pleasant voice wasn't there physically among them, just the sound of her voice had distracted him for a moment. Of course, there would always be people who would suggest the problem was with the young Marine for being unprofessionally distracted—obviously only those people who had forgotten, or were biological freaks and had somehow missed out on, the hormone load any normal 18 year-old male was carrying around in the tip of the raging hard-on he was sporting 24/7. The same hormone load that caused a kid to be willing to voluntarily risk his life to go into battle for political causes he may not fully understand. It was highly unlikely that the two reactions could somehow be separated—so that the kid's budding libido

55

could be neutered, but his willingness to commit violent acts on command could be maintained—but this was exactly the social agenda of a group of media-darling, politically-active socialists and other liberals.

Now 23, and wizened by experience, Hussar well-remembered being an 18-year-old "immortal" willing to take on the world for truth, justice, and the American way—or for pretty much any other reason that came along. And he was quite sure those memories accurately characterized every one of the young Marines in his squad right now.

But the lady with the pleasant voice was apparently the one who had analyzed Q's sample and had the questions that even the Colonel figured couldn't wait, so he better pay attention to the mission and stop wondering if the woman was good-looking.

"This is Karen Donnelly at USACEHR. OK, we understand from Major Renick that the sample was taken inside a medical facility and that you can't give us some information because of security concerns. But I would like to ask Corporal Anderson a few questions—just answer the ones you can, please."

"Yes, ma'am," Q responded.

"How was the sample taken?"

"I scanned the MEM sensor over the 3 sealed plastic vials I found. It was the Secondary detector that got the hit through the plastic."

"From what distance?"

"About a foot."

"What were the background environmental conditions: time of day, temperature, humidity, wind, atmospheric dust, number of people or animals in the area?" She was reading right off the Watch Officer's checklist in the Crisis Response Center.

Q gave approximate answers to the questions.

"Were the samples packaged in any special way?"

"It appeared the samples were being kept warm. There was packing around them—something like those chemical instant heat packs you squeeze and put on a sore muscle."

"Were there any indications of people being treated for any infectious diseases at the hospital? This would probably be indicated by an area of the hospital that was under a quarantine restriction."

"No, ma'am, I didn't really see any sick people." Since the hospital story was bogus, Q hoped this wasn't an important question. He had no idea if anyone had been exposed to any of the terrible diseases in the vials. He didn't even know if he had been exposed. Maybe they would have a different answer for her in a couple of days when they were fully into the incubation periods of the diseases. He shuddered at the thought.

"Do you have any idea of the strength of the radiation source and how long the vials have been exposed?"

"I don't know how long they've been exposed, but the radiation dose rate is approximately 1 mrem/hour. And if it helps, the radiation source is generating gamma rays of 1.8 MeV." His radiation detector had been very steady with those numbers ever since they picked up the SADM-10.

1 mrem/hour was about 25 times typical background radiation level. MeV, or million electron volts, was the standard unit of measure for the energy of a gamma ray.

In the *Tarawa's* Intel Center, Renick frowned. Although the radiation specifics were probably important to the bio researchers, any amateur quantum physicist (or somebody who didn't mind spending 2 minutes doing a web search) would eliminate medical X-ray machines, Cobalt calibration sources, and cancer treatment devices as likely radiation sources for 1.8 MeV gamma rays. The same person would probably also know that 1.8 MeV gamma rays are produced during the natural radioactive decay series of a Uranium-235 atom. Renick knew all this information because he had been instructed by the Defense Threat Reduction Agency (DTRA) cadre at Oak Ridge National Laboratory to calibrate his radiation detector sensitivity peak for 1.8 MeV gamma rays, specifically because that energy level was significant for the Uranium decay but was highly unlikely to occur from other natural or man-made emitters. Of course, the DTRA guys knew his Marines were looking for Uranium-235 decays, since weapons-grade uranium was generally enriched to greater than 90 percent Uranium-235. Anyone else would have to connect the dots to figure out 11th MEU was in the nuclear weapons business, but the dots had just gotten bigger and closer together.

Karen Donnelly had heard enough to realize this could be a very serious threat. There was still the chance they were dealing with a false detect, but the circumstances were very suspicious. To get an indication of three really bad bio agents off of three sealed vials was not good. To have found the vials carefully wrapped in some sort of thermal blanket near a gamma radiation source was even worse. To guess that the Marines had probably taken the vials off some very bad, and probably very dead, people made the situation downright frightening. She knew the Marines didn't give her the whole story, but it was clear they were chasing terrorists. What else would Marines be doing in Yemen? Suddenly, she was very glad the Marines were so intense. At least now, the vials were out of the hands of the terrorists.

"OK, that's all I have right now. Thank you very much. I want to look up some reference material, and then I would like to call back, if that's OK. Col. Danielson?"

"Gentlemen, you can imagine our desire to get the material to a lab for accurate analysis as soon as possible. We need to figure out how to do this quickly, but safely. Also, I'll have to report up my chain immediately. I don't know if you've had a chance yet to inform your superiors, but it will make things easier if we both have the same story …"

Colonel Jeffries had to cut him off the UHF SATCOM link before the good doctor took over the war, "Col. Danielson, 11th MEU is the lead on this."

And Colonel Steuben was right there to help clear things up.

"Exactly. First thing, my Marines in the field can go ahead and drop off the net. They still have a lot going on and don't need to get bogged down in administrivia. We'll see you shortly, gents," replied Steuben, as a dismissal to Sergeant Hussar and Q. He wasn't about to get into a chain-of-command and logistics discussion with a couple of O-6's while two grunt NCO's, especially two grunt NCO's sitting on a beach in Yemen waiting to get picked up, were still on the net.

"Second, I need to get back on the horn with CENTCOM to report this possible bio threat. I'm going to tell CENTCOM that the threat has not been confirmed, but we are already in contact with the experts at USACEHR and will continue the dialogue with them. I'm quite sure this situation will attract lots of attention very quickly, Colonel Danielson, and you should expect to hear from CENTCOM within the next 10 minutes."

Colonel Steuben had delayed any additional reporting until he was sure everything possible was done to protect Sergeant Hussar's squad from the possible threat. The brass would be pissed they weren't notified first, but they would just have to deal with it. No one at CENTCOM could have really helped him with this crazy bio issue (except ask a thousand questions he couldn't have answered), so he wasn't about to take the time to provide an informational report while he still had Marines in a potentially deadly situation.

"Finally, thanks for the help. We'll look forward to hearing back from Dr. Donnelly with any additional information or questions. I hope she is assigned to work this issue. Also, I need to stress again the importance of keeping this information at the Top Secret level and not sharing it with anyone who doesn't have a need-to-know. For now, I am the Classification Authority and I'm limiting that need-to-know group to the people on this radio net plus two others—your boss, Col. Danielson, and CG, I MEF as Colonel Jeffries superior. Once CENTCOM is in the loop, they will figure out who gets to know what, but for now, that's the way it has to be. Acknowledge receipt, please."

"Affirmative, I understand, Col. Stueben," answered Colonel Jeffries.

"Yes, I agree," responded Col. Danielson.

"Out here." Steuben broke the connection.

He immediately got on the net with the Senior Watch Officer at CENTCOM and reported the discovery of the potential bio agents. There had been quite a few laudatory comments when he reported the capture of the SADM-10 and the terrorist prisoner a little over an hour ago. Now his report was greeted with stunned silence.

Before they could start in on him with the questions, Steuben said, "We'll have an Op Immediate report out through DMS in the next two minutes which will catch you up. My S-3 is finishing it now. Since my Marines are still in-country, I'll need to stay on top of the local situation here until they've returned to the *Tarawa*. But we'll send follow-up reports every 30 minutes until they become redundant. I recommend we hold a VTC in 90 minutes, make that 0030 Zulu, and I also recommend you try to get Dr. Donnelly from USACEHR at Ft. Detrick on for part of the VTC. We've already had a brief technical exchange with USACEHR to help us try to determine exactly what we are dealing with here in the way of possible hazards and prudent safeguards."

He knew he was way ahead of the guys at CENTCOM headquarters in Tampa, Florida, on this one. So he might as well take the initiative and try to control the MEU's information reporting requirements. Plus, a schedule for getting updates would make the colonel on watch at CENTCOM look good—the brass would think he had a plan and was on top of the situation, so maybe they would give the MEU a little breathing room. That would buy Steuben some time to work the local situation and figure out his next moves. Of course, once the J-3 or the CINC showed up at the CENTCOM command center and demanded additional information, they would be all over him. But such was the life of a field commander in this day of instant global communications.

Telling CENTCOM he would send out Op Immediate reports via DMS, the Defense Message System, was a gentle reminder that a mechanism already existed for timely and official electronic reporting of significant issues. DMS would take a little longer than voice, but you had the luxury of the written word to staff, analyze, evaluate, and respond to.

"Uh, roger, 11th MEU, that sounds good. I'll pass on to the J-3 and get back to you," replied CENTCOM.

Now that he had the guys at CENTCOM in the loop and hot on the bio problem, Steuben called the Amphibious Squadron (the Navy cut it to PHIBRON) Commodore in the *Tarawa*'s Flag Quarters and gave him an update. The commodore, Navy Captain Ben Skwidolio, had been speechless for a good 10 seconds upon hearing of the chance discovery of the vials in the SADM-10 satchel.

They had already put together a good plan for handling the SADM-10 aboard the ship, but the situation had just become much more complicated with the need to handle potentially dangerous bio vials. Regardless of the final determination on the lethality of the contents of the vials, for now they had no choice but to treat them as extremely hazardous material. Skwidolio was very sensitive to minimizing the number of people who had any chance of coming into contact with bio material or had any information concerning what had been found. The first thing he did was call down to the Communication Center to make sure the ship's unclassified Internet and telephone connections were still deactivated. He had secured access to/from the ship for the popular "sailor" phones and for email transfer once the amphibious group had entered the Gulf of Aden. The sailors and Marines could still write emails to loved ones back home, but the emails would all be queued up in the Comm Center until the connection was restored. Then, Skwidolio called his Battle Staff together. There were going to be some very busy sailors in the next few hours.

Colonel Steuben next decided to make an informal call to Col. Bill West, a good friend and classmate from The Basic School in Quantico, VA. Unlike the other Military Services, the Marines sent all their officers to a common 6-month school, formally named "The Basic School," with typical USMC understatement, where all newly-commissioned officers were taught how to be Marine officers. Whether the officer was destined to fly a jet, join a tank or artillery battalion, run a maintenance or supply shop, or lead an infantry platoon, he started off at The Basic School and learned small-unit infantry tactics. To the other Services, this was perceived as an unaffordable luxury. The Marines laughed off such criticism, as there is not a single recorded incident of any Marine having ever suffered a luxury by the design of Headquarters, Marine Corps. Frugal stewards of the Corps' miniscule budget, the Marines made up for the small expense of The Basic School by maintaining a significantly lower officer to enlisted ratio than the other Services—after all, NCOs won battles, not officers—and by promoting their officers at a much slower rate than the other Services. So there really weren't that many new Marine officers every year to send to The Basic School.

The reason Steuben wanted to call Colonel West, rather than one of his other O-6 buddies, was because West was the Executive Assistant (EA) to Vice Admiral Gordon "Ice Man" Preble, the Military Liaison to the National Security Council. Although this communication would technically be outside the chain of command and could conceivably get Steuben in hot water—the military, in general, and the Marines, in particular, viewed the chain of command as sacrosanct—Steuben realized his situation was moving quickly beyond the military arena into serious diplomatic and political areas that the President's inner circle better start thinking about very soon. He went to his SIPRnet computer and sent a short email, "Colonel West, Call me ASAP—Steuben," to the Communications Watch Officer at the White House Communications Center. He knew the Watch Officer would get the message and immediately send a page and give a confirmation phone call to Colonel West. As the EA, Colonel West had a 24/7 job and was required to be within 50 miles of the White House and maintain "good" cell phone coverage at all times. Steuben knew West would call him within minutes unless he was deep in the middle of working some other national emergency.

He touched the intercom to the LFOC.

"Captain Garrett?" John Garrett, the MEU Assistant Air Officer, was standing watch in the LFOC as the Duty Operations Officer.

"Yessir."

"I'm expecting a call from a Colonel West. Please patch it through to me here in the Intel Center."

"Aye-aye, sir," came the immediate reply.

He didn't wait long. The intercom buzzer went off within two minutes, and West was on the Top Secret phone line.

"Wild Bill, we ran into something hot out here."

"I heard about the SADM-10 snatch and grabbing a bad guy. Good work."

Steuben wasn't surprised that his friend had already heard of the earlier success. After all, West was the one who had initially pushed for the mission on Yemen, and he had also probably drafted the note about the SADM-10 recovery to send in to the President. The man was definitely a player on the A-team. But he clearly hadn't gotten wind of the new problem.

"Turns out, that was the easy part. We expected to find and grab the nuke. But things just got a little more complicated. There is a good chance some very lethal bio agents were also in the satchel."

"Christ, was anyone exposed?" West hadn't hesitated at all. He was already working to assess the danger and solve the problem. There was a reason the Marines had sent him to support the National Security Council.

"Don't think so at this time. We still haven't got confirmation on the threat or if any of my guys are in danger. The squad is still on the beach, and I'm working with the PHIBRON Commodore, Ben Skwidolio, to get the ship ready to handle the material."

"I'm sure you'll be getting plenty of help here shortly."

"And that's why I'm calling you."

"What do you need?"

"It's what I don't need. And that's plenty of help. We'll be fine out here. CENTCOM will figure out how to get the WMD and the bad guy safely back to CONUS. That's the most important thing right now, of course, and I'm sure they will have a plan within 4 hours. But our focus has to be on getting more bad guys. What we just did is going to shake up the terrorist network big time. It's possible we set Al-Qaeda back and they'll hide out for a while, but it's just as possible they will accelerate any pending attack timelines if they think we're closing in. We need to follow up while we have them off-balance, so rather than sit back and congratulate ourselves, we need to increase the tempo and keep the pressure on them. My Intel Officer is telling me that the Al-Qaeda bio efforts were mostly in Africa, Sudan, and Somalia. We'll talk to the prisoner while he's still disoriented to see what we can get out of him and pass it along. If there are other operations being considered in this theater, people should be looking at us first. My guys are ready to go, we're just getting warmed up out here. We've been on station for a couple of months, and my staff and the PHIBRON staff have come together nicely. We're getting a real feel for the bad guys and their environment. Believe me, we've done nothing but live this situation. So that's where you come in, Bill. We're due to start heading back to CONUS in a couple of weeks. 13th MEU left California a month ago and will be on station in a few days to start the turnover process to relieve us. Normally, we would be more than ready to get off these damn ships and go home. But the truth of the matter is, it takes a while to get good, and you gotta use it or lose it. So don't let anyone stop us now, make us all heroes, and bring us back to CONUS to sell war bonds. Do some of that National Security stuff and keep us out here a while to work some more ops."

"You want to extend your time on station? OK. How about ... It is becoming increasingly obvious that with the complexity of the operational environment and the time it takes to come up to speed and work as an effective anti-terrorism task force, we ought to consider taking advantage of the expertise and location of 11th MEU and keep them on the job for a while. This will also allow a longer turnover period for 13th MEU, thereby providing them additional time to become fully engaged in the operational cycle."

"I knew you would come up with something clever."

"Here to serve. How long are you good for?"

"I figure the Navy will only be able to keep this old rust bucket working for another 4-6 weeks before she'll need to get back to a shipyard."

"Is Skwidolio in on this?"

"You bet. And we both briefed our people before we left that it was almost a guarantee the deployment would be extended for up to 90 days."

"Consider it done then. I'll talk to the Admiral tomorrow morning. Anything else?"

"Take a close look at Somalia. My Intel Officer thinks there is some linkage. We don't see everything out here, so we could be off the mark, but I would like to know."

"You got it. You need anything else, you let me know."

"OK, thanks."

"Happy hunting. Out, here." West was gone.

Steuben had gotten the ball rolling. It was time to get back to the LFOC and see how the extract was going.

# Chapter 5

Looking out to sea through his night vision sight, Hussar could just make out a lighter spot on the horizon at the line where the calm Arabian Sea met the night sky. The spot sort of pulsated on and off for several seconds before finally staying lit. As he continued to watch, the light got bigger and brighter but still shimmered in intensity. It seemed to be heading straight for the beach. Through his scope, it looked like an invisible person carrying a bunch of agitated lightning bugs in a jar was running right at him. He guessed it could be a cloud of sea mist reflecting light from the quarter moon that had only minutes before begun its westerly trek across the sky. But even with the light amplification of the night vision sight, it would take a lot of sea mist to glow so brightly. Probably at least the volume of spray whipped up by a hovercraft zipping over the water at high speed, he realized. He looked at the clock on his IDS. 0330. That should make it the extract LCAC. He couldn't tell how far away it was or how fast it was coming, but between the limited range of his sight and the LCAC being capable of making an easy 40 knots, he figured the "pilot" would very soon be looking for the infrared lights marking the beach to guide the LCAC's approach to the pickup point. Time to make radio contact.

"Chief, this is Strike One, over."

"Go Strike One, over."

"What is your ETA to the extract point, over?"

"One zero mikes, over."

"Roger, the beach is 200 yards wide and 50 yards deep. Surface is sand, almost no gradient, and zero obstacles. I'll mark the edges and back. The load is four light trucks and 15 packs, over."

"Roger, out."

It was time to turn on the beach "lights."

"Spike, let there be light!"

"You got it, Boss."

His Fire Team cracked several special "Chem-lites" and laid them out. Unlike typical chemical light sticks available in green, yellow, red, and various other colors, these sticks didn't emit anything in the visible light range. When you busted the inner seal and allowed the two liquids to mix and chemically react, the sticks only emitted light in the infrared range. So you had to be using the proper night vision equipment to even see the sticks at all.

"Chief, Strike One, we're lit."

"Roger, I have you in sight. Touch down in four mikes, over."

"Roger, out."

It had been a long and stressful night, and Hussar was ready to get the hell out of Yemen. He knew he wasn't the only one.

"OK, First Squad, saddle up. Extract starts in four mikes. Get the vehicles started. Spike's team will cover our getaway," he ordered.

The extract was relatively quick and without surprise, with the exception of his shock at seeing every sailor on the LCAC completely clothed in full NBC protective gear. It should have been expected, but Hussar had been so focused on the squad's mission that the impact of the evening's events hadn't fully sunk in yet. With his squad's possible exposure to lethal bio agents, it was obvious all of them would be treated like lepers because of the potential contamination threat and danger to others they represented. Anyone aware of the squad's situation that still required close contact with them would certainly take all necessary precautions. But it made for an eerie sight as the LCAC ramp lowered and several individuals in self-contained, airtight level A ensembles emerged from the dust and sand clouds kicked up by the boat.

In spite of the extra bulk of the NBC suits, the LCAC crew swiftly lashed down the trucks and got the craft underway again.

The Marines, with the SADM-10 satchel and the still unconscious prisoner in tow, settled into the cramped troop compartment for the ride back to the *Tarawa*.

Moving aft to the back of the small space, Gasser stumbled over a small footlocker partially sticking out from under one of the benches. Curious, he opened it and found sandwiches, fruit, and sodas that someone had thoughtfully sent along for them.

"Hey, guys, look at all this chow!" he shouted above the din of the LCAC's four large gas turbine engines.

Boner quickly saw the dilemma. "Gasser, how you going to eat any of it through your gas mask? It's a cruel joke that someone has done to us, boys. Probably one of those geeks from Echo Company."

There was an intense rivalry between different units at every echelon of the battalion, with squads, platoons, and companies all trying to better one another. The Marines are famous for "eating their young," especially during the lulls between wars when they can't direct their ferocious energies against an external enemy. Hussar's squad had gone down to the wire with a squad from Echo Company in the latest Battalion Super Squad competition before finally winning, and there was still a lot of ribbing between the Marines involved in the contest, including practical jokes. But it galled Boner to think that while they were out on a mission risking their necks, someone would come up with a plan to screw with them.

"Nah, those guys aren't that smart," chimed in Spike. "The squids probably brought the snacks along to munch on the way to the extract. They probably had a nice little picnic before they put on their zoot suits and stormed the beach," he smirked.

The Marines laughed at the image of sailors lounging around on red checkerboard blankets with picnic baskets full of food. There was always joking with the Navy to keep spirits up.

The joking didn't last very long. Almost as soon as the LCAC got off the beach, heads started dropping. Marines were known for the ability to sleep anywhere. Hussar had barely enough time to set up a watch for the SADM-10 and the prisoner before the entire room resonated with muffled snores as Marines, still wearing NBC masks, fell into a deep sleep. He had seen it coming. They had been pumped on adrenalin for almost 8 hours. You came off an adrenalin "fix" hard and quick. And the longer and more pumped you had been, the harder and quicker you came off it.

Just as the LCAC cleared the coastline and reached cruising speed, Sergeant Hussar flinched as Colonel Steuben's booming voice came through his headset.

"Sergeant Hussar?"

"Yessir."

"Quite a bit of concern about the apparent bio material you discovered. Caught a lot of people by surprise all the way up the chain of command. I expect it will take some time to sort things out back in CONUS. Congratulations, though, because one thing is for certain, if this stuff turns out to be real, and the folks that should know are now saying that is the most likely scenario, your squad just became the premier bio detection and recovery unit in the entire Department of Defense. That wasn't your intention, and probably isn't your first choice of things to be known for, but that's the way it will play out. From my perspective, by the way, this is a good thing. I've already refocused the MEU staff on planning several follow-up missions and, as we speak, Major Renick is busy pumping the national bubbas for any intel on bio threats in our Area of Operations. More on that when we get you back to the ship. Suffice it to say that hard evidence of WMD in the hands of terrorists is another big wake-up call for our country.

For now, though, first things first. We're going to have to run your squad through full decontamination. Apparently, the new MASS sensor you have can do what is called a "gross" detection, but the eggheads won't sign off to it being capable of detecting the miniscule amounts of material that could still constitute a health hazard to your squad. So there is a question of whether you were exposed to a potentially dangerous level of contamination that is not detectable by the MASS. I can't tell you whether they are just trying to cover their asses or if there is a real concern. Either way, we're going to need to decon and then quarantine your squad for the predicted worst-case incubation period, which is 36 hours."

Colonel Steuben had decided to quarantine the squad on the LCAC until the risk could be fully evaluated. There really wasn't much in the way of options. Colonel Steuben had to play it safe, although he hated the thought of the Marines successfully completing a dangerous mission and then not being able to return immediately to the ship. But after the information from USAECHR, the alarming news of the bio threat had to be taken seriously, and he couldn't put the rest of his command at risk. He had spoken with the CO of the ship, and they had a quick sit-down with the Senior Medical Officer and the MEU NBC Officer and a video teleconference with decontamination experts at Naval Sea Systems Center (NAVSEA) and at Bethesda National Naval Medical Center. Everyone had agreed the best approach would be to extract Sergeant Hussar's squad and the prisoner with an LCAC, decontaminate them at sea, and hold them on the LCAC until they were safely through the incubation period before allowing them back onto the ship. Since an LCAC extraction was already planned because they wanted to keep the trucks Hussar's squad had obtained, thanks to the efforts of a CIA operative working in Yemen, this also seemed like the easiest plan to execute. The experts had also made the point that seawater is a great decontaminant, so a seawater washdown of personnel, equipment, and even the LCAC itself would greatly aid the clean-up effort. Floating around in the Arabian Sea certainly made seawater a plentiful resource. Of course, some expert assistance would also be required, so a decontamination and monitoring crew led by the MEU NBC officer and made up of four Marine NBC specialists, several sailors from the ship's Deck Division that operated the LCACs, and a Navy Corpsman, would augment the normal LCAC crew.

The plan was set, but Steuben still wanted to walk Hussar through the details. Sometimes the guy whose life was potentially in danger demonstrated a clarity in thinking far beyond that shown by a bunch of guys sitting safely in a command center. Life-threatening situations can really help a person focus.

"Now this presents several potential problems, number one being where to put you. The options are to find a space on U.S. controlled property, like a compartment we can isolate here on the ship, a building in a U.S. Embassy compound somewhere nearby, or even just keeping you on the LCAC and towing the LCAC behind the ship. Another thought is to drop your squad in some remote location and let you chill out for a couple of days."

That was a no-brainer for Hussar.

"Sir, we're going to need to replace some gear. I obviously don't know any details of future missions, but if it would be possible for us to hang near the ship for a day or so to get squared away and then go ashore again to run another op, that would be great."

Colonel Steuben smiled to himself. That was his original thought, but the S-3, being the consummate staff officer, had wanted to lay out several options in case Sergeant Hussar's squad was in worse shape than the field reports indicated. The S-3 was right, of course, to work through multiple courses of action. After all, these were the first kills these Marines had actually performed, and a psychologist would claim the men needed some time to absorb the impact of what they had done. But the Marines don't recruit psychologists to command Marine units. It made Steuben feel good to know young men were still full of piss and vinegar and willing to take on the world. Steuben thought back to the surge of confidence he had felt upon returning from his first combat patrol in Vietnam.

"Plus, sir, the squad is really moving well together. This mission has made us even tighter than before. We're anticipating one another's actions and working well with Major Renick's analyst, Corporal Anderson. We would really like to hunt down some more of these bastards."

Steuben chuckled at that. It was almost the exact same pitch he had made to Colonel West for keeping 11th MEU on station.

"OK, that's what we'll do. We'll send over what we can to make the LCAC livable for a couple of days. Then we'll get you back on the ship and brief you up before we send you out again. Once again, good job."

Of course, that assumed the squad checked out clean. Although the ship's medical team was already preparing for the possibility of some very sick Marines, there was no use going through those details with Hussar right now.

By the time the LCAC got within two miles of the *Tarawa*, it was dawn. There was a slight wind from the east. The *Tarawa* had already turned into the wind and had slowed to a couple of knots. Careful to approach from the downwind side, the LCAC took up station about

800 meters aft of the big ship. Within minutes, the deck crew played out a tow hawser attached to a float from the fantail of the *Tarawa*. It was snagged by the LCAC crew and made fast to a block the chief had already rigged up. As the slack in the tow hawser was taken up, the LCAC coxswain turned off the primary fan, and the LCAC settled into the water as it came off its "bubble" and became a full displacement float. With the calm seas, it would be a relatively smooth ride.

Then the fun started. It took the NBC team three hours to completely hose down the entire squad and their equipment with soap and water before they were declared decontaminated. Although it was still technically springtime, the water and air temperature were both above 80 degrees, so at least they weren't having to strip naked in the cold and get sprayed with freezing water. Fortunately, the terrorists weren't Norwegian.

Because of the possibility that members of the squad ingested bio agents before they had a chance to put on their NBC gear, they still had to be kept isolated from everyone on the *Tarawa* for the quarantine period. Anyone coming over from the ship would have to be in NBC gear and then go through decontamination before returning to *Tarawa*. With the intensity of the decon process and the possible health risk, it would be fairly easy to limit contact to the absolute minimum. But some contact would be necessary. There weren't any creature comforts, or "hotel services" as the Navy calls them, on the LCAC. It was built for short duration ship-to-shore movements of Marines and equipment and was without galley, berthing, or head facilities. Sergeant Hussar hadn't thought about the accommodations until the Colonel mentioned making the LCAC livable. As his men had spent much of their time in the Corps in the field, they were used to roughing it. At least they should be safe on the LCAC and would be able to relax before getting back into action. But the *Tarawa*'s Deck Department, always the most innovative of sailors and led by a crusty, hard-livin' Chief Bos'un, had jumped at the chance to rig up some temporary facilities to help "their" Marines.

It is actually not easy to describe the complicated relationship between the Navy and the Marines. The task is made more difficult by the lack of consistency in that relationship between different locations and over time. There are distinct differences between the "East Coast" Navy and the "West Coast" (or "Left Coast" as the east coast sailors call it) Navy. Of course, personalities entirely drive the working relationship, often to excesses, but the best of this inter-service relationship happens in the "Gator Navy," as the fleet units comprised of amphibious ships are called. Sailors and Marines living on top of each other in cramped shipboard quarters quickly acquire a healthy respect for one another. Neither wants the other's job, but they both realize the importance of what the other is doing and recognize the professionalism in one another. Plus, the Gators have traditionally been the red-headed stepchildren of the Navy, generally underfunded and out of the glamour limelight, so they have a natural affinity for the maverick Marines. With the break-up of the Soviet Union and the lack of any real blue-water threat, however, the attitude of the Navy brass has improved somewhat. But the realization that there is a greater likelihood the Navy will be supporting Marine operations ashore than there is that Marines will be providing advance naval base defense in support of Navy at-sea operations is still a ways off. Traditions die hard, even the ones that need to go. Aboard the *Tarawa*, though, the sailors were eager to help. Even to the point of volunteering to put on NBC gear before going out to the LCAC.

With the help of the MEU's logistics section, the *Tarawa*'s Deck Division (or "Deck Apes" as they are generally called, occasionally with affection) were quick to load up the ship's utility boat and motor out to the LCAC. They immediately rigged up a large canopy frame in the aft part of the LCAC and secured a canvas cover over the frame. The canopy would provide welcome shade during the heat of the day. Several more trips between the *Tarawa* and the LCAC and the deck apes had set up a makeshift head and brought aboard several fresh water bladders (large collapsible storage tanks, called "camels"), a barbecue grill, a microwave, a small generator, several insulated food service containers filled with chow, along with a number of cots, chairs, and tables to set up under the canopy as needed.

Hussar's squad couldn't believe their good fortune. The Marine spaces aboard ship were cramped and poorly ventilated. Now they were able to have some space in the open air. Ironically, it had taken the possible exposure to lethal bioterror weapons to get such a good deal, but there was no use dwelling on the negative.

While the LCAC remodel job continued, a Marine from the Interrogator Translator Team came out to do the initial interrogation of the prisoner. It turned out to be a waste of time. The prisoner did not communicate at all, seemingly unable to understand the Arabic spoken to him by the Marine. The interrogator then tried basic phrases in several other languages spoken in different parts of the Middle East, all without success. It didn't look like the prisoner was going to be of much use to them. Disappointed, the Marine returned to the ship. Maybe he would get another chance when the quarantine period expired.

Later in the morning, a specially constructed airtight container was sent out to the LCAC. Without disturbing anything inside the SADM-10 satchel, Q carefully placed it inside the container, fixed it in place with the shipping material provided, and sent the container back to the *Tarawa*. As soon as the utility boat started back for the ship, Q could see and hear a CH-53E *Super Stallion* turning up on the flight deck. Within minutes, the container was pulled from the boat, sent up a weapons elevator to the flight deck, and secured inside the hold of the helicopter. The Super Stallion took off immediately to the west and disappeared rapidly into the horizon, accompanied by a flight of AV-8B Harrier jets which had taken off moments earlier from the *Tarawa*.

With that task complete, Hussar's squad serviced their weapons and then methodically went through all their gear and repaired any problems. The rest of the day they lounged around the LCAC and slept. In the late afternoon, Hussar took the squad through physical training, or PT, to keep them from getting too lazy. The corpsman came by in the evening to take temperatures and examine each of them for any signs of illness. No one showed any abnormal signs at that point, so the squad had a barbecue to celebrate.

The following day was another slow one on the LCAC. Hussar was getting antsy, wondering if anyone would get sick, and the hours seemed to drag by. Finally, at 1800, which was the designated end of their incubation period, the corpsman again evaluated each of them.

Without finding even a fever among them, the squad was deemed good to go. It was time to get back to work.

As soon as the LCAC powered up, the crew let loose the tow hawser and held station off the stern of the *Tarawa* while the long cable was reeled back in. The big ship then ballasted down almost 10 feet and lowered the huge ramp to allow access directly into the cavernous well deck. The coxswain lined up his approach, expertly piloted the LCAC into the mother ship, settled onto the designated docking spot, and then cut engine power. The deafening roar of the large gas turbine engines echoing in the well deck died immediately. As if on cue, all the watertight access doors for the well deck were thrown open and sailors and Marines came running into the space. Seconds later, as Hussar and his squad emerged from the LCAC troop compartment, a huge cheer went up. Stunned at first, and then grinning sheepishly and waving, they made their way off the LCAC and into the backslapping crowd of fellow warriors.

After a couple of minutes of spirited camaraderie, Sergeant Hussar saw his platoon commander trying to catch his eye.

"Yes, sir?"

"Well done, First Squad, and welcome back!"

"Good to be back, Lieutenant."

"Enjoy yourself here for a few more minutes, and then you and your NCOs need to get right up to Ready Room Two for debrief."

"Yessir."

Sergeant Hussar, Boner, Gasser, Spike, and Q went right into Squadron Ready Room Two, one of the spaces typically used for pilot premission briefings. Major Renick was already there and took them through a detailed debrief of the mission. The debrief was relatively easy because of all the info Q had collected, or that had been collected automatically, through the IDS. Much of it had already been sent back to the ship, so Renick just covered the "holes." The biggest hole was the stuff Gasser had collected from the little shop in the souk. Because of the interruption caused by the discovery of the bio vials, Q hadn't sent back the information and had actually forgotten about it. He knew he had screwed up big-time, there was no excuse for not having electronically forwarded the info while quarantined the last two days. He could tell Major Renick was disappointed, but Renick wasted no time on figuring out what to do.

"OK, we'll scan the business cards and send that off to CENTCOM along with the computer data Gasser collected. We'll have one of our system administrators look at what Gasser copied to the diskette, and we'll also send off electronic copies to CENTCOM, to the Fleet Information Warfare Center in Pearl Harbor and to NSA. Point made, gents, we all got distracted with the bio threat, but we need to stay on top of the information collected. It's all potentially very valuable."

Once the debrief was complete, Major Renick brought them up to speed on MEU activities of the past few days. While the squad had been relaxing on the LCAC, the MEU staff had been working under surge conditions as they tried to keep the pressure on the terrorist network. Without providing any details that could possibly compromise the operations, Renick told them two other Marine squads had been sent on missions to track down recently developed leads on terrorist activity. And then he sprung the surprise.

"Here's the big news for you guys. We just received info on suspicious activity possibly related to your bio threat. We're waiting on some additional information before we can justify mounting an operation, but Colonel Steuben has decided to send you back in-country to check it out when we get the green light for the mission."

"Where to this time, sir?" Hussar asked.

"Somalia."

The word ripped through them like a knife. There was plenty of payback due in Somalia to avenge the 18 Rangers killed in ambush in Mogadishu.

The Marines all looked at one another.

"We'll be happy to go, sir," Hussar answered for everyone.

# Chapter 6

Down in the ship's brig, the Marine guard carefully watched the prisoner Hussar had turned over to him upon the squad's return to the *Tarawa*. So far, the prisoner had been entirely uncommunicative, and the guard wondered what the guy was thinking. At first, he believed the prisoner didn't comprehend the attempts at communication by the Marines from the Interrogator Translator Team, and he figured it was because they just hadn't hit upon the right language or dialect yet. But as he had observed the prisoner over his last couple of watches, he began to think the guy was just playing stupid. He had overheard a comment that the prisoner had been captured in some crummy little village in Yemen, but he thought the guy was just a little too refined to be from that humble an environment. The prisoner's hands were soft and his fingernails were clean and evenly cut. He had intelligent eyes and was carrying plenty of "baby fat," which wouldn't have lasted long on a working man. Plus, he was at least 35-years-old, which seemed somewhat old to be running around in the middle of the night delivering WMD. But the thing that really set him off was the observation that the prisoner didn't seem to observe any prayer rituals. The guard was sure this terrorist was neither a religious zealot nor a flunky. The Marine had also heard a CIA interrogator was on his way to the ship to talk to the prisoner. The guard hoped he could meet the spook so he could pass on his suspicions and maybe even watch the interrogation.

The Marine's hunches about the terrorist were correct. His name was Heza Bin Bedhed, and he actually spoke several languages common to the Middle East and was fluent in French and English as well. He had attended American University in Beirut for two years and had also spent a year at Columbia University in New York. But shortly after returning to Lebanon, he abruptly stopped going to class and dropped out of school. He had casually fallen in with the Arab First crowd in Beirut that summer and came to view the university as a propaganda instrument of the West. Only later did Bedhed come to understand that he had been singled out and actively recruited by the anti-Western group. At the time, it just seemed like he had slowly been drawn into a circle of friends, mostly fellow students from prominent families throughout the Arab world, who disliked the Western, and especially American, influence in the Middle East. They weren't religious fanatics, although they could pretend to be and certainly used the extremists when it suited them. They were just bored, unhappy, spoiled little rich kids looking to make their mark on the world. Although his family believed he would one day continue his studies and go on to medical school, he had no such intentions.

Bedhed figured he would play stupid around his American captors, and they would think he was just one more ignorant "raghead" on some lowly courier mission. They would interrogate him as such and never guess he was much of the brains behind the fundamentalists collection of WMD capabilities. He only participated directly in missions of the utmost importance and went to great pains to conceal their secrecy. Of course, he knew the dirty little secret that occasionally the movement leadership would "allow" couriers or low-level operations to be compromised. Sometimes this was done as little "wake-up calls" to the West. More often, it was done to focus the attention of Western intelligence agencies on a certain part of the world or, more importantly, away from a specific area where something sensitive was going on that the terrorists didn't want discovered. It was sort of like watching a cat play with a mouse. When it became obvious that the Americans were starting to get close to an operation in Pakistan, for example, something would happen closer to home, in Britain or the United States, which would cause intense local attention, paranoia, and speculation. Like having some moron get on a plane wearing shoes with soles made of a very low yield pseudo-explosive and watch all the excitement generated by the moron's attempts to detonate the explosive and blow up himself and the plane.

But just because Bedhed spoke English and had briefly lived in the United States, it didn't mean he knew anything about American military capabilities or really understood the power he was actually facing. Like many foreigners, he took the general lack of restrictions in American life, what the natives euphemistically call "freedom," as weakness. He viewed Americans with a mixture of amusement and contempt, to include this Marine cretin who was so carefully watching him right now.

But there was an important reason the Marine was so carefully watching the prisoner at that moment; it was lunchtime in the brig (the Arab was the only "guest" at that time), and the Marine had specific instructions to observe the prisoner eat his meal. As soon as the guy finished up his lunch with a bowl of date pudding—provided by the cook in an attempt to provide culturally appropriate meals—the guard immediately moved up to the cell door and retrieved the lunch tray and utensils. He passed them to a waiting sailor who promptly took them away. But the dirty dishes didn't make it to the scullery for cleaning. Instead, the sailor took them to the medical ward where the eating utensils were deposited in a small airtight receptacle, which was subsequently placed in a slightly larger container alongside the individually sealed DNA swabs Hussar's men had taken off the terrorists killed in Yemen. The whole package was then whisked up to the flight deck. One of the MEU's UH-1N Huey helicopters was already turning over its engines by the time the container was loaded aboard. The Huey crew had already received a mission brief for their run to the *USS Carl Vinson*, presently operating with its Carrier Battle Group 150 miles to the east, and they were airborne within minutes. Once they reached the Vinson, the package would be transferred to a waiting F-18 Super Hornet, which would require 2 aerial refueling operations before landing at Ramstein AFB in Germany, location of the nearest American DNA analysis team. The team at Ramstein was tied into their counterparts back in the States and could share analysis duties and collaborate as required. More importantly, though, they accessed a common international database of DNA signatures that had been collected from all known terrorists and terrorist incidents. It would be their job to enter the new samples into the database and to search for matches with any samples or partial samples already in the database.

Major Renick had watched the entire operation and was glad when the DNA samples left the ship. He realized the MEU hadn't been very well prepared for handling the terrorist prisoner. Although they had a detailed plan for handling enemy prisoners (he had written it), captured terrorists were a slightly different situation. No one on the MEU staff had really expected any terrorists to survive the first mission, so there hadn't been a big push to update the plan. But Hussar had made a battlefield decision that he could grab one without imperiling his primary mission of munitions recovery, so now they had to work through the details. Although the prisoner was probably just some low-level delivery guy, he had obviously still gained a significant level of trust within the terrorist organization, or he wouldn't have been entrusted with the SADM transfer. So it wasn't at all like they had captured an enemy infantryman in battle. And once the bio threat was discovered, the guy became even more important. The Marines did their best adapting the MEU prisoner plan, which included the prisoner being kept under 24-hour surveillance and an attempt every 30 minutes by one of the Marines from the ITT to talk with him. The Marines would document whatever they picked up from the guy, analyze it locally for any significance, and then send it off to higher headquarters. As soon as the logistics could be worked out, the plan was to transfer the prisoner to Guantanamo Bay (Gitmo) for confinement.

Once the National Intelligence community found out the MEU was holding a prisoner, however, the plan and its timeline changed significantly. Back in CONUS at the nation's Intel centers, the potential bio discovery was immediately viewed as a much greater threat than the SADM-10. The analysts couldn't quite believe the terrorists would bundle together so much WMD in a single shipment, so there was huge interest in talking with the prisoner. Within a few hours, the closest suitable interrogator was located and directed to proceed ASAP to the *Tarawa* to provide an initial assessment and to accompany the prisoner on his immediate transfer to Gitmo. Since that would still take a couple of days to pull together, an order was also sent, via CENTCOM, to 11th MEU and to the Vinson to support immediate DNA testing of the prisoner. It was imperative to find out where the captured terrorist fit into the big picture and what he knew as soon as possible. Unknown to Major Renick, the national "bubbas" had picked up numerous indications that several significant and coordinated terrorist strikes were expected within the next few months. The credibility of the information supporting such threat analyses was dramatically increased with the reports coming out of 11th MEU and the "bubbas" in D.C. wanted whatever they could get from the guy sitting in the *Tarawa's* brig.

# Chapter 7

As he walked into Hangar Bay One, Hussar spotted his rein forced squad mustering in a small open area in the aft starboard corner of the hangar, beside a partially disassembled AH-1W *Super Cobra*. The *Cobra* appeared to be undergoing some sort of maintenance action on its port jet engine and, judging from the large number of Marine aviation mechanics frantically scrambling around the small helicopter, Hussar figured the *Cobra* must be slated as one of the gunship escorts for his squad's ingress flight that evening but had some problem serious enough to jeopardize mission availability. He recognized one of the aviation maintenance warrant officers, presently waving his arms and yelling at the mechanics about something they were doing wrong, as the guy in charge of whatever was being done. *I've never seen him so fired up,* Hussar thought, *it looks like even the air wingers are taking this stuff seriously.*

The aviation component of the Marine Corps has a reputation for being a bit laid back, sometimes a little slack, and occasionally a no-show. The grunts summed it up in the quip "Time to spare, call Marine Air!" Only the grunts had this perspective; however, the truth of the matter is, Marine Aviators are an awesome, professional flying force. It's just the grunts tended to dig on anyone who didn't sleep with them in the dirt, and the aviators were easy targets in that respect.

By the time Hussar made his way over to the squad, Boner (as the First Fire Team Leader, he was in charge whenever Hussar was absent) had finished lining the Marines up in a proper military formation of two ranks, with the first and second fire teams in the front rank and the third fire team and attachments in the rear rank. Boner had spent a tour at the Marine Corps Recruit Depot at Parris Island, South Carolina, and was a firm believer in straight lines and right angles. Although the other NCOs often razzed Boner about his fanatic attention to detail with close-order drill, Hussar knew that keeping the men focused on being part of a team and believing that their individual success depended entirely on the team's success was the most important thing the squad had going for them. It was such a simple idea, but in practice, a powerful discipline was required to overcome the natural egotistical human qualities of self-love and self-aggrandizement. He still got a sour taste in his mouth when he thought about how this fundamental requirement for real organizational success was totally lost on the professional sports teams of the day, where zillion dollar "superstars" had somehow become more important than team performance. He was no longer much of a fan, turned off by the "love-me" attitude of the players, coaches, owners, agents, referees, groundskeepers, etc. of the teams in any league of any sport. When a team like the Dallas Cowboys, love 'em or hate 'em, could be reduced from a tight, respectable organization to a bunch of squabbling kids complete with childish owner and coach theatrics, it was time to find something else to do on Sunday afternoons. And many like him had done just that. But those thoughts belonged in a world far away now. Hussar had real purpose in his life and wasn't dependent upon the success or failure of a local sports franchise to give meaning to his existence.

Boner called the squad to attention, executed a perfect about-face, exchanged salutes with Sergeant Hussar, executed another about-face, and took his position with the First Fire Team. Hussar put the men at ease and pulled out the equipment checklist he had made on receipt of the Mission Warning Order that morning. He had the men double up in pairs and check each other's gear as he called off the items on the common equipment list and then went through the special items list for equipment assigned to specific Marines. The Fire Team leaders had done their jobs well. Everyone was ready to go. With less than 3 hours to go before departure, Hussar dismissed the squad and sent the Marines to chow with instructions to reassemble in Ready Room Two at 2200.

As they sauntered off in the direction of the mess decks, Hussar marveled at the difference in their demeanor. It had been less than 72 hours since the squad had departed on their previous mission, but the fidgety energy the Marines had shown then was entirely replaced with a calm confidence. These warriors were now mentally prepared for anything Al-Qaeda threw at them.

His thoughts were interrupted by a piece of yellow gear grinding to a halt near him. Two Marines quickly hooked it up to an AV-8B "Harrier" and began towing the plane to one of the *Tarawa*'s large aircraft elevators. The place was getting busy as the hangar deck crew began moving aircraft up to the flight deck and staging them in preparation for that evening's flight plan. It was time to find some other place to hang out. Walking forward, Hussar found a relatively quiet vantage point near one of the numerous foam firefighting stations positioned around the periphery of the hangar bay. He wanted a few minutes by himself before things got too busy, and this spot was probably as good as any.

As darkness slowly inked out the western sky, Sgt. J.E.B. Hussar, USMC stood alone quietly in the shadows of the forward hangar bay of the *USS Tarawa* (LHA-1) and contemplated his upcoming mission. Through the open hangar bay door of the #1, starboard-side, deck-edge aircraft elevator, he could occasionally catch the moon's reflection off the calm, eerily phosphorescent waters of the Arabian Sea. He was proud his squad, 1st Squad, 2nd Platoon, F Company, Battalion Landing Team 2/1 (BLT two-one in Marine lingo), had been chosen to form the nucleus of the first "hot" mission into Yemen for Marines of the 11th Marine Expeditionary Unit (Special Operations Capable). The 11th MEU, like every other military unit, couldn't wait to get bloody in the war on terrorism, and Hussar's squad had led the charge. They had done well. Colonel Steuben's decision to send the squad right back into action almost as soon as they had returned from that first mission was a sign of their success. He was rightfully proud. But as the departure time neared, he could also sense an increasing weight of responsibility enveloping him, cloaking him in the tradition of honor and courage of previous Marines, and of his own forefathers, when called upon to face those who wish us harm and engage in battle.

The countdown clock was ticking away. Before his mind was consumed by operational details of the squad's mission, Hussar wanted the luxury of a few minutes of mental free-play. He wanted to think about Danielle and remember everything he could about her and the time they had spent together.

# Chapter 8

Hussar had met Danielle during the two week leave period the Marines of the MEU were given before they boarded the 3 ships of Amphibious Squadron 1 and began a 7 month Western Pacific (WESTPAC) deployment. Hussar certainly hadn't planned on meeting anyone special 10 days before leaving California on an extended cruise—he just wanted to go out and have a few beers. But it turned out to be one of those solid gold nights a guy has maybe two or three times in his life. He could easily recall the entire evening. It was Fat Tuesday, the traditional last night of decadence before the austerity of Lent. Many who do not actively participate in Lenten rituals still view the night as a good excuse to party, so he knew there would be lots of people out having a good time. He had called up Sgt. Alex Sargos, a good friend from his boot camp days at the Marine Corps Recruit Depot and now a fellow squad leader in 3rd Battalion, 5th Marines, to ride along. Although he and Sargos appeared to have very little in common, they had, in the strange way of the military, become fast friends as they struggled together to survive boot camp. Sargos was also one hell of a guy to go out with, have a couple of beers and blow off a little steam. His unit had just returned from a month-long field combined arms exercise at the Marine Corps Air Ground Combat Center at Twentynine Palms, CA, and he was more than ready to go out on the town. Sargos easily talked Hussar into driving down to San Diego and catching the big Mardi Gras celebration in the city's Gaslamp Quarter. The Gaslamp Quarter, a revitalized downtown area of restaurants and nightclubs marked by large mock gas lamp street lights, took up a full eight square blocks and was a vibrant party district. Hussar had heard it rocked at Mardi Gras.

By the time they showed up, there was already a huge crowd and the party was in full swing. Several of the streets were blocked off, and there were people spilling off the sidewalks onto those streets that were supposed to be open to automobile traffic. It was crazy. Neither of the Marines had ever seen anything like it. People in traditional purple, yellow, and green Mardi Gras costumes and groups of young men and women sporting the equally traditional bead necklaces were everywhere. Around 10 p.m., when the alcohol started to really kick in, women became increasingly brazen at lifting their tops to flash their breasts, and the men became increasingly brazen at taunting the women to do just that in exchange for the beads, absolutely worthless any other night of the year but definitely the coin of the realm on Fat Tuesday. As is too often the unfortunate case in such a situation, there were many more men than women in the crowd, but there hadn't been time to ponder such mysteries. The bacchanal affair had become increasingly intense, and Hussar was feeling a little hemmed in by the constant jostling of the unruly crowd. Then a marine layer of fog, not unusual at this time of year, had slowly moved in and engulfed the entire downtown area. The eerie light reflections off the fog gave a strange and other worldly perspective to the festivities and heightened the sense of living for the moment.

Hussar and Sargos were standing at the edge of a boisterous crowd gathering around one of the old buildings near the corner of 5th Avenue and Market Street. The upper floors had been converted to loft apartments, and the mostly male crowd was fixated on the 3rd story landing of the building's old iron fire escape. It was there that four young ladies of admirable endowment were waving and nervously talking to one another, getting up their collective nerve. The crowd began the taunting yell, "Show your chi-chis! Show your chi-chis!" The southern Californians had their own version of the famous Bourbon Street battle cry, and it reflected the strong Mexican influence on the area. After about 30 seconds of yelling encouragement, and in what has become a frequent occurrence during the normal ebb and flow of mood in any American crowd after the 9/11 attacks, they spontaneously rocketed into a patriotic rush and began shouting "USA!! USA!! USA!!" At that point, national honor was at stake, and the women immediately took off their tops and began waving them in the air and yelling with the crowd. The men on the street below went nuts and launched a blitz of beads at the obliging ladies. The barrage became so intense the girls had to seek refuge and clambered back into the open window they had used to access the fire escape. Everyone broke into raucous cheering, high-fiving, and dancing.

With his eye still on the disappearing hooters, which were flopping around an astonishing, and somewhat inelegant, amount for the pert breasts of young ladies, Hussar half-turned, took a step, and bumped directly into someone. The someone was a smiling, dark-haired woman of excellent proportion, who looked right into his eyes and gave him a confident "Hello." Just as the downtown area had become shrouded in fog, an alcoholic haze had enveloped Hussar, and all he could manage to eke out was a weak "Pardon me, ma'am." But the girl didn't move and didn't look away—she kept looking directly at him.

"Oh, ma'am is it? So formal. A gentleman, no doubt; a gentleman who loves to wear beads and watch women make fools of themselves," she retorted.

Hussar was dumbstruck. One second, he was enjoying the balcony show, and the next, a beautiful woman was reaming him out. Unable to pull his eyes from hers, but equally incapable of a reply, he noticed through his peripheral vision that someone right beside the girl was also staring at him.

"The street crowds are starting to get a little rough," she said, "and we are trying to get to Injun Joe's to dance. Perhaps you and your friend can be of some use and get us through this crowd?"

At the "we" Hussar glanced briefly from the girl's face, half expecting to see some ponytail-wearing, earring-sporting doofus standing next to her. Instead, he was rewarded with a smile from an attractive, possibly natural, redhead.

*Aaahh,* he thought, *these are 100 percent American babes that aren't interested in men and who look, dress, and act like women. Excellent.*

*Although the details are still sketchy, if ever there is a job for the Marines, this is it,*

"Sure, follow me," he boldly offered.

Hussar knew the bar. One of the many bars that opened after the Gaslamp Area had been revitalized was a place called Injun Joe's, after the villain character in Mark Twain's *The Adventures of Tom Sawyer.* A catchy name, it had immediately been assailed as an affront to Native Americans by the idle do-gooders who had nothing productive to do, so they spent their days feeling superior by playing head games with their fellow man. The bar name was then politically corrected to something clever about buffalos, but it turned out to be too clever to easily remember. This probably wasn't a complete capitulation since it still sounded western, but it really was a wuss job, since there wasn't anybody left who gave a crap about defending buffalos. Some of the "in-crowd" had recently taken to calling the place by its original name, even though most of those participating lacked the historical details and were in junior high when the original controversy occurred.

As Hussar turned to lead the way through the crowd, he was surprised again as the girl grabbed his arm and squeezed tightly. He was apparently not as surprised as Sargos, however, who was staring open-mouthed at Hussar and the girls. Standing behind Hussar, with his view blocked by his friend's size, he hadn't seen any of the initial exchange with the girls and assumed the crowd was too thick when Hussar didn't immediately take off. But as Hussar turned and muttered "holy-moley" under his breath, Sargos immediately saw a brunette babe holding on to the curl of Hussar's right bicep with one hand, and the hand of an equally attractive redhead with her other hand. And the redhead appeared to be reaching out to him.

"I'm in!" he gallantly offered to Hussar, as if his position could possibly be in doubt and needed clarification. "Where we going?" as he grabbed the redhead's offered hand and turned to walk by his friend.

"Injun Joe's, down at the corner."

"What's goin' on?" Sargos was still stunned at the sudden turn of events.

"Developing situation—be cool, don't be a goof, they're probably just bustin' our balls," he said, then added needlessly, "but this is some serious snapper, dude."

As he finished giving Sargos the scoop, a gang of drunken street punks lunged in at them and tried to surround the girls. The apparent leader started waving a handful of beaded necklaces in the air and started the shout, immediately picked up by the others, "SHOW YOUR CHI-CHIS!"

Without thinking, Hussar put an iron claw grip onto the punk's shoulder, spun him around so he was looking up into Hussar's face, and said "The only place those beads are going around here is down your throat, peckerhead. Now get outta here!" as he pushed the punk away from the girls.

The gang stared menacingly at Hussar, and the lead punk took a step towards him. They were used to threatening the local citizenry and were mindful of their reputations. But something in Hussar's cool demeanor and icy stare had a rapid sobering effect on their planned festivities and, like a pack of wild dogs, they quickly moved off to circle more vulnerable prey.

Once the moment had passed, Hussar realized the chicks probably thought he was a Neanderthal. He was going to screw this up if he wasn't careful. He quickly went "on mission" and began evaluating possible options with the girls. Hussar liked to anticipate and be prepared for situations, and his mind starting turning over several likely scenarios during the few minutes it took to jostle through two hundred feet of crowd before they were standing in front of Injun Joe's. The few women he had bothered to spend any significant amount of time with thought he was very intuitive. Actually, though, his mind was always looking ahead, visualizing possible events, even conversation, weighing their likelihood of occurrence, and formulating his response. Hussar couldn't "see" what was going to happen, but he could figure out what was likely to happen. He considered himself well-prepared and discounted the idea of untrained intuition as a force of nature.

By the time the four got to the bar, which was very crowded, he thought it most likely the girls had really just wanted to get to the bar and saw him as an easy way to get there. They were probably going to meet a couple of "pickles" there, or a bunch of girlfriends, and he and

Sargos would be left awkwardly standing to the side with a brush-off comment about how the "Marines had saved them." He wasn't relishing that image, and as luck would have it, it didn't play out that way at all. As he slowed at the entrance and turned to say, "Here we are, ladies" to allow the girls to easily break contact and go on to their party without escort.

The brunette invitingly said, "Come on, we owe you a beer!"

With her hand still on his arm, she led the way into the bar and found a small table near the dance floor the four of them could just squeeze around. There was a brief clumsy silence as they all pretended to look around for a cocktail waitress.

"My name is Danielle and this is Amber. Thanks for getting us here," said the brunette.

As if on cue and before Hussar could respond, the DJ stopped babbling about whatever DJs babble about, and the place exploded with Ricky Martin's "La Vida Loca" blasting through the sound system. With a "Yeah!" both girls immediately jumped up and were the first ones gyrating on the dance floor. Other people started dancing also, but they were window dressing for the two girls who were definitely into the music and very good dancers. Hussar and Sargos felt lost—should they make fools of themselves and try to dance uninvited with the girls or just sit there and stare, like many of the other bar patrons were already doing. The longer the song played, the wilder the girls danced, and the crowd started hooting and hollering encouragement to the women. Hussar liked music but rarely danced. It wasn't that he was the big, strong, silent type; he had just watched other jarheads dance and had come to the conclusion that the last thing needed in a bar were a bunch of guys with "high and tight" military haircuts bouncing around the dance floor pretending to be stoned rockers. The lifestyle clash was just too much, so he and Sargos just sat there and watched. Finally, the song ended and the girls came back to the table.

They ended up hanging there for a couple of hours, drinking a few beers, and chatting about the San Diego party scene. The girls danced several more songs and even pulled the Marines out on the floor a couple of times. Compared to the chaos outside, it seemed like a low-key evening. But Hussar was wound tight as a spring. He had trouble taking his eyes off Danielle the entire time, and whenever she casually brushed against him, it was like getting an electric shock. He didn't want to be a jerk by just staring at her, but she was mesmerizing and more than once she caught him checking her out.

Around midnight, the party was winding down. The girls were ready to go—the jig was up. It was Cinderella time.

"You girls had enough already?" Hussar said, rather than wait for the inevitable. He was rewarded with a smile and a nod of the head. *Great*, he thought, *she thinks I'm intuitive. Isn't really that hard to figure out the evening would end, is it?*

They walked the girls the couple of blocks over to the parking garage at Horton Plaza. The street crowds were thinning, and it only took a few minutes to get there. As they reached the garage stairwell access doors, Danielle turned towards him, gave him a hug and a quick kiss, squeezed a card in his hand, and told him to come see her at work. Then as suddenly as they had shown up, the two girls disappeared into the night.

Hussar looked at the card and saw it was a complimentary pass to Honey's, a well-known gentlemen's club in Pacific Beach. On the card was handwritten "Candy S-M-Th-F 7 p.m." That was interesting. Sargos was holding a similar card he had received from Amber, but with the name "Misty" and a different schedule.

"What was that?" he asked.

"Couple of strippers out slumming, I guess," Sargos answered, "or maybe out trying to drum up some new business. I'm not sure, but I'm glad they picked us. I guess these cards give their stage names and when they work. You going to stop by?"

"What, not go check it out? And then be sitting on a boat for 7 months, wondering what might have happened, the whole time kicking myself for not at least trying to see her again? It might be a long shot, but I gotta take the chance, bro. No guts, no glory. You bet I'm going. This Thursday."

And he had done just that, but it had been tough waiting the two days for Thursday to finally come around. His expectations had ping-ponged back and forth 100 times until the whole situation had become almost unbearable. That night, as he drove down to Pacific Beach, or PB as it was called, he realized he had worked himself into a funk. But he was determined to go through with it, regardless of the outcome. Reeking of uncertainty, Hussar had slowly walked in to Honey's and found a nearby chair to sit in while he let his eyes adjust to the dim lighting. He didn't immediately see Danielle, or was he supposed to call her Candy? Christ, he didn't even know that. *This is crazy,* he thought. But he ordered a beer and looked around the place. They had a pretty good-sized crowd and plenty of dancers. There were girls dancing on 2 stages, several sitting at tables talking to guys, and one giving a fat guy a lap dance in the corner. This wasn't so bad after all. As Hussar sat back and relaxed a bit, he became aware of someone staring at him. Turning to look, he met her eyes across the almost dark room. She was sitting with a couple of well-dressed soul brothers, laughing at something one of them had said. This was too weird.

Hussar drank his beer and considered his options as he watched a chick with big hooters on stage slowly fondle her breasts and then squeeze them together while she pretended to lick her own nipples. Although he had spent very little time in such places, he recognized it as a classic move. *Maybe they all went to the same school somewhere,* he thought. He was aware that Danielle was occasionally glancing over at him, but the next move would have to be hers. After all, he had dropped in on her at work. In fact, it sort of felt like he was in the waiting room at the dentist office, but the outdated National Geographic magazines had been replaced by a sexy floor show. After a few minutes that felt like an hour, he had concluded his only real options were to sit and wait like a goof or get up and leave. Buried in angst, he almost didn't see her get up and walk over to his table. But he was nervous, not blind. In the little bit of nothing she was wearing, he could see that she was very well-toned indeed.

"I wasn't sure you would come. You seemed so serious." She was there, sitting beside him again. Everything was cool.

"I was a little surprised by your card," he admitted.

They talked a bit, and Hussar told her about the two weeks off he had now but that he would be leaving soon.

"11th MEU?" she asked.

Hussar didn't answer. *So much for OPSEC*, he thought. OPSEC, or Operational Security, always broke down with people. Loose lips sink ships. The old saying "if you want to find out military troop movements, go to a whorehouse" popped into his head. *She probably heard about 11th MEU from some sailor on one of the ARG ships*, he thought with disgust.

She was amused as she watched his brow furrow while his mind worked on her question. This guy was serious.

"You're at Camp Pendleton, right?"

"Yeah."

"You know the Seaside Bar & Grille in Carlsbad?"

"Sure."

"Can you meet me for lunch there tomorrow?"

"OK."

"Noon?"

"Sure."

"Am I going to have to carry the conversation with you all the time?"

Hussar had to laugh. She said what she was thinking and he liked that. He realized he was acting like a stiff. He needed some quick words.

"Sorry," he said, "my rule has always been the person with the least amount of clothes on should do all the talking. That is especially true if that person is in fact almost naked. Since attention is already focused on that person anyway, it would be too confusing for people to pretend to be switching back and forth—naked person talking, fully-clothed dork talking, naked person talking, fully-clothed dork talking ..."

"That was pretty quick."

Hussar immediately knew it was time to go. He had come mostly because he didn't want to have regrets about not trying to see her again. He didn't really think she was interested in him, but he wasn't about to shy away from the opportunity. Now here he had been with her only a minute and he already had a date, and she thought he was quick-witted. Things could only go downhill. "Better to quit on top and leave them wanting more," as his father used to say.

"OK, I better get going—that old man over there is giving me a dirty look." It was true, there was an old guy sitting at one of the tables staring at him in a less than friendly manner.

Danielle quickly glanced and said, "Don't worry, that's Eddie, he runs the place. He doesn't like the customers getting too friendly. But I do need to get back to work. See you tomorrow." And she turned to walk away.

Hussar hung around for a few minutes, thinking he might also see her red-headed friend, and he could put in a good word for Sargos. But it didn't look like she was working that evening, so he finished his beer and made his way outside.

Since it was still early on a Thursday evening, very popular as "weekend warm-up night" everywhere in San Diego, and he was feeling quite cocky, Hussar decided to head over to Boots, a local urban cowboy bar in Mission Valley. Some of the other guys in the NCO barracks that had decided to stay local during the pre-deployment leave, or else didn't really have a place to go home to, had asked him to meet them there. He had been noncommittal, thinking if things didn't go well with Danielle he would probably just head back to base and go to the gym. But feeling as good as he did right now, he wasn't about to return to Camp Pendleton.

By the time Hussar got to Boots, the parking lot was packed and the party was in full swing. It looked like the usual mix of coeds from San Diego State University, sailors, Marines, blue collar types, folks from the small ranching communities east of town, divorcees, and young professionals "slumming" it for an evening. Even with the crowd, though, he could tell Boner and Gasser were there as soon as he walked in. He could hear Gasser's guffaw from somewhere in the back of the joint, and you could bet Boner would be with him. As Hussar made his way through the mass of people, he nodded to a few other NCOs he recognized from the other companies in the battalion. It looked like 2nd Battalion, 1st Marines was well-represented—there were more "homeless" Marines than he had thought.

Finally, he could see Boner, who appeared to be demonstrating some kind of kung-fu move to a couple of giggling young ladies and to Gasser, who was laughing so hard his face was purple. After a second,

Hussar realized it was only Boner's rendition of the latest country and western line dance that 50 people were doing in perfect synchronization on the dance floor. Rhythmless since birth, Boner's moves weren't even close, but his spasmodic movements were hilarious. Hussar saw the two corporals were lit and realized that either he would be driving tonight or they would be sleeping in the parking lot or on the beach. He eased behind Boner and was just about to put him in a "sleeper" chokehold, when he heard a loud "oooh-rah!" as he was roughly grabbed and thrown in a half-nelson. Damn, it was Spike. Hussar should have known Spike would have been lurking nearby, the three Fire Team leaders were best of friends. Hussar relaxed his body, feinted left, threw right and neatly dropped Spike almost directly on top of Boner, who had turned to see what was happening. Gasser saw his friends going down, immediately yelled "Hussar!" and grabbed him in a big bear hug. As the girls went shrieking away, Boner and Spike jumped back to their feet and gang-tackled Hussar and Gasser. They all crashed to the floor laughing, as everyone nearby scurried out of the way of the melee. Then two very large bouncers came out of nowhere ready to crack some heads, but when they saw it was just some Marines rough-housing among themselves, they relaxed and told the Marines to "Chill out or get out." The guys had a good laugh, and Boner scurried off to retrieve the frightened girls.

The four Marines partied until the place closed. Hussar, being the only one sober, then piled everyone into his truck and drove out to deserted Fiesta Island in the middle of Mission Bay so they could crash for the night. But it was a short night for the partied-out jarheads. To a blitz of swearing, Hussar woke everyone at sun-up because he needed to get back to base and get cleaned up for his lunch date.

Hussar didn't like being late. Like most Marines, he was anal about being where he was supposed to be, when he was supposed to be there. So he made it to the Seaside Bar & Grille by 1130, sat at one of the outside tables with an unobstructed view of the parking lot, and waited. He didn't want to miss her. But wearing his one pair of nice slacks and a button-down shirt, both bought for a Squad Leader's reception the Colonel had thrown at the NCO club several months earlier when the MEU work-ups were just beginning, Hussar felt a little goofy "staking out" a restaurant.

Exactly at noon, he saw her walking through the parking lot. She was dressed up in what Hussar imagined was some sort of women's business suit, with a matching jacket, skirt, high heels, and honey blonde hair, rather than the dark hair she had the other two times he had seen her. *She must have a stage wig to go with her stage name*, he thought.

"Holy cow," he said under his breath. She looked like a banker. Hussar had limited experience with people who wore suits but had once gotten a car loan and the branch loan officer was a woman wearing something similar, but lacking the physical attributes Danielle possessed. As she neared the restaurant, he reminded himself to not say anything stupid.

"Hi," she said as he stood to meet her. She then gave him a quick peck on the cheek and waited for him to pull back a chair for her. He fumbled with the chair briefly until she appeared comfortable and then sat down across from her.

"You look exquisite, my dear," he gallantly offered.

"Thank you. I didn't want you to think I run around in a tube top or a G-string all the time." She had been wearing a tube top under a denim jacket at the Mardi Gras party and, of course, almost nothing at the gentlemen's club.

Hussar played it straight. "To tell the truth, I'm not sure what I should think."

Her eyes clouded briefly and she stiffened slightly, but then she smiled and said evenly, "That's fair."

Hussar immediately noted the change in her demeanor, wondered what was behind it, and realized he had some damage control to do. The next words out of his mouth had better be good.

"People are always telling me I think too much and don't enjoy myself enough. That I should go with the flow and take things as they are."

She visibly relaxed. *Bull's-eye*, he thought.

"That's probably good advice. My friends tell me the same thing," she said as she playfully grabbed his hand. She liked his hands. They were strong and a bit rough, and she had liked them immediately. Although it was obvious from the deep curve of his pecs and the V of his lats that he worked out, it was also obvious from his hands that he actually worked for a living. She was put-off by all the pseudo-men hanging out in fitness clubs—which seemed to be on every street corner in Southern California and were now the happening places for dudes to meet chicks. Danielle thought this was inevitable in California—a fitness club was the perfect place to harmonize the narcissism and shallow relationships which seemed to characterize the Golden State. But even as the "Fitness Freaks" had replaced the "Lounge Lizards" of an earlier time, she disliked the guys whose sole physical activity was working out in the gym, mostly just pumping iron. Maybe it was her blue-collar roots. Certainly many of them were very well-defined, but they had the dainty hands of girls and couldn't run a mile.

"Well, I'm waiting," she said after a short, but comfortable, pause.

Unsure what she meant, he scrunched his face into a question mark.

"Here I sit, dressed, what did you say, 'exquisitely', and there you are, almost naked in comparison. And I know your rule about the naked person doing all the talking."

"Touché," he lamely responded.

Something had been bothering him and he felt he needed to come clean. "Better get the turd right out on the table," as the Sergeant Major was fond of saying.

"I'm leaving on a 7-month deployment in 10 days," he blurted out.

There was a pause, and she softly replied, "I think I pretty much already knew that."

Oh yeah, he had forgotten he had mentioned it to her at Honey's. But the fact of his impending departure was weighing on his mind, and he wanted to be totally honest with her. The injustice of meeting a fun, beautiful girl who liked him just two weeks before leaving on a "pump," as the Marines called their standard deployment rotations, had been one of life's little ironies. But it didn't seem to have any effect on her. He didn't know what to make of that.

Another pause, and then she said, "I'm still waiting for you to start talking, naked boy."

"OK. OK." He threw up his hands in mock resignation. "My name is J.E.B. Hussar. My friends call me Jeb. I'm 23 years old. I've been a Marine for five years and am a Sergeant in 2nd Battalion, 1st Marines. I grew up on a small farm in Patrick County, Virginia. My parents still live there. I have two brothers, one older and one younger, and a little sister. My birthday is November 10th, my favorite color is blue, my favorite foods are barbecue, crab cakes, and German chocolate cake. I'm an occasional drinker, don't use drugs, love the outdoors, never been married, and drive a pick-up truck. My goals are to get some 9/11 payback, finish college, and get a commission. Would you like to know anything else, ma'am?"

"That's a pretty good start. What does the J.E.B. stand for?"

"J.E.B. is all that's on my birth certificate. Well, I didn't get named until I was 3 months old—family tradition. I guess I was sort of a sickly baby, so my mama was always saying 'Just Eat, Baby' and the initials stuck."

Her jaw dropped. She couldn't believe he was serious, but she had heard stories about hillbillies doing weird stuff like that. It was hard to imagine a stud like him ever being sickly. "You're kidding, right?"

"Sort of," he grinned. "Actually, Patrick County was the birthplace of J.E.B. Stuart, the famous Confederate cavalry general, and I was named after him. My family goes back enough generations in Virginia that we knew the Stuarts, who were practically neighbors. But I really was a sickly baby."

"Do you have a girlfriend?"

"No, ma'am, the Sergeant does not have a girlfriend."

"And why doesn't the Sergeant have a girlfriend?" She playfully adopted his third-person speech pattern, but he could tell she was serious.

"The Sergeant does not have a girlfriend because he is an idiot." He had thought about the standard "if the Marines had wanted me to have a girlfriend, they would have issued me one" B.S., but the truth was, he sometimes felt like an idiot because he didn't have a steady squeeze. He had missed out on several decent prospects in the last 4 years, mostly from inattentiveness. His rationalization was that since he wasn't ready to get married, why should he be in a serious relationship? Steady sex wasn't really enough to make up for high-maintenance female distraction from his duties and the inevitable whining about his frequent deployments. And with most women, at least he had been led to believe from the frequent complaints of the married guys he knew, steady sex wasn't necessarily a given anyway once you got married. So he told her the truth, at least the part about him not ready to marry and not wanting to string some girl along for convenience.

"What's your story?" he wanted to shift the focus back on her.

"My name is Danielle ..." and she told him her story of growing up on a small ranch on the prairie outside Colorado Springs, with sweeping views of Pike's Peak and the entire front range of the Rocky Mountains and her desire to find out what was on the other side of the mountains, all the way to the sea. She had made it to San Diego, fell in love with the place but found it expensive, and discovered she could make 5 times as much money dancing (which she enjoyed) as she made on her first job there as a bank teller.

He was amazed at her frankness and honesty. No hard-luck story or some B.S. about being a stripper to pay her way through medical school. She was doing what she enjoyed. It was also clear that she saw herself as an entertainer. Men could pay to watch her dance seminude, but that was as far as it went.

After a casual lunch, they sat back and watched tourists stroll through the few streets of the quaint village of Carlsbad.

"So why are you hanging around here rather than going home for a few days before you deploy? Do you have something planned or are you just going to goof around?" She was curious about why he hadn't gone to spend his leave with his family.

"I was home at Christmas. Almost all my family and friends were home from school or had taken a few days off work, so I had a great visit. Wouldn't be the same now in March, of course. So I thought I would finally take some time off around here and do the tourist stuff."

"Anything specific?" she pressed on, finding it hard to believe he didn't have a plan. He seemed so intense, it was a real stretch to imagine him loitering around the world famous San Diego Zoo for a week.

"The normal Southern California places, I guess, plus I'm going down to Baja next week for a couple of days."

"Alone?" she asked incredulously.

"Sure—I'm going to be jammed on a ship with 1000 other guys for 7 months. A little space would be nice. Usually, I just go weekend camping by myself in the high desert, but I've finally got enough time off to enjoy a few days in Mexico."

"Have you ever done that before in Mexico?"

"No."

"You really shouldn't go alone."

"Why not?"

"Mexico can be a rough place."

"I was a lot more worried about this lunch with you than I am about going to Mexico." He laughed deeply with the realization that this was absolutely true.

She didn't know if he was foolish, naive, or brave.

"Maybe I should go with you," she tossed out impulsively. She was worried about him, she realized, but mostly she didn't want to pass up the chance to go off with him for a few days.

He met her eyes, which were sparkling, "To protect me? Are you kidding?" He was trying to be nonchalant, but she could tell he was stalling while he thought about it, or, more likely, tried to think of a way out of taking her.

She decided to play along to give him some time. "Aren't you guys supposed to use the indigenous population to help you accomplish your mission when you are in a foreign country?"

"Sure."

"Well, I can help," she offered.

"Really. Are you a Mexican?"

"No," she giggled, "but I live in San Diego and I've been to Mexico before."

Something of a loner, Hussar purposely hadn't told anyone else of his plans for a Baja trip. He wasn't really looking for company and, for once, he didn't want to be responsible for anyone but himself. Yet, here was this beautiful, interesting woman asking him if she could go along, and he was seriously considering it. The nature of the trip would drastically change if she went with him. He half-regretted telling her anything, but she was so easy to talk to, and he had never considered that she might want to go or that she would even be so bold as to ask him if she could go along. But now he was faced with a decision, and his analytical mind kicked in to high gear as he weighed the pros and cons.

He could probably swing this chick without taking her to Mexico for four days, so he didn't think he was facing a sex/no-sex decision. And it would be nice to lay on a beach, kayak, and fish without worrying if someone else was having fun.

On the other hand, it would be good to spend some time with a woman. A mental image of Danielle in a bathing suit with the sun behind her flashed into his head. It would be like the Sports Illustrated swimsuit edition or maybe more like a Penthouse photo shoot. His mind stuck on that image for a couple of seconds. His plans were changing—she was definitely going. He could always spend some time alone over the next few days before they left on the Baja trip.

She had sensed his initial rejection to the idea, but then she saw the worry lines in his face relax and she knew she had him.

"Can you get the time off?"

"I already have next week off," she smiled.

"Out of curiosity, when did you set that up?"

"Last night after you left, I talked to Eddie." That hung there for a second.

"For me?" Hussar asked softly.

"For you." She smiled.

Hussar sighed. He was trapped. And he loved it. She had deftly outmaneuvered him, but all he could do was chuckle.

With his face breaking into a broad grin, he said "All right, you can come along. But I'm not staying in some fancy resort hotel in Cabo San Lucas—we're camping on as deserted a beach as I can find."

She grabbed and squeezed his hand, "Yes, sir."

Hussar immediately took charge. "OK, we leave at 0500 Monday morning. That will put us at the border around daybreak, so we should be able to find a decent campsite by nightfall. My plan is to head down to Ensenada, cut across to the east side of Baja to San Felipe, and then head south and stop somewhere around Gonzaga Bay. Have you ever been there?"

"No."

"Some guide you'll be. Do you have any camping gear?"

"Not really." She was suddenly worried he might think her too high-maintenance and change his mind about taking her along.

He smiled again, "Don't tell me your Mexican excursions are limited to road trips to Ensenada and getting hammered at Hussong's Cantina?"

"Hey, I've been to Papas & Beer also!" She added somewhat defensively and then burst into laughter when she realized how ridiculous that sounded.

"Wow, you really are almost a native," he laughed. "OK, I'll go by Base Special Services and pick up some extra camping gear. Can you handle getting enough food and water to last you a week?"

"Sure."

"All right. Where do you live?"

"Right up the road. On Fire Mountain." She gave him the address and phone number. Before he could lecture her about the importance of leaving at 5 a.m., she added, "And I'll be ready to go when you stop by at 5." Without giving him time to stand up and get her chair, she leaned over and gave him a quick peck on the cheek, stood up and threw an "I better get home and pack, dear" wise-ass comment over her shoulder as she purposefully walked out of the place.

Although almost hypnotically transfixed on Danielle's derrière as she walked away, Hussar subconsciously noted the discreet glances at her departing figure by almost every man in the place, and their subsequent, less discreet appraisals of him. Most of the guys there were businessmen, many with women at their tables, and they were probably wondering what some grunt like him was doing with a robo-babe like Danielle. Hussar gave them an exaggerated shrug, as if he also couldn't figure it out and smiled the victory smile. He then dropped some money on the table to cover the bill, stood up, and sauntered out of the place with the broad goofy grin still stuck on his face.

Now that Danielle was going along on his Baja adventure, he had a lot of work to do before the trip, and his mind was starting to turn to the details. But for a few golden minutes on a beautiful afternoon in Southern California, Hussar just wanted to savor how good it felt to be alive and enjoy the sensation of a thousand pinpricks of happiness tingling his skin. *Christ, I'm almost giddy,* he thought as he consciously checked his euphoria, got in his truck, and headed back to Camp Pendleton.

Monday morning had come fast for Hussar and he was anxious to get on the road south. He was surprised to find Danielle, true to her word, standing by for the 0500 pickup with all of her stuff neatly packed. She wasn't yet fully awake, so Hussar told her to finish her beauty sleep while he drove, which she did without a fight.

By dawn, they were already at the Mexico border. A little over an hour after passing through the Tijuana border checkpoint, they made Ensenada. Hungry from driving, Hussar pulled over to grab a couple of fish tacos at one of the few food stands open at 7 a.m. Manuel, the Mexican who owned the tiny Manuel's Restaurantito and spent 12 hours a day there, seemed a little surprised to see a gringo that early in the morning. Natives on their way to work were his typical customers at that time of day. Most of the gringos got drunk and partied late and wouldn't be seen until lunchtime. But this gringo seemed different. He was strong and straight and had a confident attitude. This man didn't look like he needed the tequila to get through life. Perhaps he was a soldier, an officer, maybe one of the *Infanteria de Marina*, as Marines were known in Mexico. Manuel thought there must be many men like him in the *Estados Unidos* or the *norteamericanos* couldn't have built such a great country in such a short time. To build a powerful nation, there had to be more industrious people up north than the slackers who came down to Mexico on the weekends to enjoy the cheap tequila. People like this gringo here would work hard and accomplish great things, and the others would live in his shadow. Manuel was proud to serve the gringo and to have figured out the mystery of *Los Estados Unidos*. He cheerfully waved goodbye.

Back on the road, Hussar turned on to one of the few east-west roads in Baja, Highway 3, which runs from Ensenada to San Felipe and crosses the range of mountains that is the backbone of the Baja-California Peninsula. The road had been good to Ensenada but was not nearly as well maintained to San Felipe. Still, they made good time.

Once in San Felipe, they turned south on the coastal road, which quickly turned rough. The road was covered with sharp rocks that would shred a tire if you drove too fast across them, so their speed was limited to about 10 miles per hour. He didn't really know how far south he should drive before stopping. With the slow speed, travel time would eat up a lot of their trip if they went too far. But he probably wouldn't find the deserted beach he was looking for if he stayed too close to San Felipe. Hussar knew the reputation of most Mexican cops and had heard many of the locals didn't really like the *Yanquis*. But he figured if he went far enough south, he could get away from the border attitudes and meet more hospitable people. It was probably like that in most countries and maybe even how foreign visitors found America. Hussar had done a tour out at Camp Lejeune, NC and had made two Mediterranean MEU deployments, or "med cruises," as they were called. On one occasion, he had a few days of liberty in France. He couldn't believe the dramatic difference in how he was treated in the French countryside from how he was treated in Paris. The people outside of Paris seemed to genuinely like Americans, as judged from the amount of free food and drink he was offered. But the arrogant frogs of gay Paris were some of the most annoying people Hussar had ever encountered. He figured the border Mexicans who only encountered rude, drunk Americans were probably not very impressed with their northern neighbors, but the inland Mexicans who rarely encountered Americans would be much more hospitable. He would have to remember to avoid the general arrogance, or ignorance, of most of his fellow countrymen who called themselves Americans, casually overlooking the citizens of over 50 other countries of North, Central, and South America that were just as entitled to the term American.

After about two hours on a mostly dirt road that passed through several small coastal villages, Hussar checked his map. They should be approaching the point where a small, dry riverbed crossed the road on its way to Gonzaga Bay. Within a mile, they crested a small hill and were rewarded with a magnificent view of Gonzaga Bay, a wide beach curving into the distance, bounded by the blue waters of the Sea of Cortez and the mountain spine of the Baja Peninsula. He saw several fishing boats a few miles offshore and occasional huts irregularly spaced along the beach. He sensed they were getting close to some choice campsites.

At the next small beach town, Hussar wanted to ask around for a recommendation of a good local beach. He spotted an armed Mexican soldier standing on a corner, watching them pull into town. Unlike most of the other cops he had seen so far in Mexico, this guy was young, in excellent physical shape, and carried himself very well. On an impulse, Hussar stopped the truck, told Danielle to wait for him, grabbed something from inside a small duffel bag he had on the front seat, got out of the truck, and walked to the soldier.

*Oh God*, she thought, *he doesn't even know enough to avoid the local cops.* Hussar casually approached the soldier and with a wave of his hand and a simple "hello," struck up a conversation. The Mexican spoke passable English and was soon very impressed with Hussar's questions about the organization of the various law enforcement agencies in Baja and the role of the Mexican military. Hussar then went on to explain his duties as a U.S. Marine. It turned out the policeman had been in the *Infanteria de Marina*, the Mexican version of the Marines, and he became very friendly and was genuinely happy to meet Hussar. He told Hussar some of the best places to camp for a few days, including a spot he knew would be deserted.

In the truck, Danielle couldn't believe her eyes. He was standing there talking to this Mexican like they were old friends. Then Hussar and the policeman walked across the street and into a small building. She could only make out the word "Federales" on the small sign over the door. "Damn, he's going to get thrown in jail and never coming out," she thought aloud.

A long five minutes later, just as she was gathering her things to go find out what was going on, they re-emerged laughing and talking like they were big buddies. Then they shook hands, the Mexican turned and gave a big wave towards Danielle, and Hussar started walking back to the truck.

When he got back into the truck, she stared at him in disbelief and asked, "What the heck was that all about?"

"Just trying to get some info."

"Why was he so happy to see you?" She couldn't get over the fact that he had just walked up to a Mexican policeman and, within minutes, become best of friends. "Did you give him some money?"

"What?"

"Did you give him money?"

"No. Why would I give him money? I was just talking to the guy and it turns out we have a lot in common. He gave me directions to a great beach campsite where he goes fishing and camping with his girlfriend."

"I saw you take something out of your bag, Jeb."

"Oh, I gave him one of these." He pulled an 11th MEU T-shirt out of his bag. It had a cool drawing of a fierce Marine rifleman charging forward, assisted by all the combat power of the MEU, including ships, tanks, airplanes, helicopters, and artillery.

She thought it looked gaudy but knew it was just the kind of thing boys would like and looked at him with newfound respect. "That was pretty good thinking, Jeb Hussar." She moved his bag off the seat and slid next to him.

The campsite the policeman had told them about was only 5 miles down the road. The access wasn't marked, so if you didn't know exactly where to go you would never find the place. It was indeed the perfect spot, with a small cove and a hidden beach and not another soul around. They were both swimming within minutes and relaxing from the long drive.

In the late afternoon, Hussar took out his kayak and easily caught a couple of fish, including a nice sized grouper. After grilling the fish and having a dinner of fish tacos and beans, Hussar put a few small logs on the fire and sat back with a beer, staring into the sparks of the fire. He was glad he had thought about hauling in his own wood, as there wasn't much in the way of trees around their campsite. He had read that the area around Gonzaga Bay was so arid it sometimes went entire years without raining.

Danielle was in the tent they had raised, laying out sleeping bags and tidying up their gear. As the evening cool set in, Danielle put on a sweatshirt and came out by the fire and sat down next to him. She looked at him in the firelight and, for the first time since she had known him, she could sense he was totally relaxed. Generally, there was a certain restlessness about him. He always seemed to be on edge, as if he was anticipating some crisis that would require immediate action on his part to save the day. She supposed it was primarily a result of his combat training, but he also seemed to have some kind of instinctive awareness, like a wild animal, that she didn't really understand. But it made her feel safe. Danielle gently nuzzled into him, and he put his arm around her and drew her towards him. She turned her face up to his and he kissed her fully on the lips. It was their first real kiss. He held her tight, and his hand slowly slipped down to caress her breasts. He could feel her nipples becoming erect through the sweatshirt as she became aroused, and she took his hand and guided it inside the sweatshirt. She was naked under it. He gently massaged her breasts, and she moaned from deep inside as he continued kissing and stroking her. As the blood started rushing to his groin, he thought to move inside the tent before his legs went rubbery and he could no longer walk. With one fluid motion and without breaking the kiss, he picked her up and carried her into the tent. Laying her down softly on an open sleeping bag, Hussar shifted his attention and slowly started rubbing her pubis through her shorts. He could feel her dampness through them, which he gently pulled off her, only to find she was wearing the leopard g-string she had on the night he had stopped by Honey's. *Whoa*, he thought, *I'm going to love on the chick all those guys were drooling over.* Danielle suddenly started going wild, ripping his shirt over his head, biting his chest, and digging her fingers into his shoulders, the whole time moaning louder and louder as he continued to rub her. *Damn*, he thought, *she's close to orgasm.* And she gasped in exhilaration, just as he was thinking it. Before she could catch her breath, though, Hussar yanked off his swimsuit and was quickly inside her, desperate to catch up. They were soon writhing as one inside the small tent, filling the deserted beach and the night beyond with the sounds of their pleasure. Afterwards, they lay together without saying a word. Hussar was spent from the long day of driving and ready to go to sleep. He could sense Danielle rustling around in the tent, apparently looking for something, but he was too tired to wonder what she was doing. He then became conscious of her licking him, first slowly and then aggressively, finally startling him fully awake as she engulfed his privates. Hussar opened his eyes just as she stopped the tongue bath, and saw her, looking wild-eyed and flushed, throw back on a bottle of tequila, take a healthy slug, and then chew on a lime she had grabbed from someplace. Then she licked his stickiness again and repeated the tequila and lime action.

He started laughing. "What the hell are you doing?"

"Shots of Hussar gold," she whispered in a throaty voice.

He looked at her blankly. "What?"

"Your salt," she pointed to the man-juices still oozing out of him, "a little tequila, and a bite of lime makes a shot of Hussar gold," she explained with a feigned nonchalance.

Hussar was speechless. She clearly had the whole thing planned in advance, and it was a moment he would never forget. He realized the memory of this evening would bring a smile to his face on the long, lonely nights of the upcoming WestPac deployment.

Danielle was thinking the exact same thing. Without a word, she lay her head on his chest and was soon in deep sleep. Hussar pulled a light blanket over them to keep out the chill of the night and wrapped her in his arms as fatigue also eveloped him. His last thought as he drifted off was the hope that this wasn't all a dream and that she would still be there in the morning.

# Chapter 9

As the CH-53F *Super Sea Stallion* lifted off from the number 5 spot on the *Tarawa's* flight deck, Hussar caught a glimpse of the faces of several sailors standing watch on the bridge. Responsible for guiding the great amphibious ship safely through the dark waters of the Indian Ocean, the sailors looked like pale apparitions behind the slanted windows of the faintly lighted bridge. The helo slowly moved forward over the flight deck about 100 feet, and then hovered for 15 seconds while the flight deck crew hooked up the sling for a Light Armored Vehicle (LAV) to the helo's external lift point. The giant CH-53F bounced around a bit as the pilot tried to hold his position over a moving ship, and the port bridge wing briefly came into Hussar's field of view. He could just make out the MEU Commander, Colonel Steuben, and the Amphibious Ready Group (ARG) Commodore, Capt. Skwidolio, holding a snappy salute for the Marines aboard the aircraft as they left on another mission. That was an impressive gesture and he felt his chest swell with pride. As the *Sea Stallion* increased power to lift its load and pick up speed, Hussar turned his head aft to look out the helicopter's open cargo ramp at the rapidly fading sight of the *USS Tarawa*. He noticed the other Marines of his squad doing the same thing in perfect synchronization, as if all their heads were mounted on a common swivel.

Two more Sea Stallions, carrying the remainder of the squad, the other two trucks they had "liberated" from Yemen, and each with another LAV slung under its belly, suddenly came into view as they took up station behind, and slightly off to the side, of Hussar's lead helicopter. He knew that other air cover was also being provided, at least until they got over the African coastline, but he couldn't see either of the escort Cobras or any of the Harriers from his window.

Although the mission plan called for 3 days on the ground in Somalia, Hussar suddenly had the overpowering sense he would not be returning to the *Tarawa* anytime soon. Not ordinarily given to premonition, Hussar allowed himself a moment to turn the thought, and the surprise that came with it, over a few times in his mind. *What a weird feeling to believe you can actually foresee the future,* he thought, *and an unmerited arrogance as well on the part of those claiming clairvoyance.* But the urgency, uncertainty, and likely difficulty of the mission ahead quickly flushed his mind of all thoughts that were not mission-critical. There was still a lot to think about if he was going to be mentally prepared for all possible contingencies. Of course that wasn't really possible, but he had learned a lot on their first mission about dealing with the unexpected and was determined to train himself to consider many more scenarios this time. He touched the intercom switch on his helmet to ask the pilot to let him know when they passed over the coastline of Kenya, and for the 100th time that day, resumed the Patrol Leader's "what-if" mental exercise.

The MEU Air Officer had laid out a circuitous ingress route in an attempt to hide their insertion. To set up the ruse, the *Tarawa* had moved south out of the Gulf of Aden and Arabian Sea proper and was in the Indian Ocean about 50 miles off the coast of Kenya when the mission was launched. The flight plan called for initially flying a Super Stallion into Nairobi to deliver a Department of State diplomatic pouch to the American Embassy there and then remaining in country for several days to fly a number of training missions. That had already happened yesterday with an almost empty CH-53E. Today, that helicopter was flying the first of several training flights authorized over the sparsely populated northeastern region of the country, well east of the famous Rift Valley that bordered Somalia. Once the MEU had secured agreement by the Kenyan government to authorize training flights by the "diplomatic" helicopter, it had been relatively simple to modify the plan to allow additional helicopters coming directly from the *Tarawa* to join in on the training flights. It was on one of these additional helicopters that Hussar and his squad were now riding.

The idea was to penetrate Somalian airspace in an area poorly covered by air surveillance radars and drop the squad and their trucks off in the highlands of western Somalia. The MEU had received Electronics Intelligence (ELINT) reports from NSA every two hours for the previous three days that detailed electromagnetic emissions in the desired drop-off area. The very few radar band emissions identified in the area of interest were consistent over time and deemed routine by the signals intelligence experts. It was then a relatively simple matter to overlay radar coverage fans centered on the locations of these known emitters onto a three-dimensional electronic map. This highlighted those places devoid of radar coverage due to terrain masking that would be suitable for stealthy flight routes. Since it wasn't necessary, and far too risky, to go very far into Somalia, the planners calculated the squad could be inserted quickly and safely before anyone noticed the flight deviation. If the helicopters did in fact sense radar hits as they approached the border, however, the squad would be dropped in Kenya and would just have to cross the border on the ground and drive a little farther to the objective area.

As Hussar continued to sort through operational details important for the various scenarios he had come up with, he became conscious that several of his Marines were staring intently at him. It was almost like he was on a stage waiting for the curtain to go up. He could feel the pressure starting to build on him to perform, to get the job done quickly and to get everyone safely back home as soon as possible. *Wished they had always been as attentive during the work-ups in the training areas of Camp Pendleton*, he thought, as he shrugged off their stares and turned back to his planning.

In addition to the Marines from Sergeant Hussar's squad, Corporal "Q" Anderson from Major Renick's Intel section was again riding along to provide information management support. Also, a Navy corpsman and a Military Occupational Specialty (MOS) 5711, or NBC specialist, from the MEU NBC cell were attached for the mission. The three LAVs and their three-man crews rounded out the small force. Colonel Steuben had decided to send along the

LAVs to provide additional firepower, if required, and also to improve the squad's egress options. The team now numbered 25 Marines, but the 13 men of the Marine Rifle Squad were still the nucleus of the force. Although there had been occasional tinkering with the size of the infantry squad during peacetime lulls, often driven by the associated budget and manpower cuts which generally characterized the periods between wars, the Marines had generally used a 13 Marine squad for most of the last 100 years. It was composed of a Squad Leader, generally a Sergeant, and three Fire Teams, each consisting of a Corporal Fire Team Leader, an Automatic Rifleman equipped with the M-249 Squad Assault Weapon (SAW), a Rifleman/Grenadier, equipped with a M-203 grenade launcher attached to his M-16, and a Rifleman/Scout. The three elements of the squad provided a lot of tactical employment flexibility, especially for squads with proficient Fire Team Leaders that were operating in environments favoring small unit actions.

There was nothing magical about the number 13, of course, as it was the gritty toughness and professional competence of the Marines, and not some clever organizational structure, that caused them to be feared the world over. But given that, the modulo-3 based structure of Marine Corps infantry units was based on the operationally proven maxim that a person could really only effectively manage 3 people at a time, especially in the life-and-death situations the Marines seemed to actively seek out. So a Rifle Squad of 13 Marines made a lot of sense. Of course, attaching additional people to the squad complicated the dynamics somewhat, but Hussar handled this by keeping the "riders" near him, thus shielding the Fire Team Leaders from any disruption to their team's operational rhythm.

Hussar closed his eyes and leaned his head back. He was through "armchair quarterbacking" various mission contingencies and felt relaxed now knowing he had done everything he had time to do. He believed his squad was ready to go and would be able to handle any situation they encountered. He was confident the MEU staff, especially the S-2, Major Renick, had prepped his Marines as much as possible for the upcoming mission and was grateful for their competence. Of course, he realized some lowly sergeant sitting on a ship in the middle of nowhere would not be given all the highly classified information used to formulate the objectives of his mission. Most of the data would be Special Access – Sensitive Compartmented Information, and the "read list" would be very tightly controlled. Certainly his name would not be on the read list allowing access to such information. But Hussar trusted the people he knew in the decision-making process, just as they trusted him to accomplish the mission he had been assigned. *They had their jobs and he had his job*, he thought.

It was still a little over an hour before they reached the insertion point. *Might as well catch a little shut-eye*, he thought and immediately dropped off into an easy sleep.

# Chapter 10

About the time Hussar's squad was crossing the Kenyan coast line, Major Renick walked back into the *Tarawa's* JIC. He had taken a short break and gone below decks to the Officer's Wardroom to partake in what the Navy called "midrats," or midnight rations. Now that the MEU was engaged with multiple simultaneous operations running 24/7, the enlisted mess decks and the wardroom had expanded serving hours to better support the men working round-the-clock shifts. The food wasn't any better, just available more often, and Renick was still burping up an unpleasant aftertaste from the greasy hamburger, or "slider," he had whamoed five minutes earlier.

There had been non-stop activity in the JIC over the past two days. Once the bio threat surfaced, it was like the entire MEU staff had gone into overdrive. It was hard enough to come up with solid recommendations on where to run the next few missions and then put together the necessary intel support for each of those missions. But now they had to also deal with the added distraction of getting pinged constantly by CENTCOM and, even worse, directly by some of the intel heavyweights around Washington for information updates. The roles had reversed—previously the stateside guys were feeding him intelligence so he could do his job, but now they were pulling information from him so they could do their jobs. Renick was practically living in the JIC 24 hours a day just to keep up with the continuous demands for information. And now, with Hussar's squad going back into Somalia, something had to give. So Renick had advised Colonel

Steuben that their ability to support on-going missions was being impacted by all the external communications. Steuben had tried to prevent this very thing from happening by setting up a reporting schedule through CENTCOM, but it was probably inevitable that others would try to contact them directly. This was, after all, a very big deal and everyone wanted to get in the game. Renick was right, though, about the potential impact to on-going missions, so he put a call into the Deputy CINC at CENTCOM and requested assistance in stopping all direct contacts not initiated by the MEU. It took several hours for the word to get out, but by the time Hussar's squad left the ship, things had quieted down considerably.

There wasn't much for Renick to do in the JIC right now but wait for something to happen, so he took the time to sit back and think a bit. The on-watch sailors and Marines had everything pretty much under control, with the exception of the Intel Watch Chief who was still fiddling with the parameters for the Tactical Event Notifier. That was to be expected, though, as this mission would be the first operational use of the Notifier, or as Renick had said, "the world premiere" of the Notifier. Renick still thought the term "Tactical Event Notifier" was a fitting name for the capability he had developed, but, as they were prone to do, the grunts had quickly bastardized it. They simply called it the "Ticker," and he had finally given up fighting the change. *You would think if you invented something, you should be able to name it,* he thought, but he realized he didn't really care anymore. Lots of things that had seemed important several weeks ago were now absolutely meaningless, but he was excited to find out if the Ticker loaded on Q's computer would be useful in a tactical environment.

Created to facilitate the information flow between tactical units, the Ticker was the culmination of a couple years of thinking and "garage" development by Renick. Like most good things, it was a very simple tool from the user's perspective. To most people, it looked a lot like the stock price tickers or news tickers found on the bottom of television screens. In fact, Renick got the idea from watching a stock ticker on a TV news channel scroll by for 60 minutes while he was running on a treadmill at the gym one afternoon. He noticed after a few minutes that his eyes and brain adjusted to the presence of the ticker and that he could watch the news broadcast and still be aware of stock prices as they went by. The important aspects that he noticed were the need for very little screen "real estate" because the ticker window could be quite small, and the fact that a person's vision could adapt to the ticker and the brain could subconsciously become aware of important changes in the ticker information. Of course, the actual presentation to the user wouldn't have to look exactly like a stock ticker, but the idea was the same. This was the easy part of the concept. The hard part was identifying what information got put on the Ticker, where it came from, and how it would be distributed in a tactical environment.

Unfortunately, Marines that he originally bounced the idea off were not very taken with the concept. At the time, Renick thought this was because the idea seemed too simple, and people couldn't visualize the power behind something so easy. They didn't understand the complexity that would be required in the software that fed the Ticker and how, if done right, it could help with tactical information management. He also knew that very few Marines were visionary or capable of articulating what new technologies could be harnessed to improve their operational prowess. Marines were good at getting things done NOW, and generally poor at planning and sorting through complex situations. They have an incredible ability to "make-do" with what is available, to "suck it up" when the situation is dire, to adapt to unfamiliar environments, and to charge when surrounded. When they see something they like, for example some new Army radio, they go nuts, send messages like crazy, make it a crisis, brief all the generals, and have to immediately go out and get 50 of them or the world will end; they will buy them, without any thought to how they will train, use, or support the equipment. Those issues will turn into the next crisis and will then be handled in similar fashion. In fact, this crisis du jour approach to procurement is pretty much the de facto Marine Corps acquisition philosophy. So Renick ended up having to do the work on his own and became one of the very few Marine officers willing to take the time to attempt to actually solve a problem with nothing but his own convictions to support him.

Attitudes towards the Ticker changed immediately after the 9/11 terrorist attacks. Within hours, all the major cable news networks adopted news tickers to keep up with the rapidly emerging facts and to quickly inform people periodically tuning in of the latest developments. This desire to get out breaking stories, still too fresh to have allowed much journalistic analysis, isn't really that much different from supporting the information needs of tactical forces. Marines everywhere suddenly embraced his idea. Although the start of the continuous cable news tickers (they never went away after 9/11) was an entirely independent event that occurred after he had already prototyped his concept, it served to generate lots of interest in what he was doing and accelerated his development schedule.

There were several components of the Ticker architecture. On the user's computer, the Ticker was a small applet running in the background that accepted and parsed Extensible Markup Language (XML) messages received from an acknowledged multicast. The user could set up a custom profile to accept only certain messages of interest for presentation on the ticker. The rest would be stored for possible future reference. For example, messages dealing with events that occurred within a specific geographic area (defined by sets of latitude/longitude pairs) or messages of higher priority (which were color coded) could be accepted for presentation. The actual presentation window could be resized, anchored anywhere on the screen, or even hidden from view until a pre-defined type of message update was received, at which time the window would pop back up.

Also, if the user's computer was identified as a possible source of information (and almost all were), a set of intelligent software agents would run in the background. They could be configured to look for specific events and automatically report those events back to the Ticker server for possible inclusion in future message updates.

The message updates, Ticker Message Updates or TMUs, were IP multicast addressable and could be sent out on as many comms paths as needed to get to the desired user base. The TMUs were very small, usually only a few hundred bytes, and could be sent out periodically or as new information was generated. Typically, the individual items of the TMU would actually be hyperlinks, which if clicked on would provide the user additional local information or would redirect him to a remote site. Also, the system could be set up so that some or all user systems would acknowledge TMU receipt so information delivery could be assured. In training scenarios, the system had turned out to be quite useful and a very low bandwidth user, which was imperative for it to be tactically viable. TMUs that included such diverse information as availability of new satellite imagery, weather forecasts, intel reports, threat alerts, etc., had been successfully passed and the Marines had come to view the tool as a necessary adjunct to the Common Operational Picture (COP), which attempted to provide a consistent view of tactical unit locations.

The Ticker Server was the brains of the system. It monitored activities on the various computers supporting the operation through the use of intelligent software agents and implemented the rule set configured by the Ticker Controller. There were quite a few configuration options, which equated to complexity in the system. But it was relatively simple to develop new event objects in the object-oriented database using the available templates and graphical user interface, and once an object was created, the associated software discovery agent would also be created for deployment. The Ticker Server feeding Hussar's squad was on the *Tarawa,* and it was this application that was currently the focus of the Intel Watch Chief.

"Any problems there, Master Sgt. Davis?" Renick offered. The Master Sergeant had over 20 years in the Corps and was a leading critic of any new technology being introduced in the field.

"Sir, we don't seem to be getting any acks back from Q yet, but the system did check out OK before they left," Davis answered. Acks, or acknowledgements, were desired on this mission so the MEU would know Hussar was getting information without having to interrupt him with voice comms.

"OK, that's probably by design. Q is hooked into the helicopter's comms, but he's probably only allowed to receive right now because of their Emission Control (EMCON) status. That's also why we're running the Ticker on UHF instead of the Globalstar L-band. We wanted to avoid all the call set-up and monitoring transmissions."

The truth of the matter was that communications with the Globalstar satellites used a Code Division Multiple Access (CDMA) scheme which generated a signal characterized by Low Probability of Intercept or Detection (LPI/LPD). He had tried to convince the MEU Air Officer of this, to include showing him all the supporting technical data, so that the CDMA comms would be allowed under EMCON, but it had been to no avail. Renick was confident, though, Hussar's squad was receiving the TMUs, so not getting acks right now really wasn't that important. Once the squad got on the ground, they would verify proper functionality.

"Roger, sir, I'll quit monkeying with it then," Davis replied, and he went over to read the incoming message log.

Renick went back to his recall of the Ticker development. It had only taken a few months to get the basic prototype up and running, and then he had immediately started improving it. Initially, he had been focused on providing information to the Ticker when any one of a number of what he considered likely events, such as the issuance of a new threat report, had occurred. He then realized he could also generate Ticker messages for non-events, i.e., for situations when a specific activity was expected to happen by a certain time but in fact did NOT occur as expected. This was a new, but very important, perspective on information management and prompted Ticker messages for such things as the failure to receive a scheduled update or report on time, a tactical unit in movement not reaching an objective when planned, or a sensor not responding to an activation command.

Then Renick turned to another problem he had been thinking about for a while. It is commonly called "cueing" in the intel world, and, in the most general sense, is the ability to use an event occurrence as an automatic catalyst, or "trigger," for other events that you desire in response to the initial event. At the top of the cueing pyramid were complex multiple event chains. For example, using a "hit" from an airborne Moving Target Indicator (MTI) radar showing possible enemy battle tank movement to automatically cue another sensor, like a signals intelligence or imagery satellite, to collect on the same area to provide confirmation. This sensor then cues the generation of GPS target coordinates suitable for use in a Joint Direct Attack Munitions (JDAM) bomb, which are then passed to an orbiting F-16 as an immediate strike mission. The pilot then receives such coordinates and uses them to program and drop a JDAM bomb. Tying together that sensor-to-targeting, cell-to-shooter string would be the ultimate, and big programs with big dollars have been working on this for years. But Renick's goals were not nearly as ambitious. He just wanted to speed up the information cycle within the MEU and provide some basic decision support and information management tools.

He eventually came up with the idea of enhancing the Ticker to support the desired cueing function. He had additional intelligent agents coded that worked with the event discovery agents supporting the Ticker data gathering function and connected the new agents with existing applications. The resulting architecture allowed information gathered to feed the Ticker presentation window to also be used to trigger any number of desired responses. For example, on Hussar's first mission, miniature camouflaged radiation detectors had been emplaced by the squad UAV and set to automatically datalink back to Q's IDS. The increased radiation readings seen as the two guys carrying a large satchel walked by one of the detectors provided Q confirmation that they possessed the SADM-10 and were permissible terrorist targets. If the Ticker had been activated at the time, the sensor location and confirmatory readings would have been passed immediately back to the MEU Command Element and could have automatically triggered such things as entries in the Watch Officer's Log, update messages to CENTCOM, incident plotting on electronic situation maps, alerts to the Emergency Reaction Force standing by to fly in reinforcements, preparation for decontamination, etc. Of course, enhancing each individual software application presently used to provide these capabilities could also have produced all of these cueing actions, but that would be a piecemeal approach and difficult to actually accomplish. The genius of Renick's approach was in providing a framework, with an open and easily extensible architecture and well-defined interfaces, for providing event notification and cueing services to all applications.

*Time will tell*, Renick thought, but he had done all he could to prepare. An energetic man by nature, Renick had been on an adrenaline high for the past 3 weeks. His fellow Marines marveled at the noticeable increase in his near legendary ability to stay focused, but he was right where he wanted to be and enjoying the experience. Once it became clear 11th MEU would be in the thick of America's response to the terrorist attacks of 9/11, Renick realized the last five years of his professional life would be evaluated in a way he hadn't thought possible. He was a key member of a small, but growing, maverick element within the miniscule Marine Corps Intelligence community that understood the changes necessary to improve tactical intelligence support. He wasn't a National Intelligence community wanna-be, with their smug attitudes and super-secret information analyses and intelligence briefs presented exclusively to only a very select group of high government officials. He didn't want to be a CIA spook or spy or work deep in the bowels of some windowless building in D.C. Renick was proud to be a Marine and proud to be the Intel Officer for 11th MEU. In his opinion, the Marines rotated too large a number of their intelligence officers through tours at the Washington D.C. 3-letter intelligence agencies (DIA, CIA, NRO, NSA, etc.) in the belief the Marines would gain "broadening" experiences but almost every one of them came back pretty much useless in performing the art of tactical intelligence. They got accustomed to working in offices with a large number of analysts and eventually became dependent on the significant resources of these multi-billion dollar organizations. Neither of these attitudes was useful in the field. In fact, both were quite harmful. Renick thought it would have been much smarter to send Marines to all of the national intel organizations for a short-term familiarization period, and then get them right back out to duty with the Fleet Marine Forces (FMF).

Although Renick had been on the MEF staff at Desert Storm and was suitably impressed with the detailed analysis and technology of the people at Central Command headquarters, and the Army (ARFOR) and Air Force (AFFOR) components, with their thousands of intelligence personnel and sophisticated automated collections and analysis systems, many of these capabilities were not easily adapted to the Corps' environment. The luxury of months of planning, build-up, and practice, while, in the background, a heavily equipped, slow-moving enemy is pummeled by the largest air campaign since the Battle of Britain didn't really mesh with the Marines role as "America's 911 Force." Marines do not do well in such large, intricately planned, structured, long-term operations—which is probably why, in spite of the fact that the Marines are the acknowledged experts at difficult amphibious operations, you never hear of any Marine exploits on D-Day, even though June 6, 1944, was the start of the largest amphibious operation of all time. But you've seen many, many accounts of Marines in close combat with a fanatical enemy entrenched on numerous islands in the Pacific, where the war was characterized by a series of somewhat smaller, quick, incredibly bloody amphibious assaults. Such is the nature of shock troops.

So Renick didn't go along with the rush of many other Marines, including senior intelligence officers, into trying to grab everything the other Services had and adopting them into the Marine Corps. For starters, he knew there were 100 times as many intelligence specialists in theater during Desert Storm than there were in the entire Marine Corps. And the Marines were not about to modify force structure to significantly improve the number of Marines in the intelligence community. In fact, the opposite was true. There was constant pressure to justify any billets that were not directly Combat Arms, that is, people pulling triggers. Marines kill bad people. Everyone knows this—which is why even the mere threat of them being sent in for action is such a powerful deterrent. Renick knew there was something to the idea of exploiting technology to increase combat effectiveness, maybe not to the scale seen by his soldier and airman brethren but still something to be investigated and pursued smartly. So Renick didn't spend much of the personal time he allocated for his professional development on the research of past battles and campaigns and the exhaustive analysis of intelligence successes and failures, which were the focus of the typical well-rounded intel professional. Instead, he read the technology section of the Wall Street Journal and followed advances in mobile wireless networking and other emerging technologies in the commercial sector through subscriptions to several hi-tech trade magazines.

He certainly didn't follow the typical intel officer career path of sitting as the token Marine at one of the 3-letter intel organizations and learning how to weave the intel picture at the National level in support of National Strategy. Instead, and to the amazement of his peers, he volunteered for a tour at the Marine Corps

Systems Command (MARCORSYSCOM) in Quantico, VA. The officer assignments section at Headquarters, Marine Corps was only too happy to grant his request. Duty at MARCORSYSCOM wasn't seen as getting you on the fast track for promotion, and ambitious officers tried to avoid such jobs that weren't career enhancing. But having an officer volunteer to go there avoided the unpleasant task of sending an undesirable set of orders to another officer, so Renick was quickly sent orders to MARCORSYSCOM before he had a chance to come to his senses and change his mind.

Unlike the other Services which have extensive research & development laboratories across the nation, maintain a civilian workforce of scientists and engineers, sponsor significant academic research at country's leading colleges and universities, manage numerous multi-billion dollar weapon system procurements, and have a comprehensive acquisition career path for uniformed Service members and civilians alike, the Marine Corps manages all their procurements through a single, small, half-heartedly staffed, Systems Command organization in Quantico. People sitting in adjacent cubes in the randomly furnished spaces may be project officers for everything from combat boots to satellite radio equipment. Project officers generally manage multiple projects, and they do so without the benefit of an organization of scientists and engineers to draw from for technical expertise and program continuity. A Marine Captain who was leading an infantry company at Camp Pendleton the previous week could find himself managing a several hundred million dollar program to automate information flow on the battlefield with state-of-the-art computers and sophisticated software. It's all part of the Marine Corps strategy to do more with less (the Marines have been living this for most of their 225 year history, long before corporate America caught on to the cliché as a way of cutting costs) and also forces officers into unfamiliar environments where they are expected to excel. It's another crucible test for these officers because they are evaluated for suitability for promotion to the next higher rank based on their performance in this stressful situation. This isn't necessarily as insane as it first might appear. Unlike the other Services, the Marines bring people with operational backgrounds directly into the acquisition process of their combat equipment, so the guy buying stuff should have some idea of the intended operational use. Plus, officers generally go right back to the Fleet Marine Force after their MARCORSYSCOM tour—where, once again in operational units, they are the direct beneficiary of whatever capability they were involved in procuring and can report back on successes and failures, i.e., directly benefit from what they did right or suffer for what they did wrong. A control system engineer might call it a closed system with feedback. Helping the situation is the fact that Marine project officers often end up as participants in procurements being led by one of the other Services or of Joint programs. This allows them to basically operate a "shadow" program office, which still influences development but costs very little time and money. Unfortunately, there is also a dark side to having the FMF operator spend a couple of years at MARCORSYSCOM as the system buyer—it supports the "crisis" procurement approach discussed earlier, as each project officer tries to make a significant difference on his "watch" so he will receive a favorable evaluation.

When Major Renick showed up at MARCORSYSCOM, he was overwhelmed like every other new arrival. He quickly realized, though, that getting caught up in all the never-ending budget shuffles and programmatic bureaucracy would neither make him a better Marine nor allow him to focus on the ideas he had for tactical intelligence and direct intel support to small units.

It was clear to Renick that, from an intel perspective, not much meaningful analysis would be done at any level below a Marine Expeditionary Force (MEF), and MEFs, made up of over 40,000 Marines, deploy very infrequently. More importantly, when a MEF did go, so would a lot of other people who would bring along their in-theater intel toys, plus all the wideband communications necessary to move information to and from the CINC HQ and the supporting Washington intelligence community.

So why should the Marines spend time and money duplicating the capabilities of the other Services and mimicking their systems if the stuff was going to be in theater anyway? Was trying to repackage existing capabilities so they could operate in the harsh environments encountered by Marines really the best approach? The current philosophy seemed to be that the stuff that was great for staff officers at higher headquarters must be useful for the guys closer to the front. There were still stories from the Vietnam days of guys in the rear having easy, almost casual access, to information that could save the lives of grunts operating in the Delta less than a hundred miles away but being restricted by classification or bureaucracy or even ignorance from providing the information in a timely manner.

Renick realized that though there were problems in the national intelligence community, generally related to inadequate sharing and coordination of information, he wouldn't be the guy solving that problem. Better to focus on things he could influence. The truth of the matter was, the real problem from the tactical point of view was managing battlefield information, not providing detailed intel analysis. So Renick decided he would spend his good time, his thinking time, after the day's paperwork had been handled, looking at the problem from the opposite end. Rather than trying to figure out how far down the operational chain he could move much of the intel the geeks in the rear had, he decided to focus on how to best support a small unit that was preparing for very near-term contact, was in contact, or for which contact was imminent. Amazingly, when he had spent about a week thinking about it, he realized that much of what he was seeing on a daily basis at MARCORSYSCOM didn't pass the common sense test—the focus was on providing capabilities for missions the Marines would unlikely ever see, especially without the involvement of any of the other Services. And the other Services, with their large civilian support infrastructure and long-term perspectives, were already focused on concerns for global and regional conflicts, regardless of the specific likelihood at any given moment, because of the lengthy timelines associated with major weapon system procurements, general force modernization, working with coalition partners, etc. So why were the Marines doing the same thing?

Wanting to validate his thinking, Renick spoke to a buddy of his, who was doing the standard DIA tour, to get the latest threat analysis and forecast of likely engagements. It pointed clearly to Mogadishu type scenarios, terrorists, and urban warfare environments. Gunfight at the O.K. Corral type stuff. Essentially, the situations where many of the high-tech sensors and weapon systems, which had worked so well in Desert Storm, could be rendered almost useless by a savvy, street smart adversary.

Renick knew he was right, but he needed to sell his story. Since the pitch would have to be made to the Corps senior intelligence officers, who were not only trained to spot inconsistencies or logic gaps in any story but were the very same people supporting the present procurement priorities, he knew he had to hit a home run if any changes were to be made. More than a mere idea would be required—he had to clearly articulate the problem and recommend some possible solutions.

He started by listing some of the commonly understood problems the Marine intel community faced at the time:

-Insufficient personnel to operate all the computer systems and new software applications being procured

-Inadequate logistics to support these systems (maintenance, electrical power, environmental limitations, weight/size impacts to sealift and airlift manifests)

-Inadequate training

-The need for separate, dedicated, intel-funded communications capabilities because new systems were showing up in the FMF faster than the communications people could get additional equipment (the budget for intel systems had grown much faster than the budget for communications equipment)

-Retention problems with skilled personnel (first-term Marines with technical skills could at least double their salary the day they got out of the Corps)

He realized almost all of these problems were directly related to trying to take the systems that provided necessary capabilities at a CINC or Joint Task Force command center and shoehorn them into the tactical environment. He further realized that although he and many others thought that by working hard they could solve the above problems, the truth was they were getting perceptibly farther behind every quarter. The standard gung-ho response of "work harder" in the face of any problem wasn't much use when you are already supporting 24/7—there just wasn't any reserve left to call upon for surge requirements.

Instead of the approach of taking the intelligence systems architecture for the MEF and seeing what pieces could be deployed to successively lower echelons, such as division, regiment, battalion, etc., Renick decided he should attack the problem by identifying the intelligence and battlefield information needed by a Marine infantry squad, the basic tactical element of the Marines. From there, he would define the system necessary to provide the required data, and then as he went up the chain to platoon, company, battalion, etc., he would add in the other capabilities required at each level. It was an opposing paradigm—instead of taking a big object and trying to chip off smaller and smaller parts that still kept all the qualities of the original object, Renick wanted to take small objects and aggregate them to make bigger objects. Sort of like a Lego set. He was going to focus on the squad's most likely missions, small unit operations in fluid situations with poorly defined targets, and build from there. He came up with a basic list of squad requirements:

-Squad members need to communicate with each other.

-The squad needs to send info to higher HQ, i.e., battlefield information that they collect.

-The squad needs to receive info—images, maps, enemy movements, possible terrorist location updates, etc.—from higher HQ and other sources.

-The squad needs to be able to view the information as it is received and also at a later time.

-Squad members must be the masters of their environment and require the latest in night vision and thermal imaging equipment and other sensors.

Renick decided that "arming" the squad with information management equipment should be addressed just like any other equipment issue, be it weapons, munitions, boots, packs, chow, etc. The Marines should take what they need for the mission. His job would be to provide a set of robust capabilities that could be tailored for the mission.

As Renick tried to develop an architecture, however, he realized he needed some help. He could do the standard thing and bring in an army of "Beltway Bandit" defense contractors and consultants to do data and process modeling, trade-off studies, establish Integrated Product Teams and Engineering Working Groups, write specifications, evaluate new technologies, create Operational and System Views, etc., or he could drop by and see Ed "Alfred E." Neumann and figure it all out in a couple of hours over a few beers. Renick had chosen the latter approach. Neumann was a former shipmate from Renick's first FMF tour and had a quick, non-linear, technical mind. He could jump several steps into solving a problem while everyone else in the conversation would still be trying to define the problem. But he was a little strange. In the way the Marine Corps had always attracted quirky, colorful characters, Neumann was the last guy anyone who knew him would pick as being a future Marine.

That opinion was shared by the Marine Recruiter in South Boston that Neumann had dropped in to see one afternoon. If it hadn't been a slow day, the Recruiter wouldn't have wasted much time—the kid was definitely not Marine material, as he was physically unfit, sloppy, not serious, and a smart-ass to boot. He didn't seem to know a thing about the Marines, so he clearly wasn't really interested about joining. The Recruiter thought one of his fellow recruiters, probably the army sergeant at the strip mall down the street, was playing a joke on him. When the kid started yakking about an MIT degree, the Recruiter knew something was up—this was South Boston, after all. The last thing the Marine Corps needed was for this clown to be an officer, but it wasn't the Recruiter's problem at that point. He dealt with potential enlistees. Marine officer candidates were screened by special Officer Selection Officers, so he sent Neumann to see a Captain at the main recruiting station in Boston. The Captain had also been initially underwhelmed by Neumann and spent 30 minutes detailing the rigorous life of a Marine in the belief he would see he wasn't well-suited, but Neumann had just nodded at the Captain's comments and left with an application package. The very next day, Neumann returned with the completed forms and was on his way to Quantico within a few months.

Although he was, in fact, a graduate of the School of Engineering at MIT, Neumann had been mostly known in Cambridge for rarely studying and for playing outrageous practical jokes. He was also witty, argumentative, and monumentally bored. Even though he was a couch potato whose only exercise consisted of the occasional game of Ultimate Frisbee, the Marine Corps seemed to beckon to him with what no one else had ever offered—a sense of purpose in his young life.

Surprisingly, and without ever actually fitting 100 percent in to the culture, Neumann ended up doing 10 years as a Marine before he resigned his commission. It was said he never passed up an opportunity for an argument or a chance to make a suggestion for improvement, even at times when either was highly inappropriate. He had actually presented a number of good ideas and brought a fresh perspective to an organization steeped in tradition, but his impatience with less mentally agile people, often senior in rank, was legendary and kept him from the promotions necessary to make a successful career. Renick never knew how Neumann had even survived 10 years with the number of people gunning for him, but Neumann used to just laugh it off with a casual "I'm just a Colonel trapped in a Captain's uniform. I'll eventually be rescued." Though it hadn't quite worked out that way, his vindication lay in the fact that most of what he had predicted over the years had actually happened, and potential technical solutions he had outlined on his whiteboard, or "artist's palette" as he referred to it, were now mostly mainstream ideas. Renick had thoroughly enjoyed sitting in on Neumann's impromptu presentations, for they were intellectually stimulating and highly entertaining, as Neumann was an over-animated figure with a loud voice. Just like those stereotypical shots of the ugly American tourist in a foreign country without benefit of understanding the local language, Neumann would speak louder and louder as he tried to get his point across to his non-comprehending fellow Marines, especially once he caught the first glazed over look on the face of a non-warp speed thinker. In fact, Renick once drew a caricature of Neumann as a schoolteacher, rapping a pointer against a blackboard, on which were drawn a number of troop tactical formations, as he yelled at his students to pay attention. The students all appeared to be senior foreign military officers, in full dress uniform, sitting in the pint-sized school desks found in elementary schools, with quizzical looks on their faces. The caption read "Now pay attention, this is important!"

One of Renick's favorite Neumann stories was the time Neumann went out to U.S. Space Command for a conference on precision targeting and support of national intelligence capabilities to tactical forces. The conference was in a nice auditorium, complete with Service flags to represent each of the Services on the stage behind the speaker's podium. When Neumann went up to the podium to propose a system architecture for supporting the Marines, he had discussed the need for precision accuracy in great detail, and then proceeded to point out the improper precedence ordering of the Service flags behind him as an example of poor accuracy. From memory, he recited the DoD instruction on Service precedence and then walked over and smartly adjusted the positioning of the flags while a somewhat incredulous audience of military officers silently watched. Some poor airman, probably pumped up with all the air power propaganda the Air Force likes to broadcast—at least until things turn ugly on the ground, that is—had placed the flags in the order Air Force, Army, Navy, Marines. Neumann put them in the correct order of Army, Marines, Navy, Air Force and then continued his briefing as if nothing unusual had happened. At the conclusion of his presentation, he told the still silent audience that, like most Marines, he was really a pacifist. He then explained that Webster defined a pacifist as someone who:

-Opposed war or violence as a means of settling disputes

-Refused to bear arms on moral or religious grounds

Neumann went on to say that he agreed with this philosophy, as it could be seen historically that war was, at best, a temporary means of settling disputes and also, that he could not see any moral or religious reason to bear arms. He had joined the Marines simply to fight for fun and adventure. After that little show, Neumann wasn't asked to give any more presentations, and he had left the Marines a short time later.

But Neumann was one of the sharpest technical minds Renick knew. And he could effortlessly transition from an operational perspective to technical discussions of great depth. So he was the right guy to help.

Renick had picked up his phone, grabbed a non-secure line, and dialed Neumann's number from memory.

"Yeah?" Neumann boomed through his earpiece.

"Alfred E., the Green Machine's—What Me Worry?—kid. What'er

yer up to?" Renick had easily dropped back into their familiar banter.

"Thinkin' and drinkin'," Neumann replied. "Whatcha want?"

"Need to stop by and tilt a few with you."

"Finally gettin' around to wanting to do something useful for the sergeants, huh?"

"Yeah." Renick hadn't spoken to his friend in several months, but Neumann had immediately known what he was up to. The guy was incredible.

"'Bout time, come on by. I'm here workin' on the Graf," Neumann had answered and hung up.

As Renick pulled up to Neumann's house, he could see a plume of blue smoke slowly rising over the house and was somewhat alarmed.

Neumann lived just south of Quantico, in an old house on one of the historic navigable creeks that feed the Potomac as it winds it's way down to the Chesapeake Bay. One of his projects was reconstructing a big old wooden yacht he had bought for almost nothing. Over 50 feet in length, it had once been an excellent boat for someone wealthy. A discerning eye could still see its fine lines, and a good imagination could picture its glory days. But it had suffered years of neglect and was much closer to a junkyard object than it was to a seaworthy vessel. To Neumann, though, it was a thing of beauty, and he spent hours on it. He had named it the *Graf Neumann*, in the fashion of the WWII German pocket battleships, and he was quite proud of it. On that particular day, he was trying to resurrect the twin diesels from the dead, which explained the blue haze surrounding his house.

As soon as he saw Renick, Neumann immediately stopped what he was doing and took Renick into his spacious, but cluttered, office in the rambling house.

Without so much as a minute of small talk, Neumann was at his whiteboard and had launched into a discussion, or maybe a lecture was the more appropriate term, outlining solutions for the problems Renick wanted to solve.

First, Neumann addressed the problem of squad members communicating with one another and the rest of the world. For intra-squad comms, miniature, low-power, low probability of detection, spread spectrum, network radios with embedded encryption would be necessary. Typically, only the leaders have access to communications equipment, but radios, throat mikes, and earpieces should be available for everyone. Squad leaders may choose not to equip every Marine with a radio for a mission or may direct certain Marines to carry but not use the radios unless necessary, i.e., to allow the Rifleman/Scout to focus his full attention on his environment without distraction. It would be the choice of the Squad Leader, and not some rear-echelon procurement specialist, to figure out the equipment load for the mission.

The squad would have several gateways to the outside world via radios with software-defined modems capable of supporting multiple modulation schemes and most of the VHF and UHF bands, to include L-band mobile satellite systems. Additionally, allowance was made for a comms processor capable of joining any HF networks supporting Automatic Link Enhancement (ALE). Any squad member could be routed through the gateways to external units, but once again, the squad leader controlled access. This architecture would allow the squad to reach back to higher headquarters to get information, which is typically platoon/company/battalion for conventional operations and the MEU or Joint Task Force headquarters for less conventional operations and also capture a number of broadcasts that periodically sent updates out to the field. That had been the lead-in for a detailed 45-minute discussion on developing the Ticker and using it to support cueing functions. Neumann had then gone through the rest of Renick's list in detail, discussing how things like UAV electro-optical sensor and radio relay platforms, F-18 Hornet and P-3 Orion reconnaissance downlinks, enhanced ground-based Tactical Remote Sensor System (TRSS) sensors, etc., could be woven into the architecture.

Renick had taken lots of notes and then asked Neumann for some insight on technology tips and on how to sell the idea to the brass. Neumann had given him the name of an engineer who had worked briefly with the Army's Land Warrior program before quitting in disgust at the lack of tactical common sense behind many of the ideas. The Army had invested heavily in the program in the hope of outfitting the modern soldier as a *Star Wars* character with all kinds of new technology and cool gadgets, but the program had hit some snags with operator interface, battery life, weight, and bulkiness. But they had done some good research on ideas like wearable computers, head-mounted displays, etc., and it would be a good place to start.

Neumann also told him he would have to steamroll the military specification zealots, who mandated that equipment must be operable from minus 20 degrees Fahrenheit up to plus 150 degrees Fahrenheit or it was unsuitable for military use. The problem with this approach is that most military missions operated well within these extremes. It was sort of ridiculous to withhold useful equipment from Marines supporting the majority of operations just because other Marines supporting a few missions in extreme environments couldn't use the equipment. It was sort of like political correctness gone crazy—the acquisition guys had to be "inclusive" of all possible mission environments or else everyone would suffer. This was motivated by a desire to try to keep the supply and logistics as simple as possible and to avoid the kinds of monumental screw-ups which sent winter gear to soldiers in Cuba during the Spanish-American war and summer equipment to Marines in Korea during the brutal winter of 1951. But wouldn't it make better sense to force the logistics system to become more flexible than to continue handicapping the fighting man with less than the best? Renick made a note to make this part of his brief as well.

Neumann then told him that not all the changes would be technical; there would be some process changes required as well. A major issue to solve from the squad support perspective was the set-up and management of the support infrastructure. Since focusing this level of support on such a small unit was a new concept, some thought was going to have to go into it. Although the first level of dedicated intel support occurred at the Battalion, it was very limited in capability. For the deployable configuration envisioned by Renick, the Battalion would be the key combat element of an MEU, which had a considerable intelligence section representing all the "ints," i.e., IMINT, SIGINT, HUMINT, etc. While aboard ship, the resources of the Amphibious Readiness Group (ARG) N-2 (the intelligence officer and his staff) could also offer significant supplemental assistance. Neumann had proposed a tiered support structure, with the MEU S-2 as the first tier of support for the squad's information needs. The next tier would include other Marine intel support. Since the MEU was part of the

CINC's operational Marine Component, or MARFOR, they could tap into the resources of the Intelligence Battalion at the MEF for help. Use of the Service intel center, the Marine Corps Intelligence Activity in Quantico, would also be included in this tier. Finally, the very capable Joint Intelligence Center owned by each of the operational theater commanders, with all their ties into the National Intelligence community, would be the top tier of support. Although Neumann envisioned all information flowing through a "handler" in the MEU S-2 before going to the squad, he knew there would be times when direct communications with other assets would be desirable, certainly to provide a back-up capability in case contact with the MEU S-2 was lost for whatever reason, but also because direct contact could be more timely and effective

For the sales job to the brass, Neumann also offered some good advice, which was "brief them what they know." Although the Marines were, to a man, rugged individualists, they didn't have any organizational values that highlighted individualism. It was teamwork and doing things with your buddies that was the focus of the Marines—always had been. At its most basic level, the concept of teamwork was epitomized by the members of a Marine Rifle Squad fighting together. This would be universally accepted by Marines, as the squad and squad leaders held mythical places in Marine Corps folklore. So anything Renick would brief would not be related to the combat power of the individual Marine but to the combat effectiveness of the Marine Rifle Squad. No one would challenge that.

Neumann was right. Renick briefed it pretty much as Neumann had outlined and got quite a few head nods from the colonels. They had authorized him to pursue the concept.

Probably the biggest change Neumann and Renick discussed that afternoon could never make it in the brief to senior officers though because it was too controversial. They both recognized there would be times when it would be invaluable for a small unit in a fast-moving situation to have someone on the ground with them to sort through all the information the Marines were locally collecting or remotely receiving as the situation developed. Renick knew he would be immediately discredited if he even suggested such a thing to his superiors, and his entire message would subsequently be tainted. But he knew every young Marine analyst would jump at the chance to go in with the grunts, although most of them today probably didn't know enough to be very useful. To be a welcome asset, the Marine would need competent system administrator/maintainer skills for all the new equipment Renick was proposing, in addition to his analyst abilities, and he would have to be able to keep up with the grunts.

Sticking his neck out, Renick decided to explore the concept on his own. He contacted some friends at the Navy-Marine Corps Intelligence Training Center (NMITC) at the naval training base at Dam Neck, VA, to find out what it would take to set up the kind of course he envisioned when the time was appropriate. Then before he started fielding his new Squad Support System, as he then thought of it, to deploying MEUs, he could call in a few favors and get a couple of Marines, manifested to float with the MEU Intel section, through the course before they embarked aboard ship. At the time, he had no idea he would be an MEU S-2 in 12 months and the first guy tasked with making the concept a reality, but that was how it all worked out and now here he was.

"Sir, there's a message you need to see," the Intel Watch Chief abruptly brought him back to the present.

Renick glanced at the computer display in front of him. The Ticker, using the Intel Center profile, was running on the screen, and his eye was immediately drawn to an item titled "Prisoner likely Al-Qaeda—DNA testing" that had just come up. He double-clicked on it and read the report.

The guys in Ramstein had done a quick turnaround on the analysis of the prisoner's DNA. Pattern recognition software and DNA analysis key genome matching from a former Al-Qaeda site in Lebanon had indicated a 90 percent likelihood that the captive was Heza Bin Bedhed, a known "Arab First" member. Also, there was a report on the analysis of the DNA sample from one of the bag men Hussar's squad had popped in the alley during the SADM-10 snatch. It identified the man as being from the same family, and within two generations, of one of the 9/11 hijackers from the World Trade Center attack. This was a real bonus.

# Chapter 11

Just a few feet on the other side of the bulkhead separating the LFOC from the JIC and Major Renick, Colonel Steuben sat and calmly watched the operations map respond to reports from 11th MEU units in the field.

The MEU had been at sea for five months. The sailors and Marines would normally have started the transit home by that point in a typical 6-month MEU deployment cycle. But nothing was typical anymore, and it seemed like operational adjustments were being made daily to respond to the changing terrorist threat. Or, probably more appropriately, in response to what we were learning new every day about the terrorist threat. It was certainly a tough problem to get your hands around. Steuben and Skwidolio had discussed this with the crew when they passed the word about their request for extending the MEU deployment to allow additional time to hunt down more bad guys. Of course, men wanted to get home to their families, so there was some disappointment for everyone at that level, but to a man, the sailors and Marines responded with a grim determination to stay on station and take out as many terrorists as possible.

Steuben knew there was still a long way to go in the War on Terror and was sure there would be more unpleasant surprises along the way. The terrorists were active and effective recruiters, and there were unfortunately many areas of the world where their type of poison would sell well. The Marines would be plenty busy for a while, and America would have to continue to adjust.

A lot had already changed over the past couple of years in the U.S. of A, from the highest levels of government to the operations of small military units like 11th MEU. Civilians saw the high-profile war in Afghanistan as the immediate response to the 9/11 terrorist attacks, but there were many other important, less publicized activities that also occurred as the government shifted focus to fight the War on Terror.

The Intelligence Oversight Board, in an extraordinary session with the senior party members of the House and Senate Select Committees on Intelligence, had directed the National Intelligence community to update their analyses of terrorist cells around the world. This had been done before, but there was a new twist to this review. Terrorist groups calling for anti-American violence, or those who associated with such groups, were identified as "Hostile to the United States" and were put into the list of "Go get." There was less ambiguity in this policy than in any since the clarity of our national intent and resolve to unconditionally defeat the Axis powers in World War II.

The Bush National Security Team had a simple, and therefore clear, view of the rest of the world. Many of the key individuals in this team were from the South and West (excluding the Pacific Time Zone apologists), where there is still very much an individualistic mentality and a tradition of simple justice oriented to responding to specific wrongdoing, rather than to social engineering. If a coyote killed your livestock, he'd be found hanging off the barbwire fence. If a man stole horses or rustled cattle, he'd be found hanging from the nearest tree. Offer violence to another man, you'd better be bulletproof. "Wanted, Dead or Alive" wasn't just a clever jingo, but a factual statement. And there was a "Ride with an outlaw, die with an outlaw" attitude for those inclined to associate with criminals. The elitist liberals had mocked Bush as a "cowboy" and wrote him off as a simpleton and a loser. The Euro crowd had laughed at his seemingly limited grasp of world politics, geography, and events and felt smug about his social awkwardness. But they all failed to recognize his American connection. Americans, at least those in the football and beer crowd, don't want a slick, haute couture wearing, french-speaking, euro-butt-kissing President. There were more surprises when the nation's perspective on the rest of the world crystallized after 9/11, as Americans began viewing other countries as being either with us or against us. Such stark language prompted immediate discussions in capitals from Addis Ababa to Zagreb, as foreign governments analyzed how the no longer emasculated United States would view them in such plain terms, and what they could do to either ensure a place on the U.S. team or minimize the damage. By calling for a War on Terrorism, Bush made it clear that we would go the distance to do the right thing and not follow the "be nice to these guys, so they leave us alone" approach the Germans had used with the Palestinians after the 1972 Munich Olympic massacre and that the French have used throughout the Middle East. Bush understood that the primary function of a government was to protect its citizens. The hollow excesses, shell game economics, and flacid foreign policy of the Clinton years had shown us that there was more than "It's the economy, stupid" to keeping a nation great. And men who degraded the highest office in the land with sophomoric sexcapades only emboldened our adversaries. We had a lot of catching up to do to get us back on track.

The intelligence community went into high gear after 9/11 and uncovered numerous potential targets. Any leads deemed "likely" to be valid by the National Security Council were aggressively pursued with the full resources of the U.S. Government. There were a lot of "dead-ends" early on, and the work continued to be difficult, as the terrorists got smarter at concealing their operations. They were beginning to use minor events as diversions to mask the extensive preparations for major attacks they were doing elsewhere. Fully realizing the news media has become a reactive and speculative beast that is quick to report what happens, and even quicker to bring out the talking heads with their B.S. analysis of what it all means, the terrorists easily exploited the media to enhance the effect of the diversion. And every time a diversion was created, a lot of "likely" leads and "chatter" popped up, most of which turned out to be worthless, but still consumed anti-terror resources and allowed the terrorists to see how close the Americans were getting to catching them.

One of the tools used by the government to coordinate anti-terror activities between all the departments were weekly reports signed out by the Director of Homeland Security, which identified terrorists, suspected terrorists, any suspicious activities, and also gave a scorecard on the level of cooperation received from each foreign government. These reports received intense scrutiny from numerous mid-level officials and helped guide daily activity.

Colonel West, USMC, the assistant to the sitting Military Liaison to the National Security Council, Vice Admiral Gordon "IceMan" Preble, was one of the guys who pored over the report every week. West noticed that the names of a relatively large number of Yemenis kept turning up in the reports. They were never any of the key people thought to be terrorist leaders and most wanted in the ongoing manhunt, but there were quite a few mid and low level thugs. He mentioned his observation to the Admiral at a staff meeting one morning and was a little surprised when the Admiral didn't have an immediate response, but just stared blankly at him for a few seconds.

Preble's previous assignment was Commander, Fifth Fleet and Commander, Naval Forces, U.S. Central Command, headquartered in the Persian Gulf at Manama, Bahrain. The Fifth Fleet had operational responsibility for the Arabian Sea, Persian Gulf, Gulf of Aden, the Red Sea, and the littoral areas of countries bordering these bodies of water. Preble was the senior naval officer in the Middle East when the dastardly suicide bombing of the USS Cole was carried out in the port of Aden in October 2000. Although Yemenis had initially shown up as a big blip on the radarscope in the search for those who had masterminded the attack, analysts later believed the link to Al-Qaeda was through a terrorist cell operating out of Karachi, Pakistan, and the focus had moved away from Yemen. Since 9/11, of course, almost all the attention had been on Afghanistan and Pakistan. But Preble knew there were a great number of only marginally governed areas in Yemen, and he still believed there was a strong link to Al-Qaeda somewhere in Yemen that just hadn't been discovered yet. It was easy to view a relatively small, backwards, and generally insignificant country 12,000 miles from Washington D.C. as a homogeneous political environment, but Yemen was hardly that.

An unhappy part of the Ottoman Empire for hundreds of years, the Yemenis began taking advantage of the weakening Ottoman dynasty at the beginning of the 20th century and had gained some autonomy by 1910. Soon thereafter, the Ottomans made the unfortunate decision to ally with the Germans in World War I, and the subsequent defeat of the Central Powers in 1918 moved the Empire entirely off the map and into the history books. The northern section of what is today Yemen became the sovereign nation of North Yemen in 1918, but the British continued to maintain a protectorate around the port of Aden for another 50 years to control the strategic Bab-el-Mandeb Strait between the Red Sea and the Gulf of Aden. In 1967, the British quit the area and the country of South Yemen was formed. By 1970, a Marxist government had come to power in the south, which prompted a tremendous exodus of people across the border into North Yemen. Almost two decades of bitterness and hostility characterized the North-South relationship, but in 1990 the two countries were united and relations among the peoples improved. Yemen supported Iraq politically in the Gulf War but with little influence or power, their position, however annoying, was irrelevant. A small southern secessionist movement by the Marxist die-hards, centered on the city of Aden, occurred in 1994, but this was soon overcome. Aftershocks from the 1994 secessionist movement in the region around Aden have continued, and there is still a lot of political tension in the country. But this was just a bunch of crap from the CIA Factbook—no American really knew what the hell was going on there. Although there had been a recent reaching out to the West, the use of Aden as a refueling station for U.S. Navy ships being one example, the general poverty of the people provided fertile ground for extremist recruitment.

West's comment to Admiral Preble triggered the Admiral to act on his beliefs. He spoke to the National Security Advisor that very day, and then pushed a directive for increased scrutiny on Yemen through the National Security Council within the week. Four months later, results of the increased surveillance helped produce the intelligence that led to Hussar's mission to recover the SADM-10.

It had been an interesting chain of events and Steuben thought it bizarre, but he knew the story was true because he had heard it directly from Bill West. And now West had helped the intel community "connect the dots" from Yemen to Somalia based on input from 11th MEU. These were just a couple of examples of the changes happening to the government's normal way of doing business as a result of the terrorist attacks. *The times they were a changin'*, Steuben thought. But that was all Washington stuff. He had his own issues to deal with out here.

The MEU Commanding Officer was a no bullshit kind of guy. He wasn't particularly interested in playing it safe or covering his ass, and it showed in the way he commanded his unit and in the intensity with which he attacked every day of his life. The Marines had quickly picked up on this attitude, and they responded well to his demanding training schedule during the 12-month work-up period prior to deployment. The regimen had roughly followed the standard routine, starting with an emphasis on individual combat skills, leading to Fire Team training, then Squad level training, and on up the pyramid through Platoon, Company, Battalion, to finally include training exercises involving the entire MEU. Instead of ending the training period with the MEU exercise, which was the typical grand finale, Steuben finished it up with an additional month of independent Squad patrolling. This departure from the norm raised quite a few eyebrows among various senior officers. The Marine Corps, being a very tradition-minded organization (sometimes to their detriment), isn't one to casually make any change, much less drop a "winning" strategy used for years. But Steuben argued that 11th MEU's most likely missions would be chasing down terrorists and interdicting activities related to terrorism. For those types of operations, the Marine Rifle Squad, with suitable attachments, would often be the force of choice. Reports of the innovative, relentless training cycle Steuben put his NCOs through made believers of everyone.

When it came time to pick the Marines for the SADM-10 recovery, the MEU S-3, LtCol. Davis, recommended a team made up of hand-picked Marines from the MEU's Recon platoon and selected hard-chargers from the different line companies of the Battalion. Davis reasoned that putting together an All-Star team for the first mission would ensure success and be the quickest way to get someone with "in-country" experience in every company in the Battalion once the "veterans" returned to their normal units. But Steuben saw it differently and had emphatically overruled his Operations Officer. First, there was no guarantee when the team would return. They could become casualties, or they might be assigned a follow-on mission which would delay their return. Also, Steuben was concerned that the team might get themselves in a jam and require significant support for extract or other operations—and the support would then have to be provided by units missing key people. The primary reason, though, was that numerous athletic and operational experiences had shown him the value of men living, training, working, and fighting together as a team.

Stueben had played varsity football during his last two years at the Naval Academy. Although he had been an All-District defensive back at Burnet High in the small town of Burnet, Texas, Steuben just really wasn't big enough to play at the collegiate level when he showed up for plebe summer at Navy. He figured out very quickly during the sport screening periods that summer that about half the plebe class had played football, and many very well. When you consider that there were more men in his plebe class—all physically fit—than there were in the entire student body of his high school, the odds didn't play well. So Steuben had tried out for the plebe Heavyweight Crew team instead. The rowers he had seen around the Academy were physically and mentally tough and workout fanatics. Even though Steuben didn't know a damn thing about rowing a crew shell and didn't initially fit in real well with the Yankee preppies recruited for the sport, he needed a release from the stress of plebe life and the intense, almost mind-numbing, crew workouts were just the thing. He ended up making the team and enjoyed the time he spent at the boathouse. Steuben would never forget the feel of an eight in perfect swing, well set, racing down the Severn River, with eight guys in synchronized heaving and legs, backs, arms exploding in the agony of exertion as they totally subordinated their individuality to stroking as one.

He had decided to change course during his second year at Navy. It turned out Steuben was just a late-bloomer physically—in the fall right before his 20th birthday, all the grueling physical punishment he had subjected himself to for years seemed to suddenly pay off. He had started plebe year at 5 feet 11 inches and 175 pounds. By Christmas of his sophomore year, he was 6 feet 3 inches and 210 pounds. When he came back after the Academy's short Christmas break, he had made up his mind to try out again for the football team and had gone to see the coach. The football coach could only smile when Steuben spoke to him. He remembered the kid as having a lot of heart and being able to hit hard for his size but just not having enough size to hit hard enough. He didn't begrudge the kid for realizing at the time that he wasn't going to get to play and deciding he didn't want to hang around the team for four years just to be part of the practice "meat" squad. So the coach gave Steuben another try-out, and immediately knew he had a keeper. Not only did Steuben make the varsity football team, he became a rare two-sport athlete by continuing to row for Navy in the spring racing season.

Steuben ended up becoming a star on the Naval Academy football team as a standout linebacker, making All-Conference his senior year. Again, he learned the absolute need to subordinate himself to the team and the value of knowing what each player was going to do, where he would be, and what he was thinking. It was beat into him that this knowledge only came after months of practicing and playing together. He had also found it a humbling and motivating experience to play in the Navy-Marine Corps Memorial Stadium in Annapolis. Ringing the upper deck of the stadium were the names of significant sea and land battles, and his father had fought in one listed prominently and known as one of the bloodiest battles ever. The action took place in 1943 in the Pacific on a small atoll in the Gilbert Islands, called *Tarawa*. Every time Steuben went into that stadium he felt connected to his dad, and he thought his present duty serving aboard the *USS Tarawa* was another great tribute to his father and his fellow Marines.

Steuben also had some operational anecdotes and experiences to support his decision. One was the well-known Vietnam-era problem with rotating personnel in and out of combat units rather than rotating the units themselves in and out of action. This caused a frequent need for squad members to adjust to new personnel and led to a breakdown of the brotherhood, sense of common destiny, and esprit of combat units. Although Steuben was still at the Naval Academy when Vietnam wound down, he had talked to a number of officers who had first hand experience with the policy—to include the difficulty of showing up as a fresh Lieutenant from the States and becoming a Platoon Commander of 40 guys, no two of which had the same rotation date. It had been one nightmare among many nightmares, of course, but Steuben, like most of his contemporaries, had it burned into his brain. What Davis proposed was different from the Vietnam situation but just the idea of violating unit integrity pissed him off.

Finally, Steuben had a negative personal experience in Desert Storm that related to the idea of bringing in the "heavies" to form an A-team for the mission. With the long build-up period before Desert Storm, officers and senior enlisted started coming out of the woodwork and showing up in theater to get their "ticket punched" for being in a combat zone. Jobs were found to try to make these people useful, but the headquarters elements became bloated with the extra bodies. It was said that if you kicked all the extra people out of the high-level staffs and pushed them down to combat units, you would end up with Majors as Platoon Commanders and Gunnery Sergeants as Squad Leaders. Steuben likened it to the crowd that shows up at a fire, curious and perhaps well-intentioned but mostly impeding the ability of emergency responders to do their job.

So he had told Davis that the nucleus and basic element of small, light infantry operations was the Marine Corps rifle squad. That's how his Marines were organized, how they trained, and how they would fight. The first squad to go in would be the squad from the BLT that had won the Battalion's "Super Squad" competition prior to the MEU work-ups, because they had earned the right. The Super Squad competition basically matched all the squads, with their normal manning, against one another to use the spirit of competition to help hone their skills and pump up their motivation during training. For 11th MEU, that squad was 1st Squad, 2nd Platoon, Fox Company, 2nd Battalion, 1st Marine Regiment. Which just happened to be Sergeant Hussar's squad.

Steuben thought this was a fitting situation, as he had found out that his father and Hussar's grandfather had served together in the 6th

Marines in the famous, bloody World War II Pacific battle on the atoll of *Tarawa*. It had been a chance discovery one evening early in the MEU work-up period. Col. Stueben wanted to get to know the Marines charged with leadership responsibilities in the MEU and had invited Marine leaders, grouped by rank, to a series of barbecues at the appropriate club on Camp Pendleton. He had met the Squad Leaders and other Sergeants at the NCO club. Stueben had spoken with Hussar for several minutes and asked the standard questions about the sergeant's hometown, family, etc. and had discovered the common WWII family history. Hussar also told him of an ancestor who had served in the Texas Marines. Although Stueben was a Texan to the core and knew a great deal of Texas history, he had never heard of the Texas Marines and was disbelieving at first. But he had researched it and found there was indeed a recorded existence of such.

After successfully breaking away from Mexico in 1836, Texas was an independent nation until 1845. During that period of independence, a military force was created, mostly to protect against any attempts at re-annexation by the Mexican government. Naturally, with hundreds of miles of coastline on the Gulf of Mexico, Texas was involved in significant sea trade and had quickly established a small navy to help protect its sea lines of communication and coastal cities. In keeping with the custom of the day, detachments of Marines were established on the larger vessels. A Hussar was listed as one of the senior Marines assigned, by virtue of his prior service as a U.S. Marine on a U.S. Navy man-o-war. Stueben thought Hussar's ancestors would be proud of their progeny— he was a good kid and a fine leader of Marines.

Just then, Steuben saw the Ticker message "Prisoner likely Al-Qaeda—DNA testing" pop up on his Commander's monitor in the LFOC. It was the same message Renick was looking at in the adjacent compartment, and Steuben was just as pleased to read it. He immediately called Capt. Skwidolio to pass on the information, and Skwidolio recommended he make an announcement to all the sailors and Marines on the *Tarawa* through the ship's general announcing system, the 1MC, to share the good news. Steuben did so, and he could hear the immediate cheer roar through the ship as the men responded to the announcement.

Feeling good, Steuben hit the intercom button for the JIC.

"Major Renick."

"Yes, sir?"

"Will Hussar's squad see this message on their Ticker?"

"No, sir, their profile doesn't include this type of message. It wouldn't be necessary for their mission. We're trying to limit the number of messages going out on this initial roll-out so the squad isn't distracted by the Ticker."

"I know everything is automated, but you can still manually force a message into the system, can't you?"

"Yes, sir."

"Good. Send it out to Hussar. This message will let them know how successful their first mission was, and they should know that as they go back in-country. It's good for morale."

"Aye-aye, sir."

"Did CENTCOM already get this report?"

"I don't know, sir, but I'll find out. They were an addressee on the message that came out of the lab. Someone at CENTCOM has it by now, but I don't know if anyone has looked at it or is factoring the information into operational planning yet."

"They don't have anything like the Ticker at CENTCOM?"

"Not yet, sir."

"We could set them up though, right?"

"Yes, sir, we could give them the Ticker client, same as we could give it to the National Military Command Center in the Pentagon or even the White House Situation Room. Even better we could give them some of the discovery agents and automatically get some of what they are seeing."

Steuben considered the possibilities. Knowing how higher headquarters worked, it would end up being a one-way affair. They would suck him dry for info and second-guess what he was doing, but there was no way they would provide him immediate access to the important stuff they were seeing.

"Nah, let's hold off on that. In fact, this isn't really anything we should be advertising right now. Let's wait and see how the Ticker performs out here operationally before we say anything."

"Aye-aye, sir," Renick answered.

The secure phone at Steuben's elbow buzzed.

"11th MEU, Colonel Steuben," he answered.

"Colonel Steuben, this is Dr. Donnelly at USACEHR."

"Go," he ordered.

*Did he say "go?" It sounded more like "g-Ooooohh." Go where?* She wasn't quite sure what he meant. She thought the Army guys were bad enough, but these Marines spoke an entirely different language. It was definitely more guttural and clipped than what the soldiers around the base used. Then it hit her. The Army guys generally used too many words to describe things, often writing voluminous papers for stuff that was obvious and were incredibly fond of generating a never-ending stream of acronyms, compound acronyms, military nomenclature reference, etc., almost like they were lawyers. The Marines, on the other hand, spoke in an aggressive "shorthand" language and really used too few words. She even suspected they were actually making some of the words up as they went along and were really just using tone or inflection to communicate the actual message.

"Sir, we received your vials earlier today, and I have an update for you on the preliminary analysis we've completed so far."

Steuben glanced at the clock on the bulkhead. The vials had left the ship less than 36 hours ago, and they already had completed some stateside analysis. It seemed amazing that the vials could have made it halfway around the world so soon. Especially considering the half-dozen transfers that would have been necessary between the various legs of the long journey that started from the flight deck of the *Tarawa*. But if they really started getting into a lot of this bio stuff, Steuben thought an analysis cell would have to be forward deployed to eliminate the long transit to the lab and thereby speed up the identification time. If the Marines had been exposed to something bad in Yemen, having to wait 36 hours to find out the actual disease would probably have been too late to do them much good.

"Roger, wait one, I want to get Major Renick on the hook also."

# Chapter 12

D r. Karen Donnelly was DoD-illiterate. She had started working at USACEHR 6 months earlier, but it still seemed like she encountered an unfamiliar situation almost every day. It would have been great if these situations revealed something new and exciting related to her medical research, but they never did. It was always some arcane administrivia or bureaucratic hurdle that she had to overcome just so she could get to her research work. She wondered often in the first few months if working for the federal government was really the right choice for her.

Karen graduated from the Johns Hopkins School of Medicine four years earlier and, wanting to be in the thick of things after finishing her residency, had joined the Medical Shock Trauma Acute Resuscitation (MedSTAR) team at the Washington Hospital Center in Washington D.C. She was a high-energy person and liked the pace of the emergency room. There was plenty to do in her 12-hour MedSTAR shifts, as the Center routinely received the area's most critical emergency patients very near the thin line separating the living from the dead. Even though reports kept coming in about the dramatic decline in violent crime in the area, the mangled and drug-stupored bodies still showed up every day from the city's northeast side.

After about a year on the MedSTAR team, Karen was shocked one day to have to patch up two teenage toughs with gunshot wounds, as she had also seen both of them several months earlier for serious injuries. The very next day she treated a badly beaten woman, who was also a repeat. Karen found herself stuck in the revolving door of emergency room treatment that was common to all hospitals servicing inner city "hoods." But it jolted something deep inside her, and that afternoon, she submitted her resignation to the Director of Emergency Services. Karen Donnelly was burned out on health care. She was 31-years-old.

The next day, she loaded up her car and drove to Jekyll Island, one of the small outer bank islands off the coast of Georgia. It was here that Karen always came to find peace when confronted with the most difficult periods of her life. After her mother's death, when she was only 5, her father had brought her here every summer so the two of them could spend time together, just the two of them, free from the constant distractions of his demanding medical career as Chief of Surgery at Northside Hospital in Atlanta and the numerous relatives, nannies, and baby-sitters that were raising her. Memories of walking with her father on the island's wide, beautiful beaches and of his patient, thoughtful answers to her millions of childhood questions soothed her to the point of absolution and cleared her head for making important decisions.

After only a week on "her" island, Karen decided she would change her focus from patient care and go into medical research. During her pre-med days at Hopkins, she had taken an internship at USACEHR one summer and worked closely with one of her father's friends investigating how artificial disease vectors could be created and stimulated. It was very interesting, but at the same time, the place seemed somewhat bizarre to a young college student—everyone was so serious and single-mindedly focused on defensive preparations to counter attacks by some unknown people so evil as to want to unleash biologic warfare against an entire civilization. To a young, idealistic college student never exposed to the dark side of humanity, it was surreal.

The year at MedSTAR had changed her. She was now acutely aware of the bad in American society and could only imagine the evil that must exist in other places where groups of fanatics could work for years to prepare for the 9/11 atrocities and then be treated like heroes in certain parts of the world after committing the dastardly acts. It was mind-boggling to consider such hatred. Her experiences as an intern at USACEHR made a lot more sense to her now in light of the recent terrorist attacks. Karen felt a calling to help the cause of freedom, and probably the best way she could contribute would be by working in such a lab. As soon as she returned to the D.C. area, Karen applied to USACEHR and was hired within several weeks.

The first night she pulled duty at USACEHR turned out to be a life-altering experience for her. Dealing with the bio alarms from the Marines in Yemen who had apparently come across some really bad stuff was the most intense thing she had ever experienced. It crystallized her sense of purpose and resolved any doubts she had about what she was doing. This was action happening on a global stage, and the stakes were huge. Karen discovered it was almost the same kind of rush she had experienced at MedSTAR—not the direct life-or-death treatment decision for a critically-injured person lying on an operating table right in front of her, but the making of time-sensitive research decisions to help find answers on thwarting biological attacks. Karen knew she had done a good job tracking down the initial alarms and following up with the field unit. Even Col. Danielson had given her kudos in front of her peers and further commented that the deployed unit chasing the terrorists had specifically requested her as their liaison to USACEHR. So she had been assigned to an ad hoc operational support cell established to investigate the contents of the vials captured by the Marines and to maintain communications with 11th MEU.

The support cell put together a plan of action and identified the resources necessary to immediately start the analyses once the vials were received. Experts from outside USACEHR, to include scientists at the National Center for Infectious Diseases (NCID), were standing by to assist. It was important to analyze the material quickly, but accurately, and the plan was to divide up the biologics so that multiple independent analyses could be performed simultaneously.

The plan worked well. Within six hours of receiving the vials at Ft. Detrick, a preliminary analysis was complete and verified. The initial analysis that the Health Analysis Laboratory (HAL) computer had performed on the field spectroscopy signature provided by the 11th MEU MASS turned out to be spot-on accurate. The Marines had recovered a viral hemorrhagic fever, Ebola HF, and two strains of an influenza virus, related to Influenza A(H1N1). Although the scientists at Oak Ridge were reassured that the field detector and HAL, working together, had been able to almost immediately provide an accurate characterization of the samples, it was frightening for all to realize the Marines had basically just "happened" across the deadly material. Where else could the stuff be? Maybe other terrorists had already smuggled some of it inside the United States and were planning an attack right now. Karen shivered at the thought, but there wasn't time to be sitting around thinking of such doomsday scenarios.

While the medical research community continued into a more detailed analysis of the material and began the search for protective antigens that could stimulate the proper antibodies in humans and lead to an immunization vaccine, the support cell started preparing responses for additional discoveries. The National Intel community and CENTCOM had alerted USACEHR that other threats were being pursued, mostly on the African continent.

It was Karen's job to keep 11th MEU informed, so she had initiated the call to Colonel Steuben.

"OK, Doctor Donnelly, I've got Major Renick on the line with me now. Go ahead."

"Yes, sir. Basically, our preliminary analyses confirm our initial belief that the vials contained Ebola HF, and two, still unidentified, strains of Influenza A(H1N1)."

"OK. It's hard to figure out if that's good or bad news," Steuben observed.

"You're right, sir. We were thinking the same thing here. But it's good to know your MASS detector appears to be working properly and that the material is no longer in the hands of the terrorists."

"Roger that."

"Also, we've been told from CENTCOM," she was surprised at how quickly she was picking up the acronyms, "that you have a mission in Somalia?"

*Good*, Steuben thought, *somebody at CENTCOM thought to read in USACEHR on the latest mission.* That would keep him from wondering if he should do it. He didn't want to wait until he needed them to establish contact again, as it made better sense to have them prepped and standing by to help out. Plus, they brought a different perspective and were much closer to the thought processes needed to effectively deliver one of these bio agents to a large part of the population.

"Affirmative. Nothing to report yet, but we are "hot" there."

Steuben had something else on his mind that he had been thinking about for a while. So far, they had run into nukes and bio but no chemical weapons. Yet, the chemical threat was generally regarded as the greatest concern because chemical agents were more readily available and easier to deliver. Although there had been some coordination with the scientists at Aberdeen Proving Ground in Maryland prior to deployment, he didn't feel the MEU had ready access to chemical munitions experts. Steuben's concern was that it generally took a while to develop a decent working relationship with another command—their experience with the nuclear and biological defense communities had reinforced that thought—and he didn't want to have to work through the process in the middle of a crisis again. Steuben was also frustrated that WMD expertise was scattered among various commands, requiring his guys to figure out whom to contact depending on the specifics of the threat. Of course, the WMD cell at CENTCOM would seem to be the logical starting point, but the reality was they lacked the necessary expertise to help with specific details and all they could really do was point to the experts.

"Dr. Donnelly, I appreciate you calling with this information. Looks like the protective measures we took were both warranted and effective. I'm happy to report we haven't yet seen any adverse health issues."

"That is good news."

"Yes. Now there is another matter on which I could use your help. We're working in an environment where different types of WMD may be encountered, potentially even on the same mission. It's a little awkward for a forward-deployed unit to have to coordinate with multiple agencies depending on the specific threat. What I would like to see is some sort of comprehensive WMD office, a "one-stop shop" if you will, where I can get immediate access to whatever expertise, whether nuclear, biological, or chemical, that I need. My people here tell me this could be done electronically, so that it's really a "virtual" office and the experts wouldn't have to actually be co-located. I'll leave that to the smart people to figure out. But I would like you to be a part of that and also ask that you pass on my concerns to Colonel Danielson. We will be sending out a formal request through CENTCOM for the establishment of such a capability."

"That sounds like a good idea, Colonel. I'll see Colonel Danielson within the hour and pass on your thoughts."

It really did sound like a good idea. Karen knew how narrowly focused she and her co-workers were and suspected every other WMD researcher was probably the same way. She could only imagine how difficult it must be for a tactical unit on the other side of the world to track down information.

"Thank you. What I'm most interested in right now is some synergy between your office and the chemical people up at Aberdeen. If you would also inform Colonel Danielson of that concern, perhaps he will initiate some dialogue with the folks at Aberdeen and get the ball rolling before the formal tasking comes down."

"Will do, sir."

"Roger, out here."

# Chapter 13

Even before Hussar's squad returned from their mission in Yemen, the MEU intelligence section had been sifting through reports which identified suspected WMD-related activities in Somalia. Though there hadn't been enough detailed information to warrant a specific strike, CENTCOM had ordered the MEU to prepare to insert a team to help develop the situation on the ground. But the Somalia mission quickly took on much greater importance and focus once the information from the mission debrief of Hussar's squad had been processed by intelligence analysts in the United States.

The business cards Gasser had grabbed from the small shop he searched during the SADM-10 snatch identified the place as a "hawala," one of a group of shadowy money operations commonly used to move money to and from Middle East families and their expatriate relatives abroad. After 9/11, some of the hawalas had been linked to Al-Qaeda and they had been mostly shut down in the United States. At least the more visual aspects of the operation, such as well-known money transfer offices with suspected terrorist ties, had been closed. But the particular business referenced in the calling card was not known to have a presence in the U.S. It was, however, believed to be the largest hawala chain operating in Somalia and also had significant presence in many of the countries of Western Europe.

Even more valuable were the data files and network configuration info that Gasser had taken off the computer he had found in the small shop. Although Major Renick initially felt Gasser should have just harvested the hard drive and destroyed the rest of the computer, it turned out leaving the computer intact had led to a real intelligence bonanza. Between the spooks at NSA and Navy computer network analysts at the Fleet Intelligence Warfare Center Detachment in San Diego, every packet of information communicated between the computer in the hawala and the rest of the world was recorded and analyzed. Within two days, the intelligence people had seen enough in the content of a number of emails and web pages to believe Al-Qaeda was using the informal hawala network to communicate messages between its members relating to WMD activities. Several of the most interesting communications had come from the southwest corner of Somalia.

So Hussar's squad was being sent into Somalia through the back door of Kenya with orders to perform a limited area reconnaissance and, if required, to transition into a small raid force or act as guides for a larger raid force. This was not near as specific a mission as the squad had gone into Yemen with, and Hussar knew he was shouldering a lot of responsibility. But he also knew the rest of Fox Company was standing by as "back-up," on-call air support would be available, and several big ticket airborne reconnaissance systems were monitoring his area of operations 24/7. Plus, Colonel Steuben had made sure he understood to "get the hell out of there" if things got ugly because the MEU could quickly bring plenty of other forces into the mix to finish the job. The Colonel's point was that it was more important for Hussar's squad to verify suspected terrorist events on the ground than it was for them to actually engage the terrorists.

With this mission so different from the other operations that elements of 11th MEU had carried out recently, Major Renick had to make numerous changes in his requests for intelligence collection. Because of the notable successes of those other 11th MEU operations, however, he had been told by his counterparts at CENTCOM that he could expect to get almost any support they needed from the intelligence community. "Ask for the moon," is how the CENTCOM Intel Ops officer had put it. So he had developed a robust set of collection requirements and forwarded it to CENTCOM for review and coordination with the satellite sensor operators and the people that managed airborne sensor platforms. In spite of what he had been told, Renick knew that satellite imagery and signals collection efforts could never provide 100 percent coverage, plus the assets could always be pre-empted by higher priority tasking to support national intelligence objectives. Sometimes chasing down WMD rumors in Somalia was the top priority and other times watching Iraq, Afghanistan, or the India/Pakistan border was the priority. Either way, some theater surveillance assets would be required.

When the Collection Plan came back from CENTCOM, Renick was impressed with the amount of national and theater resources being made available. The Intel Ops officer had given him good scoop. Somebody higher up really did think 11th MEU was doing important things.

Given the nature of the mission and the great number of downlink opportunities, Renick decided to have Q take along the Manpack Terminal. In addition to the Squad UAV, with its video camera feed to a helmet-mounted display and an integrated operator joystick control, the Marines would have direct access to imagery and signals intelligence information from many of the theater airborne sensors. This would be accomplished through the Manpack Terminal's reception of the Common Data Link (CDL), a tactical Intelligence, Surveillance, and Reconnaissance (ISR) network used by all the Services. Common Data Link was an atypically appropriate and accurate name in the military world of confusing jargon and purposefully deceptive non-descriptive nomenclature. It must have slipped by the Department of Defense's Office of Deception, whose British cohorts across the Atlantic were the clever people who labeled crates containing the early armored vehicles shipped to France in 1918 with the nomenclature "tanks" in an attempt to disguise the purpose of the contents. The amateurish attempt was of questionable success, but we're still stuck with the ridiculous term almost a hundred years later. The military is generally slow to give up on anything, regardless of its relative value, so the oversight with the term CDL would probably go unchallenged.

The CDL link was based on the protocols developed in the 1980s to directly downlink sensor information from several black world aircraft programs, including the U-2 spy aircraft. The DoD had subsequently agreed to adopt the protocol and, in the early 90s, directed its use as the common data format for downlinking information from airborne ISR platforms. Because of the classification level of the U-2 program for many years, however, it wasn't until much later that any real progress was actually made in collapsing the multiple stove-piped data links that then existed to support the transfer of sensor data from airborne platforms to dedicated ground stations. It was the explosion in the number of UAVs and CDL terminals in the late 90s that really provided the motivation for implementing the common standard, and it was all based on the USAF finally (and publicly) acknowledging the value of unmanned and remotely-piloted aerial vehicles.

It had taken years for the Air Force bureaucracy, fearful for its existence and fiercely protective of its pilots, to allow any real progress with UAV programs. Getting transferred to a UAV program was pretty much a career-ending assignment for an Air Force officer. But the minor success in Desert Storm, with near-real time video to support targeting and battle damage assessment from a handful of small drones used by the Navy and Marines, showed the future of UAVs and progress began to be made in spite of the bureaucratic hurdles. In fact, a clever organizational side-step provided the final impetus. When the degree to which the Air Force was slow-rolling UAV development became fully appreciated, the DoD established a separate organization, the Defense Airborne Reconnaissance Office (DARO), and had DARO report directly to the Under Secretary of Defense (Acquisition & Technology). The Air Force brass was effectively cut out of the loop and things started moving immediately on a number of UAV initiatives. None too happy with the power transfer arrangement, a major attitude adjustment occurred within the Air Force and soon UAVs began showing up on Air Power briefing slides. In the "Battle of the Briefs" that defines military life inside the Beltway, this was an unprecedented change of perspective.

Major Renick also decided to slightly modify the internal processes of his small MEU intelligence section to incorporate the use of some software "tools" they hadn't used much on earlier missions. In addition to the Ticker, and closely coupled to it, was a link analysis tool used to help make sense out of seemingly random bits of information about people and events. Typically, the intel analyst used an in-depth under-standing of the enemy's order of battle to help anticipate his future activities and to also predict enemy responses to friendly courses of ac-tion under consideration by the commander. Since this approach is based on possessing a great deal of confidence that the enemy order of battle is well-understood, a tremendous amount of intelligence information must be generated to provide that confidence.

The U.S. spent 40 years and trillions of dollars collecting informa-tion on Soviet capabilities, exercises, commanders, etc. Based on what was collected, the U.S. then oriented much of our force structure and disposition towards countering the perceived Soviet threats. At any given time, our commanders, through the work of the intelligence community, knew what Soviet-bloc units were in garrison, which units were deployed, each unit's present state of combat readiness, where key Soviet commanders were located, the status of the Soviet Rocket Forces, locations of every fast attack and ballistic missile submarine, etc. We had everything from satellites in space to networks of undersea listening posts that covered thousands of square miles, all focused on the Soviet threat. The CIA infiltrated the Soviet political and military structure, the NSA had hundreds of Russian linguists translating bil-lions of intercepted transmissions, the NRO rolled out new spy satel-lites every year, and millions of military personnel were on watch and trained daily against Soviet threat scenarios. All of this was done in preparation for a war that never happened against a threat that had all but evaporated by 1990. We did get a consolation war, though, with Operation Desert Storm. The Iraqis were predominantly equipped with Soviet weaponry and fought with Soviet battle formations and tactics. They also used the highly centralized, rigid command structure that characterized Soviet armies. So on a very small scale, Operation Desert Storm was somewhat representative of the war the U.S. military had prepared for over the previous 40 years, and therefore gave partial vali-dation to the use of enemy order of battle as the basis for intelligence activities.

This approach is mostly useless for situations like the ones the U.S. faced in Somalia in 1993, Afghanistan in 2002, and in the War on Terror. So the analysts learned from their failures and shortcomings and came up with different approaches for ordering information into useful intelligence. One of these new approaches eventually resulted in the development of the link analysis tool Major Renick had decided to use for Hussar's mission in Somalia. Renick could no longer even remember the official name of the tool—one of the Marine analysts had named it the "Hydra," apparently in reference to the way a node would occasionally split into two nodes (when warranted by the underlying link analysis). The obvious resemblance this characteristic had to the dreaded serpent from Greek mythology caused the name to stick. The link analysis algorithms used by Hydra supported relationships between individuals, groups of individuals, communications, events, resources, places, modus operandi, etc. and helped keep track of miscellaneous and ill-fitting contacts and reports of activities until they could be "fitted" into the model.

A really good link analysis tool, like the Hydra that Renick had trained his 11th MEU intel analysts to use, adaptively adjusted to the information it was fed, hypothesized relationships between those pieces of information, and then presented the results in a graphical link diagram, which provided visualization of the links to the user. The algorithms borrowed heavily from the science of neural networks, which attempted to model the amazingly complex, adaptive pattern recognition processes of the human brain. Although neural networks had achieved only limited success with duplicating the incredible power of the human brain, they were much more successful in modeling the domain of relationships to which humans belong, which turns out to be a less complicated problem to address. By using the Hydra in conjunction with the robust data mining capability provided by the Ticker's information discovery agents, Renick was able to demonstrate the value of bringing automation to the information management issues faced by tactical units.

# Chapter 14

OK, Sergeant, we're feet dry over the coast of Kenya."
Hussar opened his eyes and looked around. Even though it
was a very dark night, he could clearly make out the curved line where
the Indian Ocean gave way to the sandy beaches. It reminded him
briefly of the beach he and Danielle had camped on in Baja California.
Gently pushing the thought from his mind, Hussar looked at his watch.
They should be at the insertion point in a little over 20 minutes. It
was time to "wake up the dead." He suppressed a yawn and looked
over his fellow Marines. Every one of them was crashed out, leaning
against the guy next to him. The loud, rhythmic thumping of the
rotors and the shrill resonance of the jet engines made the giant helicopter, as it struggled to defeat gravity and the tremendous internal
mechanical forces battling for self-destruction, a flying lullaby for the
Marines temporarily cocooned in it. Hussar gave Boner a shake and
told him to pass it on and then watched as the wake-up call rippled
through his squad and attachments.

The drop went off without a hitch, but the whole process took
longer than Hussar expected because of the need to first drop the LAVs
and then unload the pick-ups. The squad fanned out to provide security as they typically did, but instead of quickly falling into a patrol
formation and moving rapidly away from the landing zone, they held
their positions as the LAV crews manned their vehicles and readied
them for operation. Hanging around the drop point was bad tactics.
Although the spot had been carefully selected, you never really knew if

163

anyone was actually there until you showed up. Even at night when they weren't as visible, helicopters were very loud and would draw attention from anyone in the area, so the plan was always to get away from the drop point as rapidly as possible. Fortunately, the site selection was good and no one other than the Marines appeared to be in the area. After a very long three minutes, the trucks were unloaded and ready to roll, and the LAVs were up and running. The Marines climbed aboard the trucks and LAVs and started moving east towards the first day's hide position.

Q started to run through a check-out on his equipment but was stopped by the sudden appearance of the Ticker window and several messages. At first, he thought he was seeing test messages generated as part of the start-up sequence, but then realized he was getting live data, as the message "Prisoner likely Al-Qaeda—DNA testing" flashed across his screen. Q quickly read the associated report and then called Hussar to share the good news.

"Sergeant, we're already getting Ticker messages from the *Tarawa*."

"Excellent, Major Renick will be happy."

"You bet, but it gets better. The first two messages are telling us that we scored big on the Yemen mission. The guy we snatched is some kind of big kahuna, one of the bagmen we martyred was related to a 9/11 terrrorist, and the vials we found were in fact some bad bugs."

Hussar didn't say anything for a couple of seconds. His level of job satisfaction had just gone off the charts.

"That is good news, Q. Go ahead and pass the word back there, but make sure everyone stays alert on our present mission. That was then, and this is now, OK?"

In spite of his admonition to Q, Hussar wished at that moment that he could be in New York City personally telling the family of one of the World Trade Center victims that his Marines were getting the rest of the bastards, and they wouldn't stop until they had them all.

"You got it, sergeant," answered Q.

The Marines passed through the Somalian countryside and encountered very few signs of inhabitants and absolutely no other vehicle traffic on the rugged cart paths they were using as roads. The tiny villages they skirted were totally dark. Occasionally, a fire marking the location of a larger set of dwellings could be seen off in the distance, but the squad stayed well away from those sites. After about five hours of movement across the mostly open country, they made it to their first hide site and set in and camouflaged their position as well as possible.

They were deep in the lower Juba region, almost halfway between the Kenyan border and the town of Afmadow. The lower Juba region formed the southern watershed of the Juba River, the only real river in all of Somalia. The Juba provided a fairly significant natural barrier for much of its 1000-mile journey from its headwaters in Ethiopia to its mouth at Kismayu on the Indian Ocean and was a buffer from much of the violent infighting that characterized life in central Somalia and the city of Mogadishu. The lower Juba region was sparsely populated, seasonally inhabited primarily by nomadic tribes in search of adequate forage for livestock herds.

After laying low all day, the Marines were on the move again that night, this time making it within 10 miles of Afmadow before again stopping and holing up prior to the break of day. While they rested, the MEU provided several intelligence updates and informed Hussar of possible WMD-related activity being closely monitored in Afmadow. Major Renick had told him during the mission brief on the *Tarawa* that they may end up working directly with CIA paramilitary forces on this operation, and he assumed that was where the information was coming from. Of course, if the CIA guys thought the situation could be solved by judicious application of force from the sky, whether a cruise missile or a smart bomb, then that is what would happen and the Marines would egress without delay. But a strike team might be necessary to deal with many of the possible situations, and it made sense to have a team in place when sufficient information was collected and intelligence developed to warrant a ground strike. These terrorists were shadowy and fast moving. When you got the chance to engage them, you had to move quickly. Hussar's squad was in Somalia to expedite the process by having people already infiltrated and oriented to the environment when the attack orders came.

Feeling that action was imminent, Hussar worked the squad

through a couple of operational scenarios and immediate action drills. After about an hour of intensive war-gaming with the Marines, he finished with a scenario dealing with actions to be taken if they had close encounters with Somali non-combatants.

Of course, you can't hide a squad of Marines in a town in Somalia anymore than you can hide the officers of the New York Yacht Club in the McDonald's in Harlem, so the squad would continue to lay out a couple of miles in an attempt to avoid any such encounters. But if and when they were forced to interact with any of the locals, the point man would have to be one of the three black Marines in the squad. First choice would seem to be Cpl. Spike Baxter, who was the most senior and experienced of the three. But the Corporal was totally Marine and his demeanor would stand out. Probably one of the younger kids would be a better fit, and Hussar had picked Private First Class Wallace. PFC Roberto Wallace had grown up in East Los Angeles. Living on his own since he was 14, he had survived for four years on the streets, which was sufficient testament to his street smarts. Running with the other punks had seemed like the thing to do, but he realized the odds were against him living to see 19, and he needed to get out. Joining the Marines had saved his life and, even now in Somalia, he felt safer than he had many times in the "hood." The clincher for Hussar was the fact that Wallace spoke a smattering of Italian. Since the Italians had controlled southern Somalia for many years, there was a slim chance he could communicate with some of the locals, maybe at least enough to convince them the Marines were Italians instead of Americans. It was a long shot, but the Marines would adapt as best they could. After all, didn't everyone like Italians?

In an attempt to break up the intense discussion with a little humor, Hussar teased Wallace, "PFC Wallace, are you circumcised?"

"Yes, Sergeant," Wallace answered, surprised at Hussar's question.

"Keep your pecker in your pants then. The circumcision rate in Italy is 10 percent and in Somalia it's zero. You'll give us away. Plus the AIDS rate here is 35 percent—probably more like 90 percent for the type of women that a discriminating ladies man like yourself would think about scrogging. You don't want those odds, Wallace. And, if you did survive, I don't want you infecting all the whores in Thailand on our way back to the States, or I'll end up friggin' gettin' it." PFC Wallace grinned slyly, and the rest of the Marines laughed.

Ten miles away in Afmadow—Hussar had guessed correctly—there was a guy working for the CIA. And the guy, Sid Arre, was currently watching the entrance to a small hawala in the center of Afmadow. A tip from one of his sources had hinted that a transaction would be occurring today that he might find interesting. So far, though, there hadn't been much activity at the place for Sid Arre to observe. He had dutifully taken pictures of the few visitors and made notes about their visits, but he didn't feel like anything of any real significance had yet occurred. Sitting back in the shadows of the small room he had rented, he felt vulnerable. He didn't come from one of the local tribes, and although his job as a hydrologist evaluating water tables in the Juba regions gained him a certain amount of respect in drought-prone southern Somalia, he still felt uneasy. As he wrestled with his concerns, there was movement and noise in front of the hawala. An old jeep had pulled up to the doorway and dropped off a guy with a small ice chest. Ten minutes later, the jeep reappeared just as the guy came back out with the ice chest. He quickly jumped in, and the jeep took off in a cloud of dust. While furiously taking pictures, Sid Arre realized something was different about the guy when he came out. He was walking differently. As he played back the images in his mind, Sid Arre deduced that the contents of the ice chest must have been different when the guy left. When the guy came back out, he struggled to carry the small cooler. But when he had first arrived, Sid Arre remembered the guy getting out of the jeep and walking into the hawala, effortlessly swinging the ice chest by his side. It was definitely lighter going in— maybe even empty or carrying something less dense—compared to how it came out. This was a bit puzzling because the ice chest wasn't very big—in fact, it was quite small and could only hold a couple of drinks and a few chunks of ice—so he couldn't imagine what was in it now. But his job was done, so he left to file a report and sent off the pictures he had taken.

The jeep continued out of town and ended up in a small compound 10 miles northwest of Afmadow. Orbiting at 70,000 feet, a CIA-operated RQ-4A Global Hawk UAV had continuously tracked the jeep since it left the hawala. The images were being sent via satellite link to analysts at CIA Headquarters in Langley, VA. Although the East African analysts at CIA were aware of numerous suspicious sites in Somalia and frequently monitored many of them, the compound now under observation had not previously come to their attention. There had been vague reports of unusual activity, possibly a terrorist training camp, in the Lower Juba but nothing ever came of the reports. There was a great deal of excitement among the analysts that a new site had possibly been discovered. The imagery analysts cross-indexed the geolocation of the pictures from the Global Hawk with the National Imagery database and brought up a number of satellite photos of the area of interest. Pulling up imagery from the last 12 months and ordering them chronologically, the analysts were able to quickly pick out any changes in the area around the compound. They found several instances when approximately 15-20 people would gather at the compound for a month at a time. By checking the timing of the gatherings against the seasonal migration periods of the nomadic herders, it was discovered they were totally out of phase. So although almost the entire rural population living more than five miles from the Juba river was transient and based on roaming tribes of herdsmen looking for good grass, the compound in question was clearly being used for something else. In one of the photos, a small airplane sitting near a ramshackle hangar building was visible. Although there were other farms in the area, mostly in ruins because of the battles of the last 15 years and the recent 3-year drought, an airplane was definitely a rare occurrence. Lacking credible information associating the compound with terrorists, or any information demonstrating that a connection with terrorists did not exist, the CIA analysts judged the compound to be "suspicious" and nominated it for further collection efforts.

Two hours later, after the details had been "sanitized" to protect intelligence sources, Major Renick on the *Tarawa* got a copy of the report and the associated CIA analysis. He too was perplexed by what was apparently an unusually heavy ice chest. But something else was triggering his thoughts. Was the ice chest just being used as a container, or was it actually being used to keep something cold? He wondered what suspected terrorists needed to keep cold but came up blank.

*Wait a second,* he thought, *an ice chest was really a thermal container – 'ice chest' was just a commonly used term to describe the object. Thermal containers could keep things hot as well as cold, of course. Maybe the contents actually needed to be kept warm, not cold, and that's why a thermal container was necessary.* But it was always warm in Somalia, so it was hard to think of anyone there purposefully trying to keep something warmer. It was rarely below 70 degrees, although they were now in the middle of what passed for the cool season. Renick suddenly thought of the vials loaded with deadly bio toxins that Hussar's squad had found in the SADM-10 satchel. The vials had been wrapped in a thermal warming blanket to keep their temperature high enough to support continued culture growth. Maybe that was the situation in Somalia. It was the only thing he could come up with, and if he assumed it was true, the overall picture got a lot clearer: the WMD recovery in Yemen, the hawala chain, the pick-up of something "warm" in Somalia. The pieces were starting to come together.

Poring over a map of southern Somalia, Renick saw that the compound was less than five miles from where Hussar's squad was presently laid up. He smiled at their good fortune. "Rather be lucky than good", he mumbled to himself. Renick notified Colonel Steuben of the report and his concerns and then made calls to the military liaison at CIA and to the intel center at CENTCOM. In addition to voicing his ideas about the possibility of the guys observed in Somalia being couriers of bio material, Renick wanted to make sure the intel people knew the Marines on the ground had the Manpack Terminal and could receive the CDL downlink as long as the airplane wasn't more than 25 miles away.

To minimize the size, weight, and power requirements of the Manpack, several trade-offs had to be made, the most significant of which was range. But the tactical units equipped with the Manpack generally had areas of interest a lot smaller than 25 miles, so it wasn't really a limitation from their perspective. It's just that airborne sensor operators were used to working with large ground terminals that supported comms at much greater ranges, generally hundreds of miles, so they needed to understand the Manpack characteristics or they probably wouldn't be successful closing the link. As long as the range restriction was understood, everything else should be fine. The CDL community had recently developed and implemented a link auto-negotiation capability which initially established a basic transceiver configuration, and then ratcheted up capabilities to the maximum allowed by the ground station, the airborne platform, and the radio frequency propagation environment. This was similar to the process used by computer modems and was a huge step forward in improving interoperability and ease of use by units in the field over the manual configuration changes previously required.

Once he had made the calls, Renick started to get on the radio to update Sergeant Hussar when something on his computer screen caught his eye. He hadn't been paying attention to his monitor for the past 15 minutes or so, but he now noticed that the Hydra display had updated from the last time he had checked.

"Son of a gun, would you look at that!" he said in surprise, to no one in particular.

Based on data from the Ticker, the Hydra was already showing a possible link between the compound in Somalia and the bio discovery in Yemen through the hawala connection. Here he had spent several minutes thinking hard on the situation before he had come up with a possible explanation, and there it was already displayed on the Hydra. And probably had shown up on the display while he was still thinking about it. Next time, he would keep an eye on the Hydra. As he chastised himself for not using his own tools, Renick noticed another line coming from the node representing the compound, and this one went to a new location node. Clicking on it, he was shocked to find the new node represented a tiny settlement located approximately 15 miles from the compound. Must be a mistake, he hadn't seen any reports related to that location, and it certainly wasn't in the information from the CIA. Renick clicked again to get to the underlying data.

The node had been created based on information in a troubling report received moments earlier from the World Health Organization (WHO). Some sort of killer disease outbreak that claimed a 60 percent fatality rate had been reported in the settlement. Thirty deaths had already been verified, and a number of other people were in serious condition. With the ragged medical support available in that part of the world, it was often difficult to get accurate information. But the WHO doctor authoring the report had given very specific details of the disease symptoms and also discussed the effectiveness of a local quarantine. Apparently, the sparse population density and tribal segregation practiced in that part of Somalia had been key to a successful quarantine by the WHO and the infection cycle had been broken. The cause of the illness was still unknown but under investigation.

*Whoa, that was amazing news,* Renick thought, *and highly unlikely to be a coincidence.* Perhaps the terrorists were working on their delivery techniques and trying to discover optimal weather conditions for their attacks. Maybe they were trying to ascertain the effectiveness of their terrible concoctions. Whatever the reason, it looked like this was the real deal. He had the Ticker and the Hydra to thank for connecting a WHO report that he probably would have missed with WMD movements in Somalia and Yemen. Unbelievable. Renick got back on the line with the folks at CIA and CENTCOM and briefed them on what he had found. Then he finally made the call to Hussar.

Once he had been updated by Major Renick, Hussar pulled out his map and assembled his Fire Team Leaders, the LAV squad leaders, the NBC Marine, and Q and went over the latest intel. Everyone was sobered with the news of an actual strike already taking place in the area. While the leaders were still gathered, Hussar had Q and the NBC specialist verify that the MASS and other back-up chem/bio sensors were operating properly. He wanted the Marines to witness the calibration check because they needed to have confidence in their equipment, especially when it came to the ability to detect lethal NBC agents.

That evening, the Marines moved closer to what was now considered to be a terrorist compound to establish a reconnaissance base. As they moved, the Global Hawk continued to maintain a long duration surveillance to try to piece together the situation on the ground. So far, only a few people had been spotted at the compound. With the exception of the arrival of the jeep, the camp seemed to be in a dormant state. It clearly wasn't time yet to send in any troops or to bomb the place, but it was important to know how far along the terrorists were in their capabilities and plans. Certainly some sort of terrorist strike was being planned, and although it didn't appear imminent, it was very difficult to tell how far off it would be in the future. CENTCOM decided to keep the site under surveillance and wait to see if other terrorists showed up there. If a gathering did occur, the compound would be immediately targeted. In anticipation of this taking place, the *Carl Vinson* battle group was moved closer to the African coast and additional aircraft, including an E-3 Sentry, or AWACS, for aircraft tracking and control, and a U.S. Air Force Global Hawk, fitted with the enhanced Multi-Platform Radar Technology Insertion Program (MP-RTIP), were assigned to support the mission.

On the ground, Hussar's squad took advantage of the report of minimal people at the compound to perform a detailed reconnaissance of the site. Although higher than normal background readings were picked up for both chemical and biological agents, nothing specific was conclusively identified. Major Renick had told him that the CENTCOM strike planners specifically wanted to know if there was any evidence of underground bunkers or tunnels at the site. The Marines looked over the area from several different observation points throughout the night and into the morning. They had to pull back a bit before daylight to avoid detection, but the increased visibility gave the Marines some great looks. They even watched the terrorists as they started moving around in the morning in the small hut where they had apparently slept. Significantly, Hussar saw one of the terrorists carrying the small cooler he had heard about the day before from Major Renick. Nothing pointed to any underground facilities, and the fact that the terrorists were still carrying around the cooler seemed to imply that a secure storage capability did not exist.

Hussar reported this back to 11th MEU to pass on to CENTCOM. Although no one told him why there was so much interest in whether underground bunkers existed or not, he had a pretty good idea. The best way to destroy any of the chem/bio agents was to "cook" them. In fact, that was the disposal method used during disarmament activities. Hussar knew that an air-delivered Fuel-Air Explosive (FAE) air burst device would incinerate everything within 200 yards, but it wasn't necessarily a precision strike weapon and would have little effect on any material stored underground. The "targeteers" at CENTCOM were probably already thinking about their weapons employment options, and that's why they were so curious about the existence of any underground facilities.

Meanwhile, flying at 35,000 feet over the Indian Ocean, the distinctive rotating radome on the AWACS airplane was able to scan the entire southern half of Somalia for aircraft. Of course, there was very little air traffic over Somalia, as there were very few reasons why anybody who could afford a ride on an airplane would want to be anywhere near Somalia. But they did detect and monitor a single low-flying plane from the point where it first became visible approximately 20 miles northwest of Bu'aale to the point where it disappeared from radar at the terrorist compound approximately 30 minutes later. As soon as they had picked up the radar blip, the AWACS crew notified CENTCOM of the location and heading of the contact. The operator on the AWACS continued to give routine updates of the contact's information and also notified CENTCOM of a brief route excursion, which looked to the operator like the plane did a couple of passes over something on the ground before continuing on to the compound. At 70,000 feet, and actually over Somalia, the new model Global Hawk with the enhanced MP-RTIP radar was also surveilling the area. Cued by the AWACS report, the sensor operator focused the hyperspectral imagery sensor onto the area of interest and easily picked up the slow-moving airplane. As the MP-RTIP operator watched, he saw the airplane signature slow down and circle an area once and then go around to circle again. Suddenly, the airplane signature began to dramatically lengthen, almost as if the small plane was generating contrails that were visible in one of the selected hyperspectral bands. But the sensor operator wasn't the only person who saw the signature change. In addition to the data feed back to the UAV Ground Control Station, the Global Hawk was also pushing a reduced data-rate bit stream down to the Marines Manpack Terminal with Hussar's squad.

Q had set the terminal up hours before and had been waiting for a connection. He didn't know exactly what would be flying or when it would be in range, but Major Renick had told him to set up the terminal because a CDL downlink was possible. He had been ready to give up when some of the link status lights began flashing, indicating a link candidate was in the area. As Q continued to watch, a reduced frame rate picture showed up on his IDS screen. Not being a trained MP-RTIP analyst, and not privy to the AWACS communications, Q wasn't exactly sure what he was looking at on the screen. Because the CDL link carried an embedded audio channel, however, he was able to communicate with the Air Force operator and ask a few questions to get himself oriented on what he was actually seeing. After watching for 10 minutes or so, Q noticed the plane circle a couple of times and then he also saw the sudden signature change. Immediately querying the operator for clarification on what had caused the change, Q was disappointed to find out the guy didn't have a clue. When the Air Force sergeant made a comment about the similarity in appearance to contrails, Q got a sinking feeling in his gut. He knew the plane was making a chem or bio spray attack. They had circled once to check the wind, and then had come back around and flown directly into the wind over the target area as they sprayed their deadly poison. It was possible to actually see the spray initiate from the plane and the cloud plume sort of coalesce as the atomized mist slowed after leaving the spray tanks. The effects of a slight easterly wind could be seen on the plume propagation before the eventual scattering, dispersion, and ground contact of the particulates. Q could imagine the cloud engulfing an unsuspecting village. He checked his map, and sure enough, there was a small settlement indicated in the middle of the spray run. There was no time to warn the villagers—Q was convinced he was witnessing a mass murder, and there was nothing he could do about it. He told Hussar what he had seen and then got on the radio with Major Renick to report his fears.

When the small plane touched down in the terrorist compound after completing its dastardly attack, the strike decision timeline accelerated. The Americans couldn't have prevented the attack because none of them had known that a plane was going to take off from an unknown point, attack a village, and then land at the compound they had just put under observation. It was just luck that they had seen the attack at all, but they could prevent anything else from happening if they moved quickly. Everyone believed that additional WMD had been brought to the compound the day before by the two couriers from the hawala, and it was likely the terrorists were going to strike again soon. Plus, it seemed that their delivery team was in the compound, thus increasing the target value. Without hesitation, the strike was ordered by a flight of F/A-18E Super Hornets off the *Carl Vinson*. Hussar's squad was told to move away from the target area, as several BLU-95 FAE bombs would be used to ensure the job was done properly. Knowing that the FAEs were "area" weapons, he was happy to comply.

Keeping the terrorists under long-distance observation, Hussar could see they were working on the aircraft. He also noticed they all had on gas masks while they worked and one of the guys, who appeared to be messing around with the spray tank under the port wing, was wearing a full protective suit. Hussar couldn't tell if they were refilling the tank to prepare for another attack, but he assumed the worst. If the air strike didn't come before the terrorists tried to take off, he would move in and engage with the LAV's 25mm chain gun, firing High Explosive Incendiary Tracer (HEI-T) rounds in the hope of lighting off the plane and accomplishing the desired high temperature effect. There was no way he was going to let the plane get airborne again.

But it didn't come to that. Within minutes, his earpiece crackled.

"Recon, this is Diamond One, over."

"Go, Diamond. Over."

"Can you laze target, over."

"Affirmative, standing by to laze."

Knowing the power of the BLU-95, Hussar was more than happy to laser designate the target to make sure it wasn't accidentally dropped on him. Although the pilot had already been given target coordinates and a target description, he verified his information with Hussar and made sure he knew exactly where the Marines on the ground were in relation to the target. Hussar appreciated the guy's professionalism and obvious concern for where his bombs actually ended up.

"Recon, laze him, over."

"I'm on him, over."

"Roger, I got it, over."

Without warning, the first Super Hornet was suddenly over the compound and dropping two BLU-95s, which looked like very large cans falling from the sky from Hussar's position. As the thunderous roar of the jet ripped through the air and followed the Super Hornet across the valley, Hussar saw the small initial explosion to disperse the fuel mixture across the area. He was then conscious of watching the terrorists stand absolutely motionless for a second in total shock and then attempt to run away as realization of their impending fate overcame them. They took maybe two strides before the mixture was explosively ignited and they were vaporized.

The Marines started cheering and kept up the yelling as the second Super Hornet came in and dropped another two BLU-95s over the same area.

Once the strike was successfully completed, a number of other issues had to be addressed. The place where the small plane had taken off from that morning was also a terrorist site in possession of WMD and had to be destroyed. Although it took several hours to locate the facility, another strike mission from the *Carl Vinson* was called in as soon as its location was determined. CENTCOM also contacted the State Department and provided information regarding the villages attacked and the cause of the illnesses seen earlier by the WHO medical team. Dr. Donnelly at USACEHR was brought in to provide specific medical details to aid in disease identification and treatment. To protect sources, the State Department passed the action to the U.S. Ambassador to the U.N., who in turn made a call to the lead U.S. representative on the U.N. Medical Commission. The Medical Commission sent out a request to the WHO for a health team to be dispatched to the location of the most recently attacked settlement to investigate local "reports of disease," and also provided a private communication describing the "likely" diseases and recommended treatment for the victims in the first village attacked. In the old days, the U.S. government wouldn't have provided any warnings to avoid blowing the cover of an on-going operation. But things were different now, and the thought of terrorists attacking a bunch of innocent livestock herders as practice for killing a bunch of Americans made the villagers our brothers.

Hussar's squad was directed to proceed to the site of the morning's attack and take readings with the MASS to determine which agents the terrorists had used. Hussar decided to risk traveling in daylight—

he was now more concerned about stumbling into a contaminated area than he was of Somalian warlords. They used a point reconnaissance team of Q and the NBC Marine, outfitted in protective suits and equipped with the MASS, to lead the advance. Careful to approach the site from upwind, the squad was still a mile away when Hussar called a halt. Although the MASS hadn't yet detected anything, Hussar had spotted a vantage point and used his binos to survey a few buildings visible on a small hill in the distance, which looked to be about where the settlement in question should be located. What he saw surprised him. He could see at least 50 dead cows lying in the grass, and some other shapes, which he assumed were probably people, lying in a small group near the dead cattle. Hussar could feel his anger rising as he searched unsuccessfully for any signs of life. It was clear that the terrorists hadn't used bio toxins here; they had used chemical agents, probably VX2, on these poor people who herded cattle. There was nothing his squad could do for any of them. Hussar sent the NBC recon team slowly forward until they encountered enough traces of vapor to register on the MASS. There was no need to go all the way to the site or until they reached an alarm condition, as the spectroscopy results from the vapor traces would be enough for detailed electronic analysis back in the States to determine the actual agent. Q sent the report back to Dr. Donnelly for her to pass to the experts at Aberdeen. Then the squad performed a field decontamination, buried their protective suits, and got into their vehicles and began moving towards their extract point across the border in Kenya.

# Chapter 15

It was time for 11th MEU to return to California. 13th MEU had shown up on station the previous week, and the staffs of 11th and 13th MEU had already met three times in preparation for their operational turnover. Marines from 13th MEU were chomping at the bit to start their terrorist hunting—the mood on the lead ship of their ARG, the USS *Bonhomme Richard* (LHD-6), was one of great enthusiasm and anticipation. In addition to the face-to-face coordination between the principal staff officers that made up the typical MEU turnover process, Colonel Steuben also offered to cross-deck a couple of NCOs over to the *Bonhomme Richard* to provide some operational tips at the Marine Rifle Squad level. When the 13th MEU Commanding Officer gratefully accepted Steuben's professional gesture, Hussar and Boner, widely recognized as the "duty experts," were sent via helicopter to the *Bonhomme Richard* to school their fellow Marines on what they had learned in-country.

The plan was for Hussar and Boner to stay on the *Bonhomme Richard* for a week while 11th MEU started the transit east, and then the two Marines would catch a commercial flight and hook back up with their shipmates in Singapore. It would take that long for the *Tarawa* and accompanying ships to cross the Indian Ocean and pass through the Strait of Malacca to reach Singapore, and Hussar and Boner were looking forward to getting there just in time to join the rest of the MEU for a couple of days of well-deserved liberty in the wonderful island nation.

Hussar enjoyed the week on the *Bonhomme Richard*. They were treated very well, and he had the good fortune to run into several Marines he knew from previous duty assignments. Since he and Boner possessed the credentials of having "been there," the 13th MEU squad leaders were very attentive to the "lessons learned" from 11th MEU's hot missions.

Towards the end of their time on *Bonhomme Richard*, 13th MEU received an intel update concerning a suspected terrorist cell operating in Oman. Shortly thereafter, 13th MEU was ordered to depart the African coast and return to the Arabian Sea to stand off the coast of Oman in the event the Sultan requested American assistance. *It seems like the action of chasing down the terrorists was ping-ponging back and forth between the Middle East and Africa*, Hussar thought, *but at least we are hunting them near their homes and not ours.*

By the time he and Boner were ready to leave the ship, 13th MEU had moved so far east that the closest major international airport turned out to be in the city of Dubai in the United Arab Emirates. Dubai was used by the U.S. Navy as a logistics point, which made it easy to catch a lift on the chopper making the daily resupply run from the *Bonhomme Richard*. Hussar was a little apprehensive about their travel arrangements, but everything was all set up when they arrived at Dubai International Airport. An American in civilian clothes, who identified himself as a Navy Chief Petty Officer, met them on the tarmac and escorted them to an empty part of the waiting area near their departure gate. The Chief gave them their tickets, asked if they needed anything, and then retired to a chair about 25 feet away and pretended to be busy with some paperwork. Hussar realized the Chief wanted to give them their space, but he had obviously been told to stick around and make sure the two jarheads didn't miss their flight. The Sergeant had to smile at that. In the last month, he had led a squad on two combat raids, recovered a nuke and some nasty bio stuff, destroyed a terrorist training camp, called in an air attack to incinerate a cache of chemical and biological weapons, and killed several terrorists, yet someone still needed to make sure he got on the correct commercial airline flight. *Go figure*, he thought, and quickly forgot about it. He had long ago acquired the skill of being able to easily dismiss the ridiculous things others did over which he had no control. It was a mandatory skill to possess if you were going to stay in the military.

Hussar spotted an international phone and tried to call Danielle, but all he got was her voice mail. *Damn*, he thought, *it would have been great to actually speak with her, but I guess that will have to wait.* He left a nice message, though, because he knew she would enjoy hearing his voice. Now that he was out of the action, he constantly missed her and couldn't wait to see her again. But 11th MEU was still three weeks away from returning to California, and he realized he was locked in that bittersweet temporal irony where the more he looked forward to his return, the slower the time passed. Best to try to think about something else, and he spent the remainder of the wait jotting down a few training ideas for the squad to better prepare for future anti-terrorist missions.

Finally, the boarding call for their flight was called. The first leg of the trip was to Bangkok, Thailand, where they had a scheduled stop and change of planes. Both Hussar and Boner slept most of the long flight, and with the time change, they landed at the Bangkok International Airport in the late morning. Looking forward to getting out and stretching their legs a bit, the two Marines were quickly reminded they had journeyed to a very different climate region. As soon as the cabin door was opened, a fog of humidity enveloped them as if they had just stumbled into a steam room. Even so, Hussar had been to Thailand before and wished they had enough of a layover to get into the actual city and spend some time looking around. He knew the Thais as a cheerful, attractive people, and Bangkok was definitely a fun city. But they were due to leave for Singapore in less than two hours, so they had to make do wandering around the airport and buying cheap souvenirs.

The flight to Singapore was only about half-full and boarded very quickly. As was his habit, Hussar spent a few minutes before take-off looking at the emergency instructions for the big 767 airplane and also at the route map in the airlines magazine he found in the seat pocket in front of him. He wondered if their actual route would take them straight over Malaysia into Singapore, or if they would stay east of Malaysia and cross the Gulf of Thailand and South China Sea and approach Singapore from the east, or maybe even cross the "tail" of Thailand and come down the west coast of Malaysia over the Strait of Malacca with an approach into Singapore from the west. He knew there were still some unsettled border issues between many of the countries in the area, but he didn't know if that affected air travel routes. Regardless, it was certainly an interesting part of the world.

Singapore, as a former British Crown Colony, was a tiny cosmopolitan enclave of considerable wealth. Strategically sited at the eastern end of the Strait of Malacca, Singapore bordered Malaysia to the north and was elsewhere enveloped by the archipelago of Indonesia. This made for an interesting blend of people and religions; Indonesia, poor and the most populous Muslim country in the world; Malaysia, a somewhat higher standard of living and also heavily Muslim; and Singapore, proudly sporting an economy rivaling that of any country in the West and predominantly populated by Buddhist Chinese with a large, very British, expatriate community. Hussar had twice pulled liberty in Singapore and was impressed with the vigor and industry of the people and the amazing cleanliness of the place. Everything was so well-ordered and maintained, it would soften the heart of the toughest Marine Drill Instructor to look upon the spotless streets. In fact, that is how Hussar viewed Singapore—as Ready for Inspection. The first time he visited Singapore, it was during the middle of a big festival, and he thought the city had done a great job of sprucing up for tourists. It was only on his second visit, which happened during a period of relative calm, that he realized the place was always immaculate. He had a healthy respect for Singaporeans and was eager to visit the island nation again.

As the plane took off and climbed out of the notorious Bangkok haze, Hussar stared out the window, waiting to get his bearings. After about 15 minutes, he could see they were taking the westerly route over the tail of Thailand, which meant they would then be traveling right down the Strait of Malacca. It was a clear day, and he could see water and land any direction he looked. *A great day for sightseeing*, he thought. Once they reached the Strait, Hussar diligently studied the narrow passage for a while, hoping to catch a glimpse of the *Tarawa*. From 25,000 feet, there were quite a few ships visible in the Strait, which was one of the busiest and most restricted shipping lanes in the world, with over 150 ships a day transiting through a passage that was less than 1.5 miles across at its narrowest point, but none of them looked like the venerable amphib. For all he knew, the *Tarawa* was already in Singapore and his fellow Marines were out partying, but he couldn't help looking out the window until he lost sight of the Strait below him as the plane adjusted course.

With nothing else to do, Hussar relaxed and could feel himself settling into a nap. He pulled his New York Yankees baseball cap low over his eyes and got as comfortable as he could in the small coach seat. Hussar couldn't believe he was still tired, but his body had not yet fully recovered from the stress of the squad's last mission and his subconscious energy monitor wanted to take advantage of the down time to recharge his batteries. No use fighting it.

He thought briefly of Lieutenant Morando, his first platoon commander, with a smile. Lieutenant Morando prided himself on being a student of human nature and was constantly making banal observations about Marines. One of his favorite comments was "If you give a Marine a break, he will do one of three things: build a fire, get naked, or go to sleep." Hussar had laughed when he first heard Morando say it, but the next time they were in the field and there was some downtime, Private First Class Hussar had watched his fellow Marines. Sure enough, someone was building a small fire to heat some chow, several Marines were changing socks, one was taking off a field jacket liner he had been wearing under his camo blouse, another was putting on a T-shirt, and half the platoon was asleep. From that moment on, Hussar had forced himself to be more conscious about what others were doing. He realized he was so focused on his own issues that he was generally unaware of what others were doing. Pretty typical for a PFC, but he knew better. Having spent a lot of time in the Virginia countryside hunting and fishing, Hussar well knew that being predictable could lead to death. Now as a Sergeant and a Squad Leader, he trained his men to recognize the danger of falling into a comfortable routine and being predictable. But they were out of the "bush" now, and he was going to take a nap.

Boner, who had earlier gotten "naked" and changed some of his clothing, was stretched out next to him, reading a dime adventure novel he had picked up at the Dubai airport. "Just a couple of businessman on international travel," was what Danielle would quip if she could see the two of them now. He had to remember to tell her that. As Hussar drifted off, his thoughts were of Boner and the good Fire Team Leader and friend he was but how he would soon pin on Sergeant and leave Hussar's squad to go pick up his own squad of Marines. He was happy for Boner, but would sorely miss him. They had been a good team and had a lot of fun ...

Hussar felt a sharp jab and woke with a start. "What the hell?" he mumbled as he opened his eyes. He looked over at Boner, who was slouched way down in his seat and was looking back at Hussar with a finger to his pursed lips.

"Shhhh, something's fixin' to go down, man," Boner whispered.

"What are you talking about?"

"Be cool, but see if anyone is still up and checking out the passengers."

The 767 had two aisles running the length of the plane, and this particular aircraft was configured for three classes of service, with a small business class seating area between first class and coach. Hussar and Boner were seated on the port side near the front of the coach section.

"Yeah, there's a guy up and stretching on the starboard side and another guy fiddling with something in the overhead bin on the port side. They're both in the front of the business section and are taking their sweet time and looking around a bit," Hussar replied.

"They look like they could be together and maybe up to something?"

It was an international flight and there were people from many nationalities aboard, so it would be impossible to say who might be a threat. But the two guys did look like they came from the same part of the world, probably somewhere in the Middle East. They definitely weren't Swedish anyway.

Both Hussar and Boner had carefully looked over the passengers on the flight out of Dubai, trying to spot possible extremist Islamic terrorists from the Middle East. But this was pretty much a useless endeavor since almost everyone was from the Middle East, and no one was wearing an "I'm an extremist Islamic terrorist" T-shirt. In fact, everyone had looked similar except them, of course, so they had joked (quietly to themselves) that everyone else on the plane probably saw the two Americans as the threat. Hussar hadn't paid near as much attention on the flight out of Bangkok, and he didn't remember noticing either of the two guys in question when he boarded the plane. His first thought, though, was that Boner had let his imagination get the best of him. Probably something to do with the novel he was reading. Then Hussar noticed the guy stretching in the starboard aisle look over at the man standing in the port aisle and give a slight nod. Maybe just a courtesy, maybe not.

"You might be right." Hussar's brain had cleared from his nap and he was working on a plan, but there wasn't going to be much time if something was in fact going down.

"OK, you cross over to the starboard aisle and try to move forward. There's a head between first class and business you can make for that's just past the guy. I'm going to pretend to look for a magazine and try to make it all the way up to first class. Then we'll see what happens."

"Got it," Boner answered and started to get up. Just then, Hussar saw movement up near the front of the plane.

"Wait a second", he ordered. Boner slid back down in his seat. He didn't have much of a view into the first class section, but Hussar had a better angle and could even see the cockpit door. Hussar had just seen a flight attendant, carrying a tray of drinks, enter the cockpit. The two guys were still loitering in the aisles, but as they were between Hussar and the front of the plane, he saw that they had also watched the flight attendant enter the cockpit.

Then it hit him. There had to be somebody in first class who had seen the flight attendant making up a tray of drinks for the cockpit crew and had signaled the two guys now standing in the aisles. As soon as she came back out, whoever was in first class would rush the cockpit while the door was open and try to take over the plane.

"Change of plans. A stewardess just went into the cockpit. They know she's going to come out, and when she does, that's when they are going to make their move and try to take the plane. There must be more of them in first class. I'm going to go to the head in first class on the port side. You try to make it up the starboard side."

With that, Boner moved away. Hussar got up and ambled forward. He tried to appear nonchalant, but he could feel his muscles tightening for action. The number 5 kept going though his head. That's how many terrorists were on most of the 9/11 planes. So he and Boner were severely outnumbered, and the bad guys were already in better position. He couldn't count on any help, and there really was no guarantee there were only five terrorists. It was a tough situation. Wasn't there anyone else he could trust? The thought of telling a flight attendant briefly crossed his mind, but he didn't know if there was time or if it would do any good. And it went against all his training. Hussar had never been taught to call for outside help. The Marines preached self-reliance, teamwork with your buddies, and making do with what you had. If you weren't carrying it with you when you crossed the Line of Departure, forget about it. Anything else was a luxury not to be counted upon when the chips were down. After all, the U.S. Marines are the people called upon when things are as bad as they can get. When the shit really hits the fan, there's nobody else around anyhow, so the Marines have to be successful with what they have or die in place. That's all Hussar knew. So it was just he and Boner.

Hussar stopped in the port aisle and opened the first overhead bin in the front of the coach section and pretended to look for a magazine. He picked up the first magazine he found, shook his head as if unhappy with it, and then walked into the business section to continue his literature quest. By now, he was within a couple of feet of the suspect, who was still fumbling with a bag in the overhead compartment. Hussar could feel the guy's eyes boring into him as he approached, but he didn't look directly at the suspect. Instead, he stopped next to the guy, opened another overhead bin and rummaged around for a better magazine. Hussar did notice, though, that the guy didn't have any hair on his arms. Uh-oh, didn't he read somewhere about the 9/11 terrorists shaving their bodies to prepare themselves for the transit into the afterlife? He had to get up near the cockpit pronto, it was time to take the acting up to the next level.

"This one is good," he said aloud, and very clearly, in case the guy understood simple English. With that, he walked up to the head near the cockpit. As he passed through the seven rows of first class seating, he spotted three guys that were possibly connected. They were similar in appearance and, more importantly, they all seemed to have quite a bit of interest in the front of the plane. They were all staring ahead, in contrast to fellow first class passengers that were working, reading, or sleeping. Not wanting to tip them off, Hussar tried to make himself look clumsy and small. He pulled his baseball cap low, stooped over like he was much older, and shuffled into the head off the forward galley, adjacent to the cockpit door. He saw where the flight attendant had prepared drinks for the first class passengers and cockpit crew, as there were a number of cans and a couple of wine bottles on the counter. *It would have been easy for passengers in first class to notice her preparation for serving the flight crew*, he thought. He opened the head door, which was hung to open forward into the entryway of the cockpit, and stepped inside. As Hussar turned around to close the door, he saw Boner coming out of the port business class head and wander into first class. The suspect on that side, now a few feet to the rear of Boner, was staring at the back of the Marine with daggers of hatred as he walked into the first class section. At least Boner had got past the guy. They might have a chance if there really was going to be an attack. Hussar was holding shut the door to the head and had his ear to it so he would be able to hear when the cockpit door opened again. He didn't want to latch the door, as he wanted to be able to jump out without delay as soon as he heard anything going down.

After only a few seconds, his ears picked up the muffled sound of talking through the bulkhead between the head and the cockpit and then the distinctive sound of female laughter. *Christ*, he thought, *just like a couple of flyboys to be up there grab-assing while he was standing in a smelly head waiting to confront the enemy.* He was literally in the shit, while the pilots were enjoying drinks and female company. *Just like war,* he noted with a touch of envy.

The laughter had died off and he thought he heard something like "Ciao." Almost showtime. Then everything went crazy. He heard the cockpit door open and then immediately heard a lot of movement, some unintelligible yelling, and a scream all in the space of a few milliseconds as he threw open the door of the head. The door caught a guy just making a lunge for the cockpit in the shoulder and knocked him off balance. Hussar quickly kicked him in the side of the chest and sent him sprawling to the other side of the plane. As he fell, Hussar saw the guy had some kind of shank in his hand. *Damn, they're armed.* Hussar quickly glanced in the cockpit and saw a commotion as the flight attendant, knocked back into the cockpit by his forceful opening of the head door, had fallen on top of the pilot. *They'll be fine,* he thought and pushed the head door fully open to serve as a partial block to the cockpit. As he did so, he noticed a very pale first officer getting up out of his seat and reaching to shut the cockpit door. It was an awkward stretch, but Hussar knew he would get to it. There was a very determined look in his eyes that showed the first officer knew what he was up against. Hussar just hoped the guy didn't kick some critical control as he scrambled to get out of his seat, turn around, run to the door, and close it. Like shutting down an engine, or something else important. The older jumbo jets had a 3 man crew on the flight deck, but the newer models had eliminated the flight engineer position and been FAA-qualified with just the two forward-facing pilot and first officer positions. Too bad in this case, since the flight engineer would have been sitting sideways right next to the cockpit door and could easily have reached and closed the door. Of course, the terrorists would know the flight deck configuration as well, he realized. *No time for such thoughts now,* Hussar thought, *the good news is I'm in the middle between the cockpit and the terrorists right where I want to be.* He quickly turned back towards the cabin. There was a second guy coming at him, also with a shank in his hand and murder in his eyes, screaming something in Arabic. Hussar grabbed the two wine bottles off the counter and smacked the bottom of one against the counter edge. Red wine and glass flew everywhere. He was left holding the neck of the wine bottle with numerous jagged shards of glass protruding from it. It wasn't the long neck beer bottle he would have preferred as a makeshift weapon in a bar fight, but he was in first class after all. He would do his best to kick ass in a "refined" way. Hussar purged such extraneous thoughts from his mind as his adrenalin surged and he felt his "action" clock kick-in and begin slowing his perception of reality. He was in a street fight, effectively cornered with his back against the wall, facing a fanatical enemy determined to the death. Hussar could see the craziness in the guy's eyes. This one was going all the way. The guy lowered his head and charged him with the shank aimed straight at Hussar's heart. Hussar blocked by smashing the intact wine bottle (*looks like a nice Chardonnay*, he thought) against the terrorist's wrist and followed by shoving the jagged end of the broken bottle into his throat. The shank went flying and the guy went down to his knees gurgling blood. The terrorist's hands instinctively went to the gouging wound in his throat for a second, but then he willed himself to continue the attack and started grabbing for Hussar with his blood-soaked hands. Without hesitation, Hussar dispatched him with a kick to the face, snapping the terrorist's head back and breaking his lacerated neck.

Hussar glanced over to see how Boner was doing. Boner had somehow gotten hold of a laptop computer case and was pummeling a guy in the head with it. There was blood on Boner's shirt, and Hussar couldn't tell if his friend was injured or not. But Hussar wasn't about to leave his strategic spot by the cockpit door. He fully understood the concept of key terrain. He wished he could communicate with Boner, but there was so much yelling and screaming going on with the rest of the passengers that his voice was drowned out. Just then, he noticed the first attacker was starting to move around a bit, so Hussar went over and sledged the guy a couple of times until he was out and then picked up his shank. It was a hard piece of plastic, about 10 inches long with a point and a slashing edge. *Where the hell did they get these?* he wondered. There would be time for that later. There were still at least two other terrorists, the guys blocking the aisles between first class and business class. The terrorist on the starboard side was trying to help the guy Boner was fighting, but his cohort was between him and Boner in the narrow aisle, so he couldn't offer much real help. Just then, the plane went into a steep dive, followed by a series of severe turns. *Somebody finally woke up in the cockpit*, Hussar thought, *and is "jinking" to keep everyone off balance.* The terrorist on Hussar's side was moving down the aisle towards him and had to stop to keep from falling. Realizing they had lost the crucial element of surprise in their attack, the guy didn't attempt a blind rush at Hussar but approached with caution. Except for the noise Boner was making as he continued to thrash his terrorist, the whole plane had quieted down now, as people fearfully watched the unfolding drama and strapped themselves into their seats. The guy coming at Hussar paused for an extra second, and seeing what was happening with Boner, yelled something over to his accomplice, who immediately stopped trying to stab Boner and began to cross over to the port side. *These guys are focused on the objective,* Hussar thought, as he readied himself for a two-on-one attack. As the plane banked sharply to the left, Boner, who had correctly anticipated the direction of the next roll, used the momentum change to magnify the laptop case roundhouse he threw. His enemy went flying over a row of seats and crashed heavily into the side of the plane and then crumpled onto several passengers. The passengers went nuts on the guy and started beating him senseless after Boner had grabbed his shank. Turning around to see how Hussar was faring, Boner saw the two terrorists approaching Hussar and his eyes briefly locked with those of his squad leader.

Hussar let out a huge, "Thunder!!!"

To which Boner replied with vigor, "Ooo-rah!!"

And again, "Thunder!!!"

And another, "OOO-RAHH!!"

Boner jumped over to the port side and, just like that, the tables had been turned, and the two Marines had the remaining thugs surrounded. But there would be no quarter offered nor any requested, this was a fight to the finish. With annihilation on their faces and cold death in their eyes, Hussar and Boner started moving in on the terrorists. It didn't take long to end the battle. Hussar, still favoring the wine bottles over the shank he had picked up, came at the guy closest to him like a buzz saw, whipping the bottles in a flurry of swings. The guy went down with the neck of the broken wine bottle sticking out of his gut and a solid whack to the side of his head with the other bottle. Just a few feet aft, Boner led with the laptop case (he had noticed it was a Dell computer somewhere during the previous scuffle) and then came in with the shank jab under the ribs, piercing the heart of the last terrorist. The attack was over, the whole affair had lasted less than a minute.

Since no one in the cockpit had any idea what was happening back in the cabin, though, the plane was still jinking like crazy. The passengers were all terrified because it still felt like the plane was going to crash. A flight attendant stood up from the business class section and cautiously made her way towards the Marines. Although she looked like she might be Malaysian, she asked in a very proper, clipped British accent if they were all right. Hussar and Boner both nodded vigorously and assured her they were fine and the struggle was over. She made it to one of the intercom phones and, after speaking with someone in the cockpit for a good 30 seconds, was able to convince the pilot to at least temporarily stop the erratic flight movements. As the plane stabilized, Hussar and Boner went to each of the terrorists, verified that three were dead, and trussed up the other two who were both unconscious. The flight attendant made an announcement apologizing for the disturbance and assuring the passengers that everything was under control. From somewhere in the back of the plane a burst of spontaneous clapping and cheering erupted, and soon everyone was yelling and laughing. It was the bizarre behavior one would expect from a group of 120 people responding to a joint near-death experience while locked together in a thin aluminum tube flying 25,000 feet above the ground at 500 miles per hour.

When it had quieted down a bit, the captain made an announcement, "This is the captain speaking. Judging from all the partying going on back there, I'm guessing the situation has been taken care of. I would like to thank whoever was involved for what they did and also ask anyone with medical training to assist any of our passengers who may have been injured."

Hussar and Boner took up positions in the forward galley outside the cockpit door. Although there didn't appear to be any other perpetrators, the two Marines were happy to stand a little guard duty. Still curious about the terrorist's weapons, Hussar picked up one of the shanks and looked at it closely. There was a bag on an empty seat in first class that Hussar figured belonged to one of the terrorists. He carefully retrieved the bag and examined it closely to determine where the shank had been stashed. He found the answer immediately. It was a simple, but obviously effective, set-up. The bag had a rigid plastic frame to maintain its shape, but a piece of the frame appeared to be missing as the bag had partially collapsed. Hussar took the shank and, with very little effort, was able to snap it into the remaining sections of the frame. Now the bag looked normal again, and the shank was cleverly concealed. It wouldn't seem like such a shank would offer much of an advantage, but a sharp edge and point on a 10 inch piece of hardened plastic is a lot of weapon against someone who is totally unarmed.

With that mystery solved, Hussar felt he ought to notify someone on the ground of what had happened. As a Marine, he knew he had to at least attempt to keep his chain of command informed, so he pulled out his rarely used credit card and got on the airphone. It took a while to make a connection to an information operator in Singapore, who readily gave him the number to the U.S. Embassy there and connected him through.

"American Embassy, how may I direct your call?"

"The Marine House, please, ma'am."

"One moment, sir."

Marines have provided special security functions in support of diplomatic activities for hundreds of years. This activity was formalized in the Foreign Service Act of 1946 and other U.S. law provisions. Marines presently serve at over 120 American Embassies and Consulates around the world in support of the Department of State. Every Marine Detachment has a space assigned to them in the Embassy compound or in a building out in the civilian community which is referred to as the "Marine House." For some postings with large Marine Detachments, this can be a somewhat grand affair and is the center of the American social scene in the community. Regardless of the relative luxury, though, the "Marine House" provides a place for billeting and recreation, and Marines can always be found there.

"Marine House, Corporal Davis speaking, may I help you, sir?"

"Corporal Davis, this is Sergeant Hussar from 11th MEU."

"Wow, Sergeant, you guys just got in this morning. You couldn't have already got in trouble." He smirked.

*Great,* Hussar thought, *I had to get the Detachment smart-ass. Every unit had at least one.*

"Corporal, who's the senior Marine present there?" Hussar responded curtly.

"Uh, that would by Gunnery Sergeant DeVolker," the corporal answered officially. Apparently the Sergeant was a tight-ass and didn't have much of a sense of humor.

"Gunny DeVolker, 0369, just out of 2nd Battalion, 1st Marines at Camp Pendleton?" he asked incredulously. DeVolker had been his Platoon Sergeant in Fox Company as a Staff Sergeant a year earlier. It wasn't the least bit surprising that he had been promoted but quite surprising that he had ended up with the Marine Security Guard Detachment in Singapore.

"That's the one, Sergeant," Davis answered. Just his luck the Sergeant knew the Gunny, now his ass was going to be in a crack with the Gunny.

"Let me speak to him," Hussar ordered.

"Wait one." Almost immediately the Gunny came on the line, "Gunnery Sergeant DeVolker."

"Gunny, it's Sergeant Hussar."

"Whoa, how the heck are you doing? Where are you?"

"I'm not shittin' you, but ..." and he quickly told the Gunny what was going on.

"Jesus Christ," DeVolker responded when he had finished. "OK, I'll go right in to the Ambassador with this one. And then I'll get word to 11th MEU for you. They pulled in about 2 hours ago. Give me your airlines and flight number and a phone number if we get cut off. That is, if I'm even able to call you back."

Hussar gave him the data.

"OK, just stay on the line, we'll need to keep the comms up. I'll be right back."

Hussar smiled as he could picture the Gunny, a large man, get out of a chair and scramble for the Ambassador's office.

Within a minute, another voice came on the line.

"Sergeant, this is Bill Rodgers. Tell me what's going on."

"I'm sorry, sir," Hussar was confused. He didn't know a Bill Rodgers.

"It's OK, Sergeant Hussar. Mr. Rodgers is the Ambassador," DeVolker helpfully offered.

"Oh, sorry, sir." Hussar quickly retold the story.

"That's a hell of a story, Marine. Good job. I'll notify the State Department and the Department of Defense of your involvement, and I'll call the Prime Minister here and find out what the Singaporeans know. Obviously, you're not in U.S. airspace, so we have no control. I would imagine you're probably in international airspace, so I'm not sure where they will try to land you, who will let your plane land, or even who will make that decision. But let me make a few calls. You stay on the line," he ordered and was gone.

DeVolker got back on the line while waiting for the ambassador to return.

"Now you've really gone and done it, Hussar. Caused an international incident and killed some people on a commercial airplane. I haven't even been gone a year, and already you've turned into part of the criminal element," he joked.

While Hussar was on the phone, Boner noticed a sudden commotion among the passengers on the starboard side of the plane. Curious, he went over to a window and looked out. Approximately 40 feet away was a flight of 2 F-16 Falcons, fully armed. *Where did they come from so fast?* he wondered. Boner could see the pilot of the lead F-16 carefully looking them over. The 767 pilots had obviously made a distress call, and the F-16s had been scrambled to check them out—and to shoot them down if they posed a threat, Boner realized. He didn't recognize the markings on the planes, but it looked like a lion's head with a flowing mane inside the standard roundel. Boner continued to watch as the F-16s moved near the front of the 767 so they could get a good look at the flight deck of the commercial airliner and see who was flying the plane. If they didn't pass inspection, he had no doubts that the F-16s would shoot them out of the sky long before they got near any city. Although Boner had stood many inspections in his four years as a Marine, he knew this was the most important one yet because his life literally hung on the outcome. He went back and told Hussar about the F-16s with the lion's head marking and heard him relay the information to whomever he was talking with at the Embassy.

"Roger, I copy the F-16s are from the Republic of Singapore Air Force," Hussar repeated what Gunny DeVolker had just told him for Boner's benefit.

The captain's voice came back on over the announcement system,

"Some of you may have noticed the two airplanes off our starboard side. They are F-16s from the Singapore Air Force and were scrambled in response to a distress call we sent out as soon as we understood we were under attack. We have since radioed air traffic control to let them know that we are no longer in a crisis situation, but naturally they want to get some confirmation of our status before they figure out where to send us. The F-16s need to get close enough to get a good look at us here in the cockpit before they will send confirmation, so that's why they're right outside your windows. We'll let you know as soon as we hear anything else from the ground."

Ambassador Rodgers' voice came through the airphone to Hussar. "Sergeant Hussar, I've just gotten through to the Prime Minister. You can imagine there is quite a bit going on over there, but I did speak to him for a few minutes and relayed what you told me and I got some news. Although there was a great deal of concern initially that we could be in for a coordinated set of attacks as occurred on 9/11, your attack appears to be an isolated incident, at least for now. The Singapore Air Force is challenging all commercial air traffic to make sure. As far as your situation, I believe your plane will be allowed to land in Singapore because that was your original destination. I doubt if you will land at Changi International Airport since you would have to fly by the downtown area to get to Changi from where you are now, and I can't imagine the local government letting your plane get anywhere close to critical business or dense population areas. My guess is you will be diverted to Tengah Air Force Base on the northwest side of the island which, by Singaporean standards, is somewhat remote. In any event, though, once we find out for certain where you will land, I will send Gunnery Sergeant DeVolker with an Embassy car to pick you up and bring you here. The Gunny is on the phone with someone from 11th MEU as we speak, so your unit is being notified. And I—" the Ambassador had stopped in mid-sentence and there was nothing on the wire for a good 10 seconds before he came back on, "If you will excuse me, the White House is on another line, and I believe I will be giving the President an update. Once again, good job."

Hussar was starting to feel a little uneasy. This was going to be treated as a really big deal since it was the first major hijack attempt aboard an airplane since the 9/11 attacks. And it wasn't happening in the U.S. but in Asia, so the terror was now going to hit home to billions of people living in an entirely different part of the world. It would be a three-ring circus once they got on the ground, and he was already feeling a bit apprehensive about the inevitable attention they would receive.

Boner saw his face.

"What's wrong, chief?"

"Do you realize this is going to be a huge goat-rope once we get on the ground?"

"What do you mean?"

"I mean I'm talking to the Ambassador, who already spoke with the Prime Minister and is now speaking with the President. Can you imagine how many policemen we'll see when we land? How many questions we'll have to answer? Not to mention the press. Oh man, this is going to suck big-time."

The captain's voice came over the speakers again.

"Ladies and gentlemen, this is the captain. We've just been cleared to land in Singapore. However, we will not be landing at the international airport. For security reasons, we've been instructed to land at an alternate airfield. We should be landing in approximately fifteen minutes. Flight attendants, prepare for arrival."

The F-16s escorted them all the way to touch down. Once on the ground at what was clearly a military base, which Hussar assumed to be Tengah AFB, they taxied to a remote spot at the far end of the runway and came to a stop. As Hussar expected, there were soldiers and policemen everywhere. He caught glimpses of snipers locked into shooting positions and counted four armored vehicles among the dozens of police cars and SWAT vans ringing the airplane. Hussar had heard the Singapore police were among the best in the world. His occasional encounter with them on previous visits certainly gave him the impression that they were a highly professional, no-nonsense organization. He realized they were actually quite fortunate there were Singaporeans behind the triggers of all the weapons pointed at the plane right now. They could definitely have landed in worse places.

Also parked next to one of the SWAT vans were a couple of trucks configured with boarding stairs for accessing the airplane's cabin doors. A short distance beyond them, at least 10 ambulances and several buses were staged. And just outside a fence a good half-mile away, Hussar spotted a news truck setting up for a live feed. *The fun will soon start*, he thought with a sigh.

The plane's engines were immediately shut down and, as if on cue, the stairways were quickly driven up to the port-side exit doors. The on-scene police commander was apparently already in communication with the flight crew because the captain began making announcements with specific security instructions.

"Ladies and gentlemen, we will need to be extremely cooperative with the police here. I know we've all had a terrifying experience and you are probably more than ready to get off this airplane, but remember the police are not yet sure what the situation is here. Quite frankly, I don't really know yet either what all has happened, so let's just try to stay as calm as possible and do exactly as I tell you. Carefully follow the instructions of the police when they come aboard."

"OK, first thing is everyone needs to remain seated with their seatbelt fastened. Don't pull anything down from the overhead bins, and go ahead and place any other carry-on items in your possession under the seat in front of you. Do not have anything on your lap or in your hands.

It's essential that everyone keep quiet when the police come aboard. They have procedures they must follow to secure the aircraft and we don't want to distract them. It may be a little frightening when they rush aboard, but please try to remain calm, quiet, and motionless.

Once the police have secured the aircraft, medical personnel will come on board to help anyone injured. When it comes time to start getting off the plane, please remember the injured will be the first ones taken off. And let's try to be as orderly as possible. Flight attendants, please open the forward and aft port side cabin doors now."

There was a rush of air as the cabin doors were open. Immediately, a half dozen or so SWAT members, in full combat gear, moved swiftly into the cabin through each of the doors and took up firing positions. There were a couple of long seconds, frozen in time, when no one moved as the police assessed the situation, and all the passengers stared at the police. Then the police in the first class section went to each of the terrorists laying on the floor and quickly and expertly trussed their arms and legs with cable wraps. One of the cops went into the forward galley, found all the shanks Hussar had piled up on the counter, and showed them to the SWAT Lieutenant in charge of the operation. The Lieutenant made a report by radio and then walked through the entire plane, carefully looking at every passenger, before he made contact with his peer from the team that had rushed the rear of the plane. Apparently happy at what he had found, he returned to the first class section and huddled briefly in the galley with the lead flight attendant seated there. After about 30 seconds he came out of the galley, made another radio report, and then told his sergeant to take charge of getting the medical teams on board, evacuating the injured, and then deplaning the passengers. Things started happening fast at that point, as the Singaporeans clearly had a detailed plan and competent people to execute it.

Meanwhile, the Lieutenant came over to Hussar and Boner, seated quietly in the front row of first class, and said, with classic British understatement, "I understand you gentlemen had a bit of a row. Tell me about it."

# Chapter 16

It was over two hours before Hussar and Boner were able to retrieve their carry-on bags from their original seats and get off the plane. They had each been interviewed twice, individually and by different detectives, and every interview was recorded. The cops also had the two Marines walk through the entire incident, starting from the moment their suspicions were first aroused while they were sitting back in the coach section before the attack, up to the time the plane landed at Tengah AFB. To make the re-enactment realistic, several police officers stood in as the terrorists, flight crew, and any passengers that had a role in the incident. Police film crews, using several different camera angles, taped the entire re-enactment. Overall, it was a very comprehensive investigation and the two Marines, although conditioned to detailed questioning through the grilling Major Renick routinely gave them in his marathon mission debriefs, found it mentally fatiguing.

Finally, they were escorted off the plane to a waiting police car and taken to a gymnasium on the base which had been set-up as a temporary police headquarters. As he walked into the gym, Hussar was surprised to find the place still packed. It looked like no one off the plane had been allowed to leave the base yet, and there were also probably at least two cops in the building for every passenger. Apparently, everyone was being interviewed twice and filmed, regardless of his or her level of knowledge of the actual incident. Hussar sensed the police were being beyond thorough—with his military experience he had a fine eye for people wasting the time of others—and he thought the cops were stalling, keeping everyone in one place and busy while the investigators tried to piece together what had actually happened and made sure there weren't any other suspects among the passengers. Plus, the cops were probably trying to give the police in Thailand, and anywhere else they could connect to the terrorists, some time to investigate any local leads before the story broke.

As Hussar and Boner were escorted between the many tables set up for questioning, they were noticed by several of the other passengers. A buzz ripped through the place. Those who actually knew what the two Marines had done pointed them out to the surrounding people as the heroes from the flight. Since all the action had taken place in the first class section, most of the passengers really didn't know what had happened, had not seen any of the action, and had no idea that Boner and Hussar had saved the day. The word quickly spread, though, and before the two Marines had made it to a small room at the back of the building where they were being led, some clapping and yelling broke out and was quickly picked up by all the passengers and flight crew until the whole building was cheering, even the police. The Marines were embarrassed by the attention and gave a couple of waves back to the crowd before they ducked through the doorway.

As Hussar turned from the crowd to see who was already in the room, he came face-to-face with a smiling Gunnery Sergeant DeVolker.

"Hussar! I should have brought a band to welcome you, you hero, but I'm afraid I'm it," he chided his friend.

"Hey, Gunny! Thanks for coming to the rescue. Better late than never, I guess, but you really missed one hell of a party!" Hussar joked back.

They quickly fell into their old banter back and forth, mildly insulting one another for a couple of seconds. Then Hussar noticed what appeared to be a very senior policeman watching the two of them with amusement. DeVolker half-turned to the man and said, "Chief Melamba, may I present Sergeant Hussar, a slightly above average Marine, and Corporal Danzig, his stalwart assistant. Although initially quite modest in abilities, with great effort we were able to transform the two of them into the fine specimens you see before you today."

The Chief laughed. Hussar wasn't the least bit surprised that DeVolker had close friends in the police department. He was the kind of guy that could strike up a professional friendship with ease.

"I'm pleased to meet the two of you. I'm afraid we have a few more questions for you, and then I will release you to the Gunnery Sergeant. I also must inform you that you will need to stay in Singapore until we formally give you permission to leave the country. The Gunny here tells me that this will not be a problem with your unit and that he will be responsible for you while you remain our guest. Now, if you will be so kind as to tell your story one more time, I would like to hear it directly from you."

Since they had now already gone through it a couple of times, it took less than 30 minutes to get through the entire sequence of events. At the conclusion, the Marines respectfully declined the chief's invitation to join him at a press conference scheduled within the hour, and he shook their hands and let them leave with DeVolker.

When they got outside, Hussar had to laugh and shake his head when DeVolker pointed to their waiting car. It was one of the embassy's armor-plated Mercedes, complete with driver and bodyguard, parked right in front of the building. As they approached, the bodyguard hopped out and opened the door for the Marines and then stood back and surveyed the area for any potential threats. Very professional, Hussar had to admit.

Once they got inside and started moving, Hussar asked, "Where to now, Gunny?"

"Back to the embassy. You will meet the Ambassador and tell him your story. Colonel Steuben will probably be there also. They will then decide what you will do next and I will make sure you do it. Simple, huh?" With that, DeVolker got on the car phone, and Hussar heard him tell someone that they would be there in 25 minutes. He then continued, "Look at the bright side though. You slugs are going to be here for a while, courtesy of the Singapore government. While the rest of your MEU is slowly working their way across the Pacific with a bunch of squids on a couple of old rustbuckets, you two will be living large with the Gunny in the Jewel of Asia, the magical island nation of Singapore. The women here are magnificent, the culture enchanting, the food spectacular, and the bars are rockin'. And when this all settles down in a couple of weeks, we'll fly you back to California. You think you can handle that, numbnuts?"

Hussar and Boner both had to laugh, and Hussar realized how much he had missed DeVolker. The guy was a superb Marine and a real character. There was never a dull moment when DeVolker was around.

As Boner settled back for the ride and enjoyed his first ever views of Singapore, Hussar and DeVolker played catch-up on what each had been doing the past year. DeVolker had heard something of the recent successes of 11th MEU but had no idea his protégé had been a key player in many of them. In turn, he gave Hussar a run-down of all the happenings at the embassy and in Singapore generally.

There was a great deal of concern about Islamic terrorist threats in Singapore, and the police had made several arrests of suspected Al-Qaeda members. With a strong connection to the West, relative affluence, and proximity to several somewhat unstable and much poorer Muslim countries, Singapore was certainly on the target list for the extremists. It sometimes seemed like the entire country was holding its breath waiting for something bad to happen. Of course, anything American there would certainly have to be considered a likely target, and DeVolker's position at the embassy is what had led to his close relationship with a number of the Singapore police, including Chief Melamba. But the reality was that the financial district around Shenton Way was a capitalist enclave of such immense significance that it was easily the most attractive target. DeVolker speculated that one of the huge financial services buildings in that area was probably the target of the terrorists that Hussar and Boner had defeated. As they neared the downtown area, DeVolker pointed out the tallest buildings, known as the Three Tigers of Singapore, which contained many of the leading financial offices. Although individually quite distinct in appearance, all three buildings were exactly 280 meters (919 feet) tall, which was the maximum allowable height permitted by Singapore building code restrictions. Both Hussar and Boner were sobered by the view of the skyscrapers, and the magnitude of the potential catastrophe they had prevented began to sink in.

As DeVolker switched back to speaking of the country's many fine attributes, Hussar was beginning to think it may not be that bad to spend a couple of weeks in Singapore. He needed some down time. But first he wanted to find out how his squad was doing. Probably not much had happened on the transit from Somalia to Singapore, but he really missed Gasser and Spike and the rest of his Marines. It had been almost two weeks since he had left the deck of the *Tarawa* and he couldn't wait to catch up with them on some great liberty in a foreign port. *The opportunity to enjoy international travel with fellow Marines was one of the best things about being a Marine,* he thought. It really didn't get any better than that.

The big Mercedes slowed as it turned onto Napier Road and approached the impressive Embassy of the United States of America to the Republic of Singapore. The gate guard was expecting them and, after a quick glance to confirm the identity of the occupants, opened the gate for them. As the car pulled onto the embassy grounds, DeVolker pointed towards a girl walking up the sidewalk that led from the walk-in gate on Napier Road up to the embassy admin building, and said, "See there, boys, that's what I'm talking about. Singapore is a great place."

Hussar looked in the direction he was pointing and was rewarded with a spectacular full-body profile view of a honey-blond-haired woman of excellent proportion. She immediately reminded him of Danielle. He missed her deeply and realized she didn't know any of what had happened to him but would be worried sick when she found out. He needed to call her the first chance he got and tell her ... but suddenly, as if she could read his mind, the woman abruptly turned her head and looked directly at the car. He was stunned—it was Danielle.

"Whoa, stop the car!" Hussar ordered.

"What are you talking about, bub?" DeVolker responded. "We're going in to see the ambassador right now. He's waiting for us. You can chase some skirt later on tonight, stud. There are plenty of women around."

"That's my girlfriend!"

"What, have you gone loco? What are you talking about? Your girlfriend lives in Singapore?"

"That woman is my girlfriend. I don't know how she got here, but she's here. Now stop the friggin' car, dammit!"

DeVolker looked at Boner, who could only shrug. He had never seen Danielle, so he had no idea if his squad leader was hallucinating or not. Boner had taken a good look at the woman, though, and if she were his girlfriend, he'd damn sure be yelling about stopping the car, too.

DeVolker told the driver to stop the car, but Hussar jumped out long before it stopped moving. Even though Danielle had turned to look at the approaching car, she hadn't been able to see in through the heavily tinted windows of the Mercedes and had no idea her Marine was in the car. She had kept walking and was almost to the door of the administration building when he called her name.

Turning, she couldn't believe he was running towards her and just stood there staring at him.

"Oh my God! Jeb, I can't believe you just show up here now. I've been trying to surprise you all day. I spent over an hour this morning getting onto the right pier at the Sembawang Wharves so I could be there when your ship pulled in, but when the Marines started coming off the ship someone told me you hadn't been on the *Tarawa* for a couple of weeks, then I went to the visiting ship desk at the Fleet Center, and a nice Major told me you were flying in today, so I went way out to Changi Airport to meet you, and then I heard your plane was hijacked and wouldn't be landing there, so I went back to the Fleet Center and tried to find out what was going on, but nobody knew, so I decided to come here to find out what is happening. I've been stressed out all day, worried sick about you, I look a mess, and now you just come popping out of the ambassador's Mercedes like it's no big deal, and you expected to find me here. You bastard," she scolded him as she started crying.

She then pressed herself into him and kissed him. "I missed you so much. I flew all the way over here to surprise you and everything went wrong. And ... oh my God! Are you OK? What happened?"

"Danielle, slow down, honey. Everything is going to be OK. First of all, I am very surprised to see you in Singapore. I had no idea. Second, you don't look a mess, you look fantastic. Third, some terrorists tried to hijack our plane, but Boner and I stopped them. We're both OK. Fourth, I've got to go in and see the ambassador and Colonel Steuben, and I'm afraid I have to do that right now. So please come with me and I'll introduce you to the Gunny. He can figure out where you can hang out until they get through with me."

"I'm not letting you out of my sight!"

"Danielle, this may come as another shock to you, but I'm not actually in charge of the entire Marine Corps. I have to follow orders." Judging by the look she gave him, he knew that was the wrong thing to say. He had been gone for 7 months and had gotten out of practice with talking to anyone but his fellow Marines, but he better re-learn fast or he was going to be in a lot of trouble. He tried again.

"Honey, I just have this one little thing to do, and then we'll be together all night. I'm going to stay here for a week or so and then fly back to California. I won't be returning on the *Tarawa*. Maybe you can stay here with me. We'll have lots of time together. And I'm going to take a month of leave when I get back to California. Maybe we can even go to Mexico again, OK?" That went over a lot better and he could feel her soften in his arms. She was still sniffling a bit, but he decided to not make a big deal about it.

"Uh-huh, OK. Where do you want me to go, baby?"

In the car, DeVolker and Boner had witnessed the entire 90-second ordeal. They had seen it wasn't going well initially, and DeVolker had bet a beer that she was going to slug Hussar. Boner had faith in his squad leader and had readily taken the bet. When Hussar and Danielle turned and started walking towards them with Hussar's arm around her waist, Boner let out a yell of approval.

By coincidence, there was another set of interested observers of the little reunion. Unknown to any of them, Ambassador Rodgers and Colonel Steuben had witnessed the event from the 4th floor embassy office of the Defense Attaché. They had briefly stopped in to see if there had been any other reports of terrorist activities through Department of Defense communication channels and were happy to find nothing had been reported. Reassured by the lack of any additional attacks, Steuben had gone to the window to take in the view. He had seen the Mercedes pull in through the gate, and as he continued to watch, was more than a little surprised to see Sergeant Hussar jump out of the moving car and run up to and kiss a beautiful girl who had been walking on the sidewalk leading to the administration building. Steuben had no idea what was going on and had called the ambassador, whom he liked as soon as he had met him that afternoon, over to take a look.

"Ambassador Rodgers, may I present Sergeant Hussar?" he said as he pointed out the window. Rodgers walked over to the window and took a long look.

"My God, Colonel, you Marines don't waste any time. Who is she?"

"I don't know. She was just walking up the sidewalk when he jumped out of the car and kissed her. I thought she must work here."

Rodgers took another look and saw the pair get into the Mercedes. "I'm quite sure that woman doesn't work in this building, Colonel" and then, after a moment's hesitation, he added, "Although she would certainly improve the appearance of this place if she did. Or of any place, for that matter. Now, let's go back to my office and await our story."

But just as the ambassador finished his comment, Steuben noticed something else of interest. A satellite news gathering truck had just pulled up and parked across the street from the embassy compound. A technician immediately got out and started fiddling with equipment as he hurried to get his link up. Behind the truck, a newswoman and her cameraman got out of a chase car and began shooting a couple of "dry runs." Steuben called the ambassador back to the window to see all the activity, and as he was watching, another TV crew appeared and took up position.

"Looks like someone has found out about our heroes," Rodgers remarked, then turned and left for his office.

With Danielle calmed down and in the Mercedes next to him, Hussar asked DeVolker where she might stay while they went to meet with the ambassador. DeVolker immediately offered up the Marine House and began extolling the virtues of the place to Danielle. He could be a charmer, and in less than a minute he had her wanting to stay there. So after dropping her off and making sure she was comfortable, the Marines high-tailed it back to the chancellery. As soon as they got back in the car, Hussar could tell DeVolker was pissed. He assumed it was because of the delay, but there wasn't much Hussar could do about such an unexpected situation as Danielle showing up except deal with it. He wasn't about to just drive by Danielle and not stop. Still, he didn't want DeVolker to think he was a wuss, so he offered, "Hey, I'll tell the ambassador we were delayed because my girlfriend unexpectedly showed up. If he's mad, I'll take the hit, OK?"

"Damn right you would if it came up, but don't worry it won't come up because the ambassador is casual. What's really pissing me off, Hussar, is the fact that some stunningly gorgeous woman flies, on her own dollar, all the way over here to surprise you, then spends a really shitty day running all over the island looking for your dumb ass, and then fawns over you like your some kind of god when you finally do stumble across her. It's bad enough that all this has to happen on my island, but no, that's not good enough for you, you have to go and make it worse by actually finding her right here at the embassy, which is my home turf. Yeah, that royally pisses me off, Hussar." Then the Gunny's face broke into a huge smile. "But I guess it serves me right, since I trained you!"

The three Marines entered the ambassador's office and found Colonel Steuben and the ambassador casually seated in a pair of comfortable high-backed chairs. As they stood for introductions, Hussar and Boner came to attention in front of the Colonel and robustly sounded off with "Reporting for duty, sir!" The ambassador was somewhat amused at this outburst occurring in his office, but he refrained from commenting. Steuben put the Marines at ease, and the men shook hands all around and sat down.

"First things first, who was that young woman you just attacked in front of the embassy?" Steuben demanded of Hussar.

All three of the enlisted Marines were stunned and had that "just plugged up the toilet look" on their faces.

Hussar sheepishly answered, "Sir, that's my girlfriend. She was trying to surprise me by meeting me here in Singapore. She's had a rough day. She was on the pier at Sembawang Wharves when the MEU pulled in this morning and had to watch 4000 guys walk by while she waited for me to come off the ship. Obviously that didn't happen, so she finally asked someone and found out I hadn't been on the *Tarawa* for two weeks and was on a special assignment. But someone else pointed her to Major Renick, who was at the Fleet Center, and he told her I was flying in this afternoon and gave her the flight info. So she went out to Changi Airport to meet me and finds out my flight had some emergency and wouldn't be landing there. Then the story breaks that we were hijacked because someone on the plane called a relative on the ground. Not knowing what to do, she went back to the Fleet Center, but of course no one there knew anything about our situation in the air. So, in desperation, she finally decided to come here to the embassy. And we both just happened to get here at the same time."

"Where is she now?" the Ambassador asked.

"Over in the Marine House, sir."

"We can do better than that", and the ambassador picked up the phone and dialed a number. "Honey, there's a young lady, just a second … " he looked at Hussar. "What's your girlfriend's name, Sergeant?"

"Danielle, sir."

The ambassador continued with his wife, "Her name is Danielle and she's having a terrible day. Came all the way from the States to surprise her Marine boyfriend who she thought was going to come in on the ships today but instead ended up on that plane that was hijacked … No, he's not in trouble, quite the opposite really. He's something of a hero," he said this with a wink to Hussar. "I'll explain later, dear. But can you make sure she is comfortable? She's over in the Marine House. OK, thank you."

"All right, why don't we move to the conference room?" Then on the intercom to his outer office, the ambassador said, "Diane, please let the staff know we are meeting in the conference room now."

In addition to the ambassador and Colonel Steuben and the Marines, the embassy principal staff, to include the Political, Security, Administrative, and Public Information Officers and the Defense Attaché, all assembled in the embassy conference room.

"OK, Sergeant Hussar and Corporal Danzig, let's hear your story," the Ambassador ordered.

So they told it yet another time. When they finished, the room was quiet for a few seconds. Finally, the Ambassador spoke, "That's quite a story. You men should be proud of yourselves, and Colonel, these Marines are a credit to your command and the Marine Corps. I'll be more than happy to write an endorsement for any awards you decide to recommend."

"Gentlemen, because this incident happened on a non-U.S. carrier flying in international airspace on a flight originating in Bangkok and landing in Singapore, there are a lot of governments that are going to officially want a piece of this. Not to mention the incredible news value of the story."

"I've spoken to Prime Minister Wong three times already today on this matter and the President has also spoken directly with him. I also understand there has already been some progress in the investigation by the Bangkok police. Leads to Al-Qaeda have been established and several people have been taken into custody. Of course, everyone is in a state of heightened alert, but so far, this is the only incident we're aware of. OK, let's go around the table. Anything to add? Security?"

"We've taken local security in the compound to level red. The Singapore police have provided a significant augmentation to the units they normally provide outside our fences. No specific issues to report.

"Good. Defense?"

"DoD units in WestPac are in ThreatCon Delta. DoD units worldwide are in ThreatCon Charlie.

"Good. Political?"

"I've spoken to my counterparts in American Embassies in other countries in the area. There have been pledges from the governments of each of these countries to help with any investigation. This includes the Muslim countries in the area. Although it appears Singapore was the intended target, this attack, being so much closer to home, has generated an incredible sense of kinship and cooperation with the Singaporeans and even with the U.S. as the lead of the anti-terror coalition."

"Good, Information?"

"The fact that our two intrepid Marines have thwarted an attack in the air by five terrorists bent on suicidal destruction is a huge story. The word is out that the passengers who fought back and saved the day are two Americans and that they are now here in the embassy. The phone is ringing off the hook with requests for interviews. Apparently, you guys declined to stay for a press conference with the Singapore police chief out at Tengah Air Force Base?"

Hussar and Boner nodded.

"Your modesty, as well as your bravery, is duly noted. But many of your fellow passengers weren't quite as restrained, and they have done a wonderful job deifying you. Mr. Ambassador, apparently the passengers break into spontaneous cheering whenever they see these two. We have six news trucks parked in front of the embassy right now. All the major wire services are going nuts for information. Plus, I have already received indications that these Marines are to be presented medals by the King of Thailand and the Prime Minister of Singapore. Who knows what other accolades will be presented? This is a story of how two ordinary passengers, it's not well-known they are U.S. Marines, emphatically said NO! to terrorism. They saw something that wasn't quite right and took action."

"Was one of you wearing a New York Yankees baseball cap?" he continued.

"Uh, that was me, sir. They've always been my favorite baseball team," Hussar offered weakly.

"Consider the symbolism. A guy with a New York Yankees baseball cap stops the hijacking of an airplane by Al-Qaeda terrorists. It couldn't have been written any better than this. Now the Singaporeans have already told Sergeant Hussar and Corporal Danzig that they must remain in country to help with the investigation. We could force the issue and get them out of here, although I don't see a problem with them staying for a few days as we are happy to assist any anti-terror activity, of course. This is a huge opportunity for us to improve our image in the Far East. These terrorists weren't going after Americans, they were going after Asians. Of course, Singapore is a very western-oriented nation, but you can see the point. Americans prevented a terrorist attack on Asians. I've been on the phone with the information officer at the Bureau of East Asian and Pacific Affairs and they see this as a huge public relations bonanza. What we need, though, are some public heroes ..."

"Hold on, here," interjected Colonel Steuben loudly, "we're not forcing anyone to be a TV monkey. These men are Marines, not actors or propaganda props."

"Colonel, I was just suggesting ..."

"I know damn well what you were suggesting. Now, it's fair to expect some press conferences. And absolutely to expect public acceptance of awards for heroism from any of the countries involved. But it's not the purpose of these two Marines to unilaterally improve the image of the United States in the Far East." And just to show he could play the game if he had to, Steuben added, "I've already spoken to CINCPAC and to the Office of the Commandant of the Marine Corps, and that's the way it's going to be," he stated commandingly.

There was another period of brief, but this time awkward, silence. Hussar and Boner would both have rather been back on the plane fighting for their lives with the terrorists. But the ambassador had a small smile on his lips. His information officer, an Ivy Leaguer from a well-connected family, was a pompous ass, and it was good to see him taken down a notch or two by a Marine Colonel who clearly didn't give a rat's ass about such things. The ambassador let the moment hang for a couple of seconds and then smoothed the issue.

"That sounds reasonable, Colonel. Rather than being driven by the insatiable media, we'll set up a schedule of events, run it by you and the Marines for review, and then publish it. That should satisfy all our concerns, I think. Let's see, we're 13 hours ahead of the East Coast, so all of this so far has pretty much happened late at night in the U.S. I think it would be wise to give our warriors the evening off—I understand they are eager to re-join their squad and maybe spend some time with a girlfriend," he added with a twinkle in his eye. "So to get the process started, let's agree to hold a press conference tomorrow morning at 0700. That's early enough to keep the idle and curious away and will support the local news tomorrow as well as the U.S. evening news shows. Is that OK?"

There were head nods all around. Just then, the ambassador jumped as if he'd been goosed and reached into his pocket to pull out his vibrating cell phone.

"I'll never get used to this damn thing. Excuse me, please," he said and quietly took the call. When finished, he closed the meeting, "Thank you very much, gentlemen, that is all. Colonel, if you and your Marines could join me back in my office?" and he walked out of the conference room with the Marines in trace.

The ambassador's wife, Laura, and Danielle were waiting for them in the office. The girls had clearly bonded, and Hussar sensed impending trouble. He didn't have long to wait. Laura immediately lit into the ambassador for keeping "the brave Sergeant and his beautiful girlfriend" apart for some "silly meeting"—didn't he realize they hadn't seen each other for 7 months? The colonel gave a sympathetic chuckle, after all, he had a wife to answer to as well, and the ambassador quickly suggested everyone go to the Marine House for drinks and then to his residence for dinner. That comment just further infuriated his wife.

"Can't you see these young people want to be by themselves?" she chided him.

Gunny DeVolker jumped in to save the day, "Ma'am, it might be a good idea to go over to the Marine House for a few minutes. We need to make some temporary housing arrangements and also track down the rest of the Marines from Sergeant Hussar's and Corporal Danzig's squad. That will take me a few minutes, and we all might as well relax and enjoy ourselves in the meantime."

The ambassador and Colonel Steuben both looked at DeVolker with new-found respect. He had defused the somewhat delicate situation. Hussar wasn't surprised—DeVolker had always been a smooth operator and a mind reader. Hussar had just been thinking he could use a beer. So everyone headed over to the Marine House. On the way, DeVolker got a phone call from Chief Melamba.

"Gunny, The Republic of Singapore would like to put up the two Marine heroes in the world-famous Raffles Hotel while they enjoy their stay in our beautiful country. It's the least we can do while we hold them here to help with the investigation. Will they be so kind to accept?"

With a laugh, DeVolker asked the chief if he knew what he was getting into by inviting a couple of grunts just coming off a seven month deployment for a complimentary stay in one of the most famous hotels in the world. The chief said yes, the Prime Minister was quite sincere in the offer. DeVolker immediately accepted for the Marines without even asking them. The Gunny knew you were lucky to get any room in The Raffles Hotel for less than $500 a night. He had a mental picture of Hussar and Boner sipping Singapore Slings in the famous Long Bar where the Sling was created in 1915 and where they had been shaken continuously ever since. It looked like the problem of temporary accommodations for the two heroes had been solved on a grand scale, courtesy of the Singapore government. Then DeVolker had a thought.

"Chief, I need help finding some Marines."

"That should not be much of a problem, Gunny. Many work for you at the embassy and another 3000 just showed up today and have fanned out across the island. It's the biggest invasion since the Japs in 1942. From what I hear, just go to any bar downtown and you will find 20 or 30 of them."

DeVolker was astonished that the chief had made such a politically incorrect statement about the Japanese to him. The Gunny realized the Chief must think very highly of him since he had just made him a confidante, but he decided not to make a comment. There was still the problem of finding Hussar's squad and the chief hadn't picked up on his intent yet. *Sometimes there were still some minor communication problems here,* DeVolker thought.

"No, Chief, I need to find several specific Marines, not just Marines in general."

"Oh, I see. That will probably not be difficult either. Which ones?"

"I need to find the rest of Sergeant Hussar's squad. I think that should actually be enough information to track them down, they most likely are all together on liberty. If you could pass the word for "Gasser" or "Spike" to call the Marine House, that would be greatly appreciated."

"Consider it done, Gunny. Good-bye."

DeVolker reached over and roughly grabbed Hussar by the shoulder. "Come on, Sergeant, let me be the first to buy you a beer."

# Chapter 17

Hussar and Boner remained in Singapore for a little over three weeks. By the time they were allowed to leave, the furor over the attempted hijacking had died down considerably, and they were now totally bored and antsy to get back to the States. Being on deployment only sucked when there wasn't much action or if you got separated from your buddies. When either of those occurred, it really was time to go home. With the exception of having one another to hang with, the two Marines were now double-qualified to want to officially end their deployment. 11th MEU had only been in port for the first three days of their stay, and Danielle had left a few days after the MEU departed, so they had been on their own for over two weeks while they finished up with the Singaporean police. Now that their work was done, both Marines were eager to get going.

It had all turned out better than expected. They had a great time with the rest of the squad on several excellent liberty excursions generously provided by the Singapore government. Danielle loved the charm of The Raffles Hotel and got along quite famously with Hussar's friends and with the numerous bigwigs that wanted to meet the Marine heroes. Hussar was amazed at how comfortable she was around everyone—she was fun when they went out partying with a bunch of Marines, and she was also a big hit with the ambassador's wife, who took Danielle to high tea one afternoon for a glimpse of the life of the local upper class.

Hussar and Boner did end up giving several interviews and actually had a brief audience with the Prime Minister. Ambassador Rodgers had also escorted them to Kuala Lumpur for a medal presentation by the Paramount Ruler of Malaysia and then on to Bangkok for a similar event by the King of Thailand. They were treated very well in both places. Even Gunnery Sergeant DeVolker got into the act and did a first-rate job of taking care of them, calling on the Marine Detachment's tailor to custom make each of them a set of Dress Blues to wear to the meetings with royalty and important elected leaders. It was the first set of tailor-made clothes either Hussar or Boner had ever owned and with their tall, lean physiques they both looked superb. Unable to pass up the chance to dig at Hussar, DeVolker told them they looked too good for women and offered to get each of them a benny-boy to take care of them.

DeVolker was still the same incorrigible self. He had only been in Singapore a year, and he already had "hook-ups," or good deals, all over town. It seemed like everywhere they went, someone was yelling "Guneee! Guneee!" Even kids were in on it. There were over 4 million people in Singapore, somehow DeVolker knew half of them. He was living large. Because he had been promoted, though, DeVolker would be leaving soon, fleeting up to a more senior billet in Company "C" Marine Security Guard Battalion, which was based in Bangkok.

As their time together wound down, the three of them spent hours in the Marine House laughing at the stories of some of the stunts DeVolker had pulled. But Hussar and Boner had both learned a lot from the Gunny while he was their Platoon Sergeant—mostly things you wouldn't find in the Marine Non-Commissioned Officers Handbook. Hussar told the story of when DeVolker had showed him how to work the personnel assignment system.

It had been about six months before the MEU went on deployment, right before the official personnel "lock-down" date for the Battalion. This was the date when the unit was supposed to be at 100 percent manning and the personnel roster was "frozen." Theoretically, anyone going on deployment was supposed to be in the unit by the lock-down date, so they could all train together during the deployment work-up cycle and develop the necessary strong unit cohesion based on teamwork and camaraderie.

Hussar was still missing a Rifleman/Scout for Gasser's Fire Team, and he knew he would pick one up before the lock-down. He took the manning of his squad very seriously and had sat down with Gasser to figure out the kind of Marine they wanted. Of course, any Marine would work, but Hussar liked to balance out the physical and personality traits of the squad. The idea was to pull together a bunch of guys who would selflessly work well together, blending skills, egos, and motivations into a harmonious death machine. After he and Gasser had come to agreement, he approached DeVolker, then a Staff Sergeant and his Platoon Sergeant, with his request. DeVolker had listened, then laughed, and made the crack, "What did Hussar think this was, the NFL draft?" But he said he would do what he could.

The last Friday afternoon before the Battalion personnel lock-down, a bunch of new Marines, freshly graduated from Boot Camp and the Infantry Training School (ITS), showed up at the Battalion Admin office. SSGT DeVolker knew the Battalion admin sergeant, Sgt. Jeffries, very well. So when Jeffries called and told him a shitload of Privates had arrived, he knew he better get right over to the Battalion HQ and stake out his claim. He was looking for the skinny, little PFC with a broken nose and big ears that Sergeant Hussar had requested to be Gasser's Rifleman/Scout. Hussar had been very explicit with his request—a guy with minimal silhouette that could move quietly (skinny and little), was not easily intimidated (cocky, hence the broken nose), and that could hear a mouse fart at 50 feet (big ears), would be the perfect addition to his squad. When DeVolker walked into the Battalion Admin office and levied his specific request on the admin sergeant, he couldn't help but smile at the surprise on Sergeant Jeffries face.

"Son of a bitch, Staff Sergeant," he said, "I just in-processed a scrappy looking kid five minutes ago. He's definitely your Marine, Golden Gloves featherweight a couple of years in San Antone and a set of butt ears that you could hang glide with in a fair wind. Here's his file, name is Benito de la Moya, and you can pick him up out front by the flagpole."

Of course, most Platoon Sergeants knew the admin sergeant and jockeyed to get the best Marines possible for their platoons. It was a well-known scam and everyone thought they were working the system by befriending the admin sergeant. But DeVolker was one step ahead of the rest of them, for he was also working with the Gunny at ITS who was actually making the assignments to the various battalions in the First Marine Division. So DeVolker knew ahead of time which Marines were slated to come to the Battalion before they arrived, and could occasionally even influence the selection of specific Marines and the dates they actually showed up at the Battalion. It was then easy to make a very specific request to the admin sergeant, who, of course, would try to handle the most specific request first. It was human nature and DeVolker knew it.

When DeVolker showed up at the squad bay with de la Moya, Hussar and Gasser were almost speechless. DeVolker's only comment was, "Ask, and ye shall receive," and he had turned and walked out. Only later did Hussar find out how DeVolker was "helping Headquarters Marine Corps with enlisted personnel assignments," as he so eloquently put it.

Boner's favorite story was the time they had been on an Air Force base and a junior airman had thought DeVolker was his buddy. DeVolker wasn't mean, but he had given the poor kid a 15-minute lecture on why Marines were different. The airman had no way of knowing that DeVolker was a master of the good-natured ribbing Marines gave each other or that Marines saved their best for the other Services, and DeVolker was legendary in this area.

The Battalion had gone on a Military Operations in Urban Terrain (MOUT) exercise at Robins Air Force Base in Georgia. Robins AFB was home base for the E-8C Joint Surveillance and Targeting Airborne Radar System (JSTARS) airplanes. JSTARS had made their maiden operational flights during Desert Storm and were still a very significant theater collection platform. Although the Marines had several ground terminals for downlinking the JSTARS data, the terminals were held at the MEF-level. Most of the Marines in the Battalion had heard of JSTARS but were not really that familiar with its capabilities. After the MOUT exercise was completed, the NCOs had been taken on a tour of one of the JSTARS airplanes and spoke with several crewmembers. It had been very impressive and the Marines were quite appreciative. The Air Force crewmembers were also excited to meet the grunts, who operated in a tactical environment far different from the one they inhabited in climate-controlled spaces at 35,000 feet. In their enthusiasm, one of the airmen made the mistake of assuming an air of casual familiarity with SSGT DeVolker. The Staff Sergeant had been looking over the shoulder of an Airman First Class as the airman showed how he marked targets on the radar images fed to his computer screen from the large radar bulge on the airplane, which gave the JSTARS airplane its distinctive appearance. As Boner recalled, the conversation had started with something like, "Hey, Sarge, how come the Marines wear the high crown caps with their BDUs?" The airman was referring to the fact that Army and Air Force personnel wore soft, low crown, camouflaged "mickey mouse" caps with a clever little fold-down ear warmer tucked into the hat band with their BDUs, but the Marines wore an entirely different cap. Marines also made a point of "blocking" their utility covers (only the Army and Air Force called them BDUs, for Battle Dress Uniform), which entailed wetting the cover and tautly stretching and drying it over an adjustable sheet metal band, or "block." Once it dried, the cover would maintain a rigid shape when the block was removed and presented a neat, squared-away appearance. It was an innocent question, but the airman had made several important mistakes in his wording. Marine Staff Sergeants aren't called "Sarge." They are only addressed as Staff Sergeant. Marines don't wear "caps," they wear "covers." And they don't wear 'BDUs', they wear "camies," "utilities," or "utes and boots." The surrounding Marines who had heard the question cringed back away from DeVolker and waited for the fireworks and carnage to begin.

DeVolker paused for a second, as if considering whether to even lower himself to answering such a ridiculous question and then looked directly at the airman and said in a serious voice, "It's Staff Sergeant, son. I don't wear BDUs—I wear "utes and boots." I don't wear caps— I wear "covers." And the crowns of our "covers" actually all started out the same, flyboy, but you and the doggies, being flaccid, limp-dick wussies, couldn't keep yours stiff and erect." DeVolker could see the poor bastard was near catatonic with shock and remembered the Colonel's lecture about playing nice with the other Services during the operation, so he quickly broke into a grin and said "Just kidding, buddy, I'm sure our supply guys just haven't yet figured out how to buy the cool caps you fellows are sporting. Maybe when they do we'll all look the same, huh?"

Everyone within earshot relaxed and let out the breath they didn't realize they had been holding. The young airman, though, was still dazed and unsure exactly how to take this crazy Marine, so DeVolker put a reassuring hand on the kid's shoulder and proceeded to calmly educate the airman by giving him the DeVolker perspective on Service uniform policies.

"Now, the Army and Air Force are always fiddling with some aspect of their uniforms in an attempt to strike that special, stylish combination which will capture the mood of the day and resonate with the servicemen as well as the general public. The latest style change was the Army decision to outfit all their soldiers with cute little Chinese-made Monica berets, so they would all look like French peasants. Before that, the Air Force had experimented with changing their basic bus driver uniform into an imitation of the airline pilot uniform (complete with rank stripes on the sleeves!) they all aspired to wear one day anyhow. Perhaps it was part of their overall military-to-civilian transition planning they took so seriously. Apparently, it was hoped that such cosmetic tricks would suddenly inspire the soldiers and airman to be more professional. Sort of like a girl stuffing her bra—some initial appeal but eventual dissatisfaction. As for the Navy, they've pretty much just given up as a Service and left it to the individual. Witness the fact that you will never, ever find any two sailors wearing the exact same uniform.

The Marines have a different approach that was decided over 100 years ago. An ad-hoc Uniform Board was established at Quantico, staffed with the most fashion ignorant, possibly color-blind, Marines in the area that were not otherwise busy, provided with an ample supply of beer and whisky, and given one week to come up with a distinctive, appealing, and sensible dress uniform. Apparently, any and all other direction beyond the word "distinctive" was lost on the board members. They came up with a black high-collared tunic, royal blue trousers with a 2" blood-red stripe along the seam, a white belt with a large buckle, and a white hat. Everything shiny had the Eagle, Globe, and Anchor emblem. There were minor variations to distinguish the different ranks, but not many. Such audacious clothing certainly required a tough, confident, socially oblivious man to dash around in convincingly. As usual, the Marines rose to the challenge and found, or rather made, plenty of these men. Today the uniform is recognized the world over and has tremendous cachet. Not for its garishness, but because the years of association now distinctively identify the men wearing it. We like to think of it as tradition."

DeVolker had then gone on to describe the meaning and importance of every item of every Marine uniform to the increasingly amazed airman and his "associates" who had gathered around to listen. When he finished, there was total silence for a few seconds, and then the airman said, "Sorry, Staff Sergeant, I didn't realize the importance of your uniform to you. Thank you for the information."

To which, DeVolker responded with a winning smile and a slap on the back.

Besides all the quality time with DeVolker, Hussar and Boner, through all their contact with the Singapore police, became good friends with Chief Melamba. They attempted to pay back his generous hospitality by helping out, as recognized experts, with several very realistic SWAT training exercises. The Marines also went out with the chief to the firing ranges to observe a couple of live-fire exercises and shared some combat shooting tips with the policemen involved. The many professional policemen and soldiers they met validated everything they had heard about the competence of those entrusted to protect the Republic of Singapore.

All in all, it was a memorable time. Gunny DeVolker and several of their new-found friends went to the airport to see them off and, as Chief Melamba said, "to ensure there would be no further trouble or delay." Which proved to be exactly the case, as the flight to Los Angeles International Airport (LAX) was uneventful.

Since the MEU had already returned and started a post-deployment leave period, both Marines were authorized 30 days of leave and they parted company at LAX. Boner flew on to Atlanta to spend some time with his family in Kennesaw Mountain, Georgia, which is just north of Atlanta. Hussar took the short flight to San Diego, as he wanted to see Danielle before going back to Virginia. She met him at the airport, and holding her in his arms made him feel like he was home. He was surprised at the strength of the emotion.

"I got a call from Colonel Steuben today."

"What? Come again?"

"I said I got a call from Colonel Steuben today—shall I write it down for you?"

"How did he get your number?"

"He got it from his wife, I suppose. Didn't you ever wonder how I knew when you were supposed to be in Singapore? It wasn't on CNN, Jeb. Operational security and all, you know. You understand the concept. Anyway, I tried to call the ombudsman representative listed on the 11th MEU website to find out if there was a liberty port where I could show up and surprise you and keep you from chasing the native girls. The representative wouldn't tell me anything because I wasn't a wife—I think she actually used the medieval word 'dependent.' So I called the Mrs. Colonel directly and told her about our 'situation' and she gave me the details."

Hussar went blank. "What situation?"

"The fact that we weren't married, but that I so craved your body and that we had already performed numerous sexual acts, still illegal in some states even between husband and wife, but OK in Mexico. And that I was now so horny since you had been gone for 7 months that I was dangerously close to jumping the next sailor who tried to win my favor by slipping me a whopping $5 tip for a lap dance at the titty bar where I work. And she couldn't possibly allow me to so denigrate myself. I mean, a sailor for crying out loud."

Hussar was still blank.

"Jeb, I'm kidding about the last part. But the Colonel did call, and he did get my number from his wife who I did actually meet with so she could determine I wasn't a security risk before she told me about the MEU's planned liberty call in Singapore."

Hussar was lost in the details. He had just finished a 24-hour flight and was a little groggy. "Honey, what did the Colonel say?"

Sensing his fatigue and exasperation, she answered directly, "That you and Corporal Danzig are supposed to report in tomorrow morning."

"What?"

"He wants you at MEU Headquarters tomorrow morning at 0730," she quoted.

"Uh-oh. Boner is already halfway to Atlanta. We were told we had 30 days leave. No one said anything about reporting in first."

"I'm just passing the message, dear."

Hussar thought about it. What's done was done. What he needed now was a shower, a steak, a roll in the hay, and a good night's sleep. Not necessarily in that order and not necessarily only one of each. He kissed her. "Let's not let it spoil our evening. I'll take the beating tomorrow." With that, they went off and handled his bacchanal desires.

Hussar got to the MEU CP a little after 0700 the next morning. It was practically deserted, as pretty much everyone was on leave. Except him, he noted wryly. He heard a voice coming from the Sergeant Major's office and walked to the end of the hall where the brass had their offices. He knocked on the jam of the open door.

"Sergeant Hussar, come in," the Sergeant Major got up to shake his hand. "When did you get in?"

"Last night, Sergeant Major."

"Where's Danzig? Still sleeping in a bar parking lot somewhere?" he added with a grunt.

Hussar explained the snafu. When he finished, the Sergeant Major laughed out loud. It was still the same. These young Marines were poured from the same mold as the kids he knew when he first enlisted over 25 years ago and were probably the same as the previous 10 generations of Marines. Mention anything about leave or liberty to a group of Marines and they would be gone so fast you would be standing by yourself before you could finish the sentence. Everybody always got the word on "libo" as the news spread like wildfire. But call for an extra field day to clean the barracks and you would have to make 10 announcements, post flyers, make phone calls, and send pages, faxes, and emails only to have someone still not get the word. Imagine that.

"Well, that's unfortunate but understandable under the circumstances."

Hussar's jaw almost hit the floor. He had never heard the Sergeant Major rationalize anything before, and he didn't know what to make of it. While Hussar was considering this new situation, he tried to think of something to say but came up empty. Fortunately, the Sergeant Major was already moving for the door.

"OK, let's go in and see the Colonel."

The Sergeant Major escorted Hussar into the Colonel's office and quickly explained Corporal Danzig's absence. Hussar waited to get his butt chewed, but the Colonel just nodded. "We tried to get a message to you through the embassy, but apparently we just missed you. Anyway, welcome back, Sergeant Hussar. Did everything end up OK in Singapore?"

"Yes, sir. We out-briefed with the Singapore police chief and the ambassador, and they both seemed happy."

"Good, good. OK, let's get to the point." The Colonel wasn't much of one for idle chit-chat, and Hussar didn't expect anything else.

"You and Corporal Danzig are going to the White House."

"Sir?"

"Apparently you two are going to be the new face on the War on Terror. You just got back so you don't know this, but the photos of you two getting medals from the King of Thailand in the Royal Palace caused quite a stir back here. The President is not about to be outdone by some King. Anyway, you and Corporal Danzig need to go to Headquarters, Marine Corps and be at the office of the Sergeant Major of the Marine Corps in five days. The Sergeant Major here will get you all squared away with orders and a travel pay advance. Any questions?"

"No, sir, I'll get with the Sergeant Major."

Just then the MEU Executive Officer popped in with a news flash. "Sir, a staff car just pulled up front. Looks like General Morgan." And the XO ran off to greet him.

Lieutenant General Morgan was the Commanding General of the First Marine Expeditionary Force and it was, in fact, him in the staff car. Within a minute, the General, accompanied by the MEF Sergeant Major, was in Steuben's office. Everyone came to attention.

"Good morning, General."

"Colonel Steuben, sorry to interrupt. I got a call from the Commandant this morning. He wanted to make sure there won't be any problems with you and some of your Marines being in Washington next week."

The Commandant was very much aware of the significant efforts

Marines would exert in an attempt to avoid going to D.C. It was part of the Marine Corps psyche to avoid any headquarters building in general, and everything in Washington D.C. in particular. Marines weren't much for the cocktails and canapés circuit—they lacked the necessary refinement.

"But I assured him there would be no problems." The General looked directly at Colonel Steuben for confirmation.

"Yes, sir. There won't be any problems." Then turning towards Sergeant Hussar, he added, "General, allow me to introduce Sergeant Hussar, just returned from Singapore."

The General recognized the name. "Sergeant Hussar, good to meet you, Marine. I'm glad to see you could get through an entire flight without causing another international incident." He smiled at his little joke.

"Yes, sir." Hussar wasn't up to joking with the General. DeVolker would have had something clever to say, but Hussar wasn't yet that comfortable around senior officers.

The General turned serious, stared intently at Hussar, and grabbed his hand in a vise-grip handshake. "I want you to know that we're all very proud of the number you did on those Al-Qaeda thugs, and we're certainly glad you made it back safely. I'm afraid we're going to run you through a bit of a dog-and-pony show in the next few weeks, but it's important that Americans meet some of the Marines participating in our global effort to hunt down and destroy these terrorists."

Hussar could feel the intensity coming off the General. Although he wasn't personally very enthused about the idea, he understood the General's perspective and resigned himself to, as always, doing the best job he could.

"Aye-aye, sir."

The General released Hussar's hand, and by way of dismissal, said, "Colonel, I need to have a word with you about another matter." With that, the Sergeant Major and Hussar eased out of the Colonel's office and went off to contact Boner to tell him the "good news" and make the necessary travel preparations.

# Chapter 18

It had been over a year since Hussar had last been back to Virginia to visit family and friends. His parents threw what he assumed was going to be a small party to celebrate his safe return, but he was surprised when over 100 people showed up. Apparently, he was a major local celebrity because of TV coverage of his role in breaking up the hijacking attempt. The good news for Hussar is there just aren't that many people living along the banks of the Ararat River in Patrick County, or that could even find Laurel Hill for that matter, so he wasn't actually mobbed with well-wishers. Still, he did see kinfolk and acquaintances he hadn't seen in 10 years.

After the initial shock of seeing a crowd the size that was typically reserved in that part of the country for weddings and funerals, Hussar found he enjoyed himself with the solid citizens of the local communities. He realized that no matter what happened in his life, he would always consider this area to be his home. Hussar wished Danielle was there with him, but they had agreed she would wait and come out after he had taken care of his business in Washington. He wanted Danielle and his family to get to know one another without all the distraction of his temporary celebrity.

After the shindig, Hussar quickly fell into the soothing rhythms of rural life in the forested hills of southern Virginia. He went hiking and fishing with his brothers for a couple of days, and then Boner drove up from Kennesaw Mountain so they could road trip together up to Washington D.C.

"How was it?" Hussar asked his good friend about his brief vacation.

"Everyone looking at me like I was some freak circus sideshow. How about you?"

"Pretty much the same. But I suspect it will die down real fast. Neither one of us is what you would call photogenic," he added, as he playfully punched his buddy in the arm.

"You would think I could at least cash in my 15 minutes of fame for a couple of robo-babes for an entire weekend, but that didn't work out worth a damn," Boner said with a laugh. "What the hell is the use of being on TV if it's not going to turn you into a babe magnet? Girls should be offering us trim unsolicited, don't you think?"

Hussar had the visual of Boner playing the reluctant hero and trying to use his newfound celebrity to close the deal on a couple of Georgia peaches. He had to smile. He had never known Boner to have a problem with the ladies, but perhaps he had bitten off more than he could chew for once.

Hussar borrowed a pick-up truck from his older brother James for the drive to D.C. James ran a small construction business and had a number of trucks, but proudly offered up his "good" truck for the Marines to use. In a place like southwestern Virginia, this was a significant gesture and Hussar warmly thanked his brother. He and Boner started the long drive to Washington D.C. early in the morning. They had breakfast along the way and then stopped for a couple of hours at the Marine Corps Base in Quantico, VA. Both wanted to get fresh haircuts, and Boner needed to stop at the uniform shop on base to buy some new ribbons before they made an appearance at Headquarters, Marine Corps.

After their Quantico stop, they started up Interstate 95 North again, heading for the Navy Annex adjacent to the Pentagon where many of the offices of senior Marine Corps leaders are located. They had no problem getting through the huge construction mess, or "mixing bowl" as it was locally called, at the Springfield interchange of Interstates 95, 395, and 495. As they continued straight on 395, it was obvious they were going to be very early for the 1300 show time at the Sergeant Major's office. Even allowing for 30 minutes to change into their uniforms at the gym there, they had an hour to kill. *Better to stop and get some chow now while we have time rather than be hungry later,* Hussar thought. They pulled off the 395 into one of the old neighborhoods of south Arlington. As they drove away from the highway, they found themselves in one of those working-class, melting-pot neighborhoods that are a part of every large metropolitan area. Judging by the variety and number of different food stores advertising their products in various languages, it appeared there was quite the ethnic mix in the area. There were also a lot of small, older, somewhat beat-up, foreign cars parked haphazardly on the narrow streets.

Carefully navigating his way down the street, Hussar spotted a small diner up ahead that looked like it was already open for lunch. They found a small table next to the window and relaxed while they waited for their food. Outside it was an early spring day and there was significant activity in the street. Hussar didn't have a real good feel for urban life, especially in the D.C. area, but there were lots of people driving around, tradesman in work trucks coming and going, etc. He would have thought the place would be deserted in the middle of the day, with everyone at work in some factory somewhere and the kids all in school, but he realized that wasn't the case.

As they watched out the window, an old, faded blue panel truck pulled up to a small pawn shop across the street. A couple of young guys quickly hopped out and went inside. As they weren't carrying anything to sell, they must be buying something or getting something out of hock. Hussar had been to a few pawn shops—you could sometimes get good deals, but you had to really pay attention. Oftentimes, you could buy the same thing brand new at Wal-Mart for only a few dollars more. A short while later, the two guys came out carrying a large black bag between them. Although the men appeared to be in pretty good shape, they were struggling a bit to carry the bag. *Probably picked up a stereo or something,* Hussar thought. The whole scene seemed vaguely familiar, but slightly out of focus, like a memory from a night of bar-hopping. Then it hit him. It reminded him of the opening scene of the Yemen mission. Although they had been operating at night and looking through the greenish glow of night vision equipment, the image of two figures carrying a heavy bag between them to a waiting vehicle was still very familiar. He looked to Boner for confirmation.

"Boner, that look familiar?"

Boner nodded. "How long were those needledicks inside?"

"Maybe 30 seconds max."

"That's too quick to buy something. They were expected."

"Maybe they were here before, bought something big, and had to go get the van so they could pick it up," Hussar offered by way of possible explanation.

"Maybe." It was difficult to tell the nationality of the dark-skinned, dark-haired men. Once again, though, they definitely weren't going to pass themselves off as Swedish.

As the van pulled away, Hussar noticed one of the small, white, well-used cars, apparently the favorite make, model, and color in the neighborhood, pull away from the curb and follow the van. He hadn't noticed the car until then, so he didn't really know if it had pulled up with the van or not. Inside were 3 guys, all wearing caps. He watched as the van made a turn and saw the little car turn right behind it.

"You know, that doesn't look like an FBI chase car," Boner, who had also seen the car take off after the van, observed.

"Maybe the FBI is getting smarter and not driving Crown Vics in the 'hoods' anymore."

"Right. So tell me, when have you ever seen an odd number of FBI agents anywhere?"

Boner made a good point. The answer was never, at least in the movies. Like hooters, they always traveled in pairs. You would see two or four together but never three. Since neither he nor Boner had any real experience with the FBI, though, Hussar wondered momentarily if the cop movies they had both seen were accurate in this area. He decided on the spot that they were probably pretty good.

"You're right on there, my man, you never see an odd number."

The two Marines looked at each other for a long second, then Hussar said, "C'mon, let's roll!!"

They jumped up, scurried past a startled waitress, and within seconds had taken up the chase. They caught up with the van and little car just as they got to the on-ramp for 395 North. Looking ahead,

Hussar and Boner could see the Washington Monument in the distance. Neither of the two Marines were familiar with the roads in the D.C. area, but they were certainly able to recognize the various monuments.

"These guys are heading straight into D.C.!" Boner said.

They drove right by their intended exit for the Pentagon and HQMC and crossed the Potomac several hundred feet behind the blue van, but were surprised when the van merged over to the right hand lane and followed the signs for Interstate 295 rather than continue straight into the city. They took the Pennsylvania Avenue exit, crossed the Anacostia River near RFK Stadium, and turned onto the Baltimore-Washington Parkway heading north. They drove for another 10 minutes and were already in Maryland as they began to notice fewer and fewer big buildings along the highway. As they continued to head away from the downtown area, it was beginning to look like a false alarm.

"We might have been a little too quick on the trigger on this one, killer," Hussar commented. He felt a little foolish. At least they hadn't brought the entire squad along for the wild goose chase. It wouldn't do to look stupid in front of the troops. He glanced at his watch.

"We can still make it back to Headquarters, Marine Corps in time to meet the Sergeant Major. If we're going to eat, though, it's going to have to be a burger some place quick. I don't want to be late. If we do get in a real jam with time, I borrowed my brother's cell phone," he reached over and pulled it out of the glove box and turned it on so it would register in the network, "and we can call the Sergeant Major's office and act like dumbasses from California who can't tell time."

Boner winced at the thought. "Let's just turn around and go right back to Headquarters. If we get there early, we can probably find a snack shop there somewhere. If not, we'll just go hungry. Won't be the first time, right?"

"Right. OK, I'll take the next exit." There aren't many exits on the B-W Parkway, so they had to drive another few minutes before they saw an exit sign. Then two surprising things happened at almost the same time. Way up ahead, they saw the blue van and little white chase car take the off-ramp. They also noticed the exit sign, which announced in big letters, "Ft. Meade—NSA—Next Right."

"Uh-oh," Hussar said as a million thoughts crashed together in his mind. Was this the headquarters of the National Security Agency? NSA analysts were the guys who pursued the electronic leads from the info Gasser had pulled off the terrorist's computer in Yemen and developed intelligence that had proven so important to the mission in Somalia. Were the terrorists getting smarter and beginning to realize that destroying our ability to collect intelligence on them was a logical first step to destroying our political icons? After all, once our intelligence gathering apparatus was neutralized, the terrorists would have much greater freedom of movement to perform their cowardly acts. But how could he know if these guys were actually a threat?

He looked over at Boner, who had an expression of confusion on his face. Boner could only offer a "What now, chief?" in response to Hussar's look.

"We gotta stick with 'em, Boner. I know it's unlikely and the Sergeant Major is going to have our asses, but remember what Gunny DeVolker always says, 'There's no such things as coincidences.' I mean we find a couple of guys in Arlington doing something that reminds us of what we saw in Yemen, and next thing you know, we're following them off an exit to NSA. I mean, what the hell, aren't there pawn shops in Maryland?"

"All right. But if these guys are bad, they probably made us by now."

"I got an idea."

Hussar went past the exit and then slowed the truck down and made a U-turn across the median. He drove down the southbound off-ramp for the exit to NSA and stopped the truck. Quickly reaching behind the seat, he pulled up a couple of magnetic door signs that read "Hussar Excavation Service."

Seeing the quizzical look in Boner's eyes, he said, "My brother uses this truck for his business and attaches these magnetic signs whenever he's on the job site. Here, get out and put them on the doors. Lively, now," as he handed Boner the signs.

It only took a few seconds. As Boner finished, he saw Hussar had found one of the yellow lights that were generally seen flashing on construction vehicles while they were operating on a job site. The light had a magnetic base, so Hussar set it on the roof of the pick-up cab.

"OK, let's go!"

The Marines had only lost about 20 seconds, but the vehicles they had been following were already out of sight. They quickly sped across the overpass heading east, looking for any sign of the blue van.

"Do you think our camo job will work?" Boner asked.

"Probably. We're in a white pick-up, which is the most common color. There must be, what, 20 million of them? And we've totally changed the distinguishing features with the construction light and signs. Unless they got our license plate number, we'll be OK. If we get close, you can duck down so they will only see one person instead of the both of us. It will be a cinch."

Boner could tell Hussar was "in the zone." He had become very matter-of-fact and focused.

They drove on, both intently peering down the main road on which they were traveling and also scanning every side street they passed. They didn't see the van, but after driving about a mile, they passed a huge complex of buildings, surrounded by elaborate security fences and with all kinds of satellite communications antennas bristling out of it, that was set off the road about a quarter-mile.

"That must be NSA," Boner said with obvious understatement.

"Right. OK, let's assume the guys can't get on the base and will attack from somewhere close by. Maybe they have a SADM-10, maybe they have chem or bio. We'll start here and do a sector search until we find them."

"Roger, chief."

"Which way is the wind blowing?"

"Couldn't be worse. Looks to me like we are almost directly up-wind now, so if the bad guys are anywhere close they are also upwind."

There was a pause.

"Maybe that's why they chose today to pick up their package from the pawn shop," Hussar thought aloud.

"Another coincidence, huh?"

"Yeah, sure."

They began driving down several of the local streets in search of the elusive blue van and the white chase car. Nothing seemed unusual in the first neighborhood they drove through, so they returned to the main road to drive to the next neighborhood.

"Bingo!" Boner yelled and pointed.

Parked on the side of a convenience store located on the corner across from them were the two missing vehicles. The store parking lot was otherwise empty, and there wasn't a lot of traffic on the adjacent roads at that time of day. They could see that the rear doors of the van were open, but the two Marines didn't have a very good viewing angle so they had no idea what was happening inside the van. The white car, parked near the back of the van, had its trunk open. There were still two guys in the small white car, the third guy was standing outside the car smoking a cigarette. He appeared to be looking right at them.

"OK, they got us. I don't know what they are doing, but it sure the hell looks suspicious. Since they've seen us, let's pull into the store and get some snacks and try to play it off. I'll stay in the truck while you go in, Boner. Don't tip anyone off, it's possible the people in the store are involved, OK? And put this on."

He handed Boner one of his brother's yellow construction helmets. Hussar was still wearing his New York Yankees cap, which he pulled low over his eyes. They drove across the street into the parking lot and stopped in front of the store, close to the side where the blue van was parked. Boner jumped out and made a big thing of asking him what he wanted, and then slowly ambled into the store. Hussar watched for a second to make sure nothing crazy happened to Boner as he walked in, and then he grabbed a clipboard his brother had left in the truck and pretended to be studying it while he surreptitiously checked out the situation. *A baseball cap is the perfect cover for this,* he thought, as he turned his head ever so slightly so he could just see the bad guys under the bill of his cap.

It was hard to tell exactly what was going on in the van, but there was definitely movement inside the cargo compartment. Hussar tried to figure out a way to get a better angle to look into the back of the van. It wouldn't be easy, as it was positioned very well to block any view inside, but perhaps when Boner got back into the truck they could drive onto one of the adjacent streets and get a better look. Hussar rummaged through the glove compartment and pulled out the small set of high-powered binoculars he expected to find there. His brother had always been an avid outdoorsman who very much enjoyed viewing wildlife. Binoculars in his vehicles were pretty much a given. Now if they could just find a decent place, within several hundred yards, to watch what was going on, they could probably do so without being detected.

Boner finally came out of the store, carrying a bag of groceries. Hussar had noticed he was taking his sweet time, loitering in front of the snack rack like a teenager, as if he was trying to make up his mind on what to buy.

As he got in the truck, he said, "You were right. The guy in the store was peeping me like you wouldn't believe. He couldn't wait for me to get the hell out of his crummy store. There was another guy in the back of the place, who I never saw, that kept talking in Arabic with the guy up front. I don't speak Arabic, of course, but it sounded like he was asking the same thing over and over."

Hussar grabbed some snacks and started munching while he considered the situation. He could feel several pairs of eyes on them as he and Boner pretended to have a conversation, but he didn't think anyone was going to attack them directly so he made no motion to leave. With Boner now in the vehicle, he half-turned towards the passenger seat to carry on his mock conversation, which offered him a clear view of the van and car. For the first time, he noticed the van had one of the little skylight windows in its roof. Thinking about it, he realized that someone inside the van must have just cranked the window open, which had raised the plastic cover high enough so that he could now see it. As he continued watching, the skylight opened further until it was sticking up at about a 45-degree angle. Hussar caught a small flash, like a reflection of sunlight, from some part of the skylight, probably from the movement mechanism, he thought. He then saw it again and realized it was from a piece of metal, maybe some sort of pipe, that someone inside was sticking up through the skylight opening and wiggling around. *That is weird*, he thought. *Time to get a better view.*

He started the truck, backed out of his space, and pulled into the street in front of the store. As he left the parking lot, Hussar looked into his rearview mirror. He saw a guy, who must have just popped out from the back of the store—probably from a rear door—approach the van. The man was pushing a small dolly that carried two large pressurized gas bottles, of the kind commonly used everywhere from restaurants to welding shops, to provide various industrial and commercial gases. *This is getting stranger by the minute,* he thought, as he accelerated away from the convenience store.

Hussar drove about a half-mile and then pulled over to the side of the road near a small construction site.

"What are you stopping here for, chief?" Boner asked.

"Let's get some weapons." He ran out of the truck and started rummaging through a nearby pile of construction trash. In less than a minute, he had found a couple of short 2x4 boards, a 3-foot piece of 1-inch rebar, and some pieces of galvanized pipe. Hussar threw most of it in the back of the pick-up, but kept the piece of rebar in the cab with him. Boner also grabbed a few improvised weapons, with his favorite being what appeared to be a busted pick-ax handle. They jumped back in the truck, and Hussar turned it around and sped back towards the store.

"Now what?" Boner asked.

"OK, the way I figure it, those guys are fixing to make some sort of aerial spray attack. Could be chem, bio, nuclear, who knows. But they've got pressurized gas to carry the bad stuff downwind, they've got some sort of delivery system out of the top of that van, and they sure seemed like they didn't like the looks of us. I'm thinking that's three strikes against them."

He continued, "So we're going to try to get a little better look angle for confirmation before we decide to attack, all right?"

"Got it."

"I'm going to pull off on a side street up here that I think will give us a clear view. Hand me those binos, will you?"

Hussar stopped the truck again, this time at what he thought would be a good observation point. They were about 300 yards from the store but could only see the roof of the building. Need a little more height-of-eye, Hussar mumbled to himself. He jumped out, climbed in the bed of the truck, and stood up to check out the view. Still not enough. He climbed up on top of the cab and slowly raised himself up to the point where he could just see the blue van. Holding a somewhat contorted crouch position for almost a minute, Hussar scoped out the inside of the van. When he finally got down, there was a perplexed look on his face.

"What did you see?"

"I'm not exactly sure. It was definitely a more complicated configuration than I expected. I can't tell if it's a carpet cleaning operation or a terrorist cell getting ready to attack."

"Let me take a look," Boner said and grabbed the binoculars and clambered up on top of the cab of the truck.

Sure enough, it was difficult to tell. He thought briefly of the 1998 cruise missile attacks against the purported chemical weapons facility in Sudan. Over time, it had come out that attacking the site had been a mistake, as it appeared the facility was actually a legitimate pharmaceutical plant. Before they go in and crack some heads, they needed a little more to go on. Boner next scanned the little white car. There were still two guys sitting in it, the driver and a man in the back. They appeared to be having a conversation, with the man in the front gesturing wildly as he spoke. Then the man in the back seat responded, and Boner could clearly see that he had a pistol in the hand he was casually waving about.

"Jeb, the guy in the back seat of the car is waving a pistol around!"

"Is he pointing it at someone?"

"Nah, he's just talking to the guy in front, but he's waving the pistol around in his hand as he speaks."

"OK, that pretty much nixes the carpet cleaner option. C'mon, let's roll!!"

# Chapter 19

As Boner climbed back in the truck, Hussar picked up the cell phone and dialed 911. The operator in the 911 Center for Anne Arundel County, Maryland responded immediately.

"9-1-1 Operator."

"I need to speak with the FBI!" Hussar demanded.

"Sir, we handle all emergency calls. What is the nature of the emergency?"

"This is Sergeant Hussar, United States Marine Corps. Put me through to the FBI Command Center right now!" Hussar ordered.

Something in the man's voice sounded sufficiently official so that the operator decided to immediately do what he requested. There was a brief pause while the call switching occurred to bring the FBI Command Center in the Hoover Building in downtown D.C. into the multi-party call.

As she processed the connection join, the operator looked at her computer screen and then up at an electronic map displayed on the wall in front of her. Anne Arundel County had recently deployed the enhanced 911 capability to support emergency calls from cellular phone users. Enhanced 911, or E911 as it was generally called, was an FCC mandate that required wireless carriers to provide fairly precise (within 50 meter accuracy) caller location information to a local Public Safety Answering Point (PSAP) when the PSAP requested the information. PSAP was just the official government FCC term for a 911 call center. By policy, the Anne Arundel system was configured to automatically

239

request and log location information for all 911 calls. There was the concern that a 911 call could be prematurely terminated without the operator getting sufficient information as to the nature of the emergency. But if location information was at least available, some sort of initial emergency response could still be made. The actual infrastructure to support the location requests was fairly complicated, but it was well hidden from the operator. Basically, the location request was passed to the closest of several national call processing centers, which in turn passed the calling cellular phone's electronic serial number to the authorized wireless carriers in the PSAP area. The wireless carriers queried their networks to determine if the calling phone was in fact "registered'" in their network, and if so, exactly where it was located. This geo-location process could be done through radio triangulation from adjacent cell towers, or through an assisted-GPS algorithm supported by newer cell phones. Regardless of the method, the geo-positional information was sent back to the PSAP to support emergency response efforts. It all actually happened pretty fast, at least when it was working correctly, which still wasn't all of the time. But as the operator watched her screen, Hussar's location popped up on her map display. She immediately noted the proximity to NSA and wondered what was going on. It didn't take long to find out.

"FBI Command Center, Special Agent Bragg."

"Sir, this is Sergeant Hussar, United States Marine Corps. I'm watching 5 or 6 guys, possibly of Middle Eastern descent, rig what might be some sort of spraying system in an old van. Possibly to attack the nearby NSA headquarters with some WMD material. At least one of the guys is armed with a pistol."

Boner had been looking ahead while Hussar drove and spoke on the phone. As the parking lot came into view, he saw the third guy get back into the little car. It looked like they were getting ready to leave. The rear doors of the blue van were still open, but he couldn't see anyone inside from his angle. They were going to have to go in blind. He gave the pick-axe handle a tight, reassuring squeeze as he got ready to launch his own shock attack.

"Jeb, they might be leaving. We've got to take out that car first!!"

Hussar had also seen what was happening. He quickly finished his message to the FBI, "My buddy and I are going in. You had better get some people here pronto! We'll probably need some help, to include some WMD experts."

Special Agent Bragg was stunned. Was this some lunatic making a crank call? Did this, what was his name … Sergeant Hussar … say he and a buddy were going in on 5 or 6 men, known to be armed? Were Hussar and his friend armed? A WMD attack on NSA? Christ, he had just come on shift. This was going to be a long day. But after the briefest of hesitations, he pushed the emergency alert button at his desk to declare a crisis, and the greatest police force in the world sprung quickly into action.

Hussar accelerated the truck as it neared the convenience store parking lot. It was time to find out if air bags really worked. He thought briefly that his brother was going to kill him for wrecking his "good" truck, assuming he survived the incident. Oh well … no guts, no glory.

As the ¾-ton pick-up truck wheeled into the parking lot and headed straight for the little white car, there was a brief moment when everyone was looking at one another. The 3 guys in the car all seemed to hear and see the truck at the same time and were now transfixed on the approaching pick-up. Hussar and Boner were staring at the car, bracing themselves for the impending impact. Then the 3 guys appeared to simultaneously realize their predicament and fumbled with the doors in an attempt to escape. But there wasn't time, and the truck T-boned the little car and sent it flying. Hussar and Boner were thrown forward into a not very appetizing air bag lunch and had to spend a few precious seconds disengaging themselves once the truck stopped. They both jumped out, and Hussar yelled, "You take the guys in the car, I'll check out the van."

Boner quickly moved to the car, whose passenger side was completely caved in, and picked up all the weapons he could find laying around the car and off the groggy, groaning occupants. Since it wasn't possible to exit the car on the passenger side, he took up position on the driver's side and stood there menacingly with his pick-axe handle in his hands. One of the guys, coming to faster than his cohorts, looked at Boner and spat out something to him in Arabic. As it didn't sound like a compliment, Boner didn't say a word but smashed the pick-axe handle against the roof of the car. The whole car rocked and the noise was quite impressive. The guy cowed down in the car without another word.

Hussar, meanwhile, had quickly circled around to the back of the van with his piece of rebar at the ready. Expecting to have to fight off at least two lunging attackers, he was instead surprised to find the van empty. He briefly looked over the apparatus in the van—it was definitely some kind of jury-rig of a crude, but simple, design. Not an industrialized configuration by any means but possibly quite effective for a one-shot attack. Best he could figure, they were going to force the pressurized gas through a mixing tank where it would somehow attach with the WMD particles of choice, and then the mixture would be expelled through a nozzle head that was sticking out the skylight opening. *So that's what I saw earlier*, he thought. He was impressed, though. There weren't any moving parts—the whole thing was driven by commonly available pressurized gases seeking a lower pressure environment, like all gases did. Hussar wasn't an expert in the propagation of airborne particles, but it seemed to him that if they parked the van upwind and close to the NSA building and parking lot and then waited for the afternoon shift change so they could maximize the number of people caught out in the open, it might be a very effective attack. The terrorists, as he now thought of them, had probably figured out which gases would be the most effective as agent carriers and also the optimum location for parking the van before they started the attack and abandoned the vehicle to do its terrible deed. Perhaps they could even start the process remotely. He wondered if the action his squad had seen in Somalia with the chemical attacks on remote tribes was somehow related to what was now in front of him. It didn't appear that the WMD material had been added to the mixing tank yet. At least he hoped not, or he was probably exposed. There would be time to figure that out later, he was still missing a couple of terrorists and he had work to do. With a quick look at Boner to confirm his situation was under control, Hussar approached the rear of the store. He could hear sirens approaching in the distance and assumed the cavalry was on the way. Better hurry if he was going to catch the rest of the bad guys by surprise. Hussar had no idea why they hadn't run out of the store at the noise of the car crash to find out what was going on, but he had to find the terrorists and the WMD.

Carefully peeking around the corner, Hussar could see the back door was propped open. He slowly approached the door, alert for any sounds from inside, but all he could hear was a loud motor noise, probably from the compressor for the store refrigeration system. The closer he got to the door, the louder the noise got. Assuming anyone was in the back of the store, that would explain why they hadn't come out when he crashed into the car—they probably hadn't even heard the sound of the collision. Nearing the door, he could see it was much darker inside the building. *Damn, I'm going from light to dark, no fire-arm, no WMD gear—not even a gas mask, without back-up, against at least two guys playing around with WMD material. How do I keep getting into these situations?* He asked himself rhetorically. Holding his breath—he didn't want to suck in a bunch of air as soon as he entered the building in case he was immediately faced with an airborne WMD threat—Hussar eased through the doorway in a low, crouched position with his makeshift rebar weapon at the ready. An initial scan revealed a storage room, one whole wall of which was the back of the drink coolers that faced the front, customer area of the store. Hussar didn't initially see anyone in the room, but as his eyes adjusted to the light, he noticed the far corner of the storeroom had been screened off and he sensed movement there. Slowly approaching the screened area, he slightly adjusted his course so he could see through a small open area where two of the partitions didn't quite come together all the way. What he saw stopped him in his tracks and sent a shiver up his spine. There were definitely two guys behind the screens, but they were un-recognizable as they were almost completely suited up in Level A HAZMAT suits. He paused for a few seconds to try and figure out exactly what was going on. OK, it looked like neither one of the guys had their facemask on yet. That was good because it meant they had not yet gone completely self-contained with internal air supply and everything, so they probably weren't yet working with anything dan-gerous. The two were still talking to one another, possibly going over some last-minute instructions before they finished suiting up, so he eased closer to see what else of interest was visible. Behind the two terrorists, Hussar spotted the large black bag he and Boner had seen carried from the pawn shop almost two hours earlier. *Whatever bad stuff these guys have is in that bag,* he thought, *and it appears to still be "safed," since the terrorists are not completely protected.* It looked like they were close to getting ready to go, though, so now was the time for action. He had surprise on his side, plus the HAZMAT suits were very awkward to move around in, so he thought the situation was favorable. The important thing was to separate the WMD from the terrorists, and with a plan in mind, Hussar moved back a few feet and got ready to charge. He took off with all the speed and power of the middle linebacker he had once been and charged into one of the partitions like a battering ram. The partition solidly connected with both of the terrorists, knocking them to the ground and, more importantly, away from the black bag. They both started shouting in Arabic, Hussar responded by sledging them both in the face with his fist. Then while they were both flopping around on the floor like beached walruses, Hussar jumped up and grabbed the black bag and tried to make a quick getaway. He had somehow smashed his knee in the attack, so he was a little off-balance. And, unfortunately, he had forgotten that it had taken two men to carry the bag and was stopped short by its weight and his leg injury. "Damn," he muttered under his breath. This wasn't going to be a quick "purse snatch" after all. He squatted down, grabbed the bag's handles over his shoulders, and then stood up and walked as quickly as possible towards the door, grossly favoring his injured leg. The two terrorists were still thrashing around on the floor. Hussar had no idea if they had any weapons, but he didn't care anymore. He was going to make it outside that door regardless, and he willed his legs to drive on. Three more steps and he'd be there, then two, then one, and finally he burst out through the doorway into the bright sunlight.

"Freeze, don't move!!" was his welcome back into the world. Hussar stopped, and slowly lowered himself, and the precious bag, to the ground. He looked up and saw no fewer than 20 weapons pointed at him, with an FBI agent, ATF agent, deputy sheriff, or policeman behind every one of them.

"Gentlemen, I'm Sergeant Jeb Hussar, United States Marine Corps. There are two more of the bastards inside the store in HAZMAT suits. They were on the floor when I left, and they may be armed."

"Who are they?" one of the cops asked him.

"Sorry, boss, I didn't have time for a 'stop-and-chat,' so you'll have to figure that out. But they won't be hard to find as they are the only two guys in there wearing airtight suits and sporting recently broken noses, OK?"

With that, the cops rushed into the store and quickly secured the terrorists. Hussar looked over and saw Boner already talking to someone that looked like a senior Fed, even as he kept an eagle eye on the agents that were handling "his" prisoners. Hussar waved to get Boner's attention, and his trusty Corporal saw him and trotted over. The Fed bigwig couldn't believe the young Marine just ran off and left him standing there in mid-sentence. But it wouldn't be the most surprising thing he learned that day.

"Hey, chief, you all right?"

"Yeah, I dorked up my knee charging into those two," he pointed to the terrorists now being hauled out of the store by the cops, "and I didn't help it much when I tried to run out carrying this heavy-ass bag."

"You look in it yet?"

"I'm almost afraid to," but then he slowly pulled back the flaps. Inside were two black, heavy, finely-machined cylinders identical in appearance. Each was about a foot in diameter and maybe 18 inches in length. Based on his experience lugging them out of the store, Hussar guessed their weight at about 80 pounds apiece. Stamped into the top of the cylinder were the letters "AdT."

"What the hell is that?" Boner asked as he pointed to the embossment.

"Those are the initials for *Armée de Terre*, literally, Army of the Soil, the French term for the Land Army of the Republic of France," said a new voice, "and I would ask that you please not touch the nerve agent canisters."

Hussar and Boner both involuntarily cringed away and then turned to see who was speaking to them. It was a tall, thin, bespectacled man neither of them had ever seen before.

"Gentlemen, thank you. I am Special Agent Jackson from the FBI Counter-Terrorism Division. I have been looking for these two little beauties for almost six months," he said, almost fondly, of the sinister looking canisters. "Along with two more just like them that are, unfortunately, still missing. They were stolen from a French Army munitions depot near Reims, France, last year during a bloody attack by an unknown group of assailants. No one ever claimed responsibility for the assault, so we really didn't have any idea where they would show up. As such, they have been the focus of a worldwide search since the day they were stolen. I was almost beginning to believe, or rather hope, that they were lost for good and the world would never have to deal with this scourge. But now, here two of them have shown up less than 15 miles from my office."

"Did you say 'nerve agent'?" Boner asked.

"That's right. VX2, in fact. Nasty stuff, really, once it is developed. Actually, what you have here are the binary precursor reagents, in this case O-ethyl O-2-diisopropylaminoethyl methylphosphonite and elemental sulfur, that produce VX once they are combined. I suspect the reason those two goons are suited up in Level A HAZMAT is because they were preparing to do the mixing in their makeshift lab in preparation for an attack sometime later today. At least that was the plan until you two showed up.

Something had been bothering Hussar. "You said there were four of these canisters missing?"

"Yes, there were. Since we now have two, there are only two still missing," corrected Special Agent Jackson with a smile.

"I think I know where you should look for the other two," Hussar said evenly.

"Really. Where?" Jackson was very interested.

"In an old van slightly upwind from either the CIA or NRO headquarters."

Jackson immediately saw the connection. "You think they are going after our 'eyes and ears' now." It was more of a statement than a question, but Hussar responded anyway.

"I didn't until an hour ago when we followed these guys right through the heart of D.C. before ending up here outside NSA. Now, I would be willing to bet that was their plan."

Jackson looked at Hussar with newfound respect. "That's pretty good thinking." He picked up his encrypted hand-held radio.

"Let me speak to the Deputy Director." Jackson quickly outlined the situation for the Deputy Director, and then turned his attention back to Hussar and Boner.

"OK, we will follow up on your idea. In the meantime, you guys are going to have to answer some questions." Jackson paused briefly to wave over a couple of large men that were first responders from an area HAZMAT Response Unit and gave them specific handling instructions for the canisters. Then he said, "Special Agent Lee," he pointed to the man Hussar had seen Boner talking to earlier, "will take your statements. Please see him."

They were interrupted by the loud thrashing sound of an approaching helicopter, which landed 100 feet away in the middle of the blocked-off street in front of the convenience store.

"That's my chopper. I'm afraid I have to leave." Jackson started to walk off, but then stopped, turned around, and yelled over the noise of the helicopter, "Say, there was a fellow by the name of Hussar that was involved in breaking up that attempted airplane hijacking last month in Singapore. Any relation?"

Hussar grinned sheepishly, "Uh, that was me and Corporal Danzig on that one, sir."

"Really. That's very interesting. In fact, almost an uncanny coincidence, I would say." Jackson gave them a final appraising look and then turned and walked rapidly towards the waiting helicopter. As soon as he got aboard, the chopper took off to the southwest in the direction of Washington, D.C. and rapidly disappeared from view.

Special Agent Lee had suddenly shown up at their side. "If you gentlemen will come with me, we need to get your story right away."

Hussar looked across the parking lot at his brother's wrecked truck, the smashed car, and the old blue van, which was now being closely scrutinized by several FBI technicians. Beyond a yellow police line that had been set up a couple of hundred feet away, crowds of the idle and curious were starting to gather, and there were already news crews from 3 different TV stations on scene. Boner sighed at the inevitable attention they would again be receiving.

Hussar tried to cheer him up, "Look at the bright side, sport. Maybe now the robo-babes will notice you!"

He suddenly had another thought, much more sober, which made him wince. "Agent Lee, we were supposed to be at the office of the Sergeant Major of the Marine Corps over an hour ago. By now, we are officially in a lot of trouble. Can I borrow your phone?"

# Chapter 20

The FBI did in fact find the remaining two canisters of nerve agent precursors in a van near the CIA Headquarters in Langley, Virginia. They were also able to apprehend a five man terrorist cell preparing to execute a very similar attack plan. Based on interrogation of the terrorists, it appeared they were executing a coordinated set of attacks timed to occur in the middle of an employee shift change, when the maximum number of people would be out in the open in employee parking lots and easily exposed. Plus, the terrorists expected some of the deadly chemical vapors would get sucked in through ventilation systems and contaminate the building interiors as well. It was a bold set of physical and psychological attacks designed to go after the very people who were responsible for tracking the terrorists down. The terrorists considered most Americans to be personal cowards, hiding behind significant technological advantages and happy to watch Arabs die on TV from the comfort of their living rooms but scurrying to safety at the first sign of personal danger. The terrorists wanted to bring the war "home" to all the government employees and contractors that manned the U.S. intelligence apparatus, which was responsible for bringing death to the faithful from the air-conditioned comfort and safety of fortress-like office buildings.

Although the terrorist leaders were disappointed at the botched attacks, they got some validation of their attitude towards Americans. The mere threat of nerve agents being discovered in the city, once the news of the thwarted attacks hit the streets, did cause a significant amount of panic. The terrorists had hoped to see Americans dying the grotesque deaths associated with lethal exposure to poisonous gases but had to content themselves with seeing wild-eyed soccer moms picking up their kids from school and clogging up the streets with the millions of people who decided they needed to immediately leave work. It turned out to be the worst traffic jam in D.C. history, with many people not getting home until after midnight and thousands of cars being abandoned along the choked interstates. Numerous rumors of actual attacks, mixed with exaggerated accounts of the actual incidents, flew across the city throughout the remainder of the day and kept the fires of fear fully stoked. In the clear pecking order officially described in the National Command Authority Succession and Survival Plan, the President and several senior government officials were evacuated. Everyone else was left to fend for themselves, which sent a strong message of their relative importance to all the jack-ass advisors, consultants, lobbyists, bureaucrats, staff members, political party leaders, and assorted other strap-hangers, all with an inflated sense of self-importance, which were somehow able to make a lucrative living in the nation's capital. If nothing else, the American dream of the antiseptic killing of "criminals" thousands of miles away without the slightest personal threat or inconvenience was shattered, at least for the people of the greater Washington D.C. metropolitan area.

Hussar and Boner were unaffected by the brouhaha. They spent a couple of hours with Special Agent Lee, answering questions, providing the location of the pawn shop, describing the terrorist actions, etc. Hussar had also finally gotten through to the very disbelieving Sergeant Major, who told them to show up at 1000 the next morning. So when they were finished for the day with the FBI, they got their personal gear out of the wrecked pick-up, got a ride from the local cops to a nearby hotel, checked-in, and then went out to the nearest bar to eat and have a few beers.

Watching the disturbing images of a public in panic that were already coming across the TV in the bar, Hussar was philosophic, "You know, even after 9/11, I think most people still haven't come to grips with the fact that they are potential targets. They really don't understand why that is. As a nation, we've made certain decisions on who our friends are and who we don't like, on where our national interests are and where we turn a blind eye, on who we reward and who we punish. We expect the rest of the world to just accept this. That's not logical. Even among Americans, we never get consensus. It's just that most of us follow our convention of voting for our beliefs and then accepting the will of the majority. If we're not happy, we vocalize our dissatisfaction, maybe we even protest, and we try to improve our position during the next election cycle. People elsewhere that aren't a party to this convention will react differently in ways they accept as appropriate. Unfortunately, for many of them, that means violence. Violence directed at us, because we are by far the biggest blip on the radar scope, and there isn't ever going to be enough of us to prevent some of it from actually happening."

Boner wasn't used to hearing his friend talk like this, "So what does that mean for us, chief, a couple of grunts looking for a little adventure?"

"It means we'll be busy for a long time. Job security for the profession of arms, I guess, but a lot of personal risk for everyone, especially us."

"It also means I'll have another beer," he added with a smile, "because who knows if we'll ever get another chance, eh?"

"I'll drink to that!" Boner responded, glad Hussar was back to his old self. It didn't pay to spend too much time thinking about heady stuff like that, it could cause them to lose the tactical edge they depended on to stay alive. Let the politicians worry about that stuff—after all, their asses were on the line now also.

The next morning they actually made it to Headquarters, Marine Corps and checked in with the Sergeant Major. After a quick, but thorough, inspection, the Sergeant Major pronounced them "Good To Go," and took them in to see the Commandant of the Marine Corps. Colonel Steuben was already in the general's office and gave them a big smile as they entered. The Commandant stood up and came around his desk to greet and shake hands with Hussar and Boner.

"Good morning, Marines! I understand you two were involved in yet another major incident yesterday on your way to this Headquarters. I want you to know that we all appreciate your alertness and initiative. You seem to be a two-man wrecking crew for Al-Qaeda! I'm sure the President is going to want to hear all about it, so I won't make you tell me all the details right now. Sergeant Major, when do we need to leave to make it to the White House on time?"

"Scheduled to leave here in 20 minutes, sir."

"OK, good, why don't you take Sergeant Hussar and Corporal Danzig down to the Operations Center and have someone give them a short tour of what we actually do down there. I don't want these Marines to leave Headquarters thinking that the only thing us admin poges do all day is sit around here and dream up clever ALMARs to write up and send out to the FMF," he said with a wink to the two NCOs, "which is pretty much what I assumed everyone did the first time I ever came here. Then I'll meet you at the car and we can talk on the way."

Rear echelon troops were typically called "poges" and ALMARs was an abbreviation for the All Marine Notices that went out from Headquarters, Marine Corps addressing everything from promotion opportunities to the Commandant's annual Marine Corps Birthday message.

"Yes, sir!" they answered in unison.

The Commandant was right. Hussar and Boner really had no idea what anyone at Headquarters, Marine Corps actually did, but they assumed it wasn't much—or at least wasn't much that was operationally relevant. The Major who briefed them in the Ops Center convinced them otherwise in less than five minutes. After finding out they were from 11th MEU, the Major showed them how operations were tracked, such as their missions in Yemen and Somalia, the role of Headquarters personnel in supporting those ops, how the Ops Center communicated with everyone from the National Military Command Center in the Pentagon to unit commanders, such as Colonel Steuben, and how recent operations impacted major decisions made by the senior leadership of the Marine Corps. By the time they left the Ops Center, Hussar and Boner were amazed at the level of coordination, the depth of understanding, the complexity of the environment, and the amount of support provided. They had always considered themselves to be at the "tip of the spear," but had very narrowly defined the "spear" to only include other combat forces in theater. Now they realized the "spear" actually included the entire supporting infrastructure at the various headquarters up the chain of command, all the way back to Washington D.C. Of course, neither one of them ever wanted a tour of duty at Headquarters, but it was good to gain an appreciation for what was being done there.

The trip to the White House was a blur of protocol and security checks. Hussar and Boner hung with Colonel Steuben and followed his lead. After all, in the rarified air of the Commander-in-Chief's inner sanctum, a mere colonel was probably viewed as being not much higher on the totem pole than a couple of NCO's, Hussar wryly observed. They were ushered into a waiting room that already held several other people and briefed that they would spend 10 minutes with the President in the Oval Office and then go to the East Room for an awards ceremony and press conference. The aide then told them that the President's schedule was running about 15 minutes behind. Hussar was amused to notice that the aide didn't say the President was late; rather, it was the President's schedule that was behind. He also noticed that the Commandant, being someone important, had apparently been taken somewhere else to wait. The Colonel, he, and Boner were left waiting with the rest of the riffraff.

It was tough to sit right outside the office of the President of the United States and not fidget. Hussar found that he was actually nervous and his mouth was dry. There was a drink tray set up, probably just for that purpose, but he hesitated. Not knowing how long they would be waiting, it would be just his luck to have to urinate badly about the time they were called into the Oval Office. He looked over at Boner, and from his expression, guessed that pretty much the same things were going through his head.

They were finally called in to meet the President. As they walked into the Oval Office, the Commandant and the Secretary of Defense appeared out of nowhere and went in with them. Hussar thought that was a pretty neat trick. Introductions were quickly, but formally, made and a photographer, clicking away like crazy, was there to capture the entire event.

The President was the slightly awkward, good-natured guy he

appeared to be on TV. Hussar was impressed that the man immediately made them feel at ease and gave them his undivided attention. Colonel Steuben spoke first, giving the President a summary of highlights from the 11th MEU deployment, to include the missions Hussar's squad had completed in Yemen and Somalia. The President listened carefully, nodded his head, and then asked Hussar about the hijacking attempt. Again, the President was very interested, and asked a question about how he and Corporal Danzig could so quickly come up with a plan to defeat a better-armed, numerically superior, group of terrorist fanatics who had been planning and rehearsing their mission for months.

Hussar paused for a second. "Sir, we didn't really come up with a plan. We recognized the severity of the threat, responded aggressively, and adapted to the situation as it developed. Just like we've been trained."

The President mulled that over briefly, then looked at the Secretary of Defense and said, "Without the benefit of the entire military-industrial complex. Interesting."

Hussar had no idea what that meant, but it appeared the President was directing his comment at the Secretary of Defense, so he didn't respond.

An aide came and whispered in the President's ear, and the President nodded his head in response. "Gentlemen, you did a fantastic job, and your country and your President are very proud of you. If you would join me now in the East Room for the presentation of well-deserved medals?"

The White House visit had been planned two weeks in advance and was scheduled for the purpose of officially recognizing the Marines for breaking up the attempted hijacking in the skies over Singapore. It was clear that the President hadn't yet been briefed that Hussar and Boner were also the two guys who had prevented the planned chemical attack on NSA Headquarters. It wouldn't do to have the President find out this very important fact from some reporter's question.

The Commandant cleared his throat, "Mr. President, there is another matter with respect to Sergeant Hussar and Corporal Danzig."

The young aide turned and gave the Commandant his practiced and most severe look of disapproval. He had the President's schedule to keep for crying out loud. Delays couldn't be tolerated. *These generals just never seem to understand the importance of keeping a tight schedule,* he thought with visible agitation.

"And what is that, General?" The President asked evenly. He didn't like surprises at what were supposed to be routine office visits.

The Commandant sensed the tension in the room, but he pressed on.

"These Marines were also the guys who broke up the planned terrorist attack on NSA yesterday." Everyone in the room stopped for a second. The pompous aide turned white, then fumbled through some notes he was carrying. As the President's "information man," he was looking pretty stupid for not making the connection ahead of time and informing the President. Though the situation was unintentional, the Commandant enjoyed seeing the aide's obvious discomfiture, as the little jerk had routinely annoyed him for years.

"They broke up the planned terrorist attack on NSA yesterday?" the President parroted, with a look of annoyance at his aide.

"Yes, sir. While traveling here to meet you, they discovered the terrorists in the middle of preparing for the chemical attack. At great personal risk and with no regard for their own safety, Sergeant Hussar and Corporal Danzig assaulted and defeated the terrorists and secured the deadly nerve agent canisters, thus averting a potential catastrophe. They then tipped the FBI that the terrorists had probably planned a simultaneous attack on CIA Headquarters, which of course turned out to be the case. They thus directly contributed to the prevention of a second potential catastrophe. But we can have these Marines tell us about it."

Hussar realized the Commandant had somehow got information from the FBI, since very few people knew they had tipped the FBI, and he and Boner certainly hadn't told the Commandant about it. Hussar heard that many FBI agents were former Marines, so he correctly guessed the Commandant had some buddies that were in very senior positions within the FBI.

The President turned to his aide. "You'll need to delay everything by 30 minutes," and then sat down again as the aide shot out of the room like a rocket. "Tell me, gents, what happened yesterday?"

After Hussar told the story, the President again looked at the Secretary of Defense and said, "You know, we are spending almost 400 billion dollars a year at DoD and billions more in various counter-terrorism programs in other departments, none of which seems to have even remotely been a factor in the two stories we just heard from these Marines." The President was growing somewhat weary of his arrogant, acerbic, know-it-all Secretary of Defense and what he perceived to be the Defense Department's undue emphasis on technical gadgets and gizmos at the expense of building tough, well-trained, aggressive, warriors like the two Marines in front of him.

"Leave it to the Marines to remind us of what's important," the President uncharacteristically mumbled under his breath. He had a brief memory moment of his father, a proud World War II Army veteran who had died several years earlier, once telling him that the Marines were the only Service that wasn't run by a bunch of politicians in uniform. *That probably explained their miniscule budget,* the President thought, *but apparently the perceived risk of death was high enough to keep out most of the self-aggrandizing power brokers that staffed every other entity of the Federal government.* The President wondered how badly the Marines' reputed selfless devotion to duty had been corrupted by the me-first social attitudes of the last twenty years. He made a mental note to find out. With the shifting sands of world diplomacy increasingly taking up more of his time, it was likely the mettle of the Marines would again be severely tested in the months and years ahead. It was important to know, in absolute terms, who could be counted on when times were tough. If it turned out that the men now in front of him were representative of Marines in general, there was much good that could be done.

There was a silence in the Oval Office. It was obvious the President was deep in thought. Watching him, Hussar had a sense the President was wrestling with some important issue that his story had somehow triggered. Then the President nodded, as if in affirmation of some decision he had just made, smiled broadly at them, and said, "Again, well done. C'mon Marines, your fellow Americans are waiting to hear this story!"

# Glossary

**ALMAR** - All Marine Notice. A bulletin sent out from Headquarters, Marine Corps to every Marine Corps unit, typically providing information, guidance, or direction on non-operational matters. For example, ALMARs are released to direct uniform changes, list professional books selected by the Commandant to be read by all Marines, and to identify promotion and special duty opportunities.

**ARG** - Amphibious Ready Group. The smallest amphibious task force, typically consisting of 3-4 ships and used to embark and transport a Marine Expeditionary Unit.

**Basic School** - Mandatory 6-month school for all newly commissioned Marine Corps Officers. Every officer, regardless of ultimate duty specialty, is first honed into an Officer of Marines and taught the infantry skills required of a rifle platoon commander, the most fundamental proficiency of a Marine Corps Officer.

**BDU** - Battle Dress Uniform. An Army term, never used by Marines, for the "utility" uniform available in various camouflage patterns and worn in field training and combat operations.

**BLT** - Battalion Landing Team. The ground combat element of a Marine Expeditionary Unit, comprised of a reinforced infantry battalion with attachments from other combat arms elements, such at tanks, artillery, amtracs, light armored vehicles, etc. BLTs are uniquely identified by their regiment and battalion number, such as BLT 2/1 for a BLT built around the 2nd Battalion of the 1st Marine Regiment.

**Bos'un** - Boatswain. Crusty sailor in charge of all things nautical on a ship, including boats, anchors, lines, rigging, etc.

**CDC** - Centers for Disease Control and Prevention

**CDL** - Common Data Link. A military communications protocol for transmitting sensor data from airborne platforms to ground terminals.

**CENTCOM** - U.S. Central Command, headquartered at MacDill AFB in Tampa, FL is the operational command responsible for military operations from the Horn of Africa, through the Middle East, and on to South Asia. This tumultuous area of operational responsibility is home to most of the pissed-off people of the world and includes numerous inexpensive vacation spots like Somalia, Iraq, and Afghanistan.

**CIA** - Central Intelligence Agency. More descriptive slang terms, such as Christians In Action, or Cowboys Incinerating Assholes, are often fondly used instead of the official name.

**CINC** - Commander-in-Chief. Title used for the commander of major military units, such as CENTCOM.

**CINCPAC** - Commander-in-Chief of the U.S. Pacific Command

**CONUS** - Continental United States.

**CRC** - Crisis Response Center

**DAMA** - Demand Assigned Multiple Access. Marketing scheme developed by satellite terminal vendors to convince the military that bandwidth efficiency could be dramatically increased if a new technology was bought which allowed multiple users to access the same satellite channel. The marketing pitch was much more successful than the technology.

**DIA** - Defense Intelligence Agency. Think CIA with a military slant.

**DMS** - Defense Message System. Multi-decade, multi-billion dollar effort to pretend to "invent" Email for use on Department of Defense computers. Plot was almost foiled by quick-witted Pentagon employees who suspiciously noticed similarity of DMS to the Email application they were using for free on their home computers.

**DNS** - Domain Name System. Internet service which translates how we address each other (by alphabetical names) to how computers address each other (by numbers). DNS allows us to use easily remembered terrms, like www.yahoo.com, instead of trying to remember the IP address of 216.109.125.64

**DoD** - Department of Defense. Defenders of Democracy. Dead on Departure.

**DSP** - Digital Signal Processing. Mathematical algorithms used to improve the ability to recover information from signals.

**DTRA** - Defense Threat Reduction Agency. DoD agency that believes it "safeguards America's interests from weapons of mass destruction (chemical, biological, radiological, nuclear and high explosives) by controlling and reducing the threat and providing quality tools and services for the warfighter".

**DWT** - Discrete Wavelet Tranform. An advanced signal processing technique used to deconstruct complex waveforms into hopefully meaningful components for the purpose of detection, identification, classification, etc.

**EA** - Executive Assistant. In military parlance, an officer, generally a Colonel, who manages the office of a very senior commander or DoD official.

**ELINT** - Electronics Intelligence. Intelligence derived from the exploitation of electronic signals.

**FAE** - Fuel Air Explosive. A bomb which dispenses a huge cloud of flammable material which is subsequently ignited to create a thunderous fireball and explosion. Very hot, but cool to watch from a safe distance.

**Fire Team** - smallest tactical element of the Marine Corps made up of a Fire Team Leader, an Automatic Rifleman, a Rifleman/Grenadier, and a Rifleman/Scout. These are your "bros", who you depend upon the most when the going gets tough. Note: No chicks allowed in this part of The Gun Club.

**FMF** - Fleet Marine Forces. USMC operating forces make up the FMF and are part of either FMF, Atlantic or FMF, Pacific.

**FTP** - File Transfer Protocol. The standard Internet protocol to exchange files between computers connected to the Internet.

**Grunt** - slang term of grudging respect, admiration, and endearment for an infantryman.

**HUMINT** - Human Intelligence. Intelligence derived from the exploitation of information directly collected by humans.

**IDS** - Integrated Display System. Data from multiple sensors and systems displayed on a common viewing screen worn by the operator.

**IMINT** - Imagery Intelligence. Intelligence derived from the exploitation of images, generally taken by satellites or airborne collection platforms.

**IP** - Internet Protocol. Fundamental network protocol for the Internet.

**ISR** - Intelligence, Surveillance, and Reconnaissance

**ITS** - Infantry Training School. Where privates learn grunt skills.

**ITT** - Interrogator Translator Team

**J-2** - Staff code for intelligence section of a joint command

**J-3** - Staff code for operations section of a joint command

**JIC** - Joint Intelligence Center

**HAL** - Health Analysis Laboratory. Fictional name for supercomputer used by researchers at the U.S. Army Center for Environmental Health Research.

**HE** - High Explosive

**JDAM** - Joint Defense Attack Munition. Modification kit that converts unguided free-fall "dumb" bombs into accurate "smart" weapons using GPS.

**JSTARS** - Joint Surveillance and Target Attack Radar System. Severely modified Boeing 707 with sophisticated radar system that provides an airborne, stand-off, surveillance, target acquisition, and command and control center.

**LAV** - Light Armored Vehicle. For the Marines, an 8-wheeled amphibious vehicle with multiple variants, to include the basic reconnaissance vehicle equipped with a 25 mm cannon, as well as mortar, anti-tank, logistics, and command and control configurations.

**LCAC** - Landing Craft, Air Cushion. A big hovercraft that can carry over 60 tons of equipment at speeds in excess of 50 miles per hour.

**LFOC** - Landing Force Operations Center. Compartment aboard ship where the Marines control operations while embarked.

**LHA/LHD** - Amphibious Assault Ship. Primary U.S. Navy landing ship, resembling a small aircraft carrier and capable of being ballasted down to allow landing craft and amphibious vehicles to access a cavernous internal compartment while at sea. The LHA is designed to put Marines on hostile shores where they can immediately go to work pacifying the unhappy hostiles.

**MARCORSYSCOM** - Marine Corps Systems Command. Sole USMC combat systems acquisition command responsible for procuring just about everything Marines take to war.

**MASS** - Miniature Air Sampling System. Fictional device built with MEM technology and capable of detecting chemical, biological, and radiological threats.

**MEF** - Marine Expeditionary Force. Largest integrated combined arms team, or Marine Air Ground Task Force, in the Marine Corps. Standing size is over 40,000 Marines, but a MEF can become significantly bigger depending on the mission. Commanded by a Lieutenant General.

**MEM** - Microeletromechanical. Refers to a revolutionary class of microscopic device technologies that perform useful electrical and mechanical functions. MEMs are believed to have significant potential in almost every field of science and engineering and will eventually become prevalent in consumer products.

**MEU** - Marine Expeditionary Unit. Smallest integrated combined arms team, the MEU generally consists of over 2000 Marines and includes ground, air, and combat support components. Commanded by a Colonel.

**Mikes** - Phonetic M, commonly used to denote minutes. For example, "The helo is 5 mikes out. Standby to pop smoke."

**MOS** - Military Occupational Specialty. Job description.

**MOUT** - Military Operations on Urbanized Terrain. Fighting in cities.

**MPP** - Multiple Point-to-Point. A communications protocol used to aggregate a number of individual communications links into a single large channel.

**MP-RTIP** - Multi-Platform Radar Technology Insertion Program. Effort to build advanced radar for the JSTARS and other airborne platforms.

**MTI** - Moving Target Indicator. Capability to automatically identify radar images that are moving with respect to the ground.

**NAVSEA** - Naval Sea Systems Command. They build and support Navy ships and combat systems.

**NBC** - Nuclear, Biological, and Chemical.

**NCID** - National Center for Infectious Diseases. Part of the Centers for Disease Control.

**NCO** - Non-Commissioned Officer. For the Marines, Corporals and Sergeants. Staff Sergeants, Gunnery Sergeants, Master Sergeants, First Sergeants, Master Gunnery Sergeants, and Sergeants Major are collectively referred to as Staff Non-Commissioned Officers (SNCO).

**NIMA** - National Imagery and Mapping Agency. Provides geospatial data, such as imagery and map products, to enhance knowledge of the battlespace.

**NOC** - Network Operations Center

**NRO** - National Reconnaissance Office. Designs, builds, and operates the nation's reconnaissance satellites.

**NSA** - National Security Agency. The SIGINT masters. These spooks develop encryption systems that protect our information systems, but they are most famous for breaking enemy codes and exploiting the information they discover.

**OPSEC** - Operational Security

**PHIBRON** - Amphibious Squadron. Tactical grouping of amphibious ships.

**PDA** - Personal Digital Assistant. What the guy next to you on the plane is fiddling with for hours in the misguided belief that it may save him a few minutes one day.

**PSAP** - Public Safety Answering Point. The people that pick up the phone when you dial 9-1-1.

**Poge** - sometimes pogue. Term of disrespect used by grunts to denote anyone besides a grunt, but especially administrative or support types in the rear with all the hot chow, bunks, and showers.

**PT** - Physical Training

**S-2** - Staff code for intelligence section of a command

**S-3** - Staff code for operations section of a command

**SADM-10** - Soviet Atomic Demolition Munition with a 10-kiloton yield. Relatively small device that makes a big bang. Unfortunately, these devices actually existed with 1 kiloton yields, but we're not sure where they all are now.

**SATCOM** - Satellite communications

**SAW** - Squad automatic weapon. Light 5.56mm machine-gun carried by the automatic rifleman in each fire team.

**SIGINT** - Signals intelligence. Intelligence derived from the exploitation of electronic communications signals.

**SIM** - Sensor Interface Module. Device to connect multiple sensors to a computer terminal.

**SIPRNET** - Secure Internet Protocol Router Network. Encrypted Internet used by the DoD.

**SITREP** - Situation Report

**STU-4** - Secure Telephone Unit 4. Fictional next-generation device to provide secure voice and data services over commercial telephone lines.

**TCP** - Transmission Control Protocol. Fundamental transport protocol for the Internet that resides in the layer above IP. TCP is a connection-oriented protocol that provides reliable communications.

**Ticker** - Fictional capability to mine data relevant to the tactical mission and present it to the Marine in a low-profile manner as it becomes relevant. The Ticker can also be used to automatically "cue" or trigger any number of desired responses upon receipt of pre-determined information or event.

**TMU** - Ticker Message Update.

**UAV** - Unmanned Aerial Vehicle

**USACEHR** - U.S. Army Center for Environmental Health Research. Innocuous sounding title for research dealing with chemical and biological weapons.

**USMC** - The Gun Club. Uncle Sam's Motivated Combatants.

**VTC** - Video Teleconference

**WESTPAC** - Western Pacific. Generally, in reference to a deployment to the Western Pacific.

**WHO** - World Health Organization

**WMD** - Weapons of Mass Destruction

**Zulu** - Referenced to Coordinated Universal Time, the "Z" time zone is centered on the Prime Meridian passing through Greenwich, England

Printed in the United States
1164600002BA/65